PRAISE FOR

THE CELEBRANTS

A *New York Times* Bestseller
A Read With Jenna Pick
A Good Housekeeping Book Club Pick
An Indie Next List Pick
A LibraryReads Hall of Fame Pick

"It's hard to think of a novelist who handles grief with more gentleness than Steven Rowley. . . . Rowley himself nails the vibe as 'four funerals and a wedding' . . . Rowley's repartee is witty, and the importance of making sure those you love know how much they mean to you comes through on every page." —*The Christian Science Monitor*

"Rowley has created such living, breathing characters that the heartbreaking truth—this is a book about a character's impending death—is truly heartbreaking. . . . I kept Kleenex in business while reading this book, but I also laughed a whole lot. It's the sort of heartwarming story that makes me want to ring up my pals for a much-needed visit." —*Reader's Digest* (Editor's Pick)

"The author of *The Guncle* brings his signature humor and warmth to life's inevitable passages and the value of friendships over time." —*The Washington Post*

"Equal parts contemplative, heartfelt . . . The book not only serves as a reminder that life is indeed short, but also pays tribute to the healing power of friendship in times of great upheaval or loss. . . . Plenty of funny surprises . . . A truly heartrending yet convincingly uplifting conclusion . . . Unforeseen bombshells at just the right moments, and

[Rowley's] gift for taking some of life's most challenging roadblocks and turning them into opportunities for hope and genuine connection . . . What we're left with is a recipe for embracing life and all that comes with it by looking death in the eye and moving forward."

—*San Francisco Chronicle*

"'*Big Chill*, but make it Gen X-y and at least thirty percent more gay': That's one potential logline for the fizzy, emotionally intelligent latest from *Guncle* author Rowley."

—*Entertainment Weekly*

"This funny, poignant, heartfelt novel is a testament to the importance of friendship, especially when life gets hard."

—*Good Housekeeping*

"*The Celebrants* offers the combination of tears and laughs fans of Rowley, author of *The Guncle*, have come to expect."

—*Parade*

"Steven Rowley is one of those authors where if you read one of his novels, his name gets added to a mental 'TBR' (to-be read) list. That is, of course, if you love rich characters written with love and humor that you'd like to know in real life. Each of his books is so uniquely different in plot and beautifully told. . . . Rowley keenly taps into the vibe of old friendships. . . . People are craving connection now more than ever. Rowley's *The Celebrants* is not only a reminder of that, but a salve. Treat yourself, read this book, and call an old friend."

—Associated Press

"Touch[es] on family, friendship, love, and navigating issues in a funny, smart way."

—*Good Morning America*

"Rowley's accomplished style can be counted on to pull out a pocketful of energetic vitality. . . . Sophisticated madcap moments regularly rub elbows with universal bittersweetness."   —*LEO Weekly*

"A *Big Chill* for our times . . . Funny, tender, and incredibly moving, [*The Celebrants*] is a life-affirming, powerful ode to friendship that will inspire you to reconnect with your own treasured friends."
—*Serendipity Magazine*

"A little *The Big Chill*, a little *St. Elmo's Fire*, the kind of buddy book you want for the summer . . . Perfectly crafted, and author Steven Rowley packs a lot of characters in it while still leaving the tale uncomplicated."   —*Seattle Gay News*

"Deeply moving, built with both heart and humor, and addresses the deepest challenges of life."   —*Alta Journal*

"This heartwarming coming of age story follows a group of five college friends all about to enter their fifties. . . . Alternating between the present day gathering and previous 'funerals' from past years, you'll grow attached to these characters . . . and when you finish, you'll want to go hug your BFFs."   —*theSkimm*

"From the author of *The Guncle* comes the ultimate story of friend goals. . . . Throughout this ode to good friends is lots of clever dialogue and some genuinely funny moments."   —*BookRiot*

"Rowley once again displays his talent at balancing humor and heart in surprising ways."   —*BuzzFeed*

"What can stave off the fear of death, or rescue you from one of life's less fatal heartbreaks? Steven Rowley, ever warm and witty, offers up lifelong friendship, and I am inclined to believe him."

—Emma Straub, author of *All Adults Here* and *This Time Tomorrow*

"A tender, funny, bittersweet exploration of friendship, family, joy, grief, and what it means to be alive. I loved everything about it."

—Allison Winn Scotch, author of *The Rewind*

PRAISE FOR

THE GUNCLE

WINNER OF THE THURBER PRIZE FOR AMERICAN HUMOR
NATIONAL BESTSELLER · WALL STREET JOURNAL BESTSELLER ·
USA TODAY BESTSELLER
AN NPR BOOK OF THE YEAR
FINALIST FOR THE 2021 GOODREADS CHOICE AWARDS
A LIBRARYREADS PICK

"Wise and hilarious."   —*People*

"Funny, delightful, bittersweet, and eye-opening with tons of atmospheric detail about fabulous Palm Springs."

—Elin Hilderbrand, #1 *New York Times* bestselling author

"Rowley's depth and humor will warm even the most jaded hearts."

—*The Washington Post*

"[A] heartwarming, hilarious tale of family ties that even the deepest grief can't shake."   —*Southern Living*

"A formerly famous gay sitcom star is suddenly tasked with raising his niece and nephew in this sweet, saucy novel."   —*Vogue*

"In his heartwarming, humorous new novel, Steven Rowley shows readers the true meaning of family, reminding us that everyone—even parents—is only human."   —*Travel & Leisure*

"The author of *Lily and The Octopus* and *The Editor* delivers arguably his funniest and most poignant novel yet."   —*E! News*

"[A] moving, feel-good summer escape."   —*Newsweek*

"Deeply entertaining."   —*Real Simple*

"A laugh-out-loud heartwarmer."   —*Oprah Daily*

"[A] brilliant tale of loss and love."   —*Good Morning America*

"[A] funny and heartwarming beach read."   —*CNN*

"[A] feel-good story, perfect for summer."   —*AARP*

"Rowley hits the sweet spot between hilarity and heart in this endearing charmer."   —*The Christian Science Monitor*

"Often hilarious, sometimes devastating, and genuinely touching."
   —*New York Daily News*

"Chronicles grief in a way that offers a lot of comfort to the reader, and while at various points is a definite tearjerker, it often unlocks the humor and joy that can still be found after those we loved are gone. . . . Wistful, warm, and very funny."   —*Fodor's Travel*

"As hysterically funny as it is profound, *The Guncle* is the perfect summer read for anyone who's looking for a good time with amazing characters without forfeiting deep and meaningful discussions that will feel like a balm to the soul for anyone who's ever lost someone."
                                                                —*The Nerd Daily*

"Cue some family growing pains and humorous antics, and you get this heartwarming novel you'll devour in a flash."   —*theSkimm*

"A big-hearted, laugh-out-loud-funny kind of book that's sure to stay with you long after you turn the final page."   —*PopSugar*

"Rowley uses the juxtaposition of lifestyles and situations for an enormous comic harvest without once forgetting the sorrow and tragedy that have resulted in the situation. The characterizations are rich and wonderful, and Rowley writes with a tenderness, affection and empathy about life, sorrow and family that's the stuff of pure heart."
                                                                —*The Day* (CT)

"Hilarious and heartwarming . . . Auntie Mame-like laughs, lessons and hijinks ensue as Patrick—a once-famous gay sitcom star—deals with a midlife crisis while launching a second act."   —*Boston Spirit*

"A sweet story of family, with plenty of laughs and even a few tears."
                                                —*The Parkersburg News & Sentinel*

"Equal amounts of heartache and witty bon mots."
                                                                —*Palm Springs Life*

"Influenced by comic dialogue that would make Neil Simon jealous, the novel's serious undercurrent of loss gives way, in the end, to a warmth that will make readers smile. . . . A funny, gentle tale of family and friends, and a salve for the wounds they often cause."

—*Library Journal*

"Patrick is a memorable character, and it's genuinely thrilling to read screenwriter-turned-novelist Rowley's take on the mechanics of stardom. . . . There's true insight here into the psychology of gay men, Hollywood, and parenting. A novel with some real depth beneath all its witty froth."

—*Kirkus Reviews*

"Heartwarming, hilarious . . . Rowley finds humor and poignancy in the snappy narrative. . . . Readers will find this delightful and illuminating."

—*Publishers Weekly*

"Rowley's sensitive and witty exploration of grief and healing soothes with a delectable lightness and cunning charm."

—*Booklist*

"Never going too dark, *The Guncle* is a sweet family story that offers an unexpected yet inevitable ending."

—*BookPage*

"This hilarious and heartfelt story will make you laugh, cry, and want to be a better person."

—*BookRiot*

"One of the hottest beach reads of the year."

—*SheReads*

"Warm and funny . . . [Rowley] continues bringing the hits with this feel-good read that still has depth and meaning."

—*Scary Mommy*

"Beach read alert."

—*PureWow*

"A heartwarming and delightful story of love, loss, and the bonds of family." —*BookBub*

"Steven Rowley has triumphed again with his new novel *The Guncle*, an exuberant but tender story about life, death, family, and love. Rowley's protagonist is a modern-day Auntie Mame with every bit of that unflappable flapper's sharp wit and fabulous wisdom. This book is a dazzling banquet of laughter and insight; with it Rowley has proven himself to be one of the great comic novelists of our time."
—Camille Perri, author of *The Assistants* and
When Katie Met Cassidy

"Patrick, the hero of Steven Rowley's effervescent, utterly charming, and affecting novel, is the dearest friend you haven't met yet. You'll root for his two adorable charges as they navigate a terrible loss, and for Patrick's own heart to make a long-overdue comeback. A cleverly subversive story about what makes a family."
—Christopher Castellani, author of *Leading Men*

"*The Guncle* is super funny, charming, and tender. Love, loss, and Palm Springs are the perfect ingredients for a delightful cocktail."
—Gary Janetti, author of *Do You Mind If I Cancel?*

"Patrick is a famous bon vivant, caftan-wearing gay uncle with a fabulous house in Palm Springs. He's an unlikely family member to help his niece and nephew work through their feelings of raw grief after their mother dies, but it turns out he's exactly who the kids need—just as he needs them to help him address his own, less recent loss. Steven Rowley's assured and moving page-turner is studded with laugh-out-loud humor and moments of profound feeling and insight. This book hit every note on my emotional register, and

I savored it like an Aperol drunk poolside with friends on a hot, desert day."   —Christina Clancy, author of *The Second Home*

"Delightful, sharp, and very funny, *The Guncle* is the cocktail equivalent of the fourth sip of your martini while you sit poolside at sunset. I loved lingering in this world (and loved reading the dialogue out loud). A novel as much about family and friendship as it is about style and sass, it's a divine mix of *Terms of Endearment* and *The Birdcage*."
—Timothy Schaffert, author of *The Perfume Thief* and
The Swan Gondola

PRAISE FOR

THE EDITOR

A NATIONAL BESTSELLER
AN NPR BOOK OF THE YEAR
AN INDIE NEXT PICK

"Steven Rowley has hit a home run. What a stunning portrayal of family this is. At equal turns laugh-out-loud funny and searingly poignant, Rowley has created a truly unforgettable story of a son trying to understand his mother. *The Editor* is one of those exceptional stories that is both a joy to read on every page and also deeply profound and significant. It took my breath away."
—Taylor Jenkins Reid, author of *Malibu Rising* and
Daisy Jones and the Six

"Filled with whimsy and warmth, the *Lily and the Octopus* author's second novel centers on the complex relationship between a fledgling writer and his fabulous editor, the latter of whom becomes a mentor, friend, and maternal figure. Oh, and she happens to be Jacqueline Kennedy Onassis, but that's Mrs. Onassis to you."—*O, The Oprah Magazine*

"A journey of self-discovery . . . Ultimately a story not about celebrity but about family and forgiveness."   —*TIME*

"Witty and heartwarming."   —*InStyle*

"Sweetly evokes a mature Jacqueline Kennedy Onassis. In 1990s New York, James Smale is an obscure first-time novelist, but his editor is world-famous. In this delicately observed tale the steely Jackie becomes not just the midwife of the angsty gay Smale's manuscript, but of a wider reconciliation."   —*Sunday Times* (UK)

"A sweet and charming novel, perfect for fans of Jackie O."
                                                                                      —*PopSugar*

"[A] delightful slice of historical fiction."
                                                                   —*Entertainment Weekly*, "The Must List"

"[A] sharp, funny sophomore novel."   —*Town and Country*

"Steven Rowley is the best-selling author of *Lily and the Octopus*, and he's honestly outdone himself with *The Editor*."   —*Cosmopolitan*

"[A] funny, poignant novel about a young writer and his fabulous editor, Jacqueline Kennedy Onassis."   —*Orange County Register*

"The resonance of Rowley's originality and sensitivity shines on every page. He has written a refreshing, superbly crafted novel of hard-won self-discovery filled with big, well-paced scenes and a pitch-perfect blend of humor and compassion that will charm and fully engage readers. In this refreshing, imaginative novel of self-discovery, a debut author has his work—and his life—edited by the inimitable Jacqueline Kennedy Onassis." —*Shelf Awareness*

"A poignant tale . . . Rowley deliberately mines the sentiment of the mother/son bond, but skillfully saves it from sentimentality; this is a winning dissection of family, forgiveness, and fame."

—*Publishers Weekly* (starred review)

"While diving deep into questions of identity, loyalty, and absolution within the bonds of family, Rowley, author of the beloved *Lily and the Octopus*, soars to satisfying heights in this deeply sensitive depiction of the symbiotic relationships at the heart of every good professional, and personal, partnership." —*Booklist*

"Told with warmth and humor, Steven Rowley's charming second novel tells the story of a mother-son reconciliation, facilitated by a most unlikely fairy godmother. *The Editor* offers a delightful, fictional glimpse of an iconic American family—but it is, at heart, a tribute to every family whose last name isn't Kennedy."

—Chloe Benjamin, author of *The Immortalists*

"*The Editor* is an absolute delight from start to finish. Steven Rowley writes such evocative, compelling characters, and his ability to buck the cliché in favor of true nuanced emotion is a gift. Rowley's portrayal of the unconventional relationship between a charmingly uncertain James Smale and the one and only Mrs. Onassis made me laugh, nod and eventually, cry. I adored this book!"

—Sally Hepworth, author of *The Good Sister* and *The Mother-in-Law*

"The first time Steven Rowley graced us with his presence, he told us an unforgettable story about a dachshund with an octopus on her head. This time, he flawlessly gives life to an American icon. *The Editor* will have you weeping tears of joy when it's not quietly breaking your heart. It's a study of mothers and sons, unlikely friendships, and how we go about collecting the scattered pieces of our pasts. It takes guts, humor, and immense talent to write a book like this. Lucky for us, Rowley has plenty of all three."

—Grant Ginder, author of *Honestly, We Meant Well* and *The People We Hate at the Wedding*

"When you've loved an author's debut, there's a little bit of breath holding when you are presented with the second. Well, exhale, because Steven Rowley's *The Editor* is an absolute triumph! By page three, I announced aloud, 'I LOVE THIS BOOK.' And it didn't stop even after I finished it. Rowley is a master of creating characters you fall in love with, and never want to leave. *The Editor* is irresistible."

—Julie Klam, author of *The Almost Legendary Morris Sisters* and *You Had Me at Woof*

"What fun! This droll and wonderfully poignant book gives you full access to one of the most fascinating figures of the twentieth century. A delight."   —Henry Alford, author of *And Then We Danced*

"This funny, warm and thought-provoking novel is the next best thing to having Jackie O. around to make us see how the larger-than-life characters in our own histories—our mothers—are as human, fallible, and as prone to heartbreak as us kids. Keep tissues handy. I had to use a bedsheet."

—Julia Claiborne Johnson, author of *Better Luck Next Time* and *Be Frank With Me*

THE
CELEBRANTS

THE
CELEBRANTS

A NOVEL

STEVEN ROWLEY

G. P. PUTNAM'S SONS
NEW YORK

PUTNAM
— EST. 1838 —

G. P. Putnam's Sons
Publishers Since 1838
An imprint of Penguin Random House LLC
penguinrandomhouse.com

First G. P. Putnam's Sons hardcover edition / May 2023
First G. P. Putnam's Sons trade paperback edition / March 2024
G. P. Putnam's Sons trade paperback edition ISBN: 9780593540435

Printed in the United States of America
1st Printing

BOOK DESIGN BY KRISTIN DEL ROSARIO

Interior Art: Sun Over Mountains © Miloje / Shutterstock.com

For Stephanie Chernak Maurer
and the Sixth Floor

"Life is what you celebrate. All of it.
Even its end."

—JOANNE HARRIS, *CHOCOLAT*

THE
CELEBRANTS

YESTERDAY ONCE MORE

(JORDAN, 2023)

He was an astronaut, he imagined, like in one of those movies; his mission took him to a distant planet on the far reaches of the solar system, Saturn, perhaps, or Neptune. He was gone a nominal amount of time—three years, maybe five, significant but not interminable—but somehow everyone Jordan Vargas knew on Earth had aged a lifetime while he was in space. Naomi with her readers, struggling to figure out the television's remote as if the technology had eluded her, her irritated face twisted in frustration. Craig in the kitchen employing the flashlight on his phone to read take-out menus, muttering the whole time about the Big Sur retreat's soft ambient light while confusing yellow curry with green. What was the difference? *The color, yes, obviously.* But one had more turmeric. *What the hell color is turmeric?* Marielle educating them in great detail about the kittens she'd brought for the weekend. They were born without eyes, *a condition called microphthalmia*, she explained, caused by a genetic mutation that can sometimes result in smaller-than-usual tongues.

And Jordan Tosic, loyal Jordy, his husband and other half, the man who made them the Jordans to so many. (Should we invite *the Jordans*? You don't know *the Jordans*?! We love *the Jordans*!) Jordy's metamorphosis, like Jordan's own, was less shocking, as they'd been together since college and had witnessed each other aging slowly, each having had ample time to adjust to the other's weathering like the wearing of a beloved chair's upholstery over time.

Of course Jordan Vargas wasn't an astronaut, or anything close to it. He was a public relations executive, bound to Earth by gravity, a mortgage, a business he owned with his husband, and aging immigrant parents who moved the family from Bogotá when Jordan was eight to give him and his brother a better life. He was someone who vibrated not from sitting above liquid-fuel cryogenic rocket engines aboard a shuttle ready to launch, but with the genuine thrill of securing his clients ample media coverage. Or at least he used to, until slowly over the years he came to resent both the clickbaitification of journalism and the troublesome clients whom he saw more as crises than people. And it wasn't space travel that kept him away from these friends, a dangerous mission (as poetic as it might be to imagine), so much as his own busy life and the sad fact that friends—even best friends of thirty years—drift apart.

Jordan was growing impatient with Craig's inability to read a simple take-out menu. They were only in Big Sur for the long weekend; their time together, as always, was limited. He rolled up one of Mr. Ito's old *National Geographic* magazines stuffed in a rack next to him and, from the recliner where he sat, swatted the coffee table. "Jesus, Craig. How old *are* you?"

Craig sighed his displeasure.

Naomi peered over her glasses. "Don't do that to my father's magazines."

Cowed, Jordan rolled the publication the opposite way to flatten it. "Will someone help Nana with the menu? I'm famished."

"I just need to turn on some lights." Craig ran his hand against the dated backsplash in search of a light switch, managing only to trigger the garbage disposal instead.

"I told you. All the lights are already on." Naomi strained to open the remote, but the plastic latch was stuck. Her mother would use a dime to open battery compartments, but no one carried coins anymore.

"I'll help," Marielle offered. "My eyes are still *young*." She was also the youngest by a year, having skipped a grade somewhere, the only one of them yet to turn fifty. Her hair was untamed, an ashen blond with streaks of gray, and only a delicate whisper now of its former red. Of the five of them, she had updated her style the least, and she looked much like the lone female member of a once-popular folk trio—all she was missing was a tambourine.

"There's nothing wrong with my eyes. It's the light," Craig groused.

"It's not the light," Naomi insisted.

Jordy chuckled. "Unlike the cats."

"There's nothing *wrong* with their eyes," Marielle admonished, fussing over the laundry basket at her feet she'd requisitioned to make the kittens a nest. "It's just they don't have any."

Jordan looked up at Craig. "Toss me your phone."

"I only have one bar." The cell reception at the house was almost nonexistent.

"I didn't ask you how many bars you had, I said toss me your damn phone!"

Marielle, in a sincere yet comical overreaction, jumped in front of the kittens to act as a human shield and everyone laughed.

Naomi Ito, Craig Scheffler, Marielle Holland, Jordy Tosic, Jordan Vargas. They were mostly nineteen the night they met; it seemed like just moments ago. They, along with Alec Swigert, were transfer students to Berkeley who shared a dormitory floor, graduating with the Class of 1995 (except for Alec, who didn't live long enough to collect his degree).

Jordan tapped the back of his husband's hand and pointed to his own phone on the charger, thinking he had a better chance of placing a take-out order online, even with one bar of service, than Craig ever did of deciphering a printed menu. Jordy reached for the phone and Jordan could still see in his six-foot-four frame the young athlete he fell for in school. They jumped at the sound of three rapid raps, Naomi banging the remote on an end table; the table lamp's shade went askew. Naomi looked up to everyone's scorn. "What! Craig's eyes are weak, not his heart."

"We have a dog with a weak heart at the rescue, stage five murmur, a Basset," Marielle offered as she sat in the recliner, placing the kittens on her lap. She tucked her legs underneath her so that they disappeared entirely under her dress. "He made friends with a deaf Malinois. They're so cute, the two of them, so we're trying to place them together." Several years back Marielle had left her life in D.C. to open an animal rescue in Boring, Oregon. ("That's not a commentary on Oregon," she had repeated several times, as if obligated to do so by the Beaver State's chamber of commerce. "That's literally the name of the town.")

Craig peered up from the menu, raising his phone in the process and blinding Jordy with his flashlight. "Do you guys even *want* Thai? We could also just order pizza."

Naomi finally had the remote open. "These batteries are corroded. I think my mother kept replacements upstairs." She had maintained the Big Sur house as a shrine to her parents years after they died.

"What about sushi?" Jordy suggested, still rubbing the light from his eyes.

"Surprise, surprise. The Jordans want sushi."

"I'm Switzerland," Jordan insisted.

"I stand corrected. Tosic wants sushi, Vargas wants . . . Fondue."

"No sushi. I'm vegetarian," Marielle reminded them.

In unison, they shouted, *"WE KNOW!"*

Naomi headed for the stairs and Marielle followed, as if she'd been dying to get her alone.

As much as they had all aged, the house in Big Sur seemed revived, its retro style that felt so dated twenty-eight years ago when they assembled here the night Alec was buried was once again in architectural vogue. The house sat high above the water, built over a cliff between a grove of trees and craggy rocks overlooking the ocean. It was all wood paneling and glass to make the most of the breathtaking views, the whole place a paean to the American midcentury and its minimalist aesthetic. While much of the house was a single story on stilts that jutted out over the water, there was a small second story built over the back end of the house by the driveway. There were clean lines throughout; in fact the stairwell to the small upper bedrooms didn't even have a banister. In an unfortunate pun, the house was named Sur la Vie.

When the guys were alone Craig pointed to Jordy's tee. "You haven't bought a new shirt in thirty years?"

Jordy glanced down to see *BERKELEY* written in blue. "Jordan got me this for my fiftieth when I started swimming again." Jordy's doctor had told him running was taking a toll on his knees, and his Chelsea Piers health club had a pool. "I set a goal of doing the 20 Bridges Swim around Manhattan."

Craig recoiled. "You would swim in the East River?"

"It's actually the cleanest it's been in years."

"Mount Saint Helens is the most dormant it's been in years. I wouldn't lower myself in the crater."

Jordan studied a painting that hung just shy of level on the living room wall. He remembered the seascape from their first visit to Big Sur after Alec died; he hated it then, it was a shade too bright and too cheery for both their mood and the sea, but he had a certain fondness for it now that he saw the world as a darker place and welcomed a smattering of light. "You know, I think this is an actual Rembrandt."

"Funny," Craig said, obviously not amused.

"No, I'm serious, Nana. Maybe you can confirm." Nana was a nickname Craig earned in college by wearing nightshirts and falling asleep before nine.

A commotion drew their eyes up to the landing; Marielle and Naomi reappeared at the top of the stairs.

"It's true!" Marielle said, in the midst of a tense conversation. "For the last year or so at least I've been feeling like my own worst enemy." She turned to look at Naomi, expecting perhaps the sympathetic nod of female companionship.

"Is that so." Naomi clutched a package of likely expired AAAs.

Marielle nodded.

"Because I'm literally going to push you down these stairs if you don't move any faster." With her glasses and the gray in her hair, Naomi looked not unlike her late mother, and she had an inscrutable demeanor to match.

"OH MY GOD!" Marielle shrieked, grabbing Naomi's hand. "Is that a *ring*?" She studied the double gold band with an oval green stone.

Naomi snatched her hand back and headed down the stairs, Marielle in hot pursuit. "Let's not make a big deal of it."

"Does this mean you and . . . ?"

"I said, let's not make a big deal!"

"But it's jade." Where romance was concerned, Marielle was one for tradition.

"It's an inside joke." Naomi wanted off the subject as quickly as possible.

"I don't get it."

"That's because you're not on the inside." She knew her friends. There was no weaseling out of an explanation with such intense focus on her. "Jade is supposed to cure . . . I don't know, kidney ailments or something. Gary says I'm a pain in his side, but he wants to marry me anyway."

"Romantic," Jordy offered.

Naomi wasn't about to take relationship advice from the Jordans, who never had to endure modern dating. To her it was the perfect proposal.

Marielle's face lit up. "We have to celebrate!"

Jordy interjected, "We are celebrating. We're celebrating Jordan."

Naomi buried her face in her hands. "You know, I was with Fleetwood Mac when you called."

"*The* Fleetwood Mac?" Marielle asked.

"No, Fleetwood Mac and Cheese, a lounge act in Reno. Yes, *the* Fleetwood Mac." Naomi, an executive for the band's music label, had been sent out to check on the surviving members on tour.

Craig emerged from the kitchen. "So, Jordan. Are you going to tell us why you assembled us here?"

Jordan pretended to be immersed in his phone as Naomi slipped the new batteries into the remote. "Don't you think we're getting a little old for the pact?"

Marielle chastised Naomi. "You only say that because you had *your* funeral already."

"As did you, if I recall," Naomi said. "As have we all."

"Actually, I haven't," Jordy said, and all eyes turned toward him. "*I haven't!*" he stressed.

"Oh, sweet Jordy." Naomi dropped her head to feign sorrow. "Always a pallbearer, never a corpse."

Craig gathered the stack of menus. "I'm taking these outdoors where I can read them under the floodlights you use to scare the raccoons. No one follow me."

"No one is," Jordan clarified, but Craig was already gone.

"Should we tell him the floodlights are there to scare away mountain lions and not raccoons?" The batteries now secure, Naomi turned the television on to a rerun of *The People Upstairs*, keeping the volume on mute. The warm glow of the TV helped everything feel so familiar.

"I used to love this show," Jordy said.

Craig burst back inside.

Jordan looked up. "Mountain lion?"

Craig recoiled. *Mountain lion?* "No. There's a putrid smell out there."

"Those are trees. It's called nature," Naomi clarified.

Craig, who still lived on the Lower East Side of Manhattan near the gallery where he once worked, replied, "That's not it. It smells like *mulch*."

"WHAT DO YOU THINK MULCH IS?" Naomi made exasperated gestures with both of her arms to emphasize all the bark and wood that surrounded them.

Marielle checked on the kittens, then flopped on the couch, kicking one leg over the armrest. She turned to the Jordans. "You two should adopt my dogs. The Basset and the Malinois."

Jordy shot his husband a panicked look. They had just arrived at the cabin, hadn't even ordered food. Were they going to get into their news before a second bottle of wine? "It's not a good time."

"It's never a *good* time. That's just an excuse. You just do it because there are so many in need." To Marielle it was like having children. If she had waited for the right time, she never would have had Mia, and she loved her daughter (despite her complicated feelings for Mia's father).

Jordy scrambled for an excuse. "We live in the city. In an apartment. There's no room for a large dog."

"Oooooh," Marielle cooed, not ceding an inch. "I know four bonded Maltipoos." She said it in a boastful way, the way one might announce they knew Michelle Obama.

"FOUR!" Craig exclaimed.

"I'm not talking to you! I'm talking to the Jordans."

"Look at their faces! Tosic is apoplectic!"

Marielle sat up, put her hands on her hips, and said, "Aren't you supposed to be in prison?"

Craig frowned. He had been granted early release but wasn't quite ready for jokes.

If Jordan squinted he could still see them as they were when they were twenty-two, the night they first came to Sur la Vie. They listened to music that night, Sarah McLachlan and Sophie B. Hawkins and Shawn Colvin, and the Carpenters for some reason too; he vividly remembered that, as Naomi had made such a fuss. They stood around with a sort of stunned bemusement, the finality of Alec's death yet to sink in. Alec would burst through the door at any moment—they were *convinced* of it—high on his signature trail mix, a blend of ecstasy, ketamine, and god knows what else (none of them were privy to his recipe—he was like Colonel Sanders that way) and make a grandiose proclamation like no two people have ever met, or that they only existed inside him. The invincibility of youth had been pierced that night, but the air had yet to fully escape. Before that, like most young people, they had all thought they would live forever.

"Someone put on music," Naomi instructed. "It's like a wake in here."

Jordan said very plainly, "Ha."

"I will!" Marielle volunteered.

"Someone other than Marielle."

Marielle protested, but they all knew exactly why Naomi objected. Marielle liked the highlights, the songs they played on the radio. Naomi detested singles, had spent a life at war with popular music, professing only to like deeper cuts. It was that way now that she worked in the industry, and it was that way in college when they were randomly assigned as roommates, as far back as history took them. Naomi arrived with a milk crate of albums, Marielle with a shoebox of cassingles.

When Naomi looked away, Jordan slipped his phone to Marielle and encouraged her to choose. She beamed. Seconds later piano chords unspooled through the speaker; Marielle reached for Jordan's hand and together they started to dance as Karen Carpenter's rich voice, thick as cabernet, filled the room.

When I was young, I'd listen to the radio . . .

He'd teed Marielle up and she'd knocked it out of the park.

"NO! VETO!" Naomi came running to grab Jordan's phone.

"OVERRIDE!" Jordan laughed.

Naomi exhaled her displeasure. "It's your funeral," she mumbled, giving up. It had been twenty-eight years, more than half their lives, since they made their pact and that joke was never not a source of amusement.

Jordan hooked his arms around Marielle's waist like they were at a seventh-grade dance, and she placed hers on his shoulders, leaving just enough room between them not to alarm adult chaperones. She rubbed her hands over his sweater and a look of concern crept across her face.

So thin, her eyes said.

Don't worry about it, his said back.

"What about the place we went for Alec?" Jordy asked, still focused on dinner.

"Nepenthe?" It was a Big Sur institution, but Naomi hadn't been able to go back since.

"Right. It was Greek, or Middle Eastern."

"Mediterranean."

Jordan and Marielle held each other tight as they swayed to and sang along with every sha-la-la-la, every whoa-o-o-oh.

"Do they do takeout?"

Naomi grabbed her hair in fists. "I CAN'T THINK WITH THIS GODDAMN MUSIC!"

Marielle whispered to Jordan, "She called it *music*."

Jordan whispered back, "That's an improvement!"

"Craig, call them and see. They had fish, I think. And shawarma. Chickpea salad for Marielle. Just order whatever. Order everything. Baba ghanoush."

"Gesundheit," Craig said.

Jordy smirked as he reached for his wallet. "Dinner tonight is on me."

Marielle whispered, "You need to eat."

Jordan had hoped the sweater he'd chosen, in part because he was always cold thanks to both the treatment he was undergoing and his significant weight loss, but also because it was bulky, disguised just how much he was no longer himself. "I will."

It was indeed his funeral they had congregated to celebrate. Just as they had in years past gathered to celebrate Marielle's, then Naomi's, then Craig's in their individual hours of crisis and need, the result of the decades-old pact they had made in their grief over Alec to throw their funerals while they were still living so that none of them could ever question exactly what they meant to the others. *Leave nothing left unsaid* had been Marielle's motto when the idea was first hatched. If nothing else, it would be clear that they were loved. But this funeral was unlike any of their prior affairs. They were not here for Marielle in the wake of her divorce, or Naomi after her parents' private plane went down, or Craig when he pleaded guilty to art fraud. This was not their little game as usual, "funeral" as *pick-me-up*, designed to give them a chance at a new life when they felt most at wit's end with their old. This funeral was a real goodbye. Only, none of them knew that yet. Not Craig as he phoned in an order for hummus plates, not Naomi as she tried to pair her own phone with the speakers to rid her ears of seventies AM gold, not Marielle as she danced to Karen Carpenter with a partner who was likewise dangerously thin.

Because Jordan had yet to tell his friends that the cancer that started several years back in his prostate had returned with a vengeance and was now in his lungs, liver, and bones. Instead of saying that out loud just yet, Jordan Vargas imagined himself an astronaut readying for another mission, this time with no discernible end; it was easier than telling the best friends he'd ever had that he was dying.

THE
JORDANS

The waiting room inside Memorial Sloan Kettering on York and 68th was blindingly white; whoever had chosen this paint color had grossly misfired. There were hundreds of shades to choose from, Jordan thought—Polar Bear, Whisper, Frost, Pure, Swiss, Dove, Cloud, Icicle, Mist, Paper, Lace—and this was what the decorator went with? Something that reflects life's stark impermanency back in your face in the gravest moment of one's existence? Jordy reached over and gripped Jordan's thigh tightly with his right hand while flipping through his phone with the left, as if there were a person he could call to fix this if he could just think of exactly whom. The appointment had gone as Jordan feared, not as they both had hoped. But Jordan knew. It wasn't any one symptom, although he had several (including a mass he could feel in his abdomen on the right side, something tangled in his lymph nodes), but rather a deep foreboding in the way you just know when something is not at all right. His entire body felt like he'd slept on it

wrong for a month and there wasn't enough caffeine in Starbucks'
largest bucket-sized iced coffee to shake his recent malaise.

"What did they tell you when you finished your treatment last
time, five years?" Jordy asked.

"Five years," Jordan confirmed. That was what his doctors had
said after his first diagnosis and successful course of chemo. Make
it five years without a recurrence and he'd go from in remission to
cancer-free.

"And how long has it been?"

Jordan shifted in his seat; the backs of his legs were sweating.
"Four years, ten months, and three days."

"Then this has to be some sort of cruel mistake."

Two months. Sixty days. Fourteen hundred hours. The finish line
so tantalizingly close he could almost graze it with his fingertips. Alas,
it wasn't a cruel mistake so much as just cruel.

Jordy gave up on his phone. They were well-connected, but they
knew no one with the authority or expertise to fix this. "So we reset
the clock. We did it once and we'll do it again."

We. Jordan bristled. Also, it wasn't like he'd fallen off the wagon
and had to restart sobriety. Hand in a coin and work to earn it back.
If anything there was a very different stopwatch that had just started,
ticking off the time that he had left, and they were wasting precious
minutes sitting in this glaring white.

Jordy tried a different tack. "What about dinner tonight at the
Carlyle?"

Jordan turned to his husband, who was almost as white as the
walls, with an expression just as blank. "To celebrate?"

"No. To . . ." Jordy didn't know how to finish that sentence, at least
not out loud. He was already making a mental list of favorite things
he wanted to do with Jordan again before his husband was too sick to
do them. "To take our mind off this."

It would have been almost sweet that Jordy thought a good martini and lobster bisque could make one forget a death sentence if it weren't also so misguided. Jordan closed his eyes to imagine permanent darkness, but there was too much light from the windows and ambient noise to lose himself in the idea of nothingness. "Why do you think Alec occupies such a large space in our lives?"

Jordy looked surprised. "What does Alec have to do with anything?"

Isn't it obvious? Jordan thought.

"Are you invoking the pact?"

"I'm not invoking anything. I'm asking you a question."

Jordy gazed out the window at the East River and Roosevelt Island as he gave that real thought. The afternoon clouds formed a low ceiling on the concrete city that made him want to shrink into his chair. After a spell he said, "He's the embodiment of our younger selves."

Jordan clasped his hands tightly, grateful not to have had his question evaded. And Jordy's answer made a certain sense to him. Alec was the version of themselves that was forever young. In dying, he had somehow become immortal.

Jordy held up his own arm and pinched some skin at the elbow. "I mean, what is this?" he asked as the skin all but refused to snap back. He meant it to demonstrate that they were no longer young themselves, but all his gesture did was draw attention to his enviable arms; they were as muscular as they had ever been.

Jordan pushed his arm away. "That doesn't mean you're old. It means you're dehydrated." And indeed there had been a fair amount of tears in the doctor's office.

In the distance a bell rang, the same bell Jordan rang five years—no, sorry, four years and ten months—ago that marked the end of his chemotherapy. Someone else had just successfully finished their treatment. "They should have a gong for people like me." *Gallows humor,* he thought, but he did have the urge to strike something.

"You'll ring the bell again," Jordy said, but it wasn't what Jordan wanted to hear. They were going to have to accept his fate, and fast if they wanted to make the most of the time he had left.

"Lobster bisque, huh?" Jordan's mind drifted to the supposed healing power of soup. Maybe going out made some sense. They had come directly from the office for this appointment, which meant they were already dressed for dinner, and going home seemed too sad.

"I was thinking the octopus carpaccio," Jordy said, as if the real decision were in what to order. "Can you stand?"

Jordan's legs were Jell-O. "Not yet." They sat there perfectly still, studying others in the waiting room who looked equally grim. "I don't believe in an afterlife."

"Neither do I," Jordy said, but in the moment he was open to changing his beliefs.

"And yet I keep picturing Alec and me together, wandering around in some sort of heaven."

"Would that be heaven?" Jordy asked; Alec one-on-one could be *a lot*.

"Alec is twenty-two and I'm *fifty*, and people keep asking if I'm his dad."

"So you're in hell, then."

Jordan came close to smiling, but he wasn't fully able. "Yeah."

"You'll be older than fifty," Jordy said optimistically; he massaged the back of Jordan's neck how he liked. "Much older."

Jordan crossed his fingers on both hands. "C'mon, fifty-one." It had never been more clear to him that aging was a gift. But no matter how much more time he had, Alec would still be twenty-two. "I don't want to go," he whispered, his voice cracking on *go*.

"To the Carlyle, you mean?"

That wasn't what he meant, but if he had to make himself understood he might start crying again and not stop. Instead he said, "Do you think I should?"

"Should what?" Jordy asked as he continued the neck massage.

Jordan fished for his phone and scrolled back until he found the group text chain with Naomi and Marielle and Craig. It was named *NANA'S HUNGRY LITTLE PIE EATERS*. He held it up for Jordy to see.

"The pact," Jordy said, now understanding.

Jordan pointed to *PIE EATERS*. He couldn't in this moment recall the joke.

"Remember? Craig brought that pie."

Jordan didn't.

"To Marielle's."

It rang a faint bell.

Bell.

"I thought you believed in the pact even less than an afterlife."

Jordan stared at his phone. Not believing in something and not needing something were two different things. He didn't know how to explain it yet, and frankly maybe he never would, but everything from here until the end would be different. All bets were off. That was just the way it was. "Do you remember how it started?"

"The pact?"

And this time Jordan couldn't help himself, because he always smiled when his husband said *I do.*

WE'VE ONLY
JUST BEGUN

(ALEC, 1995)

Their lives changed overnight. They went to bed exactly two weeks before graduation day thinking they would live forever and woke up to the last real lesson that college would teach them: all that begins, ends. They did not live in a womb, safe until life commenced. They weren't killing time in some sort of heavenly waiting room, readying to be born into adulthood (no matter how much Berkeley felt like that for so much of their academic careers). They, like every other living thing that drew breath, were already in the throes of dying, used cars losing value the moment they were driven off the lot. And yet here they were at a starting line, comically stretching cold muscles, waiting for the *BANG* of a starter pistol, not realizing they were twenty-two years into a race that had different finish lines for them all.

"Alec was a one-man show," Craig muttered in admiration. "The problem is he hated the cast." They were gathered around an outdoor table at Nepenthe, a Mediterranean restaurant with an enormous wraparound deck built on a cliffside in Big Sur; he cut a warm wedge of pita right through the dish of cool hummus. Craig barely finished the sentence before Marielle hit him, right on the sternum.

"Ow!" Craig's mouth was full and he wiped hummus from his lip with the back of his hand. "Why?"

"That was uncalled for."

"*Hitting* is uncalled for."

All of them were on edge, as not one of them knew how to act. Jordan whispered, "Was."

"Huh?"

"You said *was*," Jordy explained. "Alec *was* a one-man show."

"What are you, finishing each other's sentences now?" Naomi thought it was bad enough they shared a name.

"It's just . . . Never mind." And then he added, "Hard to get used to."

Marielle pulled her hair back from her face. "I don't ever want to be used to it."

Naomi studied Craig as he reached for more pita. She slapped his hand away from the bread, appalled. "How can you eat at a time like this?"

"WHY IS EVERYONE HITTING ME?" Craig was hungry, simple as that. And maybe it was to fill a void that would never be filled by food, but he was new to loss, and twenty-two, not to mention a little bit drunk, and by god, he thought, it was his right to eat. He wasn't surprised by the outbursts, just annoyed they were directed at him.

Alec belonged to them, and they desperately wanted to hold on, even if any attempt they made now was glaringly too little, too late. Part of their shock was that Alec was built to last, unlike everything else in their day-to-day lives that was inherently temporary and disposable: their dormitory addresses, their phone numbers, the sheets that fit a dorm room bed (the last twin bedding they'd ever own), the milk crates that stood in for furniture, and the three-ring binders that held the endless reams of paper that college necessitated that would be unceremoniously tossed in a dumpster in the hours before graduation. Alec was beauty and permanence, marble and stone, meant to stand and draw admirers for centuries. But the truth was he was fragile too, more than they were, even, as he lacked the cynicism they all sometimes wore as armor. He was skeptical about the world, about people, but saw that as a personal failing of his, and not, as he should have, the failings of literally everyone else.

Marielle was still stewing over Craig's observation. She had every right to be the most upset with Alec, but she found herself digging in, determined to stand up for him, someone who could no longer stand up for himself. "He was aware of his flaws, that doesn't mean he hated himself." She gazed into her pour of a local white blend, one of several bottles Naomi insisted they bring from her parents' collection at Sur la Vie, even though the restaurant's corkage fee was half a day's wage on a work-study salary. "I thought you were supposed to be his best friend." She turned her glass absent-mindedly three times on the linen tablecloth. Other than Craig, no one had touched the Mediterranean plate, which now looked not unlike a pie missing a piece. "Why would you be best friends with someone who hated themself?"

Craig leaned back. "Pick a different word. He certainly spent no shortage of time numbing himself. What for, if not self-loathing?"

"Oh, that's rich. Coming from you," Naomi groused.

"What's that supposed to mean?"

"It means we never met anyone who thought Absolut was a food group," Jordy muttered.

Jordan's head was pounding. "Guys, knock it off."

"It's not even good vodka."

"GUYS." Jordan kicked Jordy under the table and closed his eyes tight. Earlier he had been grateful for his headache, leaden pressure that kept him anchored in the moment. Now his appreciation was wearing thin.

Naomi placed her hand on Craig's, a subtle gesture suggesting he take it down a notch. But he remained steadfast. "Why can't we just be honest?"

It was the last day of April 1995. The prior week had started out uneventful: Marielle had mistaken April for February and mused about the month sometimes having an extra day. Bill Clinton had declared a national day of mourning for the victims of the Oklahoma City bombing. The Dow Jones had hit an all-time high. The Unabomber claimed another victim. Normal things that happened in normal weeks. Or if not quite normal, certainly not outside the bounds of convention. Things like this happened in the world at large, not all of it making its way through the bubble of campus life. And then sometime in the early hours of Thursday, something happened to them that was very *abnormal*, and it unsettled them to their core.

"Who has a funeral on a Sunday?" Jordan grumbled, changing the subject. "Is that weird?" Raised Catholic, he couldn't remember a funeral encroaching on regular Sunday services.

"*You're* weird," Naomi said, but it was more reflex than accusation.

Warmer temperatures had arrived in much of California, in the southern parts of the state and much of the inland, but they had not yet reached the Central Coast and Big Sur. The day might have hit sixty-five around the time they were leaving the cemetery in Pacific Grove, but temperatures plummeted with the sun and they found themselves underdressed. Before dinner, Marielle had the good sense to grab a blanket from Sur la Vie, which she and Naomi currently had placed across their laps, but the men were left to fend for themselves, seated farthest from the patio's heat lamps, Craig in his vest and shirt-sleeves and the Jordans with only light blazers, Banana Republic and J.Crew.

Nepenthe offered an eclectic menu of California Mediterranean cuisine, but the food was almost an afterthought. The restaurant boasted panoramic views of the water to the south from its enviable terrace. It was a splurge for five college kids ten days shy of graduation (the menu prices reflected the scenery as much as the cuisine), but they knew from experience that Naomi would pick up the bill, as the Itos had generations of family wealth from a business none of them much understood except to say that her parents imported some things and did equally well in the exportation of others. And even if she didn't pay the tab, they all would have willingly forked over whatever cash was on hand, as they assumed incorrectly that watching the sunset over the vast Pacific would bring them some comfort and, as life was uncertain now at best, would be an experience worth the inflated fee. The only promise was today, their only future the meal they were about to order—even if most of them didn't quite have the appetite to consume it.

Jordan feigned interest in the menu. "What looks good?" Under the table his knee was touching Jordy's. Truthfully, nothing on the menu appealed. What he had an appetite for was decidedly off-menu: Jordy Tosic's naked flesh pressed against his own, back at Naomi's parents' place perhaps, where they could maybe, finally, have a blessed moment to themselves. Six days earlier, spurred by their impending graduation and the sudden realization that they were no longer going to be living down the hall from each other, Jordy Tosic had finally kissed him. It was electric, and felt, despite the fact that college and the only adult existence he'd yet known was coming to an end, like life, his life, *their* life, was finally about to begin. Since that kiss they'd had sex exactly twice, once that first night in Jordan's dorm room, as he had somehow finagled a single, and once in their dorm floor shower, very late at night where they were afforded a few clandestine moments and even though the water made everything both hotter and more

tricky for certain logistical reasons they had managed to fully consummate their relationship like, well, consummate pros. (What they did
the following afternoon in the library stairwell, while extremely hot
and Jordan wanted to count it if for no other reason than to remember
it for some future retelling of their origin story, could be defined as a
third of a sex act at best.) Two and one-third acts of passionate love.
And then Alec died, and they'd barely been alone long enough to
touch each other since. They couldn't do so openly. How do you ask
people to share in the joy of the beginning of something when stricken
with grief over the ending of something else?

"I don't know, what looks good to you?" Jordy asked, and Jordan
looked at him imploringly. *You, you oafish galoot.* In the end the group
decided to do what they often did, order a number of things to share,
since their lives were already so communal anyway. They shared the
same bathrooms, the same dining hall, the same academic spaces, and
the same residence hall. In fact, if it weren't for the obvious boundaries
formed by a cafeteria tray, delineating where one's meal ended and
another's meal began, they would have shared every meal too.

Naomi adjusted the blanket, pulling it up over her arms as she
leaned into Marielle, and they all resumed the awkward wait for their
overworked server. "I can't eat. But I'll push something around a plate
to stay here." Corkage fees would only reserve them a table for so long.

"I'll eat whatever you don't," Craig offered, thinking he was being
helpful. Instead, Naomi thought, he had never sounded more gauche.

According to the menu's boastful promotional copy, the cabin at
the center of the restaurant was once owned by Orson Welles, who
bought it as a romantic getaway for himself and Rita Hayworth;
whether the couple had spent any significant time there seemed up
for debate, which seriously undercut the brag. But it was almost befit-
ting, a cabin, waiting empty for its most distinguished resident, now
host to a party of five missing their most celebrated friend. The res-

taurant's name, Nepenthe, was from the Greek, a potion used by the ancient gods to induce forgetfulness from pain or sorrow. The bottles of wine they'd consumed thus far were all Californian and, as far as potions go, seemed to lack the same mystical powers. But the night was young and their surroundings were breathtaking and Jordan had even inquired about a bottle of ouzo, so they had not given up hope that something magical—even if it was just magical thinking—might occur.

"This view," Marielle mused, before kissing the top of Naomi's head, grateful to have been invited; the ocean was rapidly disappearing, along with the sky, in darkness, as if a painter were priming over a sunnier canvas with a dark wash to capture a night scene. The mountains horseshoed to the south, the base of them disappearing in mist, and the water, perfectly still and reflecting the sky, was marred only by a few rock outcroppings. It was almost impossible to tell if they were right side up or upside down, which also seemed apropos. "Alec would have loved this."

"If he were here he'd have hopped the railing and rappelled halfway to the beach before we would have decided on sparkling water or flat." Naomi offered a weak smile. She could all too easily picture him making friends with the sea lions that liked to sun themselves on the beaches below.

"He would have *hated* today," Craig added, thinking back on the torturous service that reflected nothing of the young man they knew. Brothers of his who shared a whisper of Alec's looks (but none of his charm) blathering on about a version of Alec they had never met. "I mean, who was that funeral even for?"

"Besides his parents?" Naomi asked.

"Oh, his parents," Marielle said, clutching her chest with obvious sorrow; only she in this moment had the capacity to acknowledge someone else's pain.

"Who did they think they were burying?"

"Certainly not Alec," Jordy said. "Their idea of him, maybe."

"You're assuming *we* knew the real Alec."

"Didn't we?" Naomi asked.

"Maybe he didn't know the real us," Jordan said, wanting to settle the debate once and for all. He picked at a wedge of pita, tossing bits of it on the terrace, feeding birds that wouldn't come until daybreak. It was an observation that stung, in part because at twenty-two they were inclined to make everything about them (as that's what twenty-two-year-olds do), but also because it fed their massive guilt. Alec did drugs openly and often. The rest of them partook as it suited them, when the mood struck, not more and not less. And only when they weren't overwhelmed with work, which, in their senior year, was almost never. And when they did, their drugs of choice differed and didn't put their lives at imminent risk. Naomi and Jordy smoked weed (and Jordy only when swim season was done); Marielle took mushrooms on occasion or Valium she stole from her mother; Jordan and Craig drank. Alec was in another league entirely; he arrived at Berkeley that way, fully (as it were) cooked.

"He might have at least appreciated the crowd." Jordy tapped his leg against Jordan's several times in what he hoped came across as more than a friendly nudge.

"That was always his biggest fear," Naomi agreed. "Not being the center of attention."

Craig suddenly pushed his seat back from the table. "All right, who's playing footsie?" He looked beneath the table and Jordan immediately retreated. The girls weren't the least bit curious, much to Jordan and Jordy's relief. Craig resurfaced and fidgeted with his napkin.

"It was not being *worthy* of attention," Marielle corrected. And that was an entirely different beast. As the youngest of six kids (and once he was no longer little), Alec would practically have to set himself on fire to get his family to notice.

"Well," Jordy said, before he spit out the pit from an olive. "He was worthy of all the attention today." He raised his glass of wine, and the others did too, but if there was meant to be more to that toast, it fizzled or was left unspoken.

I t was Marielle who had found him in the dorm lounge that morning, lying on the stained carpet as he often did when waxing poetic on life or making proclamations that had the vague ring of words written by others one might read at a liberal arts college. *Life isn't about finding yourself, but creating yourself!* (George Bernard Shaw.) The medical examiner would later tell his family that he had been gone for some time, but Marielle cursed herself nonetheless for not having an earlier class, something that might have brought her past the lounge before eight forty-five when she was on her way to Comparative Politics, a lecture on abuses of power no less, agenda manipulation, exploitation and oppression (topics on which Alec would have had plenty to say), but in the end it would not have made any difference. Alec had left them at some unspecified point during the night, after the last of them had gone to bed, before the first of them rose. Marielle had sat and squeezed Alec's hand; she had done much the same with her grandmother's a decade earlier in the moments before they closed her casket. A dead hand feels just that. *Dead*. But her grandmother's hand had skin that crêped, knuckles that had bent and protruded, and was to the touch ice-cold. Hers was the hand of an old person, who had lived a full life and had done many things with palms that were calloused, with skin nearly sloughed off. There was something wrong in holding a hand as smooth as Alec's, cold as it was, soulless, in that way lifeless things are, but weighty and smooth in other ways that suggested strength and vitality, life force that might still, in some way, squeeze back. She couldn't say how long she sat with him, his hand in hers, before her body let out a bloodcurdling scream.

Jordy came running first, as his room was closest to the lounge and he was already back from a morning swim. He and Alec had elected to remain roommates both junior and senior year, which is not to say they weren't a bit of an odd pairing. Jordy, the athlete, maintained something akin to a traditional schedule, sleeping when it was dark, waking when it was light, whereas Alec didn't see much of a difference between day and night and expressed no particular preference for either. He'd be perfectly happy to eat lunch at three a.m., and be shocked to find almost everything closed and no one willing to join him and would end up heating SpaghettiOs from a hot pot. Jordy's body was an athlete's, and he treated it as such, very particular in what he put in it. Alec's body was also one of high performance, beautiful and sleek and able to bounce back from all sorts of abuses, but it was like a sports car whose owner never saw much need in paying for premium octane fuel. When Jordy found Marielle hunched over Alec he was certain he knew what had transpired; Alec had been careless one too many times.

Jordy pushed Marielle aside that morning to feel for a pulse, and once she caught a glimpse of Jordy's resignation she scurried into a corner like a frightened animal, tucking her legs into her chest and letting her hair fall over her face. Jordy tilted Alec's head back, checking his airway, suspecting his friend might have choked on his own vomit; surprisingly the passage was clear. He began CPR, which he had first learned for a summer job lifeguarding at his community pool; in his head the whole time he was screaming *Annie are you okay?*, which was what you were supposed to ask of the training dummy—a rubber head and a chest and not much else, which to Jordy always made her seem very *not* okay at all. (*Where are your legs, Annie?*) He pinched Alec's nose and breathed into his mouth; it was one of only a handful of times in his life his lips had touched another man's and it was also the second time inside eight hours. Jordy was all adrenaline, and his breath was forceful. Alec's chest inflated, and Marielle gasped until Jordy shook his head no while returning to chest compressions. That was Jordy's breath doing the work, not Alec's. Behind her hair Marielle's face sank and in that brief moment, the last hope she had, died.

Alec are you okay, are you okay, are you okay, Alec.

Naomi was roused by the growing commotion and exhibited the type of calm that you hope for in emergencies. She was the first to pry Jordy off Alec, but he sprang right back into action attempting to save his roommate. She then tended to Marielle, burying her friend's face in her chest and pleading with her not to watch. Craig arrived next, still in his nightshirt, pushing his way through a small crowd of students who had started to gather. He didn't know what to do of any use except to go and retrieve Jordan, who, once he threw on some boxers, was finally successful in getting a beleaguered Jordy to stop. Jordy's muscles burned with lactic acid but still squeezed Jordan tight, their bodies reunited after only a few short hours, forgetting to care what others might see. The six were now five, and they would have to lean on each other in any and every way that they could.

f only he knew," Craig said, mindlessly pushing the dish of hummus away from his plate with a spoon.

"Knew what?"

"How much he was loved."

"You think he didn't?" Marielle's hackles were up in the way they often were when she came to Alec's defense. More often than not the group let this slide; if they were upset with Alec about anything it was usually in how he treated Marielle. But what Alec had done this time was an affront to them all.

"I know he didn't." The rest of his observation went unsaid: if he had, he wouldn't have been so cavalier with his own life.

"Wait. You think he did this on purpose?"

"You *don't*?" Craig scanned the others, realizing just now that this had gone unspoken.

They sat in silence as waves crashed far below on a beach none of them knew how to access. It was something they had all been too afraid to voice out loud. Had Alec, the unstoppable force at the center of their friendship, taken his own life? Was there any evidence to support this? A note? Something they would find when they returned to school from Big Sur? Jordan turned to Jordy, who was maybe the last to see Alec, given that they shared a room. *You don't know anything?* his eyes asked. *Some crucial missing piece to the puzzle?*

"Guys," Marielle said in that way she did, bucking the class she'd taken in feminist studies, which encouraged her to curb the use of patriarchal language.

"What?"

Marielle wanted to say it was an accident with the finality of a coroner reading their report. It was simply what the science said. But she didn't know this anymore than the rest of them did, and without anything nearly concrete she felt lost.

"No, really. What?" Naomi insisted.

Jordan kicked Naomi so that she would stop pressuring Marielle and, sensing movement, Craig again looked under the table to investigate.

"Nothing." Marielle pushed her chair back and stormed off to the edge to stare out at the horizon, where the very last ribbon of daylight shimmered. The way the breeze caught her hair, the way she folded her arms resolutely in the cold, the way she leaned forward against the railing as if the water had its own gravitational pull gave her the air of a fishing boat captain's wife on a widow's walk waiting for her husband to return safely from sea.

"She needs to face facts," Craig said, balling up his napkin. "It will help in the long run."

"And what about the short?" Jordan asked, excusing himself from the table to join Marielle. Ever the gentleman, he removed his jacket and slipped it over her shoulders, making her look even more like she was from another time. They watched as some sort of bird swooped low over the water, diving to catch a fish.

"How do they know how to do that? Dive in that exact spot to get fish."

Marielle stood in silence for some time before saying, "It was an accident." Her gaze still locked straight ahead. "But what do I know."

Jordan smiled gently. None of them knew exactly how long she'd sat with Alec that morning before she screamed for help. "I'd say quite a bit." She was the smartest of their group. Naomi and Jordy worked hard, and Craig was happy to rely on charm when knowledge failed him, a skill certain to get him far. Jordan himself was content to be well-liked, and he leaned on people's goodwill and his Latin good looks to gloss over any of his shortcomings. But none of that approached Marielle's natural intelligence. He stroked her hair and quietly repeated, "Quite a bit, I'd say."

The ambient din of the restaurant happily filled the long silence between them. Ordinary people on an ordinary night doing ordinary things. Laughing, ordering, talking, drinking, toasting, eating, shifting to get more comfortable in their chairs. The five of them were in a slightly parallel dimension, where they were doing most of these things too, but everything was other than ordinary. Jordan wanted to ask the diners how they could possibly be so callous.

"What do I do now?" Marielle finally asked.

"With what?"

"With my life?"

Jordan fluttered his lips until they tickled. "Anything you want."

"Be serious."

Jordan was. "It's all going to kill you. You might as well do something fun."

Marielle burst into tears, shocked that anyone could be looking for lessons so soon. Jordan threw his arms around her.

"I'm sorry, I'm sorry, I'm sorry," he stammered, realizing how flip he had been. Marielle's whole body heaved, and then she angrily kicked a pine cone off the edge of the deck and watched until it was swallowed by darkness; neither of them heard it land.

"What's going on with you and Jordy?" she asked once she'd gained control of herself.

Jordan gripped the railing until his knuckles turned white, then looked innocently back at the table. "You mean how we're platonic friends and nothing else?"

"Uh-huh."

Jordan blushed, which he hoped could be attributed to the day's waning light.

"Did something finally happen? We've been waiting for this *for years.*"

"Who's 'we'?"

"Everyone. All of us. Your crush was super embarrassing."

Jordan shook his head. How foolish they'd been, thinking no one else could see. He turned to her, suddenly panicked she might misconstrue. "It happened before Alec, I swear. We haven't been . . . Rolling around like animals during all of this." In truth, Alec's death had dampened what they had, perhaps even extinguished it for good.

Things were already so fragile, and there were major life changes on the horizon. This new challenge might be one too many to overcome, and maybe that was for the best.

Marielle took Jordan's hand. "Alec would have been happy." She looked at Jordan this time to make sure he understood.

Jordan nodded through welling tears of his own. He opened his mouth to say just as much, that their coming together was precipitated most by a certain tick-tick-tick, and the idea that they wouldn't see each other again after graduation unless they *chose* to, but he stopped himself in the nick of time; instead he rubbed Marielle's arms under his jacket, noticing they felt very spindly. "Look at the moon," he said. It was just rising above the treetops.

B ack at Sur la Vie, Naomi's eyes locked with Craig's. "Take off that vest," she instructed, like she just noticed he was still wearing it.

Craig was surprised by the sudden hostility. "No."

"Take it off!"

"Naomi. Why?"

"You've been wearing it for hours and Marielle is tired of looking at it."

Marielle, flipping through the Itos' records, sighed in protest. She didn't want to be dragged into this.

Jordy gently coughed. "It's not a vest, it's a waistcoat."

"Who are you, Thierry Mugler?" Naomi scoffed.

Jordan narrowed his eyes. *Waistcoat?* Jordy might have just outed himself with a single word.

"I'm leaving it on. I'm cold."

"It looks like you're wearing a girdle!"

"Oh my god, STOP!" Jordy flopped on the couch. "I wish I could go right from here to L.A." He had a job lined up at a marketing firm after graduation. He caught Jordan's pained expression and his heart sank; Jordan was headed to New York.

"I can't go back and take finals." Marielle had sectioned her hair and twirled one part into a spiral to chew. "Someone has to write us a note." They would all limp through their exams; the goal now was just to squeak by. GPAs were no longer as important; they all had job offers on the table. Marielle was heading to D.C., Jordan and Craig to New York. Naomi to San Francisco, where she would spend a summer in the family business working up the nerve to tell her parents that she wanted to break into the music industry.

Naomi crinkled her nose. "I don't know what Alec's plans were after graduation." She wondered in hindsight if this was a sign they had missed. Maybe he had made none.

Marielle spat out her hair. "He was going to Joshua Tree."

"To do what?"

"The planets were going to align."

"All of them?" Craig asked. "Over *Joshua Tree*?"

"Jupiter and Saturn," Marielle corrected. "And maybe Mars and Neptune. I don't know. He said it happened once every twenty years and he wanted to see it. His own Harmonic Convergence."

Jordy turned to her, confused.

"You don't remember the Harmonic Convergence?" Marielle looked around the room for signs of recognition and found none. "It was eight or nine years ago when a number of planets aligned, inspiring the first synchronized global meditation for peace. Alec had read about it in some book." It sounded exactly like Alec, and as soon as Marielle mentioned it they realized he'd talked about it with each of them; it was just that when it came to Alec, they hadn't always listened. The Harmonic Convergence occurred in the summer of 1987 when the sun, the moon, and six out of the eight planets aligned to form a grand trine. Alec, a freshman in high school at the time, believed like many that this coincided with a great shift in the Earth's energy from warlike to peaceful. He loved all that *I'd like to teach the world to sing* nonsense. "There were supposed to be these various power centers, mountaintops mostly if I recall. But you know Alec, if others went up, he would go down. He thought he could find his own power center in the desert, below sea level, where he would be closer to the Earth's core. He thought he would be most attuned to a change in vibration there, like laying his head on railroad tracks listening for a train." Alec, who set the vibe in every room he walked into. "That's how I know he didn't do this on purpose. He *had* plans. And he would not have purposefully abandoned them."

Craig didn't quite buy Marielle's assessment. "That's not a plan so much as a vacation." It was just as likely Alec thought a second Harmonic Convergence would be a good time to make an earthly exit in an attempt to join a higher consciousness. "So then what?"

Marielle looked confused.

"Because how long does that take? So he goes to Death Valley—"

"*Joshua Tree.*"

"—to hear the Earth vibrate. That takes what, an hour? A day, a *week*? And then what?"

Marielle was crestfallen, trying to hold on to certainty that seemed less and less certain by the minute. Finally, her voice cracked. "We can't let this happen again."

Naomi went to the kitchen to open a bottle of pinot, while Marielle settled on the Carpenters' *A Song for You* and pulled the vinyl from its red sleeve. The Jordans sat across the room from one another, Jordan spooked by how much the others had apparently observed and wanting to put some physical distance between himself and any growing rumors. Craig plopped in a chair with a bottle of Cutty Sark he'd found in a cabinet and proceeded to pour himself a glass, neat.

The opening chords of the Carpenters' "Hurting Each Other" unspooled from the record player. Richard's piano. A soft tambourine. Karen's low contralto. Marielle moved to the center of the room and swayed slowly in time with the music. *For nowhere in the world could there be a boy as true as you, love.* Marielle even had an unlikely resemblance to Karen; the hair was different, yes, but she had the high cheekbones and teeth that were almost too big for her mouth, and she had a look that was both wounded and impish, as if you could never quite tell what was going on behind her smile.

Naomi returned with the bottle of wine and several glasses, which she set down on the surfboard-shaped coffee table before the music finally registered. She said, with all the authority she could muster, "Absolutely not."

But the song was just hitting the chorus, and Marielle grabbed Naomi to dance, one hand around her waist, the other clasped in her own and they swayed as Karen sang *Can't we stop hurting each other.* Naomi humored her at first, as if it were any other evening and they were just drinking and getting high, dancing to all kinds of nonsensical music, but then something snapped in her and she broke free of Marielle's grip and took a step forward toward the turntable. "Turn this shit off."

Marielle blocked her, and instead turned the volume up, bleating the lyrics along with the record like an angry goat. "MAKING EACH OTHER CRY! HURTING EACH OTHER MY! WITHOUT UNDERSTANDING WHY-Y-Y!" Her lyrics did not quite match Richard and Karen's, but they were close enough to prove a point, and with each move Naomi made to get past her friend and reclaim control of the music, Marielle wailed "CAN'T WE STOP!" in time with

Karen, pounding her chest each time with her fist, until Naomi was a little unnerved and gave up, throwing her arms in the air in exasperation.

"Do any of *you* want to deal with this?" she asked of the boys, as they were better equipped to intercede. At the very least they were bigger than Marielle, and there were three of them—she couldn't block them all if they launched a coordinated attack.

"Why would we stop her?" Jordan asked. "She's on top of the world, looking down on creation."

Naomi threw a pillow at him.

"What? It's the only explanation I can find." Jordan laughed at his own joke and then so did Jordy and Craig—it was just that *stupid*—and it was weird to have laughter fill the room. Spooked, the guys looked around, as if they were uncertain where it came from.

Marielle finally snapped out of her trance when "Goodbye to Love" began, as if even she realized that was too masochistic under the given circumstances. She turned the record off and the room was silent. "Let's get in the hot tub," she said, done with music entirely.

"None of us brought swimsuits." Craig said it sheepishly, as if there weren't an easy alternative.

Marielle kicked off her heavy shoes, which landed on the floor with a thud, and pulled her dress over her head until she was standing only in a bra and panties. "So?"

Craig scanned the room to see if anyone else found this as uncomfortable as he did. His squeamishness did not stop Marielle, who was pretty tipsy on wine. "Oh, who cares," she said, spinning her undressed body. "Everyone's gay anyway."

Craig's hand shot up and he stammered, "I—I'm not."

Jordy looked conspicuously at his shoes.

"NAOMI," she barked. "Bring wine." It was rare for Marielle, the peacemaker, to command the troops and so, not knowing what else to do, they obeyed.

They had been soaking in the hot tub for a good half hour when the Jordans overheated. They emerged and sat on the edge of the deck, leaning back on their hands, two of which overlapped. It wasn't a formal declaration of their relationship, but they weren't hiding anymore either. Jordy wore black briefs and Jordan nothing, his free hand cupped over himself in a vague attempt at modesty. Craig split the difference, hovering half in and half out of the water, his white boxer shorts now a second, translucent skin.

"Nana," Marielle said, her wet hair finally tamed and slicked back.

"What?"

"You're so hairy." He reminded her of the wolf who ate Grandma, assuming her place in the bed.

Craig turned awkwardly to Naomi, crossing his arms to hide his chest. "Do you ever worry your parents will find us here?"

"I haven't seen them in nearly two years. I highly doubt they'll waltz through the door."

"Isn't that a little weird?" Marielle asked.

"Not *that* weird. I mean, I live with you guys. And I had that internship most of last summer, then went to see my cousin in Japan."

"But you'll see them soon. You're going to work for them."

"I'm going to work for their *company*."

Craig's boxers ballooned into an awkward bubble. If his vest had been a girdle, he now had a petticoat to match.

"How often do you see *your* parents? I mean, at a certain point we're kind of grown." It was something that made Alec's death all the more devastating. For better or worse, their reliance on their found family had now eclipsed any dependence on their own.

"Do you feel grown?" Marielle had a skeptical look.

"Do *you*?" It was a typical Naomi response, turning a question back on its asker, one she executed with such disdain a person could easily wither under her crippling tone and not realize until later it was a defense mechanism employed to avoid anything approaching vulnerability. But tonight, and because it was Marielle asking, she relented, a sign of just how off-kilter they all felt. "Not this week."

Marielle floated to the center of the hot tub and tilted her head back so that only her face protruded from the roiling water, her hair radiating out in all directions like rays of sunshine trying to pierce the night. She planted her feet firmly over the drain and felt a slight suction, tickling the dry, roughened skin on her soles. She often went barefoot and thought nothing of it but was surprised in this moment how sensitive the undersides of her feet were. As if he could read her mind, Jordy said, "Did you read about that girl who was disemboweled in a Jacuzzi? She sat on the drain and got stuck there, creating a vacuum seal, and then the pressure . . ." He made a horrible suction sound.

Marielle lifted her head out of the water to say, "That's repellent."

"Isn't that how we all feel, though," Craig observed, bucking Marielle's disgust. "Our insides sucked right out." He re-created Jordy's awful suction sound and added an obnoxious POP.

"STOP IT!" Marielle pushed the hair out of her face, the rest of it just covering her breasts like Daryl Hannah's in the movie *Splash*. "Your bloomers are growing," she said, pointing to Craig's boxers, which were inflated again.

"Where are you going?" Jordy asked when Craig stepped out of the tub.

"I'm getting out of this bouillabaisse." He picked at his boxers in a failed attempt to keep them from revealing everything. "Oh, fuck it." He turned away from his friends and slipped them off. Naomi and Marielle exchanged startled looks at the sight of his hairy ass.

"Nana!" Jordy barked, and he tossed Craig a towel.

"Oh, relax." Jordan stood, more confident in his nakedness. His body was almost hairless by comparison; in the moonlight his skin glowed blue like a seal's as he shook his body dry. Jordy didn't care who saw his eyes transfixed on Jordan—it was impossible not to stare.

"I wish Alec could have been there today," Marielle said wistfully.

"At his funeral?"

"We said it ourselves. If Alec had been alive to witness today, none of this ever would have happened."

Jordy looked at his watch. "Yesterday," he said softly when he saw the time. It was now just after midnight. They had survived the day.

Jordan covered himself, much to Jordy's chagrin, but he rolled the top of his towel down a few times so that it hung tantalizingly low on his waist.

Marielle lit up with inspiration. "We should have our funerals. You know, now while we're still alive to appreciate them." It was the kind of idea that seemed inspired after a night of drinking and smoking weed.

"Tonight?" Craig asked. "I'm kind of zapped."

"Not tonight," Marielle groaned, as if he'd foolishly misunderstood.

Naomi leaned back and closed her eyes; she could almost sleep right there on the deck. Jordy cycled through the usual series of stretches he did before he would go for a run and Jordan, recognizing the routine, telepathically asked, *Are you going for a run, now?* Jordy replied with a slight shake of his head as he reached for his other shin. *Are you nuts? It's the middle of the night.* And then Jordan understood this was just his way of air-drying. Craig redoubled his efforts to secure his towel around his waist so that he could be comfortable in the fact that it wouldn't fall. None of them were listening, which irked Marielle.

"Guys!"

Jordan scratched his head, trying to remember what they were even talking about. Their own funerals? "Didn't Tom Sawyer do that? And Huckleberry Finn?"

"Didn't they do what?"

"Play dead, only to pop out and yell *'surprise!'*?" He thought back to high school English. Yes, poor Becky Thatcher was beside herself. It did not go over well.

"I don't mean to trick anyone. I mean to help each other."

"I'm kind of funeraled out, if I'm being honest," Jordy said, pulling up out of a stretch. It would be helpful not to have to attend another for a good, long while.

Marielle stood in the center of the tub and faced them. "That's why we'll save them for a rainy day."

"Like you'll set up a hotline, and deliver us our eulogies?" Craig asked. "Give us a card with an 800 number and we can call anytime day or night?"

"Like a psychic funeral network." Everyone turned to Naomi, who they more or less had assumed was asleep.

Marielle looked at Craig, deadpan. "Your towel's slipping." Craig scrambled to hold it up, even though it showed no signs of falling down. His discomfort in his own body brought Marielle momentary satisfaction, since he was being deliberately obtuse. And strangely, she found it endearing.

Jordan lay flat on the deck; the cool night air was a welcome relief as they waited for their body temperatures to return to something approximating normal. "What are we really talking about, Mare?"

Marielle had always swooned when Jordan called her Mare; she liked thinking of herself as a majestic horse, and it fit with her love of animals. She eased her bra straps off her shoulders, as if they had tightened when they got wet and were cutting into her skin. "I'm talking about having our funerals while we could attend. To hear first-hand the impact we've had on other people so that we know our own lives are making a difference. I'm talking about what we should have done for Alec. Let him know exactly how much we loved him." Marielle looked to the sky for Alec. Wouldn't it be wonderful if he was now part of a celestial alignment? *Saturn, Jupiter, Alec.* "Life is short, yes. But it also can be very long. We need to prepare for that." She looked around at the rest of them, wondering if they too were nervous about all that came next.

"But what if it gets out of hand?" Jordy asked, taking a seat in their circle.

"How do you mean?"

"Come on, look at us. We turn everything into a joke."

"Well, this would be serious."

"How serious? Like what if I could use a funeral once a year? Like a tune-up, or rotating your tires. Aren't you going to get sick of putting me in the ground?"

"Some of us might enjoy it," Naomi offered, again through closed eyes.

"Metaphorically, I'm speaking."

"You're supposed to rotate your tires?" Jordan joked, but everyone ignored him, so he added, "Maybe there's a punch card. Tenth funeral is free."

"You're full of jokes," Marielle chastised.

Jordan chewed on his lip. In truth it wasn't the first classmate he'd lost. One of the students at Jordan's private primary school in Bogotá had been kidnapped when he was eight. His father was the vice president of Pepsi for Latin America or something like that and the kidnappers had asked for quite a sum; the father paid, but the boy was never found and his absence cast a long shadow. Not long after, and amid growing violence, his parents moved them to America. But perhaps uprooting the family was rash. What if it deserved more thought? Maybe Marielle was wise in looking for alternative ways to process this. "Sorry. Go on."

She accepted his apology and continued. "Funerals are onetime celebrations of someone's life. You don't throw them like birthday parties, year after year after year. That's just ridiculous."

None of them wanted to say what they were all thinking, which was that the entire endeavor seemed ridiculous, but that much, at least, made sense; there had to be some sort of limit. It couldn't be a funereal free-for-all that would overtake the living of their actual lives.

"Okay, so what are the rules, then? When can we cash in on our funeral?"

"That's up to you." Marielle rubbed her legs together like a cricket, drawing Craig's attention. He'd eaten the lion's share of everyone's dinner and now, hunger sated, he was inexplicably ravenous for something else. "It's up to each of us to choose wisely when life gets really hard. We agree right now to assemble when one of us calls, no questions asked. We say nice things about you and remind you that you are loved. That's it. Everyone goes once, and once everyone has gone, the pact is done. There's no more obligation."

"So, it's a 'pact' now," Craig said skeptically. It was not a word he had positive connotations for, and in this setting, at least in his mind, was too closely associated with suicide.

"I always wanted a pact funeral," Jordan said with his easy smile, and even he couldn't quite get it out without laughing. Even Marielle seemed buoyed by this joke. Jordy grabbed Jordan in a headlock and rubbed his wet hair so that it sprayed Craig, who sat closest.

"Gross." Craig wiped his arms on his towel before adding his two cents. "I don't know. I'm not good with compliments. They make me uncomfortable."

"Yours will be more like a roast." Naomi leaned forward and

buried her head in her hands; she was desperate to go to bed. But she agreed with Craig. She had never willingly accepted a compliment in her life and tended to think those that gave them were either weak or lying. Craig was raised by an aunt and uncle in Idaho who couldn't quite bring themselves to tell a kid that wasn't theirs that they loved him, and so he was deeply distrustful of the word. Even the Jordans, who these last few days had been in the throes of trading flirtatious and even prurient flattery, had more or less accepted that the other was suffering from some sort of love blindness and delusion, or was guilty at the very minimum of gross exaggeration.

"Just think about it," Marielle urged, certain they would see the wisdom in the light of day.

"We'll think about it," Jordan agreed, his head still in the nook of Jordy's arm.

"Are we going to talk about whatever's going on here?" Naomi asked, pointing out the intimacy of Jordy's grip.

Jordan wriggled free. "I'd rather plan my own funeral."

It was just after two in the morning when Jordy Tosic found his way to Jordan Vargas's bedroom. The rest of the house was asleep, knocked out from an uneasy cocktail of emotional exhaustion and wine. Jordy had volunteered to take the couch, thinking it would give him a plausible excuse to make his way into Jordan's bed. He was too tall, the cushions were too soft, the upholstery too scratchy. The others would understand, and while it would most definitely garner additional attention, that runaway train had already left the station. Jordy softly tapped on the door twice before letting himself inside. Jordan was in bed, facing the window, away from him, but he seamlessly pulled back the covers as Jordy slipped out of his shorts. This was how it had been with them. They didn't fumble awkwardly with one another, mash teeth or bang heads when they kissed. Their movements were in perfect concert, as if they shared a mind and not just a name. Jordy slipped one arm underneath Jordan and wrapped his other around him.

"You're going to Los Angeles," Jordan said as Jordy was kissing his neck.

Jordy stopped reluctantly, not understanding the need to dwell on anything other than the here and now.

"What are we going to do about that?"

Jordy rested his head on Jordan's ear, which didn't help his growing erection. "I hear they have an airport and everything, and planes that go to New York." He then loosened his grip, as the moment called for a certain sensitivity that a raging hard-on betrayed. He didn't *want* to have the feelings he had. To say they were inconvenient at this moment in time was an understatement. He thought his friendship with, and admiration for, Jordan Vargas would give him the perfect safe environment to finally embrace who he was and position him to go out into the world secure in his true identity. While he was hardly sixteen going on seventeen, he was ready for eager young lads and rogues and cads and a world that was full of men. Instead of sexual conquest, against his best judgment, he found himself falling in love. And from the sound of Jordan's question, he wasn't alone in this predicament. "We have options," he added, as if his observation needed clarification. And then, to change the subject, he asked, "What do you think of this whole business with Marielle?"

Jordan turned to look over his shoulder and spoke his next words carefully. "Maybe what we should be holding a funeral for is this." He didn't know if he'd survive losing Jordy if whatever this was went on any longer. Not on top of Alec. Not on top of every other goodbye that would come with his walking across the stage in a cap and gown. Not with moving away from Berkeley to start again in a new city. He rolled over fully, all dopey and eyes wet with love. What came next would be unfair to Jordy, on top of just coming out—the pressure of having to *decide*. How do you ask someone to commit to something, when neither of you knew what it was? But that was what the circumstances necessitated, that was what was being asked of them in this moment. Yet he couldn't really say any of this, not tonight, not after burying a friend and entering a pact that might or might not seem like nonsense in the morning. Not in this beautiful moment. So instead he just agreed. "We have options."

When Marielle felt certain everyone was asleep, she stepped out of her room dressed in only a threadbare T-shirt. She looked down over the railing where the hallway was open to the living area below; as dark as it was she could not tell if Jordy was asleep on the couch. She wouldn't have blamed him if he had migrated—tonight was not a night to spend alone, as long as he hadn't beat her to her destination.

There were three doors to three bedrooms and she stared at them like a contestant on *Let's Make a Deal*. Naomi was in her parents' bedroom downstairs, and Marielle's own guest room was the door farthest from the bathroom. That left her a fifty-fifty chance of getting this right, even if what she wanted was very, very wrong. It was incredible how differently the upstairs looked earlier when they had all picked rooms; why had she not paid closer attention? Or was this Alec playing tricks on her for having the temerity to get back at him in this way? That was what she was doing, wasn't it? Punishing him? It wasn't just the soul-crushing loneliness, a side effect of mourning, that was leading her to hunt down the house's last resident straight man. It was anger and the desire to lash out. If only she could remember which room Craig was in, center or right. Center. That was her best bet—to shoot straight down the middle.

The room was dark, darker than a room should be, even with her eyes now attuned to the night. It was all that damn wood paneling. Marielle's attention was drawn to the white ceiling, which was about the only thing she could make out. She gave her eyes a moment to adjust and then whispered, "Nana?"

Craig stirred when she bumped into a dresser, knocking over a framed photo. "Marielle?" He seemed half-asleep and confused and her name spilled off his tongue as if it were two—*Mary Yell*—but it was definitely Craig and that confirmation was all her nerves needed. In one swift motion she pulled her T-shirt over her head so that she stood fully nude in the moonlight. Craig wiped his eyes, not quite sure if he was seeing what he was seeing, or if he was in the grip of a dream. She pulled back the duvet and straddled him while gently scratching his chest with her nails. It was only a few seconds before she could feel him respond and he propped himself up on his elbows.

"Are you sure?" he asked, wiping the last bits of sleep from his eyes.

They preached consent to every Berkeley student, hammered it time and again, but most boys—especially the straight ones—still didn't quite get it. If Craig had cared about Marielle, truly cared, he would have known she couldn't have given it. Not because she was drunk or asleep, although maybe she was a little of both, but rather because she was out of her mind with grief. Craig was still a boy in a man's body. He didn't *not* care about her, she knew this—he would never deliberately cause her harm. So she nodded, slowly, as if she were sure, and that was all the consent Craig needed; he writhed, scrambling to remove his boxers beneath her.

She was surprised at how tender it was. She had imagined it

angry, as if Craig too felt the same need for revenge. She'd hoped he
might be aggressive, slap her a bit and throw her around so that their
sex would feel punitive. But of course he didn't and couldn't and
wouldn't; Alec's slight against him was very different than his against
her. Craig wanted connection as much as sex, even if it was fleeting;
from the moment he entered her she could see in his eyes that he was
happy to be out of the crippling loneliness he felt in his own body and
to momentarily be fused with someone else's. They found a rhythm in
their sadness, and she ultimately gave in to it, even found pleasure in
it, though it was not what she initially wanted. When it was over (which
was a little too quick), instead of feeling anger abating she felt a rush
of something new, guilt perhaps, or shame, on top of everything else,
but she was not sorry that she had come. He tried to talk to her as they
lay twisted in the sheets, but she put her hand over his mouth until he
stopped trying to speak, understanding at last that he could only ruin
it. Instead they listened to the night and the wind in the trees and the
odd car that made its way down Highway 1. The windows were
steamy, or the house was shrouded in fog; that probably made more
sense, as close to the ocean as they were. It was as thick as the fog in
her brain at night that made it difficult to form coherent thoughts or
assign words to her overwhelming feelings as she lay in the nether-
world between asleep and awake. Craig turned to hold her and she
allowed it but could only register the ways in which he was different
than Alec. His breath was different, less sharp, less wet, and she
wasn't used to so much hair on a man's body. There wasn't as much
muscle between his skin and his bones but not in a way that made
him seem soft or weak; in fact, it seemed like maybe he could take
flight. When he adjusted his body he did so with her comfort in mind,
while Alec flopped on top of her like a Saint Bernard might, drooling
and shedding, prioritizing his body and not hers. She eventually

turned away from the window, deathly afraid that before she could fall asleep Alec's face would appear in the fog.

Naomi was the last to awaken; the smell of bacon wafting under her door made it impossible to sleep in. When she emerged from her parents' room she was almost shocked to find so much life in the house, the opposite of how she was used to her time at Sur la Vie. This was like a scene out of a movie that any reasonable viewer would consider cliché: friends dancing to the radio while making breakfast, not a one of them concerned with the mess, the cracked eggshells that sat on the butcher block or the pancake batter that dripped onto the floor. Whatever sadness they had felt the night before seemed absent in the dawn of this new day, replaced with laughter and a general joie de vivre. In short Naomi hated it, in no small part because she couldn't help feel that she had been excluded from something mysterious. But maybe it wasn't as nefarious as that. Maybe it was just that in the absence of knowing how to act in the throes of grief, you behave as you've seen other people act in similar situations. Life imitating art more than art imitating life, and this art necessitated dancing. Casey Kasem clocked "You Gotta Be" by Des'ree at number eighteen in the countdown and Marielle cranked the volume. Jordy flipped pancakes on her mother's teppanyaki griddle, an offense in and of itself but one she was willing to let slide so long as they cleaned it, while Craig emptied used coffee grounds into the trash in preparation to make a fresh pot. Jordan set the table with mismatched flatware, folding paper napkins from an out-of-season holiday just so. When Naomi had had enough and desperately wanted to change the channel on the scene she said, "What the hell?"

Jordan grabbed Marielle and spun her just as she said, "I told them no bacon," absolving herself as if the bacon were the true offense in this extravaganza and not literally everything else.

But bacon wasn't a bad place to start. "Where did it come from?" The fridge had been bare upon their arrival except for condiments that might have been there since the eighties.

Jordy reached behind him for more pancake batter; it stood in a bowl with a whisk. "Jordan and I took your car into town and picked up a few things."

Naomi didn't understand why they weren't hungover like she was, unmotivated by an unforgiving pounding in her head. The idea of getting behind the wheel of a car was overwhelming, let alone operating it, keeping her eyes open and alert to navigate the cliffside driving required to get anywhere in Big Sur. Craig handed her a large mug of lukewarm coffee.

"Here. Saved you the last of the pot. More's brewing."

She stood there frozen, mug in hand emblazoned with the logo for California Route 1, inhaling the scent of black coffee; she begrudgingly found the aroma intoxicating. If they went to the general store at the campground they wouldn't have found grounds anywhere near this nice, but if they pressed on to the deli she understood. It was weird to feel like such a stranger in her own family's kitchen, but she also couldn't remember a time she had ever in her life felt this at home. Naomi turned the music down just as Sheryl Crow was asking if she was strong enough to be her man.

"Pancakes ready in two minutes," Jordy said as he flipped the last of the batch. He already had syrup warming in some of her mother's earthenware (a detail, she thought, no straight man would think of); however Jordy now defined himself, gay, bi, or some third option like queer, he was committing to his new part with gusto. And almost to prove her point, he pulled a stack of plates out of the oven, where he had been warming those too. "Sit," he said, and it was then that she noticed he was wearing the apron she had once given her mother that read *STRESSED is just DESSERTS spelled backward*. Jordy was the first person she had ever seen wear it; it had always lived in a drawer. Not knowing what else to do, she took a seat at the head of the table to watch the chaos unfold.

"I was thinking we could get something for Alec," she said. "You know, like in his memory. Sponsor a seat in the theater." She had thought overnight that there might be another solution to their desire to *do something* other than making a pact.

Marielle was the first to register what she was saying. "Alec hated the theater."

Jordan gasped. "No one *hates* the theater."

"The theater at Berkeley."

Jordan relented somewhat, as if that were a horse of a different color.

"A bench, then. With his name on it. In the park, where he liked to play Hacky Sack."

"Footbag," Jordy corrected as he brought a stack of pancakes to the table. Alec had always rebelled against corporate brand names.

The coffee now brewing, Craig joined them at the table. "Why? What did he ever do to us to warrant the horror of people *sitting* on him?"

Naomi sipped her coffee. "It's just, this pact. Really? It's all too Courtney Love." The Courtney Scale was invented late one night, maybe six months before, when they were in the dormitory lounge either drunk or stoned out of their minds. Naomi couldn't remember who came up with it; in truth it was probably something they had cooked up as a team in their usual game of one-upmanship. But at least one of them had said that everything could fall into one of three categories: Too Courteney Cox, too Courtney Love, or too Courtney Thorne-Smith, and in their altered states it was an absurdist metric that was immediately adopted into their vernacular. "It's macabre."

"That's your problem?" Marielle asked. "I was worried you would say it was too Courtney Thorne-Smith."

Craig turned to Marielle confused, and she looked at him with pity.

"*Melrose Place*," Jordy said with a mouthful. Naomi glared. He was literally getting gayer in front of her eyes.

The pancakes made their way around the table as Naomi took a reluctant bite. She hated how good they tasted and how long it had been since she'd had a hot breakfast; at school it was a meal she usually skipped. It was so exactly what she needed in the moment that she actually wondered if her friends might know better than she did what was the right cure for what ailed her. It was Monday. When she thought about the three-hour drive back to school and then exams and graduation and the packing and moving that lay ahead, she wanted to crawl back into bed and stay at Sur la Vie forever. Maybe with the plate of pancakes. And that was to say nothing of her grief over Alec or about walking away from the rest of these goofballs who had become family in the years since they transferred. What would it mean not to gripe at Marielle, or yell at the boys to keep it down? Blessed peace, maybe. But peace sounded so dull and, in this moment, incredibly lonely. Maybe there was merit in this pact of theirs and it wasn't just another of Marielle's half-cocked, new-agey ideas (as kumbaya as it sounded). She covered her mouth to keep from smiling as she remembered how Alec had insisted that they type up their new Courtney System in the computer lab like it might be more helpful in the art of categorization than systems that came before it—alphabetical, Dewey decimal, all that—and his hoping against hope that it would be the first conversation that future civilizations would data mine, thousands of years after humans were gone.

"What?" Marielle asked when she noticed Naomi shielding her face.

"I bit my tongue," she lied, but no one believed her, so she said, "Alec," and it made much more sense. They'd all had memories of him that made them smile in spite of their pain. Memories that made them feel guilty for enjoying them so soon after his passing; there would be time for that later, for reminiscing with a smile, but shouldn't now be a time for pain? "Fuck it," Naomi finally said. "I'll join your stupid pact."

Marielle threw her arms around Naomi. "See what happens when you come to your senses and lower your defenses?"

"Now *that's* too Courtney Thorne-Smith." Naomi pushed Marielle away. "Poetry," she said, then shuddered.

Marielle took a seat, bypassing the butter in silent protest over the factory milking of cows, and reached for the syrup, which came from trees, even if its extraction was a little barbaric for her taste.

"Well, if Naomi's in we have no excuse," Jordy said, turning to Jordan beside him.

"Sure, what the hell." Jordan reached out to hold Jordy's hand.

Naomi pointed at them with her fork. "Seriously," she said, her lips sticky with syrup. "Are we going to talk about this?"

Jordan shook his head no and offered his free hand to Craig; Jordy did the same with Marielle. Naomi relented and they joined hands around the table to swear an oath.

They left Sur la Vie just after two. They didn't fight, they didn't cry, they didn't even bicker when, stuck in traffic, the ride back to Berkeley took four hours instead of three. They were comforted. Because even in the midst of their greatest uncertainties a pact was born that would keep them together. Or at least a phone call away.

THE
JORDANS

"We should visit Positano," Jordy said, several weeks later in front of the fire. It was May and they had never lit a fire this late in the season, but Jordan was dropping weight at an alarming pace and as a result was always cold. They were drinking the 2006 Haut-Brion from their wine rack—a Christmas gift from one of their clients; there was no longer any reason to save it.

"We should," Jordan agreed. Their honeymoon, delayed as Jordan fought cancer the first time, had taken them to Florence and Venice and they had always promised to go back to visit the coast. Jordan found promises harder and harder to keep, but he couldn't say as much out loud.

"No, I mean really plan a trip."

Jordan wiggled his toes in his socks. "No time like the present." He offered a weak smile.

Jordy placed his husband's feet in his lap and massaged them. "Okay, when should we go?"

Jordan writhed when Jordy attempted to crack his toes. He felt too brittle for such a thing. "This summer." Jordan was satisfied with his answer; it was both specific and noncommittal.

Jordy moved the bottle of wine off the rug and onto the hearth, where it was less likely to be knocked over. "What would we be eating, if we were there right now?"

"In Positano?" Jordan closed his eyes and gave this the due consideration a good question deserves. "Risotto," he said. "With squid ink. And then we'd stop for gelato on the way back to our pied-à-terre. Pistachio, maybe. Or peach."

"You're going to use French to describe our Italian accommodations?"

"Mais oui."

"Appartamento," Jordy corrected. He had listened to one of those Rosetta Stone tutorials after they returned from Italy the last time.

"Appartamento," Jordan repeated.

"And what would we do?"

"In Positano? We'd lie on one of those beaches that has rows of chairs and brightly colored umbrellas and watch the fishermen come in." Jordan leaned in toward the fire to pretend its heat was the blistering August sun.

Jordy liked this little fantasy. "Hot Italian fishermen."

"Exactly," Jordan said.

"Not leathered old men named Giuseppe."

"A few of them are leathered old men named Giuseppe. But most of the fishermen in Positano are ripped and golden and twenty-five. And they're all named Chad."

"I didn't know Chad was such a common Italian name."

Jordan laughed. "Not Chad." He looked at the ceiling and then said, "Tommaso."

"Tommaso is a good name," Jordy agreed before releasing his feet. "Okay," he whispered.

"Okay *what*?"

"This summer." Jordy reached for the wine and filled both their glasses. "Anyplace else?"

Jordan's expression soured. He could see where this was going. "Like Big Sur, you mean?"

Jordan understood his husband's gentle approach of late but found his tender nudging perhaps even more annoying than if Jordy would just come out and say what he wanted and meant. "Do *you* want to go to Big Sur?" Jordan challenged. Jordy had every right to invoke the pact for himself if he thought gathering their friends was what was best, as he had yet to take his turn. But Jordy only swirled the wine in his glass and stared, as if the sediment of grape seeds and tartrates held fortunes and answers like tea leaves. As far as the pact was concerned, they were playing a game of chicken.

There were nights Jordan lay awake thinking he should reassemble their friends. But it was hard to explain what a terminal diagnosis felt like; he always imagined that receiving such news would be a great motivator, that one would spring into action making the ultimate to-do list filled with both things to accomplish (time to write that novel?) and places and people to see. As a public relations professional, he had to concede that bucket lists had executed an almost flawless publicity campaign. Not so many years before, he hadn't even heard the term. Now it was part of the vernacular; people even made them for their dogs and there was a film with Morgan Freeman. But bracing medical news often comes wrapped in depression and changes to the physical self, coupled with new medications that drained one of the energy needed to globe-trot. One gave thought and consideration to what was most important, and one's thinking tended to center on home. Family.

Why go off to the far reaches of biodiverse places like New Zealand to see the Emerald Lakes when you could walk the reservoir in Central Park at a slow pace and then sleep in your own bed that night? Everyone was on the same ticking clock. They might fool themselves into thinking that more time affords them opportunities to do more things, that the future is open-ended. But the world is simply too big. We weren't meant to see everything, we weren't built to do everything, we aren't capable of knowing everything. At a certain point, peace has to be found with the choices we've made.

"I've been thinking a lot about Colombia," Jordan admitted. He had an urge to return to Bogotá. It was fascinating to him, the idea that all the things that his parents escaped were now here, and all the things they wanted for their kids were now there. Random gun violence, political unrest, supply chain issues—those were all now American. Marriage equality, socialized medicine, and reproductive choice—those were all Colombian. And now the prospect of his life's end made him want to see where it all began.

Jordy set his glass down next to the bottle. "Then we should go," he said, but it was hard for him to mask some disappointment. To him Big Sur held the promise of more comfort. He worried they would debate this until it was too late to go.

"Oh, that reminds me," Jordan said. He sprang to his feet with an energy he hadn't displayed in weeks. "I got you a little something." He left the room briefly before returning with a gift bag that read *HAPPY BIRTHDAY*, spilling over with bright tissue paper.

"My birthday is in October."

Jordan shrugged. "It's all they had at Duane Reade."

Jordy forced a weak smile. He didn't want to say that it made him sad. Not because it was perhaps one of the last gifts he would receive from his husband, but rather because Jordan had always been an exquisite gift wrapper; in any given pile of gifts everyone always knew which one was from the Jordans. Now Jordan apparently didn't have the energy to try. Not only was the bag for the wrong occasion, it even had the little plastic hook still attached where it hung from a display, even though it was perforated for easy removal. Before his diagnosis, Jordan would have found a presentation like this abhorrent and worthy of bitchy critique.

"Go ahead. Open it."

Jordy pulled back the paper, revealing a box inside. He pulled out the game and gripped it with both hands, letting the now-empty bag fall to the floor.

"So we can continue the conversation after I'm gone," Jordan prompted, but Jordy wasn't amused. He tossed the gift aside and stood up to leave the room. "You remember. Like at Marielle's!"

Jordy left the room without saying a word, leaving Jordan alone with the fire and wine.

"Oh, come on, it's funny!" He picked up the Ouija board just as he heard their bedroom door slam closed.

To Jordy it was anything but.

TALKING TO MYSELF AND FEELING OLD

(MARIELLE, 2013)

M arielle met Max Dubicki inside the National Portrait Gallery her first week in D.C., and life, which had slowed to a crawl under the weight of her grief and the drudgery of packing her things to move across the country (not to mention slowly, painstakingly unpacking them once she had found an apartment), accelerated to a pace that once again resembled full speed. She had been desperate for an outing, and since she'd missed the city's famed cherry blossoms by a matter of weeks, and since it was already unseasonably muggy on this day in late spring, she decided one of the city's many museums would be ideal. She made quick haste through the presidential portraits, annoyed that they were all men. She paused only to admire the Elaine de Kooning portrait of JFK, perhaps her favorite—at least the artist was a woman and that would have to suffice until the subject could be one as well. Unlike the other portraits, which were stiff and monochromatic (Nixon's was painted by Rockwell, for heaven's sake), de Kooning's portrait screamed youth and vitality with its heavy swaths of green, blue, and gold. De Kooning, she learned, had an open marriage and carried on many affairs, most of them to advance her husband's painting career. Between painter and subject, Marielle marveled as to who might have had more trysts. It filled her with a rush of mixed emotions, the excitement of a free and offbeat sex life with the dread of it still sometimes being in service to a man. It had been only five weeks since Alec's death, and Marielle was determined in the wake of losing him to live a life in pursuit of her own pleasure and satisfaction. And then BAM—in search of a self-portrait by the artist Mary Cassatt, she ran headlong into a man—Max, he later told her—looking for the same painting. They agreed to find the portrait together, and when they finally did (the gallery, part of the Smithsonian, was a bit of a maze), Marielle was surprised by her reaction to the work—it was all so prim and *proper*; she'd rather hoped to see Cassatt express herself less conventionally. She struck up a conversation with this new man beside her about the friendship between Cassatt and Impressionist Edgar Degas. It was superficial at best, as neither of them were art scholars, relying instead on their audio self-guides; if this had been an actual date instead of an impromptu meeting, she would have called Craig in New York to prepare, since he was the expert on art.

"Do you think they had sex?" Max asked rather crudely, and, startled, Marielle started to blush. She pulled her headphones around her neck.

"Cassatt and Degas?"

"Yes."

Marielle bit her nails. "It's been my experience that most men are gay."

"Certainly not *most* men," Max protested, and in the way he said it Marielle detected a glimmer of interest.

"The good ones," she teased. "Besides. Not everything has to be about sex."

"But many things are. Don't you agree?" Max asked this in a legitimate and curious way, as if he'd have been perfectly happy to be proven wrong on the spot. Marielle, who felt tired and bloated (she'd missed her period with the stress of Alec and moving and figured today was its roaring return), couldn't muster the strength to disagree twice. "Sex between friends can be marvelous," he added, and Marielle blushed, thinking of Craig. "Let's just say we agree." Max extended his hand for the first time. After a slight hesitation she took it in her own, and she could see the flash of a new life ahead.

They were married that fall on the steps of the Supreme Court, where Max clerked for Justice Stevens. It was just the two of them (three if you counted the child Marielle was carrying) and a circuit court judge who Max played tennis with on weekends, and one of Max's fellow clerks who bore witness. Marielle wore a simple dress that had belonged to her mother and had retro puffed sleeves that delighted her; the empire waist both hid and accentuated her pregnancy, so her tailor only had to let the dress out a bit. She had wanted to invite her friends from Berkeley, but she was happy, or so she thought, and they were too close to Alec, both emotionally and to burying him, and she feared they would not understand. They would judge her as they always had, or misunderstand the invitation and assume this wedding was her already invoking their pact. Poor Marielle, the sensitive one, couldn't hack it out in the world and needed both a man and her friends to come running. They would have certainly had something to say about her being knocked up, and since she was excited about being a mother she didn't want to hear it. And she had new friends now, Max's, who supported them as a couple. Miraculously she had found someone who not only loved her but loved the idea of being a dad.

Until he didn't.

The rift started a year or so after Mia was born. She was blond like Alec, and had his pale skin, and didn't carry any of Max's Polish features. He tried to bond with her, but not very hard, and instead threw himself into his work. Or maybe his was a job that required all of him in a way that was not conducive to a new marriage and child, not that the why of it much mattered. They bought a condo in town, the down payment a wedding gift from his parents. The building was old, but the top-floor unit was newly refurbished; that didn't stop the roof from leaking when it rained, which in the spring of 1996 seemed like all the time. She'd had an internship in the office of Bob Packwood, one of the United States senators from her home state of Oregon, a moderate Republican—a dying breed—who was endorsed by women's groups for his dependable votes on a woman's right to choose. But he was forced to resign in October 1995 when allegations of sexual harassment that were long whispered came to a full-throated shout. His seat remained vacant until a special election could be held, and since Marielle was pregnant and about to be married, she didn't immediately look for other work. Packwood was a nasty man; she'd never been the victim of his abuse, but he would leer nonetheless, not even trying to hide it, the behavior of a person who'd gotten away with so many things for so long, and he'd never met a conversation with a woman he couldn't sexualize. It was crushing for Marielle, who went to Washington because she saw the good in people, and her lack of a job and her own social prospects made her further dependent on Max and his circle of friends. Once Mia arrived it was the two of them, sometimes huddled in the one dry corner of their sad condominium when it rained, always waiting for Max to come home; they were both usually asleep when he did.

Max stuck it out; it was what he thought a man did. He provided for the family, and they even eventually bought a house. But the mar-

riage was never much of a partnership and there wasn't a lot of love—
his affairs were frequent and eventually not all that well hidden. And
while he wasn't lecherous like Packwood had been, Marielle had come
to paint most men with a similar brush and she laughed when she
remembered that when she first ran into Max she had just come from
viewing a portrait of JFK. He asked for a divorce when Mia was just
shy of seventeen. She was mostly grown, Max reasoned. He had done
his job.

Marielle didn't think back to her college days often; when she did
memories were fuzzy and more like a dream. But it all came roaring
back when Mia found an old shoebox with photos and asked about
one of Alec.

"Who's he?" she inquired, and Marielle snatched the photo away,
as if Mia had employed a lustful tone.

"No one." But before the shoebox was back in the closet, Marielle
had decided to invoke the pact.

At first it wasn't entirely clear how—it wasn't like there was a Bat-
Signal or flare she could use to light up the sky. Technology had
changed in the intervening years; people had cell phones and email
now, Facebook and Instagram—it should have been easier than ever
to send her SOS. But Marielle didn't have everyone's contact information, as over the years they had drifted apart. She had seen Naomi a
few times when she swung through town, when an artist signed to her
label performed at the Kennedy Center or when Marielle had introduced her to Max when they took a family trip to Disneyland. The
Jordans were in New York, that much she knew. A quick Google
search found a website for the public relations firm they ran; those two
had to be practically conjoined. Craig was also in New York, or at least
she assumed, but he was harder to find. She found the name of a gallery on the Lower East Side that listed him as an archivist. But there
was absolutely no contact information included on the site, other than

an address. This was a gallery that traded in money, and if you had money (which Marielle didn't—at least not that kind of it), you just knew how to get in touch. To reach Craig she would have to rely on the Jordans.

And yet she hesitated when it came time to actually pick up the phone, reasoning she couldn't both come up with the pact *and* be the first one to invoke it—it just wasn't a good look. But this was a moment. Her husband was gone, and with him her youth; Mia had one foot out the door (Marielle had already taken her to tour three colleges); and she was staring down the barrel at forty. But all of that was secondary to the immense sadness she felt that other than raising Mia she had wasted her life, and it became harder and harder to get out of bed. When she finally gained the nerve to dial Naomi, she reached her at her office. When told Naomi was in a meeting, Marielle surprised both Naomi's assistant and herself by demanding, "GET HER OUT."

When Naomi's voice came through the other end of the line, it dripped with annoyance. "Jesus, Marielle, and Joseph," she said. "What are you doing calling me at work?"

"The p-pact," Marielle stammered.

"Pack of what?" Naomi asked confused.

She understood Naomi's bewilderment. Marielle was certain none of them had thought much of the pact in the intervening years. It was like a horror film she'd recently stumbled upon where a group of friends who had clashed with a demon in childhood promised to reunite in battle if the demon came calling again. So Marielle said quite simply, "I need you to come to my funeral."

After a moment of silence in which Marielle could imagine the quiet protest Naomi was mounting, Naomi said simply, "Okay."

Funerals are held by and large near where the deceased made their home; mourners are expected to travel to the deceased, rarely the other way around. But despite what felt like near-crippling depression, Marielle held an unyielding need to break out of her routine, and travel seemed as good a way as any to shake things up. After convincing a shocked Naomi that this was indeed for real, it was decided— they would all return to Sur la Vie. Marielle even mused about bringing Mia, at least for one night, so that she could introduce her to her friends before setting her loose to visit West Coast colleges, including their alma mater.

Once she relented and dropped the pretense of being put out, the version of Naomi who was always good in a crisis took charge. And Marielle was grateful; while one could have input into the celebration of one's life if they wanted, no one should truly have to plan their own funeral. Naomi even came up with a code name, as was custom for British royal funeral plans: Operation Esalen. Esalen was Big Sur's holistic learning center, whose pamphlets boasted that they embraced the "messy, imperfect practice of moving toward our highest humanity." If that didn't sound like Marielle, Naomi would eat a shoe. And there was a certain sense to following royal protocol. Only people of that rarefied stature had to have their funerals fully planned long before their actual demise.

Naomi got through to the Jordans, who were shocked to hear from her but yes, of course, immediately remembered the pact. Craig was a different animal, and she had to leave three messages of increasing urgency before he bothered to call her back. His evolution on the subject was annoying to Naomi. First he claimed not to remember their pact, then suggested he was busy and couldn't possibly be held to it, and finally seemed resigned but frustrated with the timing and cost. It would have been a lot more efficient if he had just immediately hitched his wagon to the train of their procession, but Naomi employed a rope-a-dope strategy and let him tire himself out; she knew him well enough to know he would eventually relent and agree to be there. Finally, she did her best to track down her parents to make sure that Sur la Vie would be empty; of course they were overseas and it was. Soon, dates were chosen and travel itineraries made and arrangements for Marielle's funeral were not only under way but nearly complete.

T his is weird." The words spilled from Craig's mouth, but it could have been any of them speaking. He made a full lap of Sur la Vie's main floor like it was a museum dedicated to their past, hands carefully held behind his back, not getting too close to any one thing, as if there were invisible velvet stanchions keeping him back. "I feel like I should be sad. Am I sad?"

"*I'm* sad," Marielle offered, as if her own grief might be something she could share to darken their mood.

"I brought pie," Craig offered. He'd been lugging around a bakery box from a place he loved in Manhattan.

"Enough with the pie!" Naomi walked over to Marielle and wrapped her arms around her, but since she was so much shorter it looked instead of hugging her like she was trying to perform the Heimlich. Marielle eventually wriggled free and said, "Maybe I should go lie down." She headed up the stairs to her room.

"Like this!" Craig called after her, clasping his hands peacefully across his midsection like a corpse placed in a casket. When she responded by shutting the door to her bedroom, he turned to Naomi and added, "She gets it," hoping that at least one of them did.

Naomi plopped down on the couch. "Nana, where have you *been*? No one has seen you in years." She studied him. He still looked the same, much like the Craig they knew. He had dark circles under his eyes, like maybe he'd missed a few nights' sleep, but his frame and his expressions were the same.

"The weekend's not about me."

"Yeah. But we can't really make it about Marielle until *the Jordans* arrive." She said *the Jordans* with mocking disdain. "You're not going to tell me anything about your life?"

"What is there to tell?"

Naomi hit him with a cushion.

"All of this is too Courteney Cox," he said, looking again around Sur la Vie.

"*Oh my god*," Naomi said. She hadn't thought about the scale of Courtneys in years.

Marielle whipped open her bedroom door. "I can't sleep," she said, as if she'd been tossing and turning for hours. She twirled once, but her usual behaviors didn't match her mood or the occasion. "What shall we do to pass the time?"

Naomi suggested a walk on the beach. It was out of character for her, wanting anything to do with nature, but it provoked the first smile Marielle had had in weeks.

Pfeiffer Beach lay south of Big Sur Station just off Highway 1. Naomi's rented Jeep Grand Cherokee made the turn marked Narrow Road, but just barely; if the car had been any bigger, the trek down to the beach would have been ill-advised. Once they parked it was only a short walk to the beach.

Marielle inhaled deeply the moment she stepped from the car; the ocean's tang was both salty and healing and she was overcome with shame about this whole to-do. She didn't need a funeral so much as she needed a *vacation*. She could be on a beach in Tahiti sipping a piña colada healing herself instead of waiting for her friends to deliver her last rites. But she brushed it off as Naomi and Craig exited the car. A pact was made and she herself had triggered it. They were already here and the Jordans were well on their way.

Pfeiffer Beach faced a massive rock outcropping that jutted from the ocean just a few hundred feet offshore with an open arch called Keystone. Photographers were already lining up in the sand to capture that magical moment at sunset when the sun's rays were low enough on the water to shine through. The tide was out and they trudged north, heads low into the wind, their hands in their pockets to protect them from the chill.

"What was the breaking point?" Naomi asked as they reached a tide pool and leaned over to see their reflections.

"With Max?"

"What made you call time of death?"

Marielle winced, suddenly realizing she was there for her marriage's funeral as much as her own. "It's silly."

"Everything's *silly*," Craig insisted.

Marielle dipped her head as if she agreed that life was a farce, even though she didn't believe that one bit.

"I was listening to Marianne Faithfull."

"Ugh. Self-help." Craig's face soured; it was visible even in his reflection.

"What? No." Marielle stood up straight. "You're thinking of Marianne Williamson."

"Who did you say, then?"

Naomi glared at Craig. "Marianne Faithfull. Folk singer. Used to be with Mick Jagger." Her tone dripped with disgust, as if Craig's lack of familiarity were an act of misogyny; surely he could name at least three Rolling Stones. Naomi turned back to Marielle. "Continue."

"I was listening to 'The Ballad of Lucy Jordan,' waiting to pick up Mia from school."

Naomi turned to Craig. "Mia is her daughter," as if all women needed to be contextualized.

"It's about the mental deterioration of a suburban housewife. At thirty-seven she comes to realize that she'll never drive through the city of Paris with the top down. That sort of thing."

"The warm wind in her hair." Naomi knew the words to almost every worthwhile song.

"And I thought, oh my god. *I'm* thirty-seven. That's me. I've never been to Paris."

Craig was confused. "You're thirty-nine."

Marielle glared. "Sometimes it takes years for a woman to put her needs first."

As they meandered closer to the far end of the beach the sand beneath them turned reddish, and then purple. Naomi pointed to the cliffs as explanation; the stone was a kind of garnet that gave the sand its unique color when eroded.

"Take off your shoes," Naomi ordered.

"Excuse me?"

"Take off your goddamned shoes. It's no Paris in a sports car, but when have you ever walked barefoot with purple sand beneath your toes?"

Marielle hesitated only a second before she slipped off her sandals and stepped barefoot in the sand. The beach was cold, and she immediately retreated toward the cliffs, where the sand was apt to be drier. It was still cold, but not wet, and she buried her feet deep within it. Naomi was right. Not everything had to be Paris to be a life experience. It was just that some things needed to be new, and carry with them the air of excitement that comes with the uncharted. She curled her toes in the sand until her ankles were fully submerged, and then excavated them just as quickly.

"'Purple' comes from the Latin *purpura*," Craig offered, having removed his own shoes to join them in the experience. "The color was first made from the mucus excretion of snails." He stomped around, kicking some toward the water, seemingly less concerned about the sand swallowing him.

"Why. Why would you say that?" Naomi was annoyed he would ruin the moment. Craig shoved his hands in his pockets. As an artist, now gallerist, he had always been interested in the origin of colors.

"*Rare* snails," he added, as if that was what made it better. "The color used to be associated with royalty."

"OH MY GOD. SHUT UP!"

Marielle smiled, then sat down and looked at her bare toes. Specks of sand clung to her nail polish, catching the light just so; snails or no snails, it looked like a whole galaxy existed across each pedicured nail. She had an overwhelming pang for Alec. He was out there somewhere, in the galaxy, the universe, in her too, growing smaller and smaller perhaps with each passing year but never going entirely away.

"Look," Naomi said, pointing at the photographers. There was a sudden flurry of activity as the sun shone through the arch. Their tripods were perfectly silhouetted against the pink sky like long-legged crabs holding court on the sand.

Marielle leaned back on her elbows, positioning herself to better see. It was beautiful, and for a brief, shining moment the keystone was like a keyhole, a tiny window into another, more perfect world. Soft light came pouring through, its rays catching the sea-foam and spray from the waves that crashed around it. The effect was unlike anything she'd ever seen. "Alec," she whispered as the whole tableau was bursting with his radiant energy. Then she immediately felt foolish and was grateful that neither Naomi nor Craig had heard. She then imagined for a moment this really *was* her funeral, and she was overcome with an image of Naomi and Craig awkwardly wading out to the arch with an urn filled with her ashes, ready to launch particles of her into the last of the day's magical light. She could even see Naomi turning to flip off and cuss the annoyed photographers with a record-breaking string of obscenities when they yelled at her for getting in the way of their shot.

"What?" Naomi asked, when she caught Marielle laughing.

Marielle could only reply with the truth. "You."

Back at Sur la Vie, Craig fretted over where they would start. Marielle didn't know what she expected her friends to do (this was always a problem with going first), but that *something* would start and that she would be the focus of it tickled her deep inside. Naomi said it would come to them when the time was right, and she said it with a certainty that allowed Marielle to draw hope. They would fix this, her funk, with some sort of service or incantation. The Jordans would arrive and something would begin. They might even be at the store now, buying kindling and ample supplies. Candles for prayer. Kleenex for a good cry. Charcuterie for a reception. They'd light a fire and all dance around it, burning talismans of her painful past, then eat cream cheese pinwheels or something equally horrid that you might be served at a wake.

"I ditched jury duty for this," Craig said as he worked on opening the fireplace's flue.

"What an unbelievable sacrifice." Naomi barely looked up from her phone.

"Well, I'm uncomfortable with the word 'hero,'" Craig grunted, his arm deep in the fireplace.

"Are you trying to open the flue? Or give my fireplace a gynecological exam?"

With a final push, he moved the lever. "There," he said, brushing soot off his hand. He looked up to see Marielle staring at him. "It's all bullshit anyway, jury service. Like the government wants me to drop everything to solve a crime for fifteen dollars and somehow that's my *duty*? I don't think so."

"How about more fire building and less social commentary." Marielle's heart rate was starting to rise. She was getting that feeling she had as a girl in the run-up to Christmas; it wasn't every day you got to attend your own funeral. She watched Craig light the fire, then take a seat on the edge of Mr. Ito's BarcaLounger. He had an uneasiness about him too, like he was afraid he was doing something wrong and could be scolded by Naomi's father for sitting in his chair, or worse, by some sort of god for partaking in this nonsense. Having a funeral for a living person was a deliberate act of upsetting the natural order; they'd all seen enough movies to worry they might be unleashing dark forces on their lives. A siren passed the house, adding a plaintive wail to their fears. They said nothing as it faded into the distance.

"I can't stand the waiting!" Marielle finally exclaimed.

"*You* called us here," Craig said without even a modicum of sympathy.

She fidgeted with her hair. "I know." She went to look out the window; with darkness falling, she saw mostly her own reflection. "I was going to bring Mia," she confessed, suddenly wishing her daughter were here. It would give them all someone else to focus on. "I thought she could join us for a night, and then go tour Berkeley, as she's looking at colleges, but she said she wasn't interested." Marielle didn't know what pained her more, her daughter missing out on meeting her friends, or expressing no interest in her alma mater—the place where those friendships were made.

"Just as well," Naomi said. "I heard Berkeley's over."

It was a strange phenomenon, the tendency to think your experience with something was the best and it could never be as good again. "Berkeley will never be *over*." Marielle was quite convinced the students who were there now loved it as much as they had then.

The sound of slamming car doors made them scramble to their feet. "Finally," Marielle said when she saw parking lights in the driveway go dark.

When the Jordans walked through the door it wasn't with kindling or sage, but rather groceries and a case of Pellegrino. Hugs were exchanged, those with Marielle extra tight. While squashed in the Jordans' embrace she attempted to peer into their grocery bags for evidence of magical ingredients: eye of newt, bat wing, something with apothecarial potential. She would have even settled for an offbeat choice of produce like an unidentified pepper that burned with unexpected heat, but the most unusual item on top of the bags was a container of watercress pesto. If healing were to derive from this funeral, it would have to come from within.

After dinner Craig restoked the fading fire and they gathered around the hearth. Marielle sat on the floor, pulling her knees to her chest. She took comfort in the warmth, which she drew from the reunion as much as the fire.

"It's strange, isn't it," Jordan said while Jordy massaged his shoulders.

"To be back where it all began?"

"I never thought we'd actually do this," Craig agreed.

"Then why did you agree to be a part of it?"

"I don't know, why did I shop at Structure?" Craig and Jordy laughed, remembering the defunct men's store. "Why did we listen to Ace of Base? Why did we do anything?"

Naomi reappeared with a bag of weed. "Actually, Ace of Base were Nazis, so we never should have listened to them at all."

"Ace of Base were Nazis?" Craig was incredulous. "According to whom?"

Naomi sighed, like it was an imposition to explain. "I heard their name was in reference to some submarine base the Germans had. All the best U-boat captains launched in and out of there, so it was nicknamed the base of aces."

"But they were Swedish!"

"I'm just telling you what I heard."

"If only you saw the signs." Marielle reached for the bag of weed. "Where did this come from?"

"I stashed it here my last visit. *Thank god.*"

"You keep that in the kitchen?" Marielle asked. "What if your mother finds it?"

Naomi shook her head. "What's she going to do? Ground me? I'm forty years old." She sat down at the coffee table and produced some rolling papers.

"Well, here we are." Craig held his wineglass up to the fire and gave it a swirl, studying the color of his pinot to see if it met some imaginary standard. "So, you guys are publicists and Naomi is VP at a music label."

"*The* music label," Naomi said, since she worked at the biggest one.

"And I'm nothing," Marielle said with self-pity.

"You're not *nothing*," Naomi insisted. "Nana's a gallerist. I mean, if you want to talk about nothing, that surely sounds made up."

Craig didn't protest, in part because he could see that Marielle was spiraling. She felt like her friends had all done things and had more to show for their lives. Yes, she had raised a child and none of the rest of them had, but was that what she set out to do when she left Berkeley? She felt so different from the rest of them, like she'd been plucked from another friend group and randomly dropped into this one.

"Wow, Naomi," Craig said, interrupting Marielle's train of thought. He pointed at the joint Naomi had rolled.

She proudly held up the finished product. "Oh, you *can* recognize good art. Maybe you're a gallerist after all." She fished in her bag for a lighter.

"So is this enough?" Jordy asked once the joint had been passed around. "Can we just hang out here all weekend cracking jokes and bottles of wine? I don't know about you, Marielle. But this feels good for *my* soul."

Craig reached for the blunt to take a second hit. "Or do we have to, you know, do stuff."

"You know, when you say 'do stuff' it sounds sexual," Jordan said.

Craig winked at Jordan. "We'll see where the night goes."

Marielle stewed in her own disappointment, suddenly worried she would have to do everything herself. Like a wife does. Like a mother does. She was the one most lost and yet, like always, others were leaning on her for direction. "It's not enough," she finally said. "I went from loving Alec to loving Max to loving Mia. Right now I need to love myself."

Craig put his arm around her and pulled her in tight. "Do you want us to, like, leave the room?"

Marielle gasped in horror and they all broke into shrieks of laughter. Jordan took Marielle's hand and promised they would step it up.

Together they decided Marielle's funeral would be Sunday at dusk, giving them most of the weekend to plan. Since they were all leaving early on Monday, it left the smallest window for awkward silence afterward if it turned out the whole event was a sham. They formed committees, Naomi and Craig on flowers, the Jordans taking charge of food.

"I need a job," Marielle protested at breakfast. "I can't just lay around all day."

"Isn't that literally what the deceased does?" Craig asked.

Jordy laughed. "Jealous?"

Marielle still felt left out and eventually took charge of preparing the house. She would clean and fluff pillows, and arrange the patio chairs to best fit their needs; Craig resisted a joke about rearranging deck chairs on the *Titanic*.

"What else do we need?" Jordan asked as he ticked off a list on his phone. "Programs?"

"No programs," Marielle insisted. As much as she might be tickled some day in the future finding a memento from the weekend in a scrapbook, she didn't need evidence of her own funeral for Mia to find—no matter how much it was meant to inspire her to live. "But there had better be, you know, a *program*."

They understood. This wasn't about flowers or finger foods or remembrance cards with fancy calligraphy. Marielle was the one who'd suggested the pact and it was for very specific reasons: celebration, community, love. To remind themselves that at any given moment others carried them in higher esteem than they might themselves. It was designed to lift them in their lowest moments to keep them from doing anything rash.

"Just give me something special."

Craig looked at the others, confused. "You mean like a . . . Fabergé egg?"

Marielle tapped her foot, annoyed. "Something special of yourselves."

You never married?" Craig wondered as he wandered through town with Naomi. They were looking for the florist, which Naomi swore up and down had moved, but Craig suspected from her frustrated stomping that it was more likely than not right where it had always been and Naomi was just confused. Which was fine; he was happy to be out of the house.

"Jesus Christ."

Craig thought she meant the florist. "Relax. It's around here some-where."

"Not the florist. *You*." She then repeated his question in a mock-ing tone.

"I was just asking."

"I'm not a thousand years old, Craig."

"I never said!"

"I'm forty, not Lesley Stahl. I'm in my sexual prime."

Craig laughed, because who's to say Lesley Stahl wasn't in her sexual prime. "Is there a man?"

Naomi took a few steps past a laundromat before answering.

"There are men."

Craig was impressed. And maybe a little jealous.

"Anyone special?"

Naomi whipped her head to the side to look at him. "Me. *I'm* special. And until the right man realizes that, they can all be happy with whatever bit of me they get." She waved at someone in the street, but Craig wasn't sure if it was in recognition or urging them to move along and not gawk. "What about you?"

"What about me?"

"*You* never married."

"So," he said, but with much less confidence. There were women, especially of late, but he had always been more coy, shy about sharing these things, and that much had not changed. "How come you never say hello?"

Naomi made a face. "Like on Facebook? I'd rather die."

"When you come to New York."

"How do you know when I'm in New York?"

"From Facebook."

Naomi clenched her fist. Social media was her personal nemesis. She was guilty of posting, just like anyone else—it helped her seem relevant in her job. Seeing this band. Sharing music from her label. Jet-setting all over the world. But it was going to be the death of privacy, if not civilization entirely. "I'm not there for social reasons. I'm working."

"You see a lot of concerts," Craig observed.

"Yes, that's me working. What's with the needy act?"

Craig wasn't certain. He knew (at least as far as Facebook was concerned) that she wasn't seeing the Jordans either, so it wasn't a fear of missing out. But the last time they were all together they lived under one roof, and at the time it felt like that would continue forever, that they would never again live apart. And if they did, it was almost unimaginable that they might be in the same city, even one as big as New York, and not even bother to at least say hello. "I can't tell if you're different or exactly the same."

"You're exactly the same," Naomi observed. And then added, reluctantly, "Except better looking." But she said it with her usual bluntness, which made it sound more like an insult about how he used to look than a compliment about his appearance now.

"Thanks, I think."

Eventually, they stumbled upon the florist. But instead of relief that they'd found it, Naomi felt a sort of horror induced by the artless display in the window.

"Tragic," Craig agreed.

"Small towns," Naomi griped. Even a small town with money.

"Maybe Marielle will like them." Before Craig could finish getting the words out of his mouth, he already knew that she wouldn't.

Naomi caught a glimpse of herself in the florist's window and was surprised by how tired she looked. She had been confronted the night before with a similar exhaustion staring back at her from her parents' bathroom mirror at Sur la Vie, but had chalked it up to her travels, having recently returned to L.A. from Glasgow, where she attended three nights of Coldplay shows at Hampden Park. But now here it was again, plaguing her in the light of midday, even after a decent night's sleep. She tried pinching color into her cheeks. "When did I start looking so tired all the time?"

"You want, like, an answer?" Craig queried, which was perhaps an intended dig. Truth was he was feeling pretty good about himself. Not even by way of comparison—there was nothing wrong with the way Naomi looked. He was just feeling like he had it together and he was happy that she had noticed. He'd made a name for himself at the gallery, after making several important sales including two Lucian Freuds. The few lines in his face and the gray at his temples helped him engender trust with the gallery's clientele, who were largely older and cautious and generally skeptical of youth and inexperience, especially so in the art world. His body had filled out with a bit of muscle thanks to joining one of those rock-climbing gyms, and he had money for clothes that were tailored to fit, and he was the rare straight man in a world full of women and gay men, which made him more often than not the center of (sometimes wanted) attention. He was finally who he imagined himself to be.

"Watch yourself," Naomi warned as she brushed past him to enter the florist. "I'm not in the mood for your snark."

"No snark." He had his hands up in peaceful surrender, but his words were lost under the sound of the jingle bells that hung from the florist's front door.

They looked at a few over-the-top arrangements inside the shop before Craig whispered, "Let's ask if they can do something less grotesque."

Naomi sighed. Such a waste of money. "I never understood flowers at funerals. Like, you need more death? As if there's not already a body decomposing, we need to watch even faster decay?"

"Funerals don't last long enough for flowers, or bodies, to decay."

Naomi shot Craig a withering look. "Just you watch. This one will."

"At least in this case, the body is still very fresh."

Naomi puckered her forehead. Was that a good thing? The oddity that was this affair was starting to bother her; she might have preferred Marielle actually be dead for the sake of her own comfort.

A saleswoman appeared from a refrigerated back room, the door wafting an overwhelming air of perfume as it closed. "I'm Bonnie," she said.

Naomi's reply was "Of course you are."

A re you going to be on your phone the whole time?"

The Jordans drove to Carmel to complete their assigned tasks when they were reminded that the shopping in Big Sur was limited. They found a food mart that passed muster; it carried a few recognizable brands and delicacies they might find at home in Gristedes. Deep in the wine aisle, Jordy pushed their cart past a shelf of Argentinian reds.

"The wine should be Californian," Jordy instructed, cradling his phone with his shoulder as he waited for someone to pick up. No one did and he eventually hung up.

"Did you leave a message?" Jordan asked, curiosity suddenly piqued.

"Did you hear me leave a message?"

Jordan sighed heavily and wandered ahead until a bottle of pinot caught his eye. "It's not our fault, you know. Be sure to tell them that when you do leave a message."

"What's not our fault?"

"The *season*," Jordan said, as if it should have been perfectly obvious. "We didn't program the season."

"I know that. And certainly they know that."

"I know *they* know that, but they've got to blame someone for their shortsightedness and the horrible lack of diversity."

"Well, they can't blame us." Jordy grabbed a bottle off the shelf. The label had an artistic rendering of a California condor.

"Watch them."

"They can't!"

"They'll blame us for the unfortunate press coverage *about* the lack of diversity."

"Oh. Yeah. That we will be blamed for." Jordy studied the bottle. The feathers around the bird's neck encircled its head like a decorative boa, giving it a serious, if judgmental, air. "Look at this vulture."

"I think it's a condor."

"She looks like she's been thrice-divorced."

Jordan relaxed into an easy smile. "Marielle will love that. A bird. A divorcée. Get all six bottles."

Jordy was skeptical. "Is it drinkable?"

"Not our funeral."

He pulled every bottle they had from the shelf before surveying their end of the store.

"Do you think they have an olive bar?"

Jordy waved his hand across the store, a gesture meant to ask *What do you think?*

Jordan put one foot on the cart's lower rack and leaned forward onto the handle. "Do you ever think about Alec?"

Jordy was caught off guard by the question, although perhaps he shouldn't have been. "Sure."

"We never talk about him."

Jordy did a quick count of wine bottles in the cart. *Ten.* Two bottles per for the weekend; hopefully that was enough—they weren't twenty-two anymore. "We don't talk about a lot of things," he said, which was an admitted problem in their relationship. Then, not wanting to get into it in a market in Carmel, he backpedaled and said, "We talk."

Jordan shrugged. *Agree to disagree.*

"What is there to say?" Jordy started down the aisle before turning back to face his boyfriend. "That sounded callous. I didn't mean to sound callous. It's this business with the season. It's not our fault."

"And still we're going to get blamed."

Jordy thought about their predicament for another moment while looking for the deli department. "It's no one's fault."

"It's *some*one's fault." This was the problem with being in business with his romantic partner: Jordan could never guarantee which hat Jordy would be wearing. Jordy his business partner was solution-oriented. That was good, a necessary quality to have. But Jordy his life partner was sometimes short on listening and providing comfort because he was always too focused on the business. Yes, it was no one person's fault that the current season of the distinguished theater company they represented was composed of its least diverse lineup of shows in a decade. Shows take years to make it to New York, and there's often no rhyme or reason as to which ones succeed and which falter along the way. To Jordy that might feel like the luck of the draw, the way this season's cookie crumbled. But Jordy was white, and it wasn't always his first instinct to consider the systemic problems that might have caused the diverse shows to fold out of town in the first place, or at the very least created an environment that made it harder for them to thrive. Or think to comfort his romantic partner, or see how a theatrical season that was alarmingly light on people of color might be upsetting to someone named Vargas.

"We can talk about him if you like," Jordy offered. And then quickly added, "Alec," in case that wasn't clear. Jordy felt a lump in his throat. When it came to Alec there were definitely things they had not discussed.

"I miss how easy everything was. Or how easy he made life seem." Jordan rattled their cart playfully until Jordy stood up to his full height. "Remember that time he was so fucked up he forgot where he had parked his car? And so he reported it to campus police as stolen?"

Jordy laughed. "And then stumbled upon it the next day in a completely different parking lot and called campus police again to chew them out for not finding it?" Jordy smiled. It was a typical Alec story. "Yeah, I remember. God, he hated the police."

"Always ahead of his time." Jordan waved their shopping list and motioned for them to move on. In another aisle he studied jars of pickled vegetables. "We don't have to talk about him now. This weekend isn't about Alec."

Jordy was quick to protest. "Isn't it, though?"

"The weekend belongs to Marielle."

"I guess we're all walking around with unsettled trauma."

Jordan sat with that diagnosis as he held two jars of roasted red peppers. His instinct was to deny it; he didn't feel like he was shouldering trauma. But almost as soon as Alec's funeral was over they scattered in the wind. Jordy had gone to Los Angeles and Jordan to New York. That lasted all of three weeks. Jordy flew to New York and landed on Jordan's doorstep, everything he owned in the giant duffel bag he used to carry to swim meets. "I belong with you" was all he managed to say before Jordan pulled him inside the tiny one-bedroom on West 53rd and served him some leftover soup. Jordy never left.

Jordan weighed the two jars of peppers in his hands like he was Indiana Jones about to replace a priceless relic with a bag of sand. "I'm so inspired . . ." He began, before trailing off in thought.

"By me?" Jordy asked, full of hope.

"What? No . . . By this sandwich I had."

Jordy laughed. This could have easily ruffled his feathers; he was so sure in that instant that the answer was going to be him. But this was typical of the way people in long-term relationships sometimes talked past each other, and the best thing to do was brush it off.

"You remember. That place in Little Italy? With the mozzarella and kalamata tapenade?"

Jordy did indeed remember. The sandwich was huge and he had allowed Jordy a few bites. It was the best fresh mozzarella he'd ever had. "The ciabatta was so soft."

"Right? I want to do something like that for the funeral. Olives. Cheeses. Roasted vegetables. Bread. Simple. Vegetarian. To the point. Just like Marielle." Jordan decided on the more expensive jar of peppers and placed the cheaper one back on the shelf.

"Marielle's *funeral*," Jordy said. It sounded so strange.

"Well, what would you call it? Celebration of life?" It was part of their job in PR to rebrand.

"No, 'funeral' works," Jordy said. "But it's still weird."

"You know what else is weird?" Jordan pointed to an endcap of crackers.

"That they keep making Cheez-Its in bigger sizes?"

Jordan shook his head no. "That we're doing this errand together. I see you every day. We should have split up to spend time with Naomi and Nana."

Jordy smirked.

"What?"

"I was just picturing you interrupting Naomi to tell her you were inspired by a sandwich." Jordy made a fist. "She would lay you out on the floor."

When they sat down to dinner that night it was around a table covered in white floral arrangements as tall as they were wide. Somehow, none of them realized what an impediment the bouquets would be to their sharing a meal until they were already seated.

"Did anyone think to buy flowers?" Jordan asked. He reached out and gathered a few to stand them more upright in their vase.

"This is absurd," Marielle said. "I can't see anyone." She moved left, then right, blocked in both attempts by the spectacular opulence, so that all she could see was Naomi, who sat next to her. The three men across from her were unseen, like on an old game show where women had to pick a suitor solely from the sound of his voice. She stood to strike a few of the more obnoxious displays from the table. "These have to go." She then pushed the remaining two bouquets to the end of the table and retook her seat. "That's more like it." She was relieved to finally see the faces of her friends, even if their expressions were, at best, bemused.

"A simple 'thank you' would have sufficed," Naomi said.

"Thank you? For what?"

"The flowers. We got them for you!"

"You know I have allergies! I could have gone into anaphylactic shock. Are you willing to stab me with an EpiPen?"

"I'm willing to stab you with something."

"Girls!" Jordan shouted, which gave them somewhere else to direct their ire.

They dug into the cacio e pepe that Jordan had made. The Jordans had recently returned from Italy and were having a hard time letting go of their trip.

"This is good, Jor—"

"Besides," Marielle began, cutting Naomi off, unable to leave well enough alone. "I'm more of an 'in lieu of flowers' kind of girl."

Annoyed, Naomi set her fork down. "We'll remember that when you're actually dead."

Craig, who was also on flower detail, likewise took offense. "We spent twelve hundred dollars!"

"TWELVE HUNDRED DOLLARS!" Marielle recoiled.

Naomi coughed aggressively, prompting Craig to turn red.

Marielle turned to Naomi. "Do *you* need my EpiPen?"

Craig corrected himself. "*Naomi.* Naomi spent twelve hundred dollars."

Marielle never worried about Naomi dropping money, which she had done any number of times in college without thought; the Itos had more than their share. It seemed strange, now that she had a successful career of her own in the music industry that appeared to have endless perks—concerts, travel, access to famous people—that she would object to spending on luxuries like flowers. But that was not the point. "Do you know how much good twelve hundred dollars could have done in the hands of a decent charity? That could have been my legacy."

"How can you have a legacy when you're SITTING RIGHT HERE?"

Marielle ignored her. "How can you honor our pact and make me feel like my life has value if you're not going to actually stop and value my life? I can't be in charge of everything; you're supposed to throw this funeral for me! Otherwise, what's the point?"

The Jordans looked to each other and Craig, then across the table at Naomi. Perhaps they weren't taking this seriously enough. "Since this is our very first time . . ." Jordan began, hoping she would cut them some slack.

"WHAT." Marielle dared him to finish that sentence.

"Nothing," he said, backing down.

Naomi, fork back in hand, was aggressively twirling pasta. "Maybe your problem is that *you* haven't given enough thought to who you are."

Marielle pushed her chair back from the table and was overcome by the aroma of flowers. It made Sur la Vie smell like honeysuckle, as sickly sweet as its name. They would have to put the arrangements outside for the night and risk them attracting the deer. Which might actually work for Marielle. At least flowers as food would be doing some good.

"Where are you going?" Naomi implored.

"To get another bottle of wine." No one said anything else until she returned; they just listened to the sound of her rustling in the kitchen, opening and closing a curious number of drawers. When she returned, she was holding a spatula. "I'm sorry if my life falling apart first is an inconvenience for you all."

"First?" Craig didn't like the insinuation that the rest of them would topple like dominoes.

"Oh, the gallerist has it *all* figured out." Marielle laid it on as thick as the floral smell. "How lovely for your therapist."

Craig replied defensively, "I don't have a therapist."

Marielle gasped. Everyone she knew in D.C. had a therapist.

Jordan reached across the table and took Marielle's spatula. "Mare, is that what it feels like? Your life has fallen apart?"

"WHAT LIFE?!"

The whole table jumped.

"Mia will be off to college soon. Our friends were Max's. I have no career. Look at all of you! You're so *successful*. I haven't accomplished anything."

"You raised a daughter to be a remarkable young woman."

"You don't know that."

"I know her mother," Jordan continued. "Who as a young woman cared about the whole world. I have to imagine your daughter is much the same way."

"Wait," Jordy said, Jordan's words just sinking in. "You're stepping on my eulogy."

"Eulogy?" Craig asked. Marielle grabbed the spatula back and rapped it on the table three times. Was no one listening to her?

This time Jordy took the spatula as he turned to Craig. "We wrote eulogies on the plane." He looked around the table to make sure that he and Jordan hadn't misunderstood the assignment. "Didn't you?"

"No," Craig and Naomi deadpanned. Naomi stepped into the kitchen for the wine bottle Marielle had failed to retrieve.

"You didn't?" Marielle wasn't necessarily expecting prepared eulogies, but now that she knew they were an option she very much wanted them.

"I didn't know there would be homework," Naomi called from the kitchen.

"That's the whole point! You're supposed to tell me how you feel. Nothing left unsaid, that's what we promised."

Naomi returned, filling her wineglass almost comically to the rim. "At this rate, I'll have plenty to say off-the-cuff."

A quick exchange of glances around the table. They were only one funeral into their pact and already it was an unmitigated disaster that not only was failing to bring them together, it was—if possible—driving them further apart.

"Maybe we didn't think this through."

"Somebody hand me the salad." Marielle held both hands out, expecting to be handed the oversized wooden salad bowl. When no one made a move she yelled, "SALAD!" Craig jumped and reached for the bowl, which Jordan took from his hands.

"Forget the salad," he said, setting it at the end of the table nearest the flowers. As if on cue, a white rose petal fell into the bowl from an arrangement called (much to Naomi's horror) the Cherished Friend Bouquet. "Marielle. We dropped everything to fly three thousand miles, all of us, after not having seen each other in years, to honor a pact we made as kids." Jordan looked around at his friends. "I wouldn't do that for anyone not at this table. You profoundly changed my life, Marielle, and I'm eternally grateful for you."

Jordy threw his hands in the air. "Well, now you're quoting directly *from* my eulogy. I never should have let you read it!"

Jordan turned to his boyfriend, confused. "I thought *I* wrote that."

"I wrote about gratitude. *You* wrote about inspiration."

Jordan shook his head. "Well. In any case. Forgive us if we bumble our way through the ceremony. But we're here." He retrieved the salad and handed it to Marielle as a peace offering; she tried to serve it with the spatula.

Craig leaned forward to address the Jordans. "You know I skipped jury duty for this?"

"There's no jury duty on weekends!" Marielle exclaimed, exasperated. It was just ridiculous enough that she laughed.

After dinner they changed into sweats and sleeping attire, with Nana in his signature nightshirt. "Still with the nightshirts?" Jordy asked.

Craig widened his stance as far as the nightshirt allowed. "I like a little airflow down there."

Even though they were still feeling fragile, their bodies found each other like they had in college. Jordy sat on the couch and massaged Craig's shoulders as he sat on the floor in front of him; Jordan ran his fingers through Marielle's hair, dividing it into sections to braid, while her feet lay in Craig's lap to rub. It was the kind of intimacy between friends who had spent years living together, where the only solid borders between them were the occasional locked dormitory door when one of them entertained.

Naomi joined them last, her hair wet from the shower, carrying a stack of board games. She set them on the coffee table and assumed her place in the pile while reaching for a palmier cookie. She studied the layers of pastry swirled in a knot and almost asked where they had materialized from, but she knew—they arrived with the Jordans; homosexuals never come empty-handed.

Marielle leaned forward to study the games, taking much of her hair with her.

"Whoa, whoa, whoa," Jordan said as he was dragged along with her, his fingers enmeshed in her tangles and split ends.

Parcheesi, backgammon, Scrabble, Monopoly, and a Japanese game Marielle didn't recognize. "What's this?" The illustrated board reminded her of Chutes and Ladders.

"Sugoroku," Naomi replied. "I used to play it with my grandmother."

"The board is beautiful." Marielle traced it with her fingers. "Is this a real place?"

Naomi leaned in to see what she was looking at. "Those are the Stations of the Tokaido, the stopping points on the road between Tokyo and Kyoto."

"How do you play?"

Naomi produced a bag of dice. "It's a dice game. The kanji for 'Sugoroku' both mean 'two sixes.'"

But Marielle had already pushed the game aside for what lay just beneath. There was one last box and she grabbed it.

"Oh my god," Naomi said. "I had no idea that was in there." She reached for the Ouija board and pried it from Marielle's tight grip.

"It's not yours?" Jordy asked.

"It *was*. When I was sixteen. I had it well-hidden for fear my mother would think I was into devil worship."

Craig laughed. "Not *that* well-hidden."

"She must not have known what it was if she put it in with the games."

Marielle marveled. "It's perfect."

"For what?"

"For tonight." Marielle snatched the box back, turning it over to read the backside. "My funeral eve." Marielle looked at them all as if it were obvious. *Don't you see?*

They didn't.

She was disappointed she even had to explain. "We made this pact after Alec died, and here the first time we've enacted it, we're already at each other's throats. We need to ask Alec for guidance. Ask him to show us the way."

The Jordans were exchanging skeptical glances, so it was Craig who spoke for the group. "Ask . . . *Alec*."

"That's right." It was just like Marielle to see wisdom in something and become so immediately and entirely convinced of it. She removed the box top and stared at its contents. Inside was the classic wooden board that had changed very little with time, as well as the plastic message indicator on which two people were to place their hands. "I had one just like this."

"Everyone did."

But the men denied ever owning one, although Craig copped to playing once at a high school party where they "contacted" the spirit of a child who had drowned in the pond behind the host's house a hundred years or so prior. "I never touched one or went back to that house again."

Jordan shuddered.

"Everyone relax," Marielle said. "It's just for fun."

Jordan was still spooked. "You have a perverse idea of fun."

"C'mon," Marielle protested.

Jordy cocked his head. "I'm game."

Jordan shot him a look, betrayed. *Whose side are you on?*

Craig chimed in with his vote. "If we all have to be here this weekend, Alec should have to be too."

"Exactly," Marielle agreed. "He doesn't get off that easy just because he's dead." She shoved a stack of magazines aside to position the board in the center of the coffee table and gently placed the plastic indicator on top. She then crossed her legs and pulled herself into the table.

"Who do you want to play with?" Craig asked.

"Jordan. It has to be Jordan."

Jordan was horrified. "Why does it have to be me?"

"Because you're the skeptic."

"I'm the opposite of a skeptic. I'm afraid it *will* work to a T and I won't sleep for a week."

"It's Alec we're reaching out to. You're scared of Alec?"

"Well, given that he's dead I'd say A LITTLE." Jordan looked at the others. "Jordy was his roommate. Craig was his bestie. Maybe it should be one of them."

Marielle snapped her fingers at Jordan. "Enough stalling. Sit down."

Jordan shook his head. Why he ever thought these were the people to enter a lifelong pact with he'd never know. *Youth.* In 1995 his favorite shirt was an L.L.Bean flannel that he'd made sleeveless with a sharp pair of scissors; he wore it over a string of graphic T-shirts with retro images, including his favorite, which had a gold crown and the words *Let the Wild Rumpus Begin.* No one had the taste at that age to make lifelong associates.

"Should we light some candles, or . . . ?" Marielle asked.

"Let's not go overboard," Jordy cautioned.

"Maybe we should do this tomorrow instead," Craig offered. "In the light of day. When we're sober."

"Who says we'll be sober in the light of day?" Naomi asked, clutching her glass of wine with a grip suggesting someone was trying to relieve her of it. "Besides, it doesn't work during the day. Everyone knows that."

"How come?"

Naomi didn't know exactly. "There's too much . . ." She gestured broadly with her wineglass hand, nearly sloshing pinot over the sides. "Atmospheric interference."

Craig laughed. "*Atmospheric interference?* Apparently we don't need to contact Alec. He's already here."

"Can we focus, *please*," Marielle pleaded.

"Good luck," Craig said as Jordan assumed a seat on the floor across from Marielle; he folded his legs under the coffee table.

"Oh, fuck off," Jordan replied. The three of them were clearly going to enjoy spooking him more than he was already spooked.

"No. That's what 'Ouija' means. *Good luck.*"

"How do you know that?" Naomi looked at the box skeptically. The copy said no such thing. "I've never heard that."

"I thought it was French and German," Jordy said. "Oui and ja."

"Non and nein," Craig replied, amusing himself. "We did a show at the gallery for an artist who recently died. His wife came in and did a séance to reach him and we got to talking."

"That's not weird," Jordy lied.

"She said when it came time to market the game—"

"Oh, it's not a game," Naomi interrupted, reverting to her deadly serious fourteen-year-old self.

Craig shook his head and continued. "When it came time to market the *product*, they asked the board what it wanted to be called. It spelled out *O-U-I-J-A*. So they asked the board what it meant. And it came back with *GOOD LUCK*. The end."

Jordan glanced across the coffee table. His eyes fell on a Magic 8 Ball, and for once he was glad this place had been left largely untouched since the eighties. He snatched it before anyone could follow his gaze and cupped the ball in both hands. "Has Marielle lost her mind?" Jordan then shook the ball vigorously and turned it over, waiting for a reveal. "SIGNS POINT TO YES."

Marielle took the ball from Jordan. "Is Jordan as clever as he thinks he is?" She then shook the ball and waited for the reply. "DON'T COUNT ON IT." She gave Jordan a smug yet dismissive smile. "Now, let's do this."

Jordan adjusted his posture and reluctantly placed his fingers on the board's plastic indicator as he had seen others do. He looked up at Marielle, who was nervously twisting her hair over one shoulder. "If we're going to open the gates of hell, let's open the gates of hell. Put your hands on this thingy."

Craig looked down at the board. "It's called a planchette."

"Butt out." Jordan gestured with his chin for Craig to move as his shadow was falling across the board. He then turned back to Marielle. "Ready?"

"Yes," Marielle said before placing her hands across from Jordan's. Naomi dimmed a few lights. "Wait!" She withdrew her hands. "Alec's *not* in hell. You said gates of hell and I want to make it clear that that's not where Alec is."

Jordan squinched his face. "Yes, fine. Alec is not in hell. Now put your hands on Cate Blanchett."

Marielle placed her fingers on the planchette. "You're pressing too hard. Just rest your fingers lightly."

"Light as a feather, stiff as a board. Yeah, yeah, yeah." Jordan remembered playing this very different game at a slumber party when he was nine, but it was all the same—children messing with the liminal space between life and death when they should be doing anything but. When the other kids made him "levitate," it gave Jordan night-mares for weeks, which seemed to spark in the other children great delight in terrorizing the new kid. To them it was just something else to do after they watched an episode of *Webster*.

Jordan closed his eyes and Marielle followed suit, although she opened one to make sure his were still closed; they were.

Jordan asked, "Do we ask for a spirit by name? Or start with a general question that any of the dead could answer?"

Jordy peeked inside the box to look for instructions; there were none. "I don't know. Naomi?"

"Just Alec. Alec, if you're there, please show yourself."

"What is he going to say? Just, like, 'Hey'?"

Jordan turned to Craig. "Knock it off."

And then they sat there, perfectly still, with their hands on the planchette. Nothing happened for so long that Jordy clocked a full two minutes on his watch *after* the silence seemed interminable. Craig quietly shed his slippers and Naomi pushed a vase with plastic daffodils away from the board, as if it might get knocked over in a sudden explosion of supernatural energy. Then, only then, did the planchette start to move.

It charted its own path around the board, almost as if exploring the edges, before making its way back toward the center, settling finally over the letter S. Naomi, Craig, and Jordy exchanged looks, while Jordan and Marielle kept their eyes tightly closed. All of them, it seemed, were holding their breath.

"So, not 'Hey,' then," Craig whispered before he was shushed.

Again, on its own time, the planchette moved. It shot to the upper right corner of the board, startling both Marielle and Jordan, and then lazily fell to the bottom left, where it set up camp, seemingly in no-man's-land.

"Is that it?" Jordy whispered.

"The board needs time to warm up," Naomi said, as if it were a perfectly logical explanation to give. Although it was not any of their strengths, everyone silently agreed to be patient. And their patience was soon rewarded with the letter *G*.

"Is anything happening?" Jordan asked.

"You don't feel it?"

"I feel it moving. But I have no idea if it's saying anything." To his credit, Jordan didn't so much as peek.

"Just let the board do its thing," Naomi said. She had surprised herself by how into this she was. The Ouija board held a powerful grip on her in her teen years when she and her friend Kendra would spend hours chatting with a spirit named Gail, who just happened to talk to them about all the things that occupied the minds of fourteen-year-old girls, but she would have said she had long outgrown it.

Jordy took Naomi's hand, a gesture she wouldn't normally allow, but the planchette was on the move again. This time its journey was short, and it quickly settled on the letter *O*, where it circled the oval letter before heading back to the top right corner, where it stopped. The color drained from Jordy's face.

"All right. What is happening?" Marielle implored. "Anything?"

"Nothing," Craig said, and Jordy immediately snapped in his direction.

"Nothing?"

"Yeah. Just nonsense."

Jordy looked to Naomi. "That wasn't nonsense."

"Are you sure?" Naomi asked.

Marielle took her hands off the planchette and opened her eyes. "Which is it? Nothing or not?"

"Not," Jordy insisted. "*S-G-O.*"

"What is that, like an airport?" Craig asked.

"S'go?" Jordy asked. "What Alec used to say whenever he was

trying to get any of our lazy asses off the floor to go along with one of his dumb ideas? *Let's go?* S'go?"

And indeed Alec would stand over them and say "s'go, s'go, s'go, s'go," a hundred times if necessary, until the two words mushed into one ugly consonant cluster and you would get up off the floor and go along with him if for no other reason than to get him to stop making that wretched sound.

"Damn." Jordan shivered.

Naomi looked at them, vindicated. "I told you it was not a game."

Craig was not yet convinced. "Jordan could have been steering the planchette."

"I wasn't steering anything."

"Occam's razor. That's all I'm saying."

"I didn't even remember Alec used to say that!"

Craig sat up on his knees and pointed. "Jordy did! And he could have told you."

Jordan threw his arms in the air. "Believe it or not, we're two different people and in the past eighteen years we've found other things to talk about than the three of you."

Marielle coughed. "Four of us." Everyone stared and so Marielle said, "Alec too." Because that was indeed who they were currently talking about. She steadied her arms on the coffee table and braced herself, then looked around the room like she was following a fly. If Alec was there in the room, she wanted to know exactly where. For a second she thought she felt fingers gently playing with her hair, and she flinched.

"You okay?" Naomi asked.

Marielle was not okay. Alec used to play with her hair exactly like that. Not sensually, not teasingly, just matter-of-factly, except for the few times he chewed on it specifically to drive her mad. But she couldn't say that without seeming unhinged; Alec communicating with them through a board from beyond the grave was one thing, Alec in the room with them was quite another.

Jordy looked at his watch. It was past eleven, even later given the time difference, but he was not yet feeling tired. "Now what?"

Marielle swallowed twice and found renewed determination. "I want to hear what the fucker has to say."

Jordan turned back to Marielle. "Okay then, that settles it. S'go."

Marielle cracked her knuckles. "S'go." The board was clearly now warm.

"Take three deep breaths," Naomi said in a hushed tone like she was leading a meditation workshop.

All of them did as instructed, not just Marielle and Jordan, and quickly the room grew silent. The two active participants locked eyes, then closed them in unison as they reached for the planchette. And that was how things remained for three and a half minutes.

"Nothing's happening," Craig whispered as he glanced at Naomi, afraid of incurring her wrath.

"The board went cold," she said, and it sounded perfectly logical. "Just give it time."

Jordy stood up from the couch and paced quietly by the windows and Craig silenced his phone; they moved with almost balletic precision, as if any movement that was not deliberate might upset the apple cart for good. Finally, when none of them could stand it anymore, the planchette moved, jerky at first, with hesitation, before swirling across the board like ice on a hot griddle and slowly gliding to a halt.

"*M*," Naomi said, giving the letter a long tail—*emmmmmm*, the sound like a Buddhist chant.

"Shhhhh," Marielle said with equal duration, but she didn't open her eyes.

The planchette remained parked over the *M* for thirty or so seconds before it slowly started to drift.

"Stop moving it," Jordan whispered.

"I'm not," Marielle whispered back, and she wasn't. But she understood why Jordan thought she was. The sensation was strange, different this time, almost as if her arms were asleep or she'd just finished an exhausting workout. She was aware that they hung from her shoulders, but she did not have control over or the strength to move them. They were like ghost appendages sewn onto her body, hard at work on a job for someone else.

"This feels weird," Jordan said. "Wrong."

"Stop talking." Naomi's eyes were glued to the board.

Under their guidance, the planchette moved just past the *I*, to the *J* and then the *K* and then the *L* before coming back to the *I* and stopping.

"*I!*" Jordy exclaimed a little too loudly. Even Jordan was annoyed by it.

"Everyone be quiet!" Naomi ordered.

"*M-I*," Craig whispered. He couldn't help himself. "Michigan? Wasn't that Alec's safety school?"

"Yes, that's exactly it," Naomi deadpanned. "He's telling us he'd have rather gone to Michigan and made friends that let him *rest in peace*."

"OH MY GOD, WHAT DID I SAY!" Marielle shouted. Jordan flinched and the planchette lurched forward again like a car that had just been jump-started. Jordy reached out and grabbed both Craig and Naomi by their arms. They all three looked at the board and watched as the little plastic piece moved first down toward the numbers before sliding back up to the start of the alphabet. It paused there for a moment and then, surprising everyone, jerked down to the bottom of the board, resting on GOODBYE.

Jordan and Marielle opened their eyes together. "What happened? *M-I-what?*" Jordan asked.

Craig looked from the board up to his friends. *"M-I-B."*

"Mib? What the hell does that mean?"

Craig contorted his face with confusion. *"Men in Black?* The Will Smith movie?"

Naomi reached forward to swat him on the back of the head. "Will Smith movie. If they're showing Alec Will Smith movies, he really *is* in hell."

"It's about ghosts, isn't it?"

Jordy looked to Craig. "I think aliens?"

"Aliens, ghosts. What's the difference?"

Naomi grabbed her hair and spun around twice in frustration. "For the love of god, stop talking. It wasn't *B*, you moron, it was *A*. *M-I-A*."

Marielle started trembling, slowly at first, in her fingers and hands, but it soon radiated to her whole body. When the others finally noticed and looked at her to see if she was okay, she screamed, "WHICH WAS IT?!"

"B! It was *B*. Jordy?" Craig looked at Jordy to be the tiebreaker.

Jordy glanced at Jordan. *"A*. I'm standing right here in the middle, looking straight down at the board." He extended his arm along his eyeline like he was explaining the Zapruder film to the CIA. "It was definitely *A*."

Spooked, Marielle scrambled from the table, overturning the board in the process.

"That makes more sense," Craig said, somehow missing Marielle's reaction. "Missing in action. I mean, that's literally Alec this weekend. *M-I-A*."

Jordan elbowed Craig, signaling for him to shut up. He nodded to Marielle. "It's not *M-I-A*, you idiot. It's Mia."

"Who's Mia again?" Craig asked, confused.

Naomi shot him a death glare.

"Mare's daughter."

Craig looked down at his feet, feeling stupid. *Right*. They used to be so close they all knew what the other ate for lunch. Now he couldn't even recall the name of Marielle's daughter; in fact, he barely remembered she had a kid at all.

Marielle shook like she had just been fished from the sea. The others gathered around to comfort her. Naomi spoke first. "What does Alec want with your daughter?"

Marielle was quiet for so long Naomi wondered if she had been heard. She was just about to ask again when Marielle replied, "I don't know. Nothing!" It was meant to sound casual, but she knew as soon as it came out of her mouth she'd overreached.

Jordan came to her rescue. "Well, he loved you. That much is clear. It would make sense that he wants to know about your life."

"Maybe he's feeling left out because he didn't get to meet her," Jordy added.

"*None* of you have met her."

Naomi had once or twice, but she let it slide.

Jordan sat next to Marielle and pulled her close. The trembling slowed but didn't stop, and her teeth chattered like she had a fever. "It's just a game," he said, and cut Naomi off with a gesture before she could once again claim otherwise. "One we should put away right now. This is your weekend. We're supposed to be doing things to remind you how much you're needed here. Not trying to communicate with *there*."

The very mention of Marielle's daughter had already done that for her. She didn't have the luxury Alec had; she was responsible for more than herself. And she didn't want Alec anywhere near Mia. He had toyed with her own emotions enough for a lifetime; he had no right to her daughter's.

Even if she might also be his.

———

Naomi placed a slice of the mixed-berry pie Craig had brought in front of Marielle and joined her at the table. Marielle spun the plate, as if that might help her decide where to dig in. "Don't scratch the table," Naomi scolded. It was just the thing that would get her in trouble with her mother. She then joined Marielle with tea.

"This is just too strange. I'm sorry I dragged everyone here."

Naomi shrugged. Maybe the ceremony of it, but not the reasons behind it. And she was coming around on the weekend as a reunion. "Maybe not."

"I'm too in my head about what happens up here, above ground, we spend so much time focused on it. In reality, we will spend most of our time . . ." Marielle pointed beneath them.

Naomi blew on her mug of tea. "That's deep."

Marielle offered a weak smile in response. "Not that deep. Think more like six feet."

"You don't believe in an afterlife?"

"I want to," Marielle replied as she took her first bite of pie. "Oh my god, I don't know who brings pie to a funeral, but this really is delicious." She covered her mouth as juice from a blackberry ran down her chin.

Naomi reached for a fork and helped herself to a bite. "I don't. For the record."

"Don't believe? Or don't want to."

"Both." Naomi never saw much use for religion. To her, life was just a temporary interruption to an eternity of nonexistence. She didn't feel the need to make sense of it.

"You're a huge comfort."

Naomi didn't see it as her job to comfort so much as to challenge Marielle's status quo. Her friend was depressed, that much was obvious. She needn't be; this too shall pass. "There's nothing wrong with wanting to make the most of your moment. But that starts by living in the present."

Marielle tilted her head curiously as she added the sweetener to her tea.

"You're upset about the past. Your marriage. Alec, still. You're stressed about the future. What your life will be when Mia moves out. Who are you alone? But really, there is only the here and now. There is only the Marielle at this table." Marielle tapped the teaspoon inside her mug and it sounded like the chimes of a bell. Naomi could feel her already resisting. "You should meditate. It's done wonders for me."

"You . . . Meditate?"

"Don't sound so horrified. I do Zazen. Most simply it means seated thought, or seated meditation. You're seated, in any case. And you empty your mind of all judgmental thinking. Words, images, beliefs. You have to let them all float by without grabbing for them." Naomi pushed back her chair and stood. "I have yet to let go of *all* my judgmental thoughts, but here. Let's try it."

Marielle looked panicked, a deer caught in the headlights.

"Sit." Naomi abandoned her tea for the floor. "Cross your legs. Back straight. Your spine should be erect, but settled." With that she leaned forward, slowly returning herself to a proper upright position. Marielle didn't quite understand why she should leave a perfectly comfortable chair to sit on the floor, but she knew better than to challenge her host. "Come on. How am I the one teaching you? Put the back of one hand against the open palm of another." Naomi demonstrated by placing her hands in her lap.

Marielle did her best to approximate Naomi's posture. "Now what?"

"Now lower your eyes halfway."

"Halfway? Why not all the way?"

"Because it's halfw— I'm not making this up."

Marielle did, and realized how hard it was to keep her eyelids only partially closed. They grew heavier than she'd ever remembered them feeling. Open, they were nothing, weightless, insignificant, feathers; half-closed they were garage doors, broken, requiring a jack to keep them from crushing anyone unlucky enough to be caught underneath. Her lashes fluttered, growing more and more Velcro-like, as if any moment now they would stick. "And?"

"And what?" Naomi grumbled, as if she were already deep in her own meditation.

"And what do we do now?" Marielle asked, annoyed.

"Let go."

"Of what?"

"Your thoughts."

"Which ones?"

"ALL OF THEM."

Marielle had read a study recently that said some people didn't have inner monologues. That their brains were free of the narrator that was so active in her own, never more so than in the quiet moments before sleep (when sleep came) and now (apparently) meditation. That they experienced emotion without coupling words with it. She wondered how they ever knew what to say out loud, if they didn't say it in their own heads first, or how they composed an email, or decided what to order from a menu, or released the stress and anxiety that came with cussing people out silently to themselves. Letting go of thoughts only replaced them with a running commentary about how difficult it was to let go of them. A worry about empty spaces, and if her brain might collapse in on itself if it wasn't running an endless narration about anything and everything she experienced, and what she might look like with a dented skull. She laughed at the idea of getting a Bumpit for balance, one of those ridiculous mail-order products to poof hair. And then she stifled her laughter just as quickly, as she was afraid of Naomi's wrath. She then wondered why she had a friend she was afraid of, why she kept her, why she *valued* her. *Because*, she reasoned. Naomi wasn't overly concerned with her feelings and therefore would always tell her the truth. Even if the truth was that she needed to release her thoughts. Only then, in thinking of Naomi, did her head begin to quiet.

"Have you let go?" Naomi eventually asked.

Marielle never realized how tightly she held on to everything. "Almost," she said.

There were footsteps in the hall. "What are you doing?" Craig ambled into the kitchen; with her eyes half-closed, she could only make out his hairy legs, which stuck out from under his nightshirt, and then wondered when the last time was she had shaved her own. *Dammit.* She was supposed to be letting these things go.

"We're meditating."

Craig cocked his head. *Are you sure?*

Marielle sighed. "Naomi is meditating. I'm trying to quiet my inner everything."

"Your teeth are blue."

"Pie" was all Marielle said.

Pie was not quite what Craig wanted this late at night, so he opened the kitchen cabinets one at a time until he spotted a jar of organic peanut butter; he found a drawer with spoons on the second try.

Naomi opened her eyes and glared. "I thought you went to bed."

Craig ran his fingers through his hair, giving it a healthy shake; it was matted on one side, as if he had attempted slumber before giving up. "Couldn't sleep. It's too quiet."

"New Yorkers." Naomi shook her head in disgust.

Craig opened the jar of peanut butter, removed a healthy

spoonful, and put it in his mouth. "Thith ith dithgusting." He looked at the label. "No thalt, no thugar. Whoth ith this?"

"Whose do you think?"

Craig screwed the lid back on the jar and threw the spoon in the sink. It landed with a clang that rattled the women out of their hopes of finding inner peace. "Theh Jordanth," he said in a tone that made them sound like the Lex Luthors to his Superman. Craig turned on the faucet and drank from the tap. "So tonight was weird," he said, wiping his mouth with the back of his hand.

Marielle narrowed her eyes and held them like she had tried to while meditating.

"Let me ask you something. I was doing some math upstairs."

Marielle quietly bit her lip, but Naomi jumped right in. "You were doing *math*."

Craig took a deep breath, as if he were the one meditating. "Is there something we don't know about Mia?"

"You don't know anything about Mia," Marielle said with motherly protectiveness.

"I mean. Just. With the Ouija board and everything."

"Go to bed, Nana," Naomi instructed.

Marielle stood and washed her hands in the sink with dish soap with a surprising intensity, lathering soap halfway to her elbows, as if she were scrubbing in for some sort of procedure.

"Because I was doing the math—"

"Again with the math," she said as she angrily turned off the faucet. She could see where this was going, but Naomi had yet to catch on. "What do you have, flash cards to put you to sleep?"

"I wasn't doing the Pythagorean theorem or anything," Craig continued, undaunted. "You said Mia was seventeen?"

"Yes."

"When's her birthday?"

Naomi was now lying on her back on the floor. "Why, do you want to add it to your calendar?" She ran her finger along the baseboard under the cabinets. Spotless. Her mother must have hired a house-keeper before their visit. "I can see up your skirt," she said to Craig.

Craig jumped two steps back. "Maybe I'd like to send her a card."

"Okay, that's creepy," Naomi reprimanded. But once she coupled Craig's question with her still-adolescent belief in the power of the Ouija board—it (or Alec) *had* spelled *Mia*, after all—she dropped her protest and shifted her focus from Craig to Marielle with an equal intensity. "Wait, when *is* her birthday?"

Marielle was cornered. "It's January sixteenth." It was clear what they were gunning for. "But she was born premature."

Her friends looked at her with healthy skepticism. "How prema-ture?" Craig asked.

"You want my medical records?"

The truth was they'd *all* been unsettled by the Ouija board. It wasn't that they expected nothing. The board was like that; it always coughed up just enough to give you chills if you were willing and able to do the required mental gymnastics to make sense of it. Even healthy skeptics could easily be swayed. But none of them, even Naomi, who believed in it most, were expecting the board to offer up something so concrete. Marielle in particular was unnerved; when Mia had de-clined to tour Berkeley she was relieved, realizing she wanted to keep her daughter as far away from this weekend as she could. She didn't need Mia imagining Marielle's funeral for real. She was still so young and just starting to flex a degree of independence, but she still needed a mother, and mothering, even in the midst of Marielle's own midlife breakdown.

"Alec is not Mia's father," she stated flatly, hoping to stop that rumor before it could spread.

"Do you have a picture?" Craig asked.

"Oh my god," Naomi protested. "Who are you, Maury Povich?" But then her curiosity got the best of her and she turned back to Marielle. "Do you?"

Marielle was now trapped. She couldn't plausibly deny having one, not in the age of smartphones. And the fastest way out of this would be to give them what they wanted, hoping they didn't see anything in particular that spurred them on further. So reluctantly she offered her phone to the wolves. On her lock screen was a picture of her daughter from junior prom. The phone's clock was across the girl's face, which both Craig and Naomi found strange and annoying (certainly there was a better way to crop a photo for such use) and it took them a moment to focus. As best as they could tell, the girl, while beautiful with a shy smile, was not a splitting image of their late friend.

"Satisfied?" she asked as she pulled the phone from their grip.

"She's stunning, Mare. Just like her mother." Sensing they had pushed her too far, Naomi nudged Craig a few steps back from Marielle.

"Now, if you would both excuse me. Tomorrow is my funeral, and I should at least get a decent night's sleep."

Once they heard Marielle climb the stairs, Naomi busied herself straightening a few things on the counter, then hung the tea towel over a cabinet door to dry. "Well. She doesn't look like Alec," she said, when they had been silent for too long.

"Not really, no." Craig was still focused on his hands, where Marielle's phone had just been, the image of the girl burned in his retinas, almost as if he were holding it still.

Naomi kicked him in the shin. She didn't understand why he was just standing there motionless, like he actually had seen a ghost. There was no reaction, so she did it again. When she still failed to elicit a response, she turned off the kitchen lights and retreated to her room for the night. "Good night, Nana."

Craig stood in the dark, coupling the photo with a very distant memory, one that was hazy to begin with (thanks to the fog of alcohol and grief) and that both he and Marielle had each worked deliberately to suppress in the intervening years. But, back in the house, together again as they were, the memory was an echo just starting to shake loose, and Craig felt weak, like he needed to sit down. Instead, he braced himself against the Formica countertop and convinced himself he hadn't seen what he just had.

N aomi feigned a cough and under her breath mumbled, "Nerd alert," when Jordan emerged from his room.

"What, this?" Jordan futzed with a tie that he had paired with his cardigan sweater. None of them had packed suits, but it *was* a funeral and he thought there should be a certain decorum. "I wanted to show respect."

"It's a fake funeral," Craig protested.

"Maybe it's a fake tie," Jordan offered, but they all knew there was exactly a zero percent chance of it being a clip-on.

"Where's the guest of honor?" Naomi asked, glancing at the time on her phone. Six o'clock. While they had been dreading this moment all weekend—for the sheer awkwardness of it, if nothing else—now that it was here they just wanted to get it over with.

Craig bowed his head. "Gone in sleep, she's earned her peace."

Naomi turned sharply toward him and glared.

Craig stifled a laugh. "She is taking a nap, is all."

Naomi shook her head.

"It would be funny if she really were, you know . . ." Craig made a motion like slitting a throat.

"Murdered?" Naomi said, appalled.

Jordy shook his head. "It's a pact, Craig, not an Agatha Christie novel."

Naomi pushed forward toward the stairs. "Someone wake her ass up so we can get busy laying her to rest." When the guys once again proved useless, she stomped up the first two steps just as Marielle appeared on the landing looking refreshed and ready to be mourned.

"She has risen," she said, doing a little twirl at the top of the stairs. "Your chatter down here was enough to wake the dead." She too had dressed for the occasion, all in black, in a dress that had hung in the back of her closet for cocktail events where she had to be on Max's arm; she wouldn't need it for such occasions anymore.

Jordan finished knotting his tie as Marielle descended the stairs, vindicated by her more formal attire. Given that this was the first time they were doing this, he held firm in his belief that their cues should be taken from the "deceased."

The flowers had been arranged outside on the deck, where they looked less overwhelming; the Jordans had arranged the chairs in a semicircle per Marielle's considered instructions. There was a seat for each of them, four mourners and a mournee, under the shade of the alder trees. Craig had suggested relocating the couch up front for Marielle to lie in repose and they had all had a few laughs over it, but in the end it was just too weird (and too on the nose for the therapy this was meant to be).

Inside, the table was set for a feast, more of a cleansing for the evening's awkwardness than a wake. By then the stilted centerpiece of their weekend would be over and they could laugh about the absurdity of it all. Jordan had pieced together the perfect charcuterie board and while Jordy helped by making roses out of some salami, the tray remained largely vegetarian with bread for those who might want sandwiches. There were plates stacked at the head of the table, the fanciest they could find, from the Itos' wedding china. Glasses for each were staged next to the wine, minus one; Naomi had filled hers early.

They stood in a circle, uncertain how to begin. "We need a ring-leader," Naomi observed.

Marielle looked cross. "It's not a circus."

Naomi scoffed—*Isn't it?*—and Marielle wondered how much wine she had drunk. "Master of ceremonies, then." Marielle frowned. That wasn't any better.

"'Officiant,' I think, is the word you're looking for." Jordan volunteered to fill that role.

"Is that a good idea?" Jordy whispered, like he was afraid this might open them up to liability or a lawsuit.

"Well, it's a little late to find someone else. One of us needs to step up."

Craig pitched his tent in Jordy's camp. "Maybe we should have hired someone. I mean, isn't it usually someone a little less . . . Involved?"

"Because of the emotional burden of having someone lead a ceremony in the throes of their own personal grief. But given that Marielle is standing right here and the sun is shining and today is mostly for her benefit, I think the rest of us can keep our grief in check." Jordan scanned their eyes for any further objections to his volunteering, turning last to Marielle. "With your blessing, of course."

Marielle took Jordan's arm and leaned in, grateful. He led her out to the deck where the low sun dappled their chairs through the leaves and helped her into the centermost seat like she was infirm. The others followed and took their places around her, Naomi's hair sticking to her lipstick when it was caught in a light breeze. Jordan assumed his spot in front of them as Naomi tied back her hair like they were about to really get into it.

"Dearly beloved," Jordan began, and even he knew it was a misstep.

"Oh, for heaven's sake," Craig muttered.

"Scratch that. That was my bad." Jordan cleared his throat. "Friends, Romans, countrymen."

Marielle looked behind her, as if there would be rows of other guests from which to pluck a replacement. It struck her now how sad this was, having only four people in attendance. She longed for her daughter, who gave her reason to live. She longed for her parents, who had always made everything somehow okay. She even yearned for Max, whose heart she wanted to see just as broken as her own. But it wouldn't have been appropriate to have any of them there. Only these four would do. That was the point of the pact. As much as these were the people she relied on to build her up, they were also the ones she would allow to see her when she was down. Even if they felt somewhat like strangers now, they had seen things, they had witnessed her when she was young and raw and exposed, in the time before she'd learned how to hide her fragility. They had known her before who she was now.

"It's hard to do this without a joke," Jordan confessed, and then he wiped his hand across his face, erasing his wry smile. "We are here today to celebrate the life of Marielle Holland, someone who has had an extraordinary impact on all of our lives. We met in college at Berk—" Jordan tripped over Berkeley; of course they all knew where they went to college, why had he bothered to say it? "Berkeley, when we were both nineteen."

"I was eighteen," Marielle corrected, and Jordan gritted his teeth. There was a reason funeral honorees were supposed to be dead.

"She entered our lives before we were twenty, when the whole world felt exciting and fresh and possible. The first thing you need to know, Marielle, is that we have loved you since the moment we met."

Marielle's face scrunched with extreme displeasure.

"What now?" Jordan asked when her look could no longer be ignored.

Marielle shifted in her seat. "You have loved me?"

"That's right. Since the first night we met."

"*Have* loved."

Jordan looked to the others for backup. Did they know what she was after?

Marielle scoffed. "What the hell tense is that?"

"Tense?"

"Verb tense. I've run that sentence back and forth in my head and I don't get it. You *have*, present, *loved*, past, *me*, noun." Marielle shook her head, as if realizing for the first time that a funeral for a living person was ridiculous, just as the rest of them were finding meaning.

Jordan hung his head in defeat. "I'm sorry! You're sitting right there!"

"So?"

"Do you know how hard it is to give a eulogy for a person making faces in response to everything you say?"

Marielle didn't know and doubted anyone did. "What did you expect? I'm an open book."

Craig leaned in and whispered, "How about you be less of an open book and more of an open casket."

"FROM THE TOP, PEOPLE!" Naomi stage-directed, as if they'd just mounted a disastrous dress rehearsal.

Marielle relaxed back in her chair as Jordan cleared his throat to begin anew.

"There's something about transferring to a new school that forces you to prioritize. You've already made one misstep in your young adult existence and you realize that life is about choices. The places you live. The things you study. The beliefs you hold. And the people you surround yourself with. Marielle, Jordy, Naomi, Craig, Alec, and I were assigned to the same dormitory floor. We did not choose that, some random housing office algorithm did. But the friendships that stemmed from a serendipitous assignment were something we cultivated, something we treasured, and something we held on to for dear life."

Jordan looked around. He'd finally found a rhythm that held their attention, and Marielle's seemed particularly rapt.

"I was intimidated by Marielle the night we first met. I think in the wake of our transfers we were all trying to figure out who we were. Not her. Marielle knew who she was as much as anyone I'd ever met, and it showed in the ease and confidence with which she interacted with everyone. Everything about her was consistent. Her clothes, her hair, her easy smile, the way she tilted her head down but still met your gaze. The way she took up space in a room, there, present, while still creating space for others, particularly if you came from a different background, a different walk of life. And here I was, this kid with immigrant parents from Bogotá, barely out of the closet, licking my wounds from a disastrous freshman year where I had trouble not just making friends, but meeting *anyone* with whom I had an intellectual or emotional spark. But there was Marielle, her name French like an ethereal goddess, collecting us one by one in the dormitory lounge, making introductions as if she had known us for years and not minutes. She remembered each of our names, which I guess is no great feat when a full third of us were named Jordan. But it was the way she employed them, not as some power move to prove that she was in charge, but to humanize us. On a campus of thirty thousand students, right from night one, Marielle made us feel seen."

Jordan thought back to his first days at Berkeley. He had transferred from a much smaller school that was closer to home in New Hampshire, where he began after his parents balked at California. But it wasn't far away enough and it certainly wasn't anonymous enough for a closeted kid desperate to break free—three people he knew from his high school class had also enrolled there. His misery was apparent over the Christmas break and he was able to sell his parents on

Berkeley, somehow: his plane ticket to the West Coast was also his ticket to freedom. Only, California was big—like, *really* big—and the following September when he landed three thousand miles from home new fears immediately took hold. What if he arrived in a safe space to make a pronouncement, only the place was so vast that all of his declarations would be swallowed by the wind? To come out, he thought, you had to have someone to come out to.

"And that was Marielle," Jordan said when he got to that place in the story. "That very first night she had taken us under her wing, as if she had been a resident fixture at Berkeley and not just as new to the school as we were. Maybe that shouldn't have been a surprise. As a girl she tended to strays in her hometown, feral cats and a lost pup, and a collection of transfer students were just that—*strays*. The freshmen had each other, and the bonds of newly found freedom waiting to be flexed. But we transfers were fewer in number and carried a bit more of the weight of the world. We weren't giddy in the same way, screaming through dormitory halls, speculating what the cafeteria might have to offer. We were more serious, except maybe Alec, desperate to make up for lost time. None more so than me, who not only was looking to make up for a lost year but also a lost sense of self. By two in the morning on our first night on campus, I had spilled my whole story to Marielle, the two of us tucked in the back of the third-floor lounge while my future love excitedly debated French cinema with his new roommate, Alec—who if I recall was probably pulling his leg, making up directors and films with names like *La Clé Perdue* Jordy only pretended to know—and Craig and Naomi chimed in like two cranky old Muppets from the sidelines."

"What is La Clé Perdue?" Craig asked, not remembering.

"The Lost Key. But I heard 'Perdue' and thought he meant chicken." Jordy covered his face and groaned at the memory.

"My point is, we were *all* figuring out this thing called life, and in truth we probably are still. But there is always someone a little farther down the path, and if they have a kind heart, if they truly care about others, every so often they turn back and light the way. Marielle, I know you think you are lost, but it's only because you are out ahead. It's someone else's turn to hold the lantern now, so please let us do that for you. Look for our light. You were there for us then, we are here for you now. I *have* loved you since the moment we met." Jordan paused for protest that never came. "And we love you still."

Jordan took a step back, as if away from a lectern, unsure if his speech met the moment. This had been a good weekend. He went into it feeling silly, as did Jordy—all of them, really—and they had some-how found meaning in a pledge they had made and friends they had met now more than half their lives ago. There was no crowd to survey as there might be if he were speaking at an actual funeral. But the faces he saw—Naomi, Jordy, and Craig—all carried the same look of relief that he did. Their turns to speak were still ahead, but the ice had been broken and the mission confirmed: *leave nothing left unsaid.* Jordan turned last to Marielle, who shared the same look as her friends and seemed, for the first time that weekend, genuinely happy.

When they all had a chance to speak and Marielle's funeral was done, they went indoors and Jordan re-created his perfect sandwich from the spread they had bought, and made one for everyone else too. The mood in the room lifted for the first time that weekend, as if they had performed an exorcism as much as a remembrance. Marielle was the life of the party, a weight lifted from her as if she had molted her skin and been reborn as someone new. Maybe it wasn't a funeral she needed so much as permission. A reminder that after raising a daugh-ter to near adulthood, it was okay to indulge in finding her own iden-tity again. To remember who she was beyond a mother, beyond a wife. She ate her sandwich, satisfying a deep hunger she didn't know was there. As she looked around the room, Marielle smiled and thought it was okay—at least for tonight—to finally let go. She closed her eyes and an elusive meditative state finally came. All that existed was this moment, all that mattered was the beauty of right now. She repeated that as a chant.

The beauty of right now.
The beauty of right now.
The beauty of right now.

She continued until Naomi broke her concentration. "Let's never do that again."

The others laughed and raised their glasses in agreement.

CHEERS.

THE
JORDANS

Jordan stood in his closet doorway waving a fistful of belts. His thin figure was cast in silhouette by the raw lightbulb behind him, making him look crooked and frail, a glimpse of old age that might never come. "What about these?"

"What about them?" Jordy was dismissive, no longer able to fake any enthusiasm for this task.

"Are you going to want them?"

"Aren't you going to need them?"

Jordan studied the belts as if he hadn't considered this. His pants *were* getting looser, maybe he should keep one or two; but it wasn't like he could take the rest with him. But which two? Which shoes did he need to match? This was already harder than he had anticipated.

Jordy sat on the edge of the bed, mesmerized by his husband's shadow, which stretched to the far corner of their bedroom, like one long string bean, or a series of beans laid end to end. It was raining, a late-spring thunderstorm sending heavy drops against their windows, making for a surprisingly dark Saturday afternoon. "You're tired. I don't see why we have to do this now."

"I'm not tired."

"Who do you think you're fooling?"

There was no point in denying the undeniable, especially with someone who knew him so well. "I'm only going to get more tired."

Jordy didn't want to fight, nor did he want to imagine a time in the near future when he was left to clear out his husband's closet alone, so he let Jordan continue. "What's the collective noun for beans?"

"A hill of beans," Jordan said without hesitation.

"Yeah, that's for like black beans, or kidney beans. I mean for string beans."

"Could you please focus?" Jordan was growing impatient. "You know my family's going to be ruthless when it comes to this."

"Your family loves me."

Jordan said nothing, preferring to let that hang in the air.

"You think they're going to take your *belts*?"

"They're locusts. They're going to try to take everything." Jordan didn't know how else to explain his parents, or their desire to hang on to everything after once leaving so much behind.

Jordy felt a deep rage without moving so much as a muscle, not believing the time for this was now—there were better things they could be doing with their weekend. He remembered the gift of rainy afternoons when they were younger, when the two of them would crawl into bed and not get out except for take-out menus and to buzz food deliverymen in. "Let them try," he muttered.

"What?" Jordan lowered the belts and their tips pooled on the floor like snakes. *A knot of snakes.*

"I said, we're married. LET THEM TRY."

Jordan frowned. "You're not going to let them have *anything* to remember me by?"

"Yes, that's what I said. They can't have anything. Thank you for allowing me to be heard." Jordy was honestly confused as to what was expected of him. "I don't understand the point of this exercise."

Jordan sat down in their reading chair, exasperated. "I want to have some say in all of this. That's the point."

Isn't that what wills are for? Jordy screamed to himself. But his frustration passed quickly and he crossed over to Jordan and began rubbing his back. "Fine. They can have your belts." And they sat there for a moment as the room got even darker.

"You should go for a swim." Jordan found himself wanting to be alone more and more, already pulling away. He also knew he would get more done without Jordy.

"What's your ECOG?"

It was something they discovered on a cancer website—the ECOG Performance Status. Zero was fully active. Five was dead. "I'd say I'm a three."

"Capable of only limited self-care."

"Sounds about right."

"Then why would I leave you to go for a swim?" Jordy glanced up at the window and thought he could swim simply by stepping out their front door; there was no way he'd make it to the pool in this rain, even if he were so inclined. "Why won't you let me take care of you?"

"Why won't you let me take care of *you*?!" Jordan was frustrated by how much Jordy had already sacrificed to be by his side. It was as unnecessary as it was suffocating, and it made him feel nothing but guilt. "You don't get it."

"No. I don't. There are so many better things we could be doing with our time."

"Like spending it with friends?" The subject of Big Sur had continued to surface, Jordan swatting at it each time like they were in an endless game of Whac-A-Mole. He didn't want to be seen in his current state, he didn't want the pity, he didn't want the exercise of sitting through some fake funeral when the prospect of a real one loomed over both of their heads. But Jordy was like a dog with a bone, and a hypocritical one at that—the pact was there for him too. If he really wanted to see their friends that badly, he could pull the trigger himself.

"I know you think this is helpful, but please don't get rid of your things. Remember Mexico? You were meant to have nine lives."

Jordan looked down, exposing his neck for Jordy to further massage. He remembered Naomi's funeral all too well. "Eight, after that trip."

"S'go," Jordy said, employing Alec's favored contraction. He gestured toward the doorway, but the *where* was left unsaid.

Jordan's mouth drooped in the way it sometimes did right before he erupted in anger; Jordy recognized that face from when things would fall apart at work. But Jordan didn't have the energy to lather himself into a full rage and his anger dissipated, the buildup to a sneeze that never came. He looked down at his hands, still holding the belts. "What a strange invention," he said, letting the belts go, their buckles hitting the floor with a sharp clunk. "Why not just invent pants that fit?"

"Why not skirts?" Jordy offered. "Shapeless elastic-waisted skirts for everyone. Problem solved." Jordan expelled a puff of air and relaxed; Jordy had stanched the bleeding.

"You should be in charge of more things." This was Jordan being conciliatory.

"I should."

"Just not today. Today *I'm* in charge. And I want to do my sweaters next."

Jordy pressed down on his husband's shoulders to keep him from getting up. Jordan squirmed, but ultimately was no match. He was feeling weak, and this exercise was emotionally draining. And to top it off, it wasn't what he wanted to do either. It was rather misguided frustration over the one thing he *wanted* to have a say in and couldn't. "Or we could just lie down for a spell."

Jordy led him to their bed and gently placed a pillow underneath Jordan's head as it found its usual resting spot in the crook of Jordy's arm. It still felt like a fight was coming; hopefully it was their relationship that had nine lives.

WHY DO STARS FALL DOWN FROM THE SKY

(Naomi, 2016)

*T*hirty-two feet per second, per second.

The equation ran through Naomi's head like a Buddhist chant, something meant to bring comfort (it was math, after all, or physics—what was so terrifying about those?), to lose all meaning until it was just that—a chant—quieting her mind and her soul until all she could hear was the sound of her own breathing. Instead it wreaked havoc like a ticker at the bottom of a screen during a gruesome event, growing louder and louder and seemingly faster and faster as it heralded more lives lost, more devastation, more ways in which the world would never quite again be the same. *Thirty-two feet per second, per second. Thirty-two feet per second, per second. Thirty-two feet per second, per second.*

But in reality it simply was what it was, the gravity behind her parents' demise, the mathematical truth of it, nothing more, nothing less. Fumiko and Takeshi Ito fell from the sky, their incapacitated jet gaining speed at that alarming rate, for just over ninety seconds. And now it was background noise in their daughter's life, hold music, a store's unpleasant Muzak, as Naomi imagined the fear that must have gripped her parents in their final moments. Though she *couldn't* imagine it, not really; the only image she could muster was of her parents buckled in their seats—devoid of expression—perhaps holding hands, but probably not, looking stoically ahead as her mother, sixty-eight, and her father, seventy-one, met their fate.

They had reached out on Naomi's forty-third birthday just three weeks before, but she was traveling, partying it up with girlfriends in Montreal, employing, poorly, French she hadn't much used since college ("Excusez-moi, une autre boo, boo, *boîte*? Non, *bouteille* de champagne, s'il vous plaît"), and while she had seen their incoming call—she had even held it up for her friends, who oooooooohed in unison, causing Naomi to laugh—she hadn't answered and the call unceremoniously went to voicemail. It was something she could have treasured from them, a last gift, a last wish, a last recording of their voices, if they had expressed their feelings or shared with her their pride (she had seen a 9/11 documentary where surviving loved ones were comforted by such calls of love), or had said anything other than what they had—a curt *happy birthday*, followed by dead air, followed by her dad mumbling something in Japanese. Now it was a cruel reminder of everything that had remained unsaid. How she, their very American daughter, needed more than her Japanese parents, who were raised very differently, had been able to give. She sat with her grief alone for two days before calling Marielle.

"Time for another funeral?" Marielle asked, almost giddy by the idea of someone other than herself triggering their pact.

"My parents are dead," Naomi replied, very matter-of-fact. It was not the funeral she was hoping for, but Marielle was on the next flight.

They were an odd couple, Marielle and Naomi, but they were the women in their group and they found value in being aligned. After

Marielle's funeral they had promised to stay in better touch, and they did for a time before they fell back to old ways. Naomi was at the height of a career that sent her all over the world chasing the hottest musical acts; Marielle was at the start of a new one, a reinvention that took all of her energy and most of her time. As Mia left for college in Massachusetts, Marielle departed for her home state of Oregon, settling in a town called Boring, of all things (although she found this new version of herself anything but). She got a job with an animal rescue and took over the nonprofit after only a year when the proprietor unexpectedly died. Naomi had visited Marielle in the midst of this chaos, on her way back from Seattle after seeing a band that she said played rock and roll the way it was meant to be played, which in Naomi's mind meant rooted in blues and Blackness. Naomi seemed both at home and out of place in Boring, which was mostly quiet and quaint. Marielle did her best to play up her town's virtues; it might not offer rock and roll the way it was meant to be played, but it did have a diner on the outskirts of town that had one of those revolving dessert cases where you could choose a single slice of coconut cake or banana cream pie, or a pudding parfait in a cup. Their visit had been awkward at first, as if they hadn't just recently reconnected, and then they found their groove over coffee and pie, and then it grew uncomfortable again when it became clear Naomi thought Marielle had taken an extravagant gift (her funeral) and squandered it, stuffing it away in the back of a closet, or worse, had returned it for cash.

But she was still Naomi's first call, and Naomi didn't quite know exactly why. The funeral they'd cobbled together for Marielle was already almost three years behind them, and it wasn't even real, but the weekend had—even more than Alec's actual death—made Naomi question her own mortality. She was not married, she did not have kids. She had a career, and a few friends who were really colleagues with whom she spent most of her time. Her parents were distant, but they were her family; as long as they were out there somewhere she was able to think of herself like anyone else. Grounded. Connected. But now they were gone and she hadn't prepared for that. *Why?* The manner of their deaths was unusual, but the fact that they predeceased her was not. How had she not imagined how untethered and alone she might feel once they were really gone?

Marielle dove into planning mode as soon as she landed. "Do you want to go back to Sur la Vie?"

Naomi thought of the house and how empty it had always felt, full of things but not people. And how supremely abandoned it would feel now, knowing her parents would never return. Plus, there was work to be done both at her parents' home in Corte Madera and at Sur la Vie, going through their belongings deciding what, if anything, to keep. Also, although down her list of reasons, the thought of the Ouija board scared her and she preferred not to be anywhere near it. "No," she answered firmly. "Anywhere but Big Sur."

Marielle hugged her tight, something Naomi loathed but tolerated in this case. "A destination funeral," she mused, marveling at the idea. "I like it. Where shall we go?"

Naomi thought for a moment of all the travel she'd done with her parents in her youth, grasping for somewhere—anywhere—they'd not been together. She wasn't really sure why Mexico sprang to mind, but as soon as it did it seemed right. "Puerto Vallarta," she said.

Almost immediately Naomi regretted choosing a destination that required her to board a plane. But travel was such a huge part of who she was, and she feared if she hesitated to fly now she might never fly again. Craig connected through San Francisco so he could attend her parents' wake. The Jordans sent their condolences; they were slammed with work and had only a few days to sneak away, so it was either Naomi's parents' funeral or her own, and Naomi decided her own was more important (funerals are, after all, for the living), so they arranged to fly directly to Mexico to meet there. The Jordans did, however, come through with reservations at Casa Kimberly, Elizabeth Taylor's former home in Puerto Vallarta overlooking the waters of Banderas Bay; it had recently been restored into a boutique hotel and they had a client who knew the owner. There were only three suites available last minute and not the four required, but they all begrudgingly agreed that they could rough it. For once it was not expected that Naomi foot the bill, although, with her parents now gone, she was about to come into a windfall.

They arrived in Mexico on a Sunday, just as vacationers were leaving. Departing travelers looked tan and rested and truly sorry to return home, something Naomi took as a good sign. The hotel sent a van to the airport, which the three of them took—it was small and drove more like a sedan; the Jordans were to meet them at the hotel. The car made its way into the city, then up a small cobblestone street, twisting its way into the foothills, and the driver had to pull all the way to one side whenever another car heading the opposite direction wanted to pass; the neighborhood reminded Naomi a bit of Laurel Canyon back in L.A. It had recently rained, the roads were slick, the sky still partly gray, but errant sunbeams lit stucco homes in a way that Craig said reminded him of the palette of Diego Rivera. Eventually they arrived at a white building that was flush with the sidewalk. Naomi looked skeptically at their hotel; above them was a small footbridge, the Puente del Amor, which ran all the way over the street. The house across from them had been Richard Burton's when he came to Puerto Vallarta to shoot the film adaptation of Tennessee Williams's *The Night of the Iguana* and he had gifted Casa Kimberly to his love Elizabeth Taylor for her thirty-second birthday—but not before he built the footbridge so they could sneak back and forth and evade the paparazzi; they were both at the time married to others. From their vantage point on the street it didn't look like much. There was no driveway, or even an entrance that looked particularly grand. If it weren't for the bridge, which she recognized from photos, Naomi might have assumed they were being swindled, that their driver had brought them to the wrong address. But she stepped out of the van feigning confidence, and as the hotel's porter removed their luggage from the back she spied a statue of Burton and Taylor kissing just inside the door. She looked up again, determined this time to remain open-minded, tipping the driver generously before stepping inside the hotel. The Jordans were waiting for their friends in the courtyard.

"¡Bienvenida a Puerto Vallarta!" Jordan exclaimed, the one fluent Spanish speaker among them. Naomi had forgotten how sexy she used to find him when he spoke his native language, when she eavesdropped on him talking to his family on the pay phone in their dormitory hall, and she was equally surprised to find that the effect it had on her had not dimmed. When she embraced Jordan hello, she tried not to make a big deal of it, even when he held her hand on the way to the elevators. "Lo siento por tus padres," he whispered. "I'm sorry about your parents." All Naomi could do was nod. She was sorry too.

Upstairs, the two women giggled as they explored the rooms, then settled on the Velvet Suite, as the bed faced the balcony and it had the most stunning views, but they warned Craig not to get too comfortable in the Sapphire Suite next door. He might enjoy a room by himself tonight, but they were reserving the right to each have a night alone.

"Dinner at the Iguana," Jordy informed them. The reservation for the night had been made.

The Iguana was the hotel's open-air restaurant and tequila bar. The surrounding hills focused their gaze over the city and then to the water, where the day's waning sun sparkled over the water like flashbulbs in Elizabeth's eyes. They snacked on ceviche and fried squash blossoms as they perused the drink menu, settling on several bottles of a Mexican chenin blanc, then soon adding a bottle of Don Julio Gran Patrón Platino. It was the most expensive on the menu—a splurge for sure, but the conversion rate worked in their favor. Marielle had a poblano chile in puff pastry, the lone vegetarian item on the menu, while she encouraged the others to share, seafood mostly along with some carnitas. Naomi sat facing the ocean, and for much of the meal she was transfixed on the horizon, as if she might spot her parents' plane approaching the shore to safely land. At one point, the Jordans, on either side of her, each put a hand on her shoulders.

"We've reached the tipping point," Naomi said, pouring a shot of Don Julio; it burned with a smoky finish.

"How do you mean?" Jordy asked.

"I just figure at a certain point, life takes more from you than it gives." She slammed her empty glass on the table for effect. In their first forty-some years it had taken Alec, their grandparents, an aunt and uncle here and there; they were perhaps easy pickings. *Now—* Naomi shuddered, hesitating to finish the thought. *Now all bets are off.*

Just as the mood was turning macabre, a mariachi band descended the stairs, twenty men in dove-gray suits with appliqués that ran down the sides. The members ranged in age from twenty to seventy and were every shape and size. When they began to play, their music filled the room in a way that made Naomi and her friends feel incredibly alive. She had heard every kind of music the world over and had access to the finest seats and venues. She was used to attending shows in enormous stadiums from the second or third row, and yet this moment felt incredibly intimate. The trumpets and guitars were expected, even the harpist who stood in the back, but the band had a surprising number of violins, at least seven by Naomi's count, something she thought her mother would have enjoyed, and suddenly she was very aware that she had to be a witness to this scene on their behalf and she was overcome with emotion. The music filled her soul, as if it had found a secret way in and the instruments were tailored to hum at a frequency that resonated only with her. She desperately wished she believed in a heaven where her parents could look down and see this. And then she was immediately comforted by the fact that she didn't; her parents had already looked down on her enough.

The sky was purple now, dusk had fallen, and the band's jacket buttons and oversized belt buckles sparkled underneath the restaurant's overhead lights, causing the members to glint as angelically as their sound. They played for twenty minutes, perhaps twenty-five, and the entire restaurant's attention was rapt, as if even turning away for a second to take so much as a bite of a lobster taco might cause them to miss something spectacular, a moment they could witness only here and only now, as if the entire band were composed of shooting stars. And then just as quickly as they descended on the restaurant, they retreated back up the stairs, and rapturous applause filled the room where melody had just been, like a sorbet between courses of music and quiet chatter.

Naomi leaned into Jordy's meaty shoulder, and he made room for her there; she imagined what it would be like to have a man who approached his size, how she could get used to being enveloped like this and kept safe when the world felt like it was spinning out of control. (She had weighed more than her last boyfriend, who was the human equivalent of a paper clip.) "That was something," she said, and Jordy beamed, happy in the knowledge that he and Jordan had picked the right spot. After their meal, fireworks filled the sky, white and gold bursts blooming against the darkness, framed perfectly between the restaurant's open-air windows, momentarily illuminating the city that sat below them. Naomi felt like Elizabeth Taylor, at least in this moment, loved, wanted, living a magical life that burst from a movie screen in full Technicolor glory. Her parents might not have voiced their appreciation for her, at least not often enough. But others had, lifelong friends who dropped everything to be with her when she needed them, filling the empty space in her life with music.

"Were those just for me?" Naomi asked of the fireworks.

"Of course!" the Jordans confirmed, and it made her happy they cared enough to lie.

Back in her room, they piled onto Naomi's bed, looking like a bus shelter poster for a show about models they all watched in the nineties. "Do we *have* to have my funeral?" she whined.

"No." Craig ran his fingers through her hair. In his mind she'd been through enough.

"YES," Marielle insisted. And then, when she realized everyone was stunned by her insistence, she added, "If I had to do it, you have to do it too."

"If I recall," Naomi began, "you weren't such a fan in the moment. You diagrammed everyone's sentences."

Marielle thought back on her outburst and covered her face, embarrassed. "Yes, but look what it did for me."

Naomi rolled her head in Marielle's direction. "You live in an animal shelter in tedious Oregon."

Marielle shook her head. "The town is called Boring."

"The town is Boring. I'm calling Oregon tedious."

"Make fun all you want, my funeral did me a lot of good, especially after I returned home."

"Like a leave-in conditioner." Naomi fanned out her hair on the bedspread like it was at its most shiny.

They all laughed, even eventually Marielle. "Exactly, it . . . Volumized me." She smiled at her own conditioner pun.

Naomi was tipsy and she continued to pout. "I don't want to live in the forest and rehabilitate possums."

Marielle smiled, knowing Naomi would find her own way forward. "You will."

Jordan crossed to the window to take in the views. "I thought we could have your funeral on the beach."

Naomi thrashed in frustration. "I've been to enough funerals this week." It had only been one, but it was for two people and she reasoned it ought to count double. "Can't we just get drunk instead?"

"You *are* drunk," Jordy pointed out.

"Mind-numbingly, blackout drunk," Naomi specified, and she meant it. She wanted to stop feeling *everything*. She reached for the phone in the room, but Craig intercepted. She sulked and he placated her by playing more with her hair.

"Where did you find that suit?" Craig reached for her lapels.

Naomi glanced down at her clothes. It was one nineties trend she'd leaned into in college: boxy men's clothes that hung off her frame, giving her a limp, androgynous shape behind which to hide. It advertised a queer identity, at least politically, and allowed her cover in the event of a crush, like the one she'd once had on Craig. She'd seen Julia Roberts pull off this style after *Pretty Woman*, although in a more feminine way; Naomi looked more like Winona Ryder, which was just fine with her. She'd found the suit hidden at her parents' this past week as she wandered through their house alone, alongside some of the rest of her clothes from that time, and it was just about the only thing that brought comfort. "You like it?"

"You look just like you did in college," Craig said.

She had paired the suit with a white tank for the Mexican heat, and the jacket's double-breasted front splayed open. She felt both sexy and safe, vulnerable and protected; she noticed Craig's response was a nonanswer but decided not to care. "I'm regressing," she said before anyone else could suggest it.

"I think that look is ripe for a comeback," Marielle concurred, to which Naomi purred. She remembered that Celine Dion had worn such a suit backward, white if she remembered, to the Oscars in 1999, which more or less killed the look for good. After that, Naomi had abandoned her suits alongside the other trends she shed with the century.

"Let's go to the beach," she suggested. As soon as she said it she realized she had an overwhelming need for fresh air. "I want to roll around in the sand like Deborah Kerr in *An Affair to Remember*."

"You mean *From Here to Eternity*."

But the water was too far away, at least in Naomi's intoxicated state, and as impressed as she had been earlier that the Jordans had found this place for them, she was now equally annoyed that anyone would book a hotel in Puerto Vallarta that wasn't right on the beach.

"How about from here to bed," Jordy suggested. The Jordans had been up early to catch their flight and the time difference was working against them. They begged off to bed, and Marielle was likewise ready to retire. Naomi didn't want to be alone with her thoughts, so she followed Craig to his room, as it had a sizable balcony.

"Some night," she said once they were alone. She meant it both sarcastically and genuinely, and she took another lap around Craig's suite to make sure it wasn't nicer than hers. She counted the windows, took in the view, inventoried each tiny soap, until she was satisfied their rooms were on par.

"Is it over?" Craig asked, producing a bottle of tequila from behind his back.

Naomi's eyes widened. "Nana," she cooed. "When did you do that?" She rushed him, pressing her body against his, slipping the bottle from between them. Craig laughed at the image of his own grandmother, who once produced buttered toast from a paper napkin in her purse. It pays to be prepared.

"Let's just say, I ordered ahead."

Naomi found two glasses in his bathroom and poured them each a drink. "To your health," she offered.

"To *yours*," he corrected, and they each took a swig.

Naomi laughed. *To her health?* That didn't exactly square with one's funeral. An ornate claw-foot tub stood in the middle of the bathroom and she climbed in, ushering Craig to join her. Together they sat in the dry tub—dry, that is, unless you counted the tequila.

"How are you holding up?"

Naomi looked away. Against the far wall was a showerhead. No divider, no partition, no curtain. Open to the rest of the bathroom and the balcony and, beyond that, the city. She gestured at it with her glass. "Is that supposed to be sexy?"

"It's a little sexy," Craig replied.

Naomi pictured Craig naked and wet, showering to get ready for dinner, and decided it *was* a little sexy. "Huh," she said as this new information sank in. And then after a minute, "I'm fine," even though she wasn't. And finally, "What a waste." She wasn't sure entirely what that last observation meant. What a waste of a beautiful night in Mexico? What a waste that she now would never get what she needed from her parents? What a waste that she once bent to their wills, thinking she ever would?

"Let me ask you something," Craig said. Naomi's legs were between his, and she playfully rested one foot in his groin. He didn't react, which was difficult for her to read, so she left her foot where it was with no particular agenda other than hoping he'd notice. "Do you think Marielle's hiding something?"

Naomi leaned over, pretending to look under the tub.

"Mia," Craig explained. He finally noticed her foot and started massaging it, while still leaving her heel in his lap.

"I don't think Mia would fit under there." Naomi returned to a reclined position as Craig found a particular spot in her instep. She moaned, leaning her head over the back of the tub.

"I don't want to talk about Marielle," she said as Craig continued massaging her foot.

"What do you want to talk about?" Craig looked down, finally noticing that her other foot was suggestively in his lap.

"Pan Am," Naomi said.

"Pan Am?" Craig asked skeptically. They were in high school when the airline went under.

"That's what I said. Pan Am."

"I think they no longer exist."

"There's a course that Pan Am used to offer on the fear of flying, it was the first of its kind. I heard a piece about it recently on NPR. Now almost every major city with an airport has one. Did you know that?"

Craig thought for a moment. "I did not."

"They should have courses for all of our fears."

Craig thought about his own—success, Brooklyn, snakes—and what coursework for those might entail. "Do you think you should take such a class?"

Naomi had thought about it. In many ways the fact that she was even here was a miracle, and she was already having doubts about making it home. But she shuddered at some of the things she remembered hearing on the radio. That one person in three had some kind of fear associated with flying; one person in six was unable to fly because of it. Anxiety before flying was often worse than anxiety *while* flying, and cruising was often the hardest for people, as there was turbulence, ample time for minds to wander while they were at the highest point in the sky. The final descent often brought relief to people, even though statistically it was far more dangerous, as there were so many maneuvers to complete and mechanical operations that could go wrong. She wondered why this was all in her head now, other than she had always found it to be a basic and uninteresting fear, something else that made her look down on people, and now she found it an unfounded one too. One in *three* people? Grow up. She didn't want to become part of that statistic. "No," she answered. "When it comes down to it, I think I should do the opposite." She downed her tequila, pouring herself more from the bottle before removing herself from the tub. She pushed open the doors and walked out on the balcony, leaning against the railing and spreading her arms wide. "I think I should learn how to fly."

Craig sprang from the tub, adjusting himself in the process, worried Naomi might drunkenly fall. Because of her height, the ornate metal railing hit her well above the waist, and instead she just leaned forward, arms outstretched as if she were Kate Winslet on the bow of the *Titanic*. "Easy there," he said, and guided her arms back to her waist. She took a long sip of tequila, sloshing a little over the side.

"What's in tequila?" she cooed, wiping the corners of her mouth with the back of her free hand.

"What's *in* it? Agave."

"Agave," she repeated. "Soothing." She mimed spreading it up and down her bare arms.

Craig slipped the glass from her hand before she dropped it over the hotel's side. "I think you're thinking of aloe."

"I am. I *am* thinking of aloe. See? You get me." She pushed Craig in his chest, causing him to take a few uncomfortable steps toward the railing; he flinched, as his center of gravity was much higher. "I don't know who I am anymore."

Craig held her face in one hand and squeezed her mouth open like a fish's. "Your name is Naomi. You're in Mexico with your friends."

"No. I know *who* I am." It wasn't her identity that was uncertain, her question was more existential. She had built an entire suit of armor to protect her as she waited for her parents' approval; wearing it colored all of her relationships. Now she was a superhero in a world suddenly devoid of villains. Was she supposed to hang up her cape?

"Okay, let's get you back inside," Craig said, peeling her off the railing. Naomi looked down at her red arms; she had somehow started to burn on their very first afternoon.

"We should get some. Agave."

"Aloe," he corrected, putting his arms around her and leading her back to the suite's double doors.

"Aloe, yes. I'll bet the hotel has some." She was slurring her words, so Craig lifted her onto the bed, setting her gently on the left side. Without missing a beat, Naomi picked up the hotel phone and was pleasantly surprised to hear it ringing, as if she'd dialed. "It's ringing."

"You're calling the front desk. Hang up, we'll get you agave tomorrow."

"Aloe. You'll get me *aloe*, tomorrow."

Craig slapped his forehead with the palm of his hand.

"Buenas noches, front desk. I would like to be able to fly." Naomi winked at Craig to prove she was in command. "No. No. No avión. No airplanes. Just flying in the open sky." She paused while the front desk took that in. "Mm-hmm, mm-hmm." She looked up at Craig. "Parasailing or skydiving?"

Craig looked horrified. *"Neither."*

"Skydiving!" she exclaimed, as if it were the only legitimate choice. "For five people." Another pause. "Para cinco personas. Sí." Naomi smiled from ear to ear in a manner Craig found deeply unsettling.

"Okay," he said, reaching for the phone in her hand. "Maybe that's enough talking on the telephone for tonight."

But Naomi held on strong. "It's my funeral, and I'll jump if I want to. When? Monday. I guess that's today."

"It will be all our funerals if you don't hang up."

Naomi held on to the receiver long enough to hear one last thing. "Okay. That makes sense. Gracias." She released her grip on the phone, causing Craig to topple backward. Once he caught his balance, he returned the phone to its receiver. "They're going to look into arrangements in the morning and call me back," Naomi said, to make sure Craig knew he hadn't won.

"Okay." Craig was humoring her, knowing she would drop this nonsense when she sobered up. "Why don't you spend the night?" he asked, but she was already mostly asleep.

The sunrise woke her early, as no one had closed the blinds, and her head pounded from tequila. She called the front desk to order bottles of water, the large kind, as big as they had, along with a pot of coffee.

"Sí, señora. Also we have made a reservation for you and your friends at Skydive Vallarta at two."

"Skydive Vallarta?" Naomi croaked, unsure as to what he was referring to.

"Sí. I have a note here you wanted to fly."

Naomi hung up the phone and lay back on the bed, the plush pillow cradling her head. She placed a second pillow over her face. *She wanted to fly?* That vaguely rang a bell, but skydiving was not flying, it was falling—diving was plunging, plummeting—it was all right there in the name. She didn't stir again until room service knocked.

At breakfast, Marielle announced she might like to do some shopping, as they had passed several cute shops on their way into town; Jordy mentioned he would like to go for a run. They were crowded around two small tables pushed together in a nearby café that also sold books. Both assumed there would be prep work to be done ahead of Naomi's ceremony but didn't see why they couldn't also squeeze in some fun.

Naomi picked at her huevos rancheros. "That's fine, just be back after lunch because we have skydiving at two." She added a few dashes of Tapatío to her eggs, as if nothing of consequence had been said.

Jordan took a sip of his iced coffee and was surprised by a sprinkle of cinnamon. "I'm sorry?"

"This afternoon at two."

Jordan set his coffee down. "It wasn't the time that's unclear."

"We're going skydiving. I had the hotel make us a reservation."

"I'm not going skydiving."

"You *especially*," Naomi announced. "You're the only one here who speaks Spanish. You'll have to help us pass the course."

"Yo hablo español," Craig said, but Naomi just looked at him with pity.

"Naomi, is this what you want?" Marielle asked, sipping a hibiscus iced tea. She had seen a video on the news once of a couple that were married mid–free fall; they held hands as a pastor fell in formation alongside them. Perhaps a funeral could be held in the same way, although she imagined it would be difficult to hear. And while the news program hadn't specified, she highly doubted the bride's parents had been killed in an air disaster.

Naomi considered this. "No, not really." And yet she was still fixated on the idea. "But I decided we're doing it anyway." In her mind this was now a game of chicken. She didn't want to go any more than they did, but there was no way in hell she was going to be the one to back down. "Besides, it's my weekend. You have to listen to me."

"I think when it's your weekend, you're supposed to listen to *us*." That was the point of the pact, at least as Craig saw it, to help the person in crisis understand how much they were loved.

Naomi rolled her eyes. She was never one to behave in ways that were expected. "The arrangements have all been made."

Jordan pushed his plate away from him. Instinctively he knew his only chance at surviving this misadventure would be on an empty stomach.

The hotel's van brought them to Skydive Vallarta, a small operation with an airstrip on the outskirts of town. The plan was to take off from there, jump, and land on a soft, sandy beach nearby, where another van would be waiting. They rode mostly in silence as the Mexican countryside whirred by. Jordan stared down Marielle, imploring her to speak up and put an end to this nonsense. Marielle in turn looked at Craig, who then looked at Jordy, who looked back at Jordan in a standoff that had become very, well, Mexican. The van's driver whistled obliviously to fill the silence as they picked up speed out of town.

They took every subsequent step that afternoon deliberately, convinced with each passing moment that Naomi would snap to her senses and call off this whole charade. During a break in their course Jordan took their instructor, a man named Eddie with an enormous mustache that seemed in danger of blowing clean off his face in the acceleration of free fall, aside and talked to him for a time in Spanish; Eddie even placed his hand on Jordan's arm in solace. But when Jordan rejoined the group he made no mention of the conversation, even when Naomi pressed him with one of her icy glares. They read the paperwork, which was in both English and Spanish, balking at the dramatic language that suggested everything that could go wrong, including but not limited to death. They still signed their lives away, thinking their feet would never leave the ground. They sat through the briefing, then were suited in jumpsuits and measured for harnesses. They learned about how their parachutes were packed and who had packed them, then practiced landing by jumping off platforms two feet from the ground. It was a technique to protect their ankles, but none of them knew how two measly feet could prepare them for fourteen thousand; their ankles would certainly know the difference, no matter how soft the sand was beneath them.

"Are you kidding me with this?" Craig whispered to Jordy, but of the five of them, Jordy, the sporty one, was having the most fun.

"It's great, isn't it?" Jordy answered as he jumped off his box a fifth and then a sixth time.

Jordan asked a lot of questions to stall for time ("What are parachutes made of?" "Shouldn't we wear some sort of helmets?" "Has anyone ever hit a bird?"), but instructor Eddie never strayed far from his script. And then, two and a half hours later, they had completed every last bit of the training they could possibly do on the ground. Eddie ushered them onto the tarmac, where they exchanged worried glances while looking back at the relative safety of the airfield's hangar. The first jump at Skydive Vallarta was always tandem, which meant an experienced diver would be lashed to their backs. Everyone was introduced to their partners on the tarmac; they had been paired mostly by size. Jordy was assigned a strapping skydive enthusiast named Diego, who had thousands of diving hours under his belt. This riled Jordan, who was given Yolonda, who was also strapping but in a way less attractive to him. Marielle had Rosalita, who actually did put her at ease, and Craig was partnered with Mateo, whose handshake he felt was too enthusiastic given the circumstances. Lastly, Naomi was paired with Santiago, who, while short, had a weight lifter's build. She eyed him skeptically like he might fall like a brick. Together they walked toward the plane like astronauts in *The Right Stuff*; Jordy could even imagine a soundtrack swelling, real *Top Gun* stuff, Kenny Loggins perhaps or Cheap Trick. There was, of course, no music but instead a wind picking up, nothing of too much concern, at least not to the professionals, but enough to swallow their instructor's excited proclamations, leaving them alone with their innermost thoughts. They felt certain that this was the moment Naomi would call things off. When she felt all eyes on her she just smiled, even though she too thought this game of chicken had gone way too far.

Marielle turned to the boys and swallowed hard, even though her throat was dry. They tried to express their assurances that things would be okay—they might have to go up in this plane to humor their friend and see her through her crisis, but there was no way in hell they were jumping out of it. "Wait, what did he just say?" she whispered hoarsely, nodding in Eddie's direction. They'd missed his latest instructions. Jordy gestured for her not to worry, Eddie had merely been running through a highlight reel of his best material, adolescent jokes that were designed to put people at ease. Little did he know this was a crowd of tough customers who were not so easy or generous with a laugh.

The plane was a Cessna 208 Caravan, designed to hold a dozen or so passengers in its unpressurized cabin, with an additional two seats in the cockpit. The high-winged plane was powered by a single turboprop engine in tractor formation with fixed landing gear that brought Naomi some comfort, even though the whole idea was to abandon the plane before needing it. They approached the Cessna skeptically, each in their jumpsuits, with varying degrees of dread. "Is it safe?" Naomi asked Jordan.

But Jordan was distracted, making a particularly sour face. "My jumpsuit has a stain on it." He pulled the blotch from his chest up to his nose, and it smelled like curdled ranch.

"Naomi?" Craig prompted, certain this was when they would

make their escape. But Naomi's eyes were fixated on a man approaching them: tall, attractive, with short shorts like Magnum, P.I., and a shirt unbuttoned to his navel exposing a hairy and muscular chest.

"Is that our pilot?" she asked, already struck by Cupid's arrow. The Jordans were likewise enamored, and when they turned to respond, Naomi was already scrambling aboard the plane.

As the rest filed inside, they were seated next to their jump partners, except for Naomi, who somehow freed herself from Santiago's watchful eye and wormed her way into the cockpit—fixing her hair from the wind while looking for anything she could use as a mirror. Santiago sat behind her, Naomi insisting Jordan stay close to translate her attempts at flirtation with the pilot, convinced that a lasting connection couldn't be made on goo-goo eyes alone.

"Come here often?" Naomi asked their pilot as he hopped into his seat. He wore aviator glasses in which she could see her reflection and she gave her hair one last pass. He then removed them to look in her eyes.

"Yes, but everyone always . . ." He made a sign like people jumping, adding a dramatic whistle to denote falling. "Is it something I say?"

Naomi laughed. "No, you're fine." She took in his deep brown eyes. "Very fine." She winked at him and then turned to Jordan. "Translate that. Make sure he understood."

Jordan shook his head, embarrassed. "I think we *all* understood."

She flashed the pilot another smile and he made a show of prepping the cockpit for takeoff, fine-tuning several dials and making notes on a clipboard; it was all very official in case there was any doubt as to who was now in charge. Naomi ate it up. The back of the plane filled with chatter, their group now swollen to double its size. Excited Spanish trampled nervous English, and Naomi took great comfort in the cacophony, as it was the very opposite of her parents' often disapproving silence; it felt to her like healing. Her inner child reached out and flicked the first switch in between her and the pilot. He flicked it back. She flicked it again. He flicked it back and wagged his finger.

"Why? What does that do?" she asked.

He answered in Spanish. Naomi turned to Jordan for translation. He leaned forward and Naomi indicated to the pilot to repeat himself, which he did.

Jordan understood and laughed nervously.

"What did he say?"

Jordan looked admonishingly at Naomi. "He said 'ejector seat.'"

Naomi looked at the pilot, who again used his hands to mime someone expelled from the plane, this time up and not down, complete with his signature whistle.

"Charming," she said, stone-faced, but then the corners of her mouth betrayed her and she was smitten all over again.

The pilot looked back over his shoulder and spoke Spanish to their tandem divers; they cheered. Naomi turned back to see if her friends were cheering too and only Jordy was. She wondered if it was because living with Jordan he understood most Spanish, or if he was simply the most game for this adventure. As the engines whirred to life, she made a note to ask him later—if there was a later. The pilot slammed his cockpit door closed three times. For luck? Or did it have a hard time staying closed? Santiago likewise sealed the rear. It fell quiet inside the plane, like rolling up car windows on a freeway when they had for a while been down. Suddenly, Naomi was overwhelmed with everything she didn't know about flying *or* jumping. Just as her friends were stunned she had yet to back out, it had never occurred to her that they would let things go this far. The pilot made one last gesture encompassing the instrument panel and made an admonishing sound.

Tsk tsk tsk. One thing was clear, from here on out she was to keep her hands off the controls.

O nce they hit cruising altitude, Naomi was living a waking dream. The horizon was a stunning blue that didn't look real, and the only clouds visible were perfect puffs of spun sugar candy sparsely dotting the passing sky; it was almost like she could reach out and touch them. Their aircraft was a tight squeeze of a hug, so warm and sturdy that the idea of jumping from its safe environs was comical. Naomi sat on her hands to contain her excitement and to give herself that extra half inch of a boost to see everything out the window more clearly. When she turned to Jordan, she didn't even realize what she was saying until it was already out of her mouth. "I want to fly the plane!" She had to shout to be heard over the noise.

"YOU WANT TO WHAT?"

"I WANT TO FLY THE PLANE!"

Jordan recoiled. He didn't think that was a good idea. Naomi indicated the pilot. *Tell him.*

No.

Naomi bit her lip. *TELL HIM.*

NO FUCKING WAY.

Marielle leaned into Craig and spoke loudly into his ear. "Are we really doing this?" It almost seemed inescapable now, like they had passed some point of no return. And yet the real moment would come when they opened the plane's door, so there was still plenty of time to back out.

"Beats me!" Craig hollered. He looked to Jordy and raised an eyebrow. Jordy bobbed his head so slightly in return it could have just been the plane's vibrations. Not knowing what else to say, Craig yelled,

"I'm not the one calling the shots!" He gave a thumbs-up to his diving partner, Mateo, who clasped his hands around Craig's fist.

Witnessing this, Diego shouted, "CARPE DIEM!"; it didn't need translation.

"Mine speaks Latin!" Jordy boasted to Jordan. He responded by high-fiving Diego, and their hands remained clasped as they held intense eye contact.

"I can see you, you know!" Jordan shouted, looking at his love holding hands with another man.

"Isn't he great?" Jordy shouted back, undeterred, a smile spread across his whole face.

Jordan turned to his own partner in this mess, Yolonda. She reminded him of a lesbian poet they once knew in the West Village who uncomfortably referred to her bathing suit area as a flower bed. He smiled, but not anywhere nearly as wide as Jordy had; she responded by tightening his harness until he couldn't easily breathe.

Naomi tugged on the pilot's sleeve. After a beat he turned to face her. She mimicked driving a car, wildly turning an imaginary steering wheel back and forth, as if she were racing the Autobahn, and then when she felt that was clear, she stuck out her thumb and pointed to herself. "Me. Avión."

"YOU JUST SAID YOU ARE A PLANE," Jordan hollered.

Naomi smiled at the pilot undeterred. "*Fly* a plane! I want to fly the plane."

"PLEASE. I'M BEGGING YOU. STOP."

Naomi put her hands on the controls in front of her, even though she was quite sure they weren't engaged. The pilot flicked on the autopilot and removed the cans over his ears.

"¿Qué?"

Naomi pointed to herself, and then to the controls. The pilot grinned as if pilots loved nothing more than budding aviation enthusiasts. He pointed to a few instruments on the panel. "Gasolina. *Fuel*. Altitude. Velocidad. Ah . . . You say, *speed*. Presión."

Naomi looked at Jordan, confused. Jordan leaned in to look at the dial. "PRESSURE," he said, and Naomi immediately understood. No gauge was needed to tell them they were under an enormous amount of it.

The pilot pointed at a sequence of numbers. "Navigation." Either he knew that one in English, or the Spanish sounded almost the same. He then slowly disengaged the automatic pilot and took control of his yoke with one hand. With the other, he gently placed Naomi's on hers.

She gripped the yoke tight, as if she were all that was keeping the plane in the air, and stared directly out ahead of her. Instinct told her it was her job to keep the plane level, and so she pointed the nose at the horizon, looking through the blades of the nose's propeller as if her vision were X-ray.

"Heh?" the pilot said, asking her how it felt to be in control. She peeled her eyes from the course just long enough to notice that his hands were still clearly in command. He followed her eyes and loosened his grip, first holding the yoke with his fingertips before releasing it altogether; he was Superman giving Lois Lane the opportunity to fly.

Naomi was gripping the yoke with such fervor, her knuckles began to turn white. She could feel the sweat growing beneath her palms and took a few deep breaths. To be in control of the aircraft, she had to be in control of herself, and the most important thing was to remain calm. She fanned her fingers out, away from the yoke, while keeping it tightly wrapped in her thumbs. And then, when she re-formed her grip, she had control of it, instead of it having control of her.

"I'm doing it?" she asked. "I'm flying?" She turned to the instructor and the plane immediately took a gentle dive. But instead of retaking control, the pilot leaned over and placed his hands on Naomi's, pulling the yoke back toward her until the plane was level again. He left his hands on hers until he was confident she had a feel for it, then returned his attention to his side of the cockpit. "This is great. Truly fantastic!" She searched for the words in Spanish. "Esto es fantástico." She spun around to make sure Jordan was watching. "SEE?" Jordan was turning green.

The pilot snapped his fingers to return her attention to the task at hand. Naomi's face flushed hot with embarrassment; she wanted to prove she was a worthy pilot not just to those whose lives she held in her hands at that very moment, but also, she realized, to her parents, who were maybe somehow there. She held the yoke steady and allowed herself to take in the surroundings below. They were hugging the coast, which was surprisingly green; the beaches were sporadic and thin. The water sparkled, which differentiated it from the sky, and the city population was growing more sparse as they flew.

"My parents died in a plane crash," Naomi confided, but the pilot had his headset back on; she repeated herself even louder. "PLANE CRASH." The words had overtaken her. The dam burst and she began to sob.

Alarmed, the pilot pulled the headset from one ear. "¿QUÉ?"

"PLANE CRASH! EVERYONE DIED! THE WHOLE PLANE!"

A look of sheer panic came over his face and he spun around to Jordan to help understand. Jordan threw up his arms in disgust. The situations Naomi got them in. "Sus papás!" he began, just as they hit an unexpected bump. "ACCIDENTE AÉREO. TODOS MURIERON."

"¡¿UN CHOQUE?!" the pilot shouted, and suddenly everyone was keenly listening in—Marielle, Jordy, Craig, and five highly qualified and now highly alarmed jumping partners. They looked at the cockpit and saw Naomi sobbing, uncontrollably now, as if she had witnessed some impending horror that had yet to register with them. And it was in that moment that the plane hit its largest bit of turbulence yet and Naomi, who was still holding on to the yoke, screamed. In a panic she pulled back, and then overcorrected by pushing the yoke back toward the instrument panel, and the Cessna's nose tilted ever so slightly down.

It was Santiago who acted first. As Naomi's companion he was seated alone, closest to the jump door. He sprang into action like he'd been a capitán in the Mexican army, ripping open the door with his powerful arms, and the plane was suddenly filled with the deafening rush of wind. Everything that followed happened in a blur.

Mateo fastened himself to Craig's back, checked the straps, and lurched for the open door. Marielle caught Craig's face, framed against the open blue sky in the doorway, panicked and confused and out of focus.

"What the hell?!" was all he could manage before they were— *whoosh*—gone.

Marielle screamed when they disappeared, causing further alarm. Whether it was in response to the threat of their plane crashing or the jump door being opened, the rest of the instructors clipped themselves to their assigned partners with methodical precision, a drill they had been forced to practice hundreds, if not thousands, of times. Rosalita backed her way to the doorframe, dragging an alarmed Marielle, as Santiago did a quick double-check of their gear. He tapped Rosalita's shoulder twice to give the all clear, and she said "GO TIME" in Marielle's ear.

"GO WHERE?" Marielle felt a tipping sensation and gravity start to take hold. Rosalita didn't have time to respond, but it didn't matter; she was well aware of the answer. Suddenly she was on her back like an overturned turtle and the plane was somehow above them and everything beyond that was blue.

Inside the fuselage, Diego struggled with Jordy, who both was more of a physical match and had the mental preparation of seeing two of his friends being thrown from the plane. Jordy braced his long legs against the seat in front of them, momentarily wedging them in. He had been the most game to jump, but he knew he couldn't leave Jordan behind—not like this. He exchanged glances with his hapless boyfriend, who looked as pissed as he'd ever seen in his nearly twenty-five years of knowing him. But then Diego put his meaty arms around Jordy's middle and Jordy gave in to the hunky man's embrace. He looked one last time at Jordan apologetically, as if to say *I'm only human* and also *If I don't make it, it's up to you to explain this to my mother.* And then suddenly, instead of leaning into his wedged position, he leaned back into Diego, their cheeks momentarily touching. And then he fully hopped back to the door, as if the only two options were to jump and remain in Diego's embrace or stay on the plane and lose the solace of it; somehow the former seemed more inviting. Jordan reached out his hand for Jordy's and for one brief, shining second their fingertips grazed like they had modeled for Michelangelo's *The Creation of Adam.* But the instant Santiago tightened a last strap and gave his signature double tap, Jordy and Diego were gone.

"WHAT HAVE YOU DONE!" Jordan yelled at Naomi as he stared at the gaping opening in the side of their plane where the love of his life had seconds before been. "ALL OUR FRIENDS ARE GONE." And then, as if it bore repeating, "ALL. OUR. FRIENDS. ARE. GONE."

In the chaos, Naomi had long since let go of the yoke, and she turned around with genuine remorse. But Naomi was incapable of letting anyone see her real emotions, so instead she wiped her tears and yelled back with equal bluster, "DON'T YOU YELL AT ME!"

Jordan retracted his chin so far it almost came out the back side of his neck. "I *HAVE* TO YELL AT YOU BECAUSE THERE'S A HOLE IN THE SIDE OF THE PLANE!"

"THAT'S NOT A HOLE, THAT'S A DOORWAY! STOP BEING

SO DRAMATIC!" And then Naomi looked around to see everything rattling: seat belts, cushions, water bottles, clipboards bungeed to seat backs, all harmonizing together as if to say loudly in one voice, *What difference does that make?* She looked startled, as if she were confused as to where her friends had gone.

"DRAMATIC?!" Jordan suddenly felt himself being pulled from his perch near the window, and he grabbed on to the back of the pilot's seat. "OH NO YOU DON'T." His hands were sweaty and it was almost impossible to maintain a grip; he knew it was Yolonda pulling him as much as the suction from the open door, but that knowledge was not any more comforting.

"JORDAN. DON'T GO!" Naomi dropped her faux outrage and now pleaded with her friend to stay, as she didn't want to be the last of them left on the plane with a pilot who, while comforted that he had regained full control of his aircraft, was visibly angered by the havoc swirling around him.

Jordan squirmed and screamed "I HATE YOU!" at Naomi and he tried his best to lunge for her; alas, he was no match for Yolonda, who was, much like the pilot, not even a little amused. "OH MY GOD YOU'RE FREAKISHLY STRONG!" Any thoughts he might have had that they were mismatched in size were now, well, out the window, along with his friends. The more he wriggled, the more she tightened their straps until it felt like resistance was futile. "Oh, screw it," he said, and then shot Naomi one last look: *We will continue this on the ground.* He pressed his goggles tightly against his face and then took a perch in the doorway. Santiago did his thing and Jordan could feel the double tap right through Yolonda's shoulder, as if they were truly conjoined. *This is it*, he thought, and instead of being pulled backward out of the plane as the others were, he leaned forward, tucking his chin to his chest, and counted three somersaults until Yolonda pulled them out of their roll.

Santiago gripped the open doorway and waved to Naomi. "COME ON!" He made several urgent gestures, beckoning her his way, and she firmly shook her head no. A plane might have been the death of her parents, but jumping out of one felt like it would be hers. Today might have been her misguided idea, but there was no way in hell she was leaving her seat. Santiago grabbed the seat back in front of him and managed two steps toward Naomi before she screamed the type of high-pitched, earsplitting scream that gets teen actresses careers in horror films. Santiago stopped in his tracks, confused as much as frightened, and tilted his head like a dog. On the ground he would slowly back away from Naomi to de-escalate the crisis, but aviation had different rules. He shouted in Spanish at the pilot as Naomi looked for an additional seat belt or shoulder harness she might use to strap herself further to her chair. The pilot shouted back and instinctually she turned to Jordan to translate before remembering he was no longer there. *Oops*, she thought. Eventually Santiago talked himself out and the pilot swatted him away, giving him permission to be the last one to jump. Santiago gave in, checked his own straps for safety, and looked at Naomi one last time. She shook her head *absolutely not* and he rolled his eyes. *Suit yourself.* He then got down on one knee, crossed his arms over his chest, took a deep breath, and tumbled out of the plane.

Naomi and the pilot were all that were left. She sat embarrassed in her seat, not knowing what to say. Language barrier or not, there wasn't an icebreaker in the world that would meet this moment. The pilot flicked several switches and reengaged the autopilot, then turned a stern finger to Naomi. "NO TOUCH." And then, to drive his point home, he grabbed one of her wrists, moving her hand toward the yoke before slapping it gently away.

"I GOT IT. NO TOUCH!" She sat on her hands just to prove it.

The pilot looked at her with distrust, then unbuckled himself from his seat. He made his way back to the open door, and suddenly Naomi panicked, convinced he too might jump. *Wake up, wake up, wake up*, she thought, as if this were a nightmare from which she could emerge. He didn't have a parachute and was the only one on board not even wearing a harness, but that didn't calm her nerves or make her think any less that she was about to be abandoned. Just as hard as she tried to strap herself to her seat, she now was just as desperate to free herself from it in order to keep from being left alone on this plane. But her nightmare endured and she couldn't find the buckle to her seat belt and in desperation she tried to undo her harness. She scrambled until a loud noise caught her attention, then a second, and then the fuselage went quiet.

Naomi scrunched her eyes closed. *This is it*, she thought. She was now alone. How could grief over losing her parents lead her to die in the exact same way less than ten days apart? It wasn't just a cruel twist of fate, it was a comical one to be retold later at her expense. But there it was. It wasn't that she could feel her parents' disapproval, although she could; it was that she could feel their resignation. *Here comes our daughter, unmarried, no kids, couldn't even hack it two weeks without her parents before she got herself in a dire situation*. She disappointed them in life, she would disappoint them in the afterlife. She could so clearly picture them, just getting the swing of things wherever they were when told to make room for one more. Retirement, relaxation, rest. As her mother would say, easy come, easy go—an importer-exporter to her core.

She felt the hand on the back of her seat before she saw the pilot's arm as he twisted his way back into the cockpit. She lunged for him, arms open to grip him in a tight hug, but she was still strapped in place and her arms were too short to reach. The pilot, clear now to hear his own thoughts, mustered enough sympathy to lean in and hug his chaotic passenger; she gripped him tight and did not let go. "I thought you left me," she said. And then, as if he were a lover and they'd had a yearslong affair, she added, "Don't you *ever* leave me!"

Naomi turned over her shoulder to see that he had closed the fuselage door. Her heartbeat calmed, now that they were both sealed inside. They could head back to the airstrip and land.

"Tus padres, ¿eh?" he asked, referring back to the start of this mess.

"My parents, sí." And then they both nodded as he took the plane off autopilot and radioed the tower. She didn't understand his message, but she hoped like hell he was telling them that they were preparing to land. Then, almost to confirm that that was indeed what he had said, the plane began to veer gently to their left.

Naomi steeled herself for scorn as she stepped off the Cessna, so she kept her eyes on the ground. As she hopped off the plane she landed squarely on her heels, sending a painful little jolt up her spine; she'd already forgotten their lesson jumping from boxes, or she had never really taken it in. She actually appreciated the shooting pain up her legs, payback for not jumping from higher up. She straightened her jumpsuit, as if presentation were key in remaking her friendships and working her way back into their good graces. Her parents were gone in an instant, plucked from the sky; she was not ready to lose all the people she'd known second longest in a similar—although, since they were standing in front of her, admittedly less tragic—fashion. When she peeled her gaze from the tarmac she saw Jordy first, standing side by side with Diego; as the tallest they were hardest to miss. Craig was there, and Marielle too, clustered together with their diving partners, as if they had been friends with them for years. She saw Jordan last, his hands on his knees, looking as if he might dry-heave.

They were all celebrating, language apparently no longer a barrier, and Marielle, hopped up on adrenaline, was bumping chests with the men. Beside them on the ground were colorful parachutes on the gray tarmac like bright splotches of paint on an artist's palette. As much as she didn't want to feel the heat of their anger as she approached, she even more so did not want to feel their indifference. She cleared her throat when she was within earshot.

"There she is!" Marielle said, but without a triumphant chest bump.

"What's up, guys?" she asked, going for nonchalant. "What happened to landing on the beach?" Her voice sounded reedy and thin.

"Yes, well," Jordy said, and then he coughed into his hand. "Turns out our jump didn't go exactly as planned." And everyone laughed except Jordan.

"What's with him?" Naomi asked.

Jordan turned his head and growled, "YOU." He lunged like a wolf, Yolonda and Jordy holding him back by his harness, which was still strapped tightly around his chest.

Naomi lurched back, startled. "What did I miss?" she asked, as if that weren't the understatement of the century.

"Jordan's chute didn't open," Craig said somberly.

"It *what*?"

"DIDN'T! OPEN!" Jordan had the air of someone who was just calming down when anger took fresh root. He lunged at Naomi a second time. "I'm going to kill you!"

"What?"

"Murder you where you stand!" Jordan yelled.

"You can't say that to me!" Naomi was indignant. "I'm an orphan!"

To Jordan this was a minor detail. "GOOD! THEN NO ONE WILL MISS YOU!"

Yolonda muttered something to him in Spanish and it distracted him long enough to turn away from Naomi.

"No, that's *not* what reserves are for," Jordan shot back. "Reserves are meant to be there *for reserve*."

"A reserve to be deployed," Marielle countered.

"If the reserve is deployed, then there's no longer a reserve! Then what? CHAOS? TERROR? DEATH?!"

Naomi clutched her head. She wished everyone would stop shouting. "Everyone stop saying 'reserve' and someone tell me what happened!"

Jordan pulled out of his somersaults with his arms and legs spread wide, like he'd seen in photos of flying squirrels. His whole face was flapping in the wind, his mouth open and dry like he was having dental X-rays. He looked down at the ground and it was a patchwork quilt so far beneath them that it didn't seem to be getting any closer, at least not rapidly or in the way he'd imagined falling would feel. Because he wasn't falling; *he was flying*. He wasn't even aware of the woman on his back. It had angered him on the ground that he wasn't partnered with a man; as they were pairing up it seemed being tethered to someone he found wildly attractive like Mateo would be the fulfillment of some sort of wish—what was Craig going to do with Mateo? The thought seemed silly now, adolescent. He was so high up, he imagined a curve to the Earth, his goggles perhaps acting as the most subtle fish-eye lens. Yes, commercial planes flew at a higher altitude, more than twice than where he was now, and a lucky few had been to space for heaven's sake, but in that moment it felt like no one had ever been that high. Below him a pop of color bloomed like a yellow rose— Jordy's chute, he hoped.

He felt the double tap on his shoulder and laughed to himself. *Santiago, is that you?* Did these skydiving instructors know any other commands? He brushed Yolonda's hand away, his arm fighting against the air as if he were trying to gesture deep underwater. But she immediately tapped him again, more urgently this time. *Tap, tap. Tap, tap. Tap, tap.* His chute. It was time to pull the cord.

pulled the cord and nothing happened!" Jordan yelled, as if Naomi had packed his parachute herself. Yolonda put a hand on his shoulder in an attempt to calm him again. He was safe, he was on the ground. But he was still reliving the experience and he wanted Naomi to live it too. Jordan pointed his finger like a dagger and took a menacing step forward before stopping. "It's like what Pinochet used to do. Throw people out of planes to their deaths!"

"Wasn't Pinochet Chilean?"

"Yeah?"

"Aren't you from Colombia?"

"So?"

"And didn't you have *two* parachutes? I mean, you're here, aren't you?"

Jordan glanced down at his finger, as if surprised to find it attached to his hand. Naomi was right. He *was* here. Even if just moments ago he thought he would not be, that it was the end. He was here. He was upset, yes. But was he being overly dramatic? He lowered his finger and stood stunned, like a dog who had just been scolded.

Jordan glanced at the altimeter on his wrist, which read just over four thousand feet. It was another source of amusement, like he had logged dozens of jumps and was capable of making his own very determined altitudinal calculations. He had enjoyed every second of free fall, and was feeling grateful for the day, for Jordy, for Naomi even, for his life. He went from enraged to joyous in the time it took to pull out of three somersaults. He placed his hand on the pull that sat up near his shoulder, just as their instructor, Eddie, had taught them in their brief training on the ground, closed his eyes, and readied himself for what came next. You weren't yanked upward like you see in movies; instead Eddie said it was more like coming to a screeching halt from an alarming rate of speed. Either way, he expected to feel whiplash and since his harness also fastened between his legs he braced himself for discomfort.

But discomfort never came. For a fraction of a second it felt like nothing happened, and he knew immediately something was wrong. As unaware as he was of Yolonda's body in free fall, he was now hyperaware of her presence, her adrenaline flowing directly into him. He tried to look up, but with the wind in his face he could only turn his neck so far. There was a parachute just above them, he could just make that much out, but the canopy had failed to fully bloom. He panicked and began to kick against an invisible current as the parachute seemed to drag them horizontally but failed to make much of a dent in their speed as they headed now straight for the ground. He no longer imagined a curve to the Earth; he no longer felt very high at all, certainly not nearly high enough. He could only imagine every bone in his body breaking at once and a last gasp before certain death.

Yolonda wrapped her arms around him, pinning his own to his side in an effort to stop his flailing, and with one hand reached toward his waist for the parachute's release. As the tangled lines of the chute disconnected from their rig, Jordan realized that the partially deployed chute *had* slowed their free fall, at least somewhat, and once released of it they picked up speed again toward the ground.

Yolonda then extended Jordan's arms into an outstretched position and similarly spread his legs with her feet. She wrapped her arms around his torso again and reached this time to his left, pulling the reserve cord swiftly with both hands. Jordan, an avowed atheist for years, accessed his inner Catholic and prayed. There was no reserve for the reserve, certainly none that he was aware of. All of their eggs were in this one final basket; like Humpty Dumpty there would be no putting them back together again. The entirety of his relationship with Jordy ran through his head as he closed his eyes tighter than they'd ever been. And then there was a loud flapping *whoosh*. The reserve opened precisely as it should and they went from falling through deafening winds horizontally, stomachs parallel to the ground, to hanging in a vertical position and everything falling quiet, except for the pounding in his ears of his own heart.

"Line over!" Yolonda shouted in Spanish as some sort of explanation for their predicament, as if he could possibly understand what that meant. He looked at the altimeter. Twenty-one hundred seventeen feet. Lower than they should have been, but with room still to maneuver even if there was no time to waste. She placed his hands along with hers on the steering cables and gave a little tug on each. "Left, right," she said, this time in English so there was no room for confusion. He knew instinctually they had less time to prepare for landing than the others would have, so when she pulled left to steer them from power lines, he pulled as hard as he could too.

When they were finally standing on the ground he had never been more excited, and when he felt one last double tap on his shoulder he screamed "WHAT?!" before realizing Yolonda, shorter than him by four inches, was unable to quite reach the ground. He turned red and lowered himself, giving enough slack in their rig so that she could safely detach. When she did, Jordan hugged her—perhaps more tightly than he had ever hugged a woman who was not his mother. As much as she was not his first choice in jumping partners, she was the only one he wanted now. He barely registered their screams as Jordy, Marielle, and Craig, who had witnessed part of this horror unfold, came running over the crest of a neighboring hill. They didn't stop until they were in each other's arms.

Well. Shit." It was meant to be a preamble to something more eloquent, but it was in fact all Naomi could think of to say. Was she really almost responsible for one of her friends dying? Did she hold some responsibility for what happened to her parents? Was she responsible for anything at all? The murmur of excitement; Naomi felt the energy around her change. Everyone turned and ran from her, Jordy last, who stopped to give her a squeeze on her arm that was meant to be comforting, an opening for forgiveness.

Then, across the tarmac, Santiago appeared carrying his wadded-up parachute under one arm. The others cheered when they saw him, a decorated soldier returning from war. Naomi was mad. All she had done was try to explain what had happened to her parents, the reason they were up in the sky. It was just a simple bid for connection with another person after suffering a stunning loss. Santiago, bloated bundle of testosterone that he was, was the one who started tossing people from the plane in midair. If anyone was Pinochet in this scenario it was him. Why was he the one getting the hero's welcome, and not her, she who had conquered a fear? She stewed in the van on their ride back to Casa Kimberly, while the others traded notes on their experience, mostly forgetting to include her.

At the hotel, Naomi evicted Marielle. "Go room with Craig," she said, physically pushing her toward the door.

"Are you sure you should be alone?" There was nothing you could do to Marielle that would keep her from worrying about others, not even throwing her out of a plane. The fact that she was the only one being nice to her right now somehow enraged Naomi even more. "You'll be down for dinner? The Jordans made reservations on the beach."

Naomi shook her head yes, as it was the fastest way to get Marielle out of her room, but she stopped shy of an audible confirmation. When she closed the door, she listened as a strong sudden afternoon rain started to fall.

Later when Naomi caved and walked along the beach to join her friends, the sun was already starting to dip; she carried her shoes in her hand. In the distance was the brand-new sail sculpture on Los Muertos Pier, spiraling out of the ocean to dizzying heights, and she felt like she was inside someone's vacation postcard. Clouds dappled the sky after the storm and she knew they were in for another glorious sunset. Before their trip to Mexico, she never knew skies could hold so many rich colors. On one side of the boardwalk was a string of restaurants packed with rowdy singles who never wanted to be far from the party (or a bar); on the ocean side, tables covered in crisp linens waited, romantic tableaus for couples still recovering from a day in the sun. Ahead, laughter eclipsed the surf. Her friends. She could see them surrounded by tiki torches stuck in the sand, their flames dancing in the ocean breeze. She had instructed them to go ahead, as she needed more time to build the nerve to face them. Still, she was already feeling like an outsider after the events of the day, and this only added to her feelings of isolation. It stung.

Suddenly, she wished she *were* dead; then she wouldn't have to claw her way back into their good graces. They would have to forgive her, and in the moment that held some appeal. As she approached their table, her sundress blew poetically in the wind, causing her to look much like the melodramatic ghost she imagined herself to be. Jordan spotted her first and reached for a bottle from a champagne bucket to pour another glass—either a gesture of forgiveness or a selfish bit of fortification.

"Your new friends aren't joining us?" Naomi asked as she struggled to even her chair in the sand. It was classic Naomi, come out swinging instead of hat in hand.

"Oh, no you don't." Craig scoldingly waved a finger.

"Don't what?" Naomi asked.

"I thought you were working on removing your armor," Marielle said gently. "Now that you don't need it anymore."

Had she said that out loud? Maybe at her parents' funeral. But that no longer seemed right; then she'd just be naked. Unable to meet their gaze, she feigned interest in a menu.

Jordan handed her the glass of champagne. "Fishing for pity is a waste of your time."

"No, a waste of my time would be live-tweeting *Glease*."

Jordan gasped and sank back in his chair. "You follow me on Twitter?"

"Not anymore." Naomi raised an eyebrow.

Marielle was confused. "Wait. What's *Glease*?"

"The kids on *Glee* put on a production of *Grease*. Glee, Grease, *Glease*."

Jordan's face grew hot. "Okay, that's enough about *that*."

Naomi pointed to several mounds of green mush. "What is this?"

"It's a guacamole flight," Jordy explained.

"A guacamole *flight*?" Naomi repeated, the idea of it ridiculous, but also she would have thought they had all long lost their appetites for anything even remotely pertaining to air travel. But she helped herself to a chip, sweeping it through the mound of avocado that looked most mild. She then laughed, almost maniacally, and then, surprising even herself, she burst into tears for the second time that day, and then covered her mouth, afraid of them seeing food in her teeth.

"Okay," Craig whispered, always uncomfortable with a public scene. Marielle threw her arms around her.

"Today was not your fault," Jordy said, placing his hands over hers while elbowing the guacamole flight to one side.

Jordan shot him a look. "It's kind of her fault." While not angry, he was still feeling salty.

Naomi shoved another chip in her mouth, hoping it would get her to stop crying. But it was not the mild end of the flight but rather the spicy, and her tears doubled until she wondered whether she had the mild or spicy end of their *actual* flight, and she went back to laughing again. The whole thing was just so absurd.

"You're a mess," Jordan said, releasing the silverware from his napkin and handing it to Naomi to dab her eyes. "But I want to tell you something. I learned something today, and I want you to learn it too. We think we have control over everything—we hold on *so* tight— and the truth is we don't. We don't have any control at all. Not over the big things. It wouldn't have been all that extraordinary if my chute didn't open. Unlucky, maybe. But not extraordinary. People die all the time, many tragically and before their time. Some people fall from the sky. But in those moments I found comfort in knowing I wasn't in charge."

"Yeah, Yolonda was in charge," Craig blabbed.

"Not even. I'm lucky she kept her cool, but even she couldn't control everything. I think it helps us all if we all just let go. And the funniest part? Once I was safely back at the hotel and had calmed down, all I wanted to do was grab a parachute and go again."

Naomi's eyes were still wet and she scrunched her toes in the sand. "I'm sorry I missed out."

"Don't be that sorry," Marielle blurted. All eyes turned to her. "It's just. At one point . . . No, never mind."

"At one point *what*?" Jordy asked. The others were equally curious.

Marielle lowered her voice. "No, I can't." She covered her face in humiliation, but it was too late to turn back now. "There was a string of drool that came out of my mouth."

"That's disgusting," Naomi muttered.

"Thank god Rosalita was wearing goggles," Craig said.

"We were *all* wearing goggles! That's not the point."

"Then, what is the point?"

"I DON'T KNOW!" Marielle shouted before burying her face in a menu.

Naomi looked around the table at her friends and felt like a crisis had been averted. The importance of their pact was only now sinking in. She didn't understand it before, found it reactionary—the invention of underbaked minds; today she saw real wisdom in it for the first time. "Thank god for you. All of you. I mean it. If I met me today, I wouldn't recognize myself." It wasn't just the random grays she kept finding in her hair, or the puffiness under her eyes that took half the morning to disappear, although both were reasons to think of herself as someone else at first glance. It was that she found herself so unmoored by the loss of her parents, when she'd spent her whole life acting like she didn't need them. "But I have you to remind me who I am."

"Someone who would watch their friends sucked out of a plane?" It was darker now, and Jordan's face was lit mostly from tiki torches. Naomi was struck by how handsome he looked.

"Watched *in horror*. I don't get enough credit for that part. Besides. Now you've proven you have nine lives."

"Nine total, maybe. Only eight left."

"Seven more than any of us," Craig noted.

Naomi raised her glass of champagne. "However many. The life I want to live is with all of you."

After they said their good nights, the Jordans retreated to the Puente del Amor under the light of the full moon. Jordan encouraged Jordy to do his best Richard Burton as he snapped photos of him coming across the bridge.

"I said Richard *Burton*."

"Who was I giving?" Jordy asked, confused.

"Richard Simmons?"

Jordy raised his arms in defeat and made like he was headed back to their room.

"Come on. Sultry, *angry*. Look like you want to rip my clothes off."

"I do want to rip your clothes off," Jordy said, thrusting forth an obvious bulge in his pants. One of the gifts being in a foreign country gave them was a jump start to their libidos. "Did you look up that thing?"

Jordan was confused.

"You remember, the last time we . . . You said you would check online."

"Oh, *that* thing." The last time they had sex there had been blood in Jordan's semen. Not a lot, but enough to be disconcerting. "Nine times out of ten it's nothing."

"And the other time?" Jordy pressed.

Jordan tapped his foot impatiently. "Kind of killing the mood here. Can we get back to—"

Jordy retreated for a do-over. The air had cooled significantly now that it was past midnight, and Jordan rubbed his bare arms with a slight chill. He took in the bridge. The thick balusters that were like majestic chess pieces as they rose to support the rail with uplighting that made them stand out. The lush green ferns that framed it on either side. The ivory-tiled dome that capped the roof on Burton's former home. The streak of moonlight across the night sky. It was so very much like a movie set itself that it didn't stretch the imagination to picture two stars embracing as they hovered safely above the prying eyes of the paparazzi. Finally, Jordy crested the bridge in full Burton mode; it took Jordan's breath away.

"Damn, that's hot."

Jordy wrapped an arm tightly around Jordan's waist. "Queens, queens. Strip them naked as any other woman and they are no longer queens."

Jordan laughed. "Are you doing Antony from *Cleopatra*?"

Jordy smirked, busted. And then his eyes turned serious, remembering their day. "I don't want to live in a world without you in it."

Their mouths met with the kind of teenage hunger that tended to dissipate over the years. When the moment had passed and they turned to head to their room, Jordan said, "You won't have to. Apparently I have eight more lives."

Craig and Marielle lay awkwardly on top of the duvet, pillows cradling heads that were heavy with the sweetness of champagne. The ceiling fan above them provided a gentle breeze while the blades lulled them into a passive state of semiconsciousness.

"Kicked out of my own room." Craig turned to Marielle. Until she spoke he wasn't one hundred percent sure she was even awake.

"It's okay to take turns," he replied, like she was a toddler who needed encouragement.

Marielle replied with a flutter of her lips that suggested she might have a case but that she was too drunk and too tired to present it to a jury. "Can you believe today?" She stretched like a cat. "I have a daughter. I can't go around jumping out of planes."

Craig blanched at the idea that her life was any more important because she was a mother. "I can't either. I like my life. In fact, I'm quite attached to it."

"Your life as a gallerist?"

Craig let her dismissiveness slide. He was happy where he was at, having taken on more responsibility at the gallery, learning the art of appraisal from the gallery owner for insurance and values for donation and sale. He'd even appraised an original by Dutch Abstract Expressionist Aernouk Janssen for a couple divorcing so that they could squarely divide their assets; he'd worked hardest on that appraisal, as there had been only a few recent sales for comparative purposes. Not that it mattered. In the end, in a fit of rage, the husband had taken a chain saw and split the artwork—frame and all—in two. (The wife had returned to see if there was any value in her broken share and Craig had to break it to her, gently, that there was not.)

Had Marielle taken a swipe at his personal life, he might have been more affected. He'd had his share of women. None of them stuck around more than six months to a year, but that was mostly by his design. And he seldom grieved these relationships; there was never time with another always waiting in the wings. He loved where he lived; New York was truly the city that never sleeps and he was never at a loss for cultural stimulation. He had friends, not many, but enough so that he was never alone.

"How is Mia?" Craig finally asked.

Marielle's body tensed at the mention of her daughter's name, but in the moment she didn't know why. "Going to Wellesley. She'll be a sophomore in the fall."

"One of the Seven Sisters."

Marielle turned to face him surprised. "How do you know about the Seven Sisters?" She said it like someone had betrayed state secrets.

"My cousin went to Smith. She had a sweatshirt or something. I borrowed it once and she yelled at me."

"Oh," Marielle said and then paused. "I always forget you didn't have a family."

Craig studied the ceiling fan. The blades looked like they were accelerating, messing with his perception of time. "I had a family."

She took his hand in hers. "I meant that you were raised by your aunt and uncle."

Craig had thought about mentioning that biographical nugget to Naomi earlier, as if being abandoned by his parents might bring her comfort in losing hers, but he couldn't find a way to do it without making it sound like a competition. "Do you ever wonder what Alec would be like at forty?"

Marielle didn't hesitate. "I don't have to. He'd be exactly the same. Except somehow even better looking. That fucker."

"Alec would have jumped out of the plane. In fact, he would have been first." Deep down, Craig knew that was the difference between them—on some level the rest of them would always have to be dragged. Just as it was up to him to drag answers out of Marielle if he wanted to put his nagging questions about Mia to rest. It took him a minute to gather the nerve and when he finally said "About Mia . . ." Marielle's eyes were firmly closed. Craig watched her sleep for a moment, then nestled into her, making himself as comfortable as he could, and when he eventually drifted off to sleep they were still holding hands.

They met on the beach at sunset. The tide was receding and they stood close enough to the water so that the sand felt mushy under their feet. They stood in a row as they faced the sea, Marielle on one end, also holding a simple bouquet of daisies, looking more like they were about to baptize someone than eulogize them. The sky was orange along the horizon, then blue, then red, then purple at the high point in the sky; the ombré effect mirrored across the ocean, then onto the wettest sand where the ocean lapped the shore, sandwiching them in color. Moored boats rocked gently in the rippling water, maybe forty feet offshore.

"Do we have to go back?" Marielle asked; it felt like they'd stepped into a dream. And there was something almost cultlike about the way they were standing, as if they could decide en masse not to and just walk straight out into the ocean, never to be heard from again. No one answered, but mostly because they too were wishing they could stay.

"I want to give the eulogy," Naomi said, breaking free. She took a few steps toward the water before turning back to face her friends.

"You want to give the eulogy," Jordan repeated skeptically.

"Yes."

"Your *own* eulogy."

"That's right." She challenged the group to deny her. Only Craig dared to speak.

"But the point is to remind you that you are loved."

"I know I'm loved. I pay for everything."

Jordan faked a cough.

"It was a joke, Ebenezer. Thank you both for this lovely weekend. I'm just saying it's *self*-love that's currently my problem. And so I would like to say a few words to myself. Unless anyone has a problem with that." She looked at each of them individually. "Good. It's 2016. Hillary's about to be president. Get used to taking orders from a girl."

Naomi wore a huipil she'd admired in one of the local shop windows; it was white mostly, gloriously embroidered with the brightest of flowers and snaking green vines made of thread. It was perfect for both the tourist on her last night and the ministerial role she assumed now.

"We are here today to remember Fumiko and Takeshi Ito, as well as their daughter, Naomi, or the version of her that perished with them when their plane crashed into the sea." Already she was fighting back tears. She took a deep breath to see if she wanted to do this. She certainly didn't have to, this was all her idea and her friends were more than ready to step in—no doubt they would say lovely things. Lovely, and wrong. On her third deep breath, her body full of oxygen, it registered that forward was the only way through. "Naomi wanted to please her parents. She had, ever since she was a little girl. But her parents were—how do I say this judiciously—*not easily pleased*. They had high expectations of her, and often their expectations were met, but never with praise or celebration. Just new and loftier hopes. There were plenty of things that made Naomi an individual. Loyalty, strength, a caustic wit, kindness . . ." Craig raised a finger to object and Naomi cut him off at the knees. "If you say one word, I will drag you into this water and hold you under until your body goes limp." Craig lowered his hand while the others smiled; Naomi was still Naomi. "Those things were not celebrated either. Instead she just drifted along, hopeful always, yet disappointed too, masking hurt with that aforementioned wit."

Naomi looked at the Jordans, who had turned inward and were embracing each other tightly. Marielle placed a hand on Craig's shoulder, the other on the crook of his arm. All four of them were looking at Naomi with eyes full of love, as she had always wished her parents would.

"She played in the school orchestra, bassoon if you can believe that, but second chair and not first. She made the National Honor Society, but to her parents' great horror was third in her graduating class. She got into Stanford, which earned her a quiet dinner alone with her parents, but after a disastrous first year she transferred to Berkeley, which earned their scorn instead. She continued in her love of music, but didn't pursue it in the way they approved. Concerts?

Contracts? Schmoozing artists? What did any of that have to do with the bassoon? She never married, or had kids, which didn't upset them as much as she imagined it would; by then it was just one more disappointment on a long list."

Naomi explained how after a time she was harder on herself for many of these things, internalizing her parents' disappointment. She sabotaged her year at Stanford in a kind of mental collapse. She didn't want her parents to have even one thing to be proud of if they wouldn't meet her halfway on anything else. She thrived at Berkeley, but it came with a cost: a deep understanding that she would never be the daughter they wanted. And yet she held out hope that one day they would come around. These were just the awkward, transformative years where they would learn to relate as adults and soon she would have the agency to reason with them. To explain her own self-worth. And she lived with that hope, that eventually she could make them see things her way. As long as they were out there, traveling the globe, they might one day fly home to her. Instead, they flew off into the ultimate sunset, leaving their only child's hopes dashed in the wreckage.

"But endings are also beginnings," she continued. "Opportunities for a new life. And so tonight we say goodbye, not only to Fumiko and Takeshi, who were good people, products of their own parenting, their own upbringing, racism, hardship, discrimination, and their own experience of the world. But also to their daughter, Naomi, the daughter who was never enough."

Marielle stepped forward first. She took Naomi's hand.

"In her place we celebrate a new Naomi. Accomplished. Funny. Okay, Craig, maybe not *always* kind, but hardly ever mean. She's flawed."

"She's beautiful," Marielle added, handing her the bouquet of flowers, and the Jordans took that as their cue to take their place beside Marielle. Craig joined them last and they all placed a hand on her, welcoming her rebirth.

"She's confident. Selfish at times, but also giving. She doesn't work out as much as she should, and she eats too much dairy, which is . . . *Not good*, flosses only on Wednesdays, she Ubers everywhere because she's too lazy to drive, and she often pushes people away. But she also kicks ass. At her job. In the world. In *life*. That Naomi. She is enough." Her friends tightened their grip on her and she started to cry. "She is enough. She is enough. She is enough."

The sun had fully disappeared below the horizon, the sky now a beautiful bruise, purple and black, as it would remain through the night, waiting for the sunrise to heal it. They laid the flowers in the water and watched them gently float out with the tide, then stood perfectly still to take in their surroundings. The lapping of the waves, the light breeze in the sky, the laughter from another group of friends, younger, echoes of their past selves, standing farther down the beach. The little birds running along the shore, plucking delicacies from the sand. The smell of salt in the air and a slight waft of fish from the fishing boats that docked just to the south after a hard day's work at sea. Everything that reminded them they were alive. They were here. And it was beautiful.

Naomi took a deep breath. "You are enough," she said one final time. "And now you are finally free."

Craig offered her a Kleenex from his pocket and kissed the top of her head. "You played the bassoon," he whispered. Naomi accepted the tissue, then swiftly hit him in the back of the head. "Ow!" he exclaimed, rubbing his noggin as the others laughed.

Two weeks later, Naomi quit drinking.

THE
JORDANS

It was an ongoing argument, which day served as their anniversary. The day they met at Berkeley? They were barely friends at the time—the studious Latino and the strapping swimmer (in fact, when Jordan said he was from Colombia, Jordy assumed he meant the university)—but it was certainly the start of something new. The day they first consummated their relationship? That time was too muddled with memories of Alec's death. Their wedding anniversary? That was merely a day they picked after Jordan's first diagnosis, to distract from the chemo he'd started and so they could take a few photos before he lost his hair. When they tied the knot, they'd been together for decades; marriage equality wasn't even the law in New York until 2011. How could that be their anniversary? So, when looking to celebrate, they more often than not settled on the day in early June, three weeks after graduation, when Jordy packed his duffel, left Southern California, and buzzed Jordan's fifth-floor walk-up in New York City. When

Jordan said "Come in," they both knew he meant not only into his home but also into his life.

The only food Jordan had to offer that first night was leftovers from his mother's visit the week before, some of her homemade ajiaco, a kind of potato and chicken soup, and a few beef empanadas; Jordy scarfed it all down. "Do you eat like this every night?" he had asked, impressed, suddenly realizing maybe he didn't know who Jordan was outside school. Jordan smiled and told him not to get his hopes up. Eventually they learned to cook together, although Jordan had more of a knack for it.

Which is why, in part, Jordan was surprised when he returned home from a walk in Central Park. "What's this?" The smells wafting from the kitchen awakened an appetite that lately had been mostly dormant.

"Your mother's soup," Jordy answered. Jordan peered farther into the kitchen in a panic, afraid he would find Carmen Vargas there ready to scold him for not wearing a jacket outdoors even though it was seventy degrees. He had told his parents that the cancer was back, but he had downplayed its seriousness. They were both in their eighties, and he worried it might be a terminal diagnosis for them too. "Relax, she's not here."

Jordan exhaled. "With three different kinds of potatoes?"

Jordy pointed to the colorful peels on their cutting board.

"What's the occasion?" Jordan asked.

"What's the occasion? It's June."

Jordan started humming a few bars of "(I Like New York in June) How about You?"

"June fourth . . . ?" Jordy clarified.

"Our anniversary." Jordan offered a weak smile; it frustrated him how much his brain was in a fog and how he had to work that much harder to access things that used to be front of mind. "You're making the soup."

"Yes, but the empanadas I got from the place."

The place. Jordan loved when they traded in the secret language of relationships. "Did you pack a duffel? Are we going to reenact the whole night?" He changed his tune to the theme from *Three's Company. Come and knock on our door* . . .

"I thought maybe dinner and we could take it from there."

Jordan was relieved. His body was no longer capable of re-creating *everything* they had done that first night. He felt so brittle at times lately he worried about snapping in half.

"Want some wine?"

Jordan glanced approvingly at the label on the bottle Jordy had selected. Of course he wanted wine, but it didn't mix well with his meds. "I think I'll pass, but you have some." He instead leaned his face over the simmering pot on the stove and inhaled deeply. "You found guascas?" he asked, referring to the soup's signature herb.

"At the Latin American grocer where we took your mom. When was that, last October?"

Jordan was impressed he remembered. "How did you know how to make this?"

"I asked her for the recipe."

"And she gave it to you?"

"She gave it to *you*. I'm just the one putting it together. Believe me, it was all I could do to keep her from coming down to make it herself. But I told her it was our anniversary and we would have her over another time." Jordy led his husband to the small table under the window so he could sit down. He handed him a card. "Here. Open this."

Jordan studied the envelope as he flipped it from front to back. "I didn't get you anything."

"Just a lifetime of happiness."

"Puke."

Jordy protested. "Oh, come on! That was swe—"

Jordan held up a finger to pause him while he took a few deep breaths to stave off a wave of nausea. "No, I thought I was really going to . . . It passed."

"Oh." Jordy laughed. Cancer once again stepping on romance.

Jordan slid a finger under the envelope's seal; inside was a card and two plane tickets.

"I took a chance on the dates." Jordy looked hopeful as he waited for a response. "But of course we can change them. I hope you still want to go." Jordan had an inscrutable look. "Wh-what?"

Jordan studied the print on the tickets. JFK to Bogotá. Jordy had really listened and taken him seriously. "When you showed up on my doorstep that first night with all of your belongings, you know, when you surprised me from L.A. . . . I never told you this, but I was actually seeing someone. Had just started. Seeing someone."

Jordy took a step back from the table. The soup was now boiling and he turned off the burner. "Oh."

"There was a moment—just a moment—where I wasn't sure I was happy to see you. I mean, of course I was happy to see you. I didn't know if I was *ready* to see you. In fact, I thought it might have been him who was buzzing my apartment."

Jordy didn't know quite what to say. He wasn't aware they had any more secrets. Of course there were little omissions and skeletons they kept tucked away; those existed in every relationship. The pants Jordan bought him that he pretended to like but secretly hated because of their tight fit. The package of Nutter Butters he kept stashed in the office for himself. A few flirtations in the steam room at the gym. But nothing potentially life-altering. "Okay . . . ?"

"Oh, don't give me that look. Like you haven't sat on any big secrets."

Jordy swallowed, remembering Craig's funeral. "I thought we moved past that. It's unfair that you—"

Jordan spoke over him. "What I'm saying is . . ." He then lowered his voice when Jordy ceded focus to him. "What I'm saying is, when I woke up the next morning everything felt right, and I've been glad every day since it was you."

"Then that's all the present I need." Jordy leaned down to kiss him. "Happy anniversary, my love."

"Happy anniversary," Jordan said, wondering how soon they would eat.

THERE'S A
WONDER
IN MOST
EVERYTHING
I SEE

(CRAIG, 2018)

Two million apiece was a high asking price, but it was far from an exorbitant amount. At least not for the international buyers a gallerist like Craig Scheffler regularly came in contact with who could spend four million dollars before lunch with little more than a phone call to move cash around. Craig didn't think what happened next would spiral into such a big deal, although of course it was going to, given both his negligence in the situation and the dark cloud that hung over him ever since childhood when he was given up by his parents to live with an aunt and uncle in Idaho. The problem escalated because, despite the ease with which his buyers spent it, four million dollars wasn't nothing—even to the wealthiest collectors—and that kind of money came coupled with pride. Or maybe the problem stemmed from this being a record sale for German contemporary master Jürgen Förg; his pieces had never demanded so much. If the sale out of New York hadn't made headlines in the art world, maybe no one would have noticed Craig's mistake. Or it could have been simply bad luck that the winning bidders themselves, Laurence and Tibby Hough, were the type that were always ready to raise a fuss. They fiercely protected their wealth (which Laurence had earned managing hedge funds and Tibby had inherited from her banker father) by elevating an already litigious nature to practically its own art form. They were never going to go quietly into the proverbial good night, or allow a simple refund from the gallery to correct the mistake. Or maybe it started long before that. Maybe this nightmare began in November 1970, when Alec (because, of course his name was Alec) Wildenstein, then just thirty years old, became the first individual ever to purchase a painting for more than a million dollars, prompting a modern run on exorbitant art sales; Velázquez's portrait of his assistant Juan de Pareja went on sale at Christie's auction house in London with an opening bid of £315,000 and after a dizzying one hundred and thirty seconds sold for a jaw-dropping £2.3 million. Or maybe it all started in the ancient civilizations of Egypt, Babylonia, and China, where the very concept of art collection began. Or maybe—*just maybe*—fault lay squarely with the cave dweller who was first unsatisfied with drab stone walls and decided it would be best to decorate them with imagery.

Or perhaps the entirety of the blame lay at Craig's own feet, which was what made him decide to plead guilty to fraud. Since no rational judge would allow into evidence receipts of a painting sold in 1970, or his pontifications on Babylonia and Egypt and people who lived in caves, the evidence instead would focus on *his* actions in the matter at hand and, crucially, his silence after the fact when he should have spoken up. Was the gallery negligent in a manner that rose to criminal, or were they simply inept? Was Craig himself guilty the moment he established credibility to forged paintings by lending his expertise or when he was silent when nagging doubt set in? And did his silence cause another party (namely, the Houghs) to surrender something of value (in this case their money), which was the very definition of fraud? His conscience said yes, and the gallery needed a scapegoat. His bank account agreed, at least so far as telling him he couldn't afford the high-priced lawyers he would need for a lengthy trial and would be outgunned by both his employer and his clients.

The night he decided he would plead guilty, Craig was home alone drinking from a bottle of peanut butter whiskey that a twentysomething woman named Farrow with whom he was sleeping had gifted him as a joke. It tasted god-awful, but it had an intoxicating smell, and after two glasses of the swill he decided to call Marielle. Why Marielle? He didn't know. In many ways their relationship was strained, him having pressed her several times now about Mia, but she would also be the most gentle, the least judgmental, and the time difference between New York and Oregon worked in his favor. And in the moment he genuinely missed her, and the company of a woman his own age.

"I fucked up," he said when she answered her phone, and it took her a moment to place who was calling.

"Nana?"

"I fucked up, Marielle, and I'm in some deep trouble. I think I'm going to jail." He then replayed those words, realizing how dramatic they sounded, like he was calling her for help in disposing of a body. So he clarified, "I fucked up at work. At the gallery." And then repeated, "At work," just to make sure he had alleviated her fears. She didn't say anything right away, so he added, "I thought I would hear cows on your end or something."

"Cows?" she said, confused.

"You know like mooing. Oinking. Animal sounds. From your sanctuary."

After another beat Marielle asked, "Did you apologize?" At first Craig thought she was referring to his crack about the cows, but then he realized she meant for messing up. It was typical Marielle. In her experience, not nearly enough men apologized for their misdeeds, and she felt a lot more could be accomplished in this world if they did.

"It's a little more complicated than that."

"Maybe it's not," she suggested, but of course she knew from the sound of his voice that it was.

"I apologized," Craig admitted, both to ward off this dead-end line of questioning and because it was true. He'd apologized to the Houghs over and over at the behest of the gallery's owner, Martin Blythe (who himself had apologized repeatedly to protect the reputation of his gallery), but against the advice of counsel who felt apologies were tantamount to admissions of guilt. "But when what you did can be seen as illegal, apologies are often not quite enough."

Marielle sat with that a moment, parsing his words. "*Can* be seen as?" she questioned. "Isn't something illegal or not?"

"How long did you spend in Washington?" Craig asked, assuming nowhere was the definition of legal more flexible than in the city in which legislators thought the laws they passed were merely suggestions for their own behavior at best.

"You're going to tell me it's complicated again, aren't you."

"It's complicated." Craig exhaled, defeated.

It had been two and a half years since they'd gathered in Puerto Vallarta and he hadn't seen all of them since. The Jordans a handful of times, since they too lived in New York. They would get together for dinner at some hot restaurant they had connections to, and once they had invited him to the opening of some experimental play about Andy Warhol's Factory years they thought would be right up Craig's alley, but which he had somehow found both pandering *and* pretentious. He stopped by the hospital when Jordan was undergoing treatment for cancer of some kind; Craig asked Jordan then if he was going to trigger the pact, but Jordan assured him it was not that serious—a few rounds of chemo and he would be back on his feet. His doctors had caught it early, in his prostate if Craig recalled, and they would monitor him every few months. Naomi he saw once as she swung through town chasing a transgender pop star who was poised to break big. Naomi could be counted on for a good time and seemed to be thriving after her own funeral and the events of Puerto Vallarta. She took him to some club where she sprang for VIP service, paying a thousand dollars for a bottle of mid-shelf Scandinavian vodka that she didn't drink, just so they could have a place to sit. She introduced him to several young women, backup dancers who toured with the pop star, and that night he ended up bedding two. Marielle he had not seen at all, as she was now settled in Oregon and as far as he could tell made little money, toiling away in the nonprofit world. (Or what money she did make went right back into her work raising animals, or whatever it was that she did.) He wondered what Mia thought of her mother out in the Oregon wilderness tending to wounded chipmunks, but by now he knew better than to inquire.

"That's lawyer speak," Marielle said, not accepting that it was complicated at all. They had been quiet for so long, Craig almost forgot he was on the phone. He didn't answer, so she asked, "You do have a lawyer, don't you?"

"I have a lawyer," he said, even though when laying out his case, his attorney made him feel less at ease and not more. Three hundred dollars an hour to make him feel like shit—and she wasn't even a partner. Craig took a final sip of the peanut butter whiskey before dumping the last of the bottle down the drain. Whoever had invented the drink should be shot.

Marielle chuckled nervously in the silence.

"What?"

"This has been an enlightening conversation," she said. And Craig understood. He hadn't been very forthcoming.

"Let's talk about you," he said.

"Why?"

"Because I like hearing the sound of your voice."

They spoke for two more hours.

There had been a lot of pressure on Craig to authenticate the paintings as original Jürgen Förgs; it had been some time since the gallery had made a big sale and so his assignment was clear—these paintings *needed* to generate buzz and excitement. And Craig wanted them to be real. As Martin Blythe wanted them to be real. As collectors circling rumors of these works wanted them to be real. It was better for everyone if they were real. The works themselves certainly looked authentic and he didn't mean from a first or casual glance. Förg had a unique, surrealist style, creating blurred portraits where every stroke of paint seemed both important and an afterthought. Craig had conducted a near-microscopic study of the brushwork, as well as a careful inventory of the paint itself, as two authenticated Jackson Pollocks that sold through a neighboring gallery had recently been proven fakes (and were the subject of several civil suits) when pigment in the yellow paint had been discovered not to have existed until a good fourteen years after Pollock's death in a car crash. Because of this, the art world (and the FBI) were on high alert. Everything he could see and test passed muster, and it would have been a no-brainer to declare them real if it weren't for their uncertain provenance. The paintings came to the gallery through a new and unfamiliar dealer who said the works had been owned by an Israeli collector who was pressured by his wife's mother, a Holocaust survivor, to unload them, even though

Förg was born well after World War II. Provenance, a detailed history of a work's ownership, was everything in authentication, and while this new dealer (who introduced herself as Mrs. Khan) was long on story, she was short on documentation. And in recalling the ordeal to the FBI, Craig realized Mrs. Khan, like Jürgen Förg himself, specialized in blurry details that made everything seem important. It wasn't until much later that he realized he himself had filled in many of the details he found missing, that she had said far less than he'd originally heard.

Craig was officially fired from his job on a Thursday, when word leaked that he planned to plead guilty; it was all the cover Martin Blythe needed to terminate him. He was leaving the gallery with a box of his personal belongings when he saw his friends, all four of them, standing together on the sidewalk, hands on their hips like the Justice League: the Jordans flanking Naomi, Marielle slightly in front, looking like a gang of schoolyard bullies, waiting to rough him up after school. Craig stopped in his tracks, his box drooping in one of his hands until a small potted plant tipped over, spilling half of its dirt.

"SURPRISE!" they yelled in unison. Naomi then blew one of those paper party horns that unfurls like a long tongue.

"Fuck me," Craig said, dropping his box on the ground. "Who are you supposed to be?" he asked. "The Sharks and the Jets?" He snapped his fingers a few times for emphasis.

"Don't try to win me over with a musical theater reference," Jordan said. "We're mad at you and I'm . . . Well, I'm not that cheap."

Jordy interjected, "You're exactly that cheap."

"Shh. Whose side are you on?" Jordan stepped forward and hugged Craig tightly.

For a second Craig was confused and wasn't sure exactly why they were there. He worried as Jordan held him that maybe his cancer was back. There were only so many times they could gather for fake funerals before they would have to assemble for something more real. They weren't there for Jordy, that much was clear—he was too even-keeled for this foolishness. But as he placed his chin on Jordan's shoulder and looked squarely at Marielle, Craig understood that this was not about Jordan's or anyone else's crisis. Marielle and Naomi had already had their funerals, so that meant they were here for him. "But I didn't trigger the pact," Craig pleaded, honestly bewildered.

"I did," Marielle confessed.

"You went already, like six years ago. We were all there." The pact was silly in many ways, but one thing Craig always admired about it was that its scope was both limited and clear. "One ride per customer, those are the rules."

"I triggered it on your behalf." He looked at Marielle like she'd slapped him across the face. "You scared me to death on the phone, Craig. Guilty? *Prison?* Honestly, what did you expect me to do?"

Craig let go of Jordan, patting him twice on the chest like he was making sure he was real. "So, Naomi gets the destination funeral, and I get, what—the surprise?"

"Surprise!" they shouted again, this time half-heartedly, as if even they found it silly. Jordan punctuated his declaration with an attempt at jazz hands.

"So what happens now? Is this, like, a kidnapping? Throw a bag over my head and toss me in a van?"

"Oh, for god's sake," Jordan protested. And then he turned to Marielle to make sure he hadn't misunderstood the plan. "Are we—? NO. No one is tossing you in a van."

"Not even him?" Craig pointed at Jordy, who in any operation would easily be considered the muscle.

"NO!" Jordy protested. "What do you think this is, rendition?"

Craig tilted his head. Maybe being sent overseas shouldn't be dismissed out of hand. "Perhaps I could use a country without extradition to the U.S." He scratched his head. "Okay, so no van. But, like, where are we going?"

Naomi stepped forward and walked her fingers up his chest. "We were hoping you'd take us back to your place." She said it with her fake flirtatious voice, the one she'd used since college to mock how easy men were to toy with; the sad part was how often it worked.

"My *apartment*?" Craig was appalled.

"What, did your cleaning lady not come?" Naomi was getting bored of this sidewalk routine.

"Marielle got Big Sur. You had Mexico. I get my *apartment*?"

Jordan surveyed the group. "Where did you want to go?"

Craig gave this the legitimate thought the question would require if real. "Dubrovnik."

Marielle pulled her chin into her neck. *"Dubrovnik?"*

Craig looked at her, confused by her reaction. Jordan interjected, "It's in Croatia."

Marielle stomped one foot. "I KNOW WHERE DUBROVNIK IS!"

Jordan took a step back.

Naomi dropped her sexy voice. "Why do you want to go to Dubrovnik?"

"Lots of people want to go!" Craig explained. "I read about it in *Travel and Leisure*. It's one of the most popular destinations in the Mediterranean." While the gallery had put him on leave he'd read a lot of travel magazines, imagining some future cell lined with their covers in the absence of a window.

"Yes, but why now?" Jordan asked. "You want to ring some bells? Travel round the world to meet the girl next door?"

Craig turned to Jordan, confused. "What?"

"'Ring Them Bells.' It's Kander and Ebb!" Jordan was exasperated and pointed at Craig. "You're the only one allowed to make a musical reference?"

Craig shook his head. "Okay, well clearly Dubrovnik is out. What about Spain?"

"What about your apartment," Naomi persisted.

"What about Atlantic City?"

"What about your apartment."

"What about . . . *The Plaza*?"

"I think you're under the mistaken impression that this is a negotiation."

Craig nudged the box of his belongings with his foot. "So what you're saying is not only do I not get to pick the time of my own funeral, I don't even get to pick the place? Do I get anything whatsoever? Finger foods? A stripper that jumps out of a cake?"

"Ooh, cake," Marielle said, dessert suddenly sounding good.

Naomi grabbed his hand and tugged. "This isn't your bachelor party, stud, it's your funeral."

"You get to be the guest of honor." Marielle tried to sound hopeful.

Craig sighed deeply. They had to go *somewhere*. There was no way in hell he was doing this here on the sidewalk like some sort of cheap street theater; he'd rather jump into traffic. He motioned for Jordy to pick up his box, given that he was the muscle. Jordy obliged and scooped up his belongings, and Marielle and Naomi linked arms like they were off to see some wizard. "Okay, but when I die for real, someone better scatter my ashes in Dubrovnik."

Craig wanted to explain his predicament in clear and legal terms, yet it was all but impossible, as he barely understood the truth of the situation himself; all he knew was that it felt like he had been held underwater for months, and the only way he could take a breath was by accepting a plea. And any explanation was made more difficult by his friends' presence in his NoLita loft like they were back at Berkeley deciding if it was worth walking to the dining hall on meat loaf night or if they should pool their money for Chinese. Naomi was even rummaging through his cabinets for clean drinking glasses, yelling at him the whole time about his lack of provisions.

"Where are the rest of your plates?" she shouted.

Craig didn't know what to say; everything he had was there. "At the cleaners," he lied, which seemed to further raise her ire.

"Why are your ceilings so high?" Marielle asked as she lay on a scatter rug looking up. The cavernous nature of his loft unnerved her.

"Why are *you*?" he countered.

"What is your problem?" Naomi hollered, either about his defensiveness or his kitchen, which admittedly was in disarray. You would be just as likely to find a spoon in a cabinet as you would in a drawer, and to illustrate that she pulled an espresso cup from his toaster oven.

"What is my problem?" he repeated, to buy himself time as he thought. They were numerous, to be honest, but when he really focused on her question the answer he kept coming back to was this: *People fall in love.* That was his problem. People fell in love. With other people. With themselves. With possibility. With the past. With the future. With life. With objects. With ideas. Alec with drugs, Marielle with her husband, Naomi her parents. Wasn't that what was at the root of these reunions, and what brought them here to his house? Humans led with their hearts and it took all five of their senses (six, if you count common) time to catch up. Brains would always try to keep pace, but brains were easily tricked, filtering everything as they do through the heart's chosen lens. But love was too hard to explain, so instead he just said, "Nothing. I don't have a problem."

Craig eyed the Jordans, who were admiring the art on his walls. None of it was as notable as the works in his former gallery, but he did have an eye for artists that were on the rise and investing in them before they took off. He was drawn to both figurative and pop art with a few geometric paintings mixed in and had amassed an impressive collection.

"Where did these pieces come from?" Jordan asked, as if they might have been on loan from the Met. "Are any of these yours?"

"They're all mine."

"No, I mean, did you paint any of them."

It had been a long time since he painted, and Craig shook his head no. "They came from different galleries. Some from the artists themselves."

"We don't invest in enough art," Jordy noted, slapping Jordan on the arm. They were wearing rings now, Craig noticed, and wondered why he had not been invited to some sort of ceremony.

"They're not investments," Craig protested, although they were; several were now worth quite a bit.

"Then how did you choose them?"

Craig didn't know how to explain other than to say, "They chose me."

It's something many people don't understand about art. You fall in love, much in the same way you do with anything else—slowly, over time, or head over heels all at once. Especially with art. Always emotion first. Which is a good thing! The purpose of art is to evoke, to awaken, to enliven, to anger, to romance, to shake the soul alive. An analytical mind putting reason, meaning, or even something unseemly like a price spoiled everything we love about, well, love itself. The mystery of it. The thrill. The reckless abandon of so completely surrendering ourselves to the object of our desire. The exhilaration. The shortness of breath. The physical response at an almost cellular level. Critical evaluation had its place and an important one at that, but often that kind of left-brain thinking was best delegated to others, lest it get in the way of a great and torrid affair. That often meant that it fell to the hands of someone in Craig's position to provide a much-needed critical eye, as it should—he had the requisite training and experience to provide one. But even those in positions of power in the art world also wanted to fall in love.

And they did.

Which sometimes clouded their judgment, as it did Craig's when he first laid eyes on two forged paintings supposedly by Jürgen Förg.

Naomi gave up on her search for glasses and started assembling five containers of any type they could drink from. A mug. A jelly jar. An eight-ounce measuring cup. A small colander, although on second inspection she realized that would not do. "How do you live like this?"

Marielle raised her hands to the loft's ceiling, amazed at how it looked even higher than it had before. "Leave him be."

"It's like you're still in college," Naomi griped before she pulled back, concerned about Craig's mental state as much as anything else. Marielle after all had heard something in him that had caused her to sound the alarm.

"Guilty," Craig said and, overwhelmed, he climbed out the window onto the fire escape to stare at the southern view of his neighborhood. Next week he would enter a courtroom, pressed to see if he understood the charges leveled against him and asked to enter a plea. Would he be able to say that again in a court of law?

Knock, knock." It was Jordan crawling out onto the escape to join him. "You're missing all the fun."

Craig glanced back inside. Naomi was showing off the "cups" she'd found while Jordy and Marielle looked on. "Oh yeah. It looks a laugh a minute."

Perhaps *fun* was the wrong word.

"Sorry," Craig apologized. "You're not catching me on my best day."

Jordan looked unconcerned. "There haven't been a lot of best days lately, have there." He could have been talking about either of them or the general state of the world. "So what's it like being interviewed by the feds, is it like the movies? A bright light shining in your face, obliterating theirs?"

"I wish. Instead I could read their disappointment all too well." It wasn't until the end of their interview when an FBI agent shot him a skeptical look that Craig realized Mrs. Khan's name was a homophone for *con*. How had Craig not seen it? Alas, she was an artist too; he felt like the dumbest person alive. "Will you come see me?" Craig sat on the metal landing, realizing he should have brought a cushion.

"In the pen?" Jordan smiled.

"That's when I should have triggered the pact, once I was safely behind bars. That way you couldn't overstay your welcome."

"Getting on your nerves, are we?" He leaned against the fire escape's railing, studying the neighboring buildings. A man was cooking naked in an apartment directly across from them. God, he loved New York. "You came to see me in the hospital, I'll come see you in jail."

Craig wasn't sure that was an even trade. "There's no such thing as a surprise funeral, you know."

"I know," Jordan said.

"Maybe if you're hit by a bus. But even then, BAM, the *surprise* is that you're dead." Craig repositioned himself, but anything approaching comfort was elusive. "You're wearing rings." He pointed to Jordan's left hand. "Thanks for the invite."

Jordan looked down as if surprised by the ring. "Yeah, we got hitched early last year. It just made sense once I was sick. We went to City Hall. I wanted to do it before I lost my hair."

"He must really love you if he said yes while you had cancer."

Jordan glanced over his shoulder at Jordy inside. "Or maybe he thought it would be a short commitment."

It had been a casual affair. They had brought a witness to City Hall, a client of theirs who was also a friend and Broadway producer, and afterward they had dinner at Joe Allen's. There was no fuss, and given the treatment Jordan was facing, the mood was somewhat subdued. More often than not he forgot the whole thing had happened; it took someone pointing out his ring or using the word *husband* for him to remember they were married at all.

"Four funerals and a wedding," Craig joked.

Jordan laughed. No one would make a romantic comedy about them.

"Does it feel different?"

"Being married?"

"You guys have been together a long time."

Jordan fiddled with his ring. "Most days, no. But I had a bad reaction to the first concoction of drugs. It was kind of touch and go there for a minute. It felt different then." Jordan remembered how relieved he was that no one could prevent Jordy from being by his side, especially as he spent yet another of his nine lives.

"I bet you're one of those assholes who looks good bald. Like Sinéad O'Connor or Elmer Fudd."

Jordan laughed. Those were the options? "When it grew back, it was blond. I looked like one of those gays having a midlife crisis, which I probably was. But it didn't last."

"The crisis?"

"The blond." Jordan smirked. "The crisis may be ongoing."

Craig looked up at Jordan. His hair was back to its usual chestnut brown, although now with a few streaks of gray.

A burst of laughter came from inside. Craig turned his head plaintively away and looked out at the street. He grabbed on to the bars of the fire escape with both fists. "I guess I should get used to these."

Jordan leaned down and mussed Craig's hair. "Come on. Everyone's waiting for you inside."

Craig, in the midst of a story, kneeled on the floor across from his friends, who were clumped on the far side of his coffee table, as if he were interviewing for a job. "I'm telling you, I woke up on the floor." He was relaying how Alec had come to him in a dream three nights prior. Take-out containers of sushi were spread out across the coffee table, and Craig reached for a piece of yellowtail. "We were fighting. Verbally at first, you know how it was with Alec, he always knew just how to goad you. He kept saying 'Enjoy prison beer,' which I think is slang for piss. Jordan, you would know . . ."

"WHY WOULD I KNOW?!"

"And then out of the blue it got physical."

"Sexual?" Naomi asked, hoping this story was about to get good.

"No! What's wrong with you? Like shoving. Hitting. Biting."

Jordy looked up from his food. "Sounds sexual to me." Jordan pretended to gag. Marielle poked Jordy with her chopsticks.

"And when I woke up, I was on the floor." Craig added wasabi to his soy sauce and stirred it around. He surveyed the spread of food between them; there was enough fish here for twenty people. "Why are you all sitting over there? Guilt is not contagious." Craig then smelled his shirt to see if he needed to shower.

Marielle reached for pickled ginger to spice up her vegetarian roll. "So what are you saying?"

"About Alec? I'm just telling you what happened." Craig set his chopsticks down in a manner that probably seemed more dramatic than he intended. "We fought, he pushed me, I wound up on the floor."

Naomi choked on a bite of hamachi, and soy sauce ran down her chin. "A ghost pushed you."

"You know how best friends are."

Naomi wiped her mouth with a paper napkin. "The ghost of your best friend pushed you out of bed and you landed on the floor."

Craig raised his right hand like he was swearing an oath.

"Well, I call bullshit," Marielle said, toying with what to eat next. Jordan reached for his Asahi and then, remembering what Craig had said about prison beer, grabbed a bottle of water instead.

"You're so sure that didn't happen."

"Yes!"

"Why?"

"Because Alec would never do that."

The Jordans and Naomi laughed, not at the absurdity of such a statement but at the perfect truth of it.

"You just had a different relationship with him, that's all." Alec would never have pushed Marielle. Craig and Alec, however, had more of a brotherly vibe, and they would sometimes let their testosterone get the best of them and wrestle themselves into a frenzy. Jordy was his roommate, Marielle his on-again, off-again love interest, and Naomi her own force of nature. But Craig and Alec vibrated at their own frequency, having deep talks about their lives and the diminishing power they might have as straight men in the world they were about to inherit. Without Alec, Craig was always disappointed to find himself feeling like an outsider. Not in a hypermasculine way, like he expected to be at the center of things. But five was already an odd number, and when there were two more natural pairs, one person was likely to feel excluded.

"What were you two fighting about?" Marielle asked, sounding a little irked. "When he 'pushed' you out of bed."

"It was nothing."

"It wasn't nothing, you ended up on the floor."

Craig pointed to her. "You said Alec wouldn't do that!"

Marielle waved him off, her sleeve just missing the shishito peppers.

"It's stupid. All I did was ask him how he was and he said, 'Ask Jordy.' And I said, 'Why would I ask Jordy?' because he and I weren't supposed to keep secrets. And he just said it was easier to tell Jordy and that's when he lost it."

The reaction was swift. Jordy kicked Craig under the table, hitting one of the table's legs in the process.

"Whoa," Jordan said as he scrambled to make sure nothing spilled.

"What the fuck?" Craig rubbed his knee in pain.

Marielle was confused. "Jordy, why did he say to ask *you*?"

Jordy's face turned bright red. "How should I know? Ask a Ouija board."

"Oh, no!" Jordan exclaimed, still spooked from the last time.

"What's with him?" Naomi asked. She pushed a bottle of beer in Jordy's direction.

Jordan turned to see sweat forming on Jordy's face. "White people and wasabi," he said, almost apologetically. It never ceased to amaze him how bland Jordy needed his food.

As if he'd actually ingested too much wasabi, Jordy accepted the beer and pounded half of it back. "Really, people. It was just a dream," Jordy managed, wiping his forehead on his sleeve. "Let's just drop it, okay?"

"Jordy." Jordan put a hand on his husband's arm.

Craig backed away from the table. "Fine. Forget I said anything."

Marielle pushed her plate away from her until it bumped a container holding a half-eaten roll topped with crunchy potato strips. "Oh, for god's sake. Is this what it's like to have brothers? You've got to stop thinking of me as fragile. I don't need protection from every little thing. Especially when it comes to Alec."

Jordy pretended to cough and excused himself from the table. He headed to the kitchen, but since it was open concept he really had nowhere to hide.

"What?" Marielle asked, now convinced he was hiding a secret. She got up from the table to confront him. "Don't you run away from me, Jordy Tosic."

Jordy opened the fridge like he was looking for something important. He pulled out a glass jug of real maple syrup. "Why do these bottles always have such tiny handles?" Indeed two handles sprouted from the neck like little ears.

Marielle grabbed the syrup and slammed it down on the counter. "Jordy!"

He was cornered. "Alec made me promise I'd never tell."

"Oh my god, you mean my dream was right?" Craig clasped his hands over his mouth; unbeknownst to the others it was to cover a growing smile.

Naomi was growing agitated. "Well, now Alec *is* telling us to ask you." She looked up at Craig's tall ceilings to address their ghost. "WHICH IS IT, ASSHOLE?"

"I'm sorry!" Jordy exclaimed, as if it were meant for Alec as much as anyone actually in the room.

Marielle grabbed Jordy. "Oh, for the love of god. ALEC'S NOT HERE."

Jordy glanced over at Craig. If he was indeed pushed out of bed, *something* was hovering nearby. Couple that with their Ouija experience from years before and the guardian angel who opened Jordan's reserve parachute and it was easy to imagine Alec wasn't quite as absent from their lives as they might think.

"Oh, for god's sake! No one pushed Craig out of bed. He fell because he's a loser and a drunk." Marielle looked over at Craig. "No offense."

Ouch, Craig thought, but it was a small price to pay for what he had set in motion. "None taken."

"Now you can take your chances that a ghost will hit you, or you can pretty much be guaranteed that I will. Which is it?"

"You're nonviolent," Jordy protested.

Marielle made two adorable fists. "I'm feeling pretty feisty today!"

"For fuck's sake, Jordy," Naomi implored. She was hastily closing take-out containers, deciding for everyone that this meal was done. She snapped the final polystyrene container closed on Jordan as he reached for a piece of sashimi.

"FINE!" Jordy blurted, covering his eyes with his hands. It had been long enough and he was tired of carrying it alone. It had been years. It couldn't still hold the same power it had when the secret was fresh—*could it?* He took one last deep breath before detonating his bomb. "Alec had HIV."

The air went out of the room. Jordan sat with his chopsticks frozen, Naomi stopped stacking the take-out containers, and Jordy pressed his palms against his eyes even tighter, all bracing themselves for Alec's wrath from beyond the grave.

But nothing came.

Marielle mouthed the word twice before she could actually put sound to it. "What?"

Jordy turned away from them and rested his head on one of Craig's large floor-to-ceiling windows. "He tested positive for HIV."

"When?"

"I don't know exactly. About six weeks before he died."

"No, no, no, no, no," Marielle repeated, as if denial itself could make it not true.

Naomi rushed over to Marielle to comfort her. "Why did he tell you and not any of us?"

Jordy rolled his forehead against the window's cool glass in an attempt to quell the pinpricks he felt in his skin. "We were roommates. We told each other things."

Naomi turned to Jordan. "Did you know about this?"

Jordan didn't have to answer. It was obvious from the way he looked at Jordy that he did not, and his not knowing was its own kind of betrayal.

No one said anything else, and so Marielle wrested herself from Naomi's grip, walked over to Jordy, spun him around, and slapped him. *Hard*. The stinging sound made the other three jump. "I have been over this and over this. For years! Twenty-three years. Trying to figure this out!" Her eyes welled with tears. "You had no right to keep this from me. Do you hear me? NO RIGHT!"

Jordy knew deep down it wasn't a secret he should have ever kept. That this was the inevitable reaction, which became its own reason to do the unreasonable. It had become a vicious cycle. "Alec said he was going to tell you."

"Well, he didn't."

"He told me not to say anything until he could."

"Well he couldn't very well tell me ONCE HE WAS DEAD!" Marielle turned to the others to make sure they were on her side; they were. "What if he had given it to me? What if I had it when I got pregnant with Mia?" Marielle gasped at the full horror of it. "What if I gave it to Mia?"

Jordy took a step toward Marielle, who retreated. "None of that happened. He stopped being intimate with you the moment he found out."

"With *me*."

"With anyone!"

"So what? Do you think he was just magically infected the morning he found out? How fucking stupid are you?"

Jordan half-heartedly intervened. "Mare," he said, but there was only so much he could do when she was right.

"I guess I convinced myself he had. Told you, I mean. Then the call you made, when you shared the news that you were pregnant." Jordy tried to get her to look at him. "Do you remember?"

"Do I remember telling you I was pregnant? What does that have to do with anything?"

Jordy took a deep breath. "You called and you said you took two pregnancy tests, but you didn't tell anyone until a blood test confirmed it. Those were your exact words."

"What, do you have my medical records? How do you remember my exact words?"

"I wanted to tell you. I wanted to tell you when he died. Then graduation happened, and we went our separate ways, and I was figuring things out with Jordan—"

Jordan held up his hands. "Don't drag me into this."

"And when you called to tell us you were pregnant, that you'd had a blood test, I figured everything was okay."

Marielle shook her head. "Leave nothing left unsaid. The whole point of this pact. *What a joke.*" She narrowed her eyes and made sure Jordy met her gaze. "You're a goddamned coward." Since Craig's apartment was a loft, there were only two doors to slam—and she wasn't about to lock herself in the bathroom. Instead, she grabbed her coat and stormed out the front entrance. Once she was gone, it became obvious how much city noise, even with the windows closed, you could hear.

Jordy turned to Jordan. *What was I supposed to do?*

Jordan shot back, *It's a little late for my opinion now.* Jordan scratched his chin, seeing Jordy in a whole new light. For better or worse they were the Jordans, one more than two, and they often bought into their own myth. But every once in a while it was clear the Jordans were a fairy tale, that no one knows every one of another person's secrets, and he wondered what other mysteries there might be between them through the years. It was one of Alec's favorite sayings—*no two people have ever met*—and Jordan suddenly understood what he meant for the first time. But it didn't help anyone to voice that out loud, so instead he said, "Well, I'm not surprised. Alec thought monogamy was a type of wood."

Naomi shot daggers in his direction.

"What?"

Too angry to speak without saying something she would most certainly later regret, she grabbed her own coat to go after Marielle and exited without saying a word.

Once Craig was alone with the Jordans he pumped his fist in the air. "Well, that ought to do it."

Jordan turned to Craig. "You manifested this?"

"That's right."

"On purpose?"

"Yup."

"There was no dream?"

Craig looked at him with pity. "You think a ghost pushed me out of bed? No! I overheard Jordy on the dorm pay phone one night and tucked that in my back pocket."

Jordan spun around to Jordy. "You told other people and not me?"

Jordy struggled to recall. "My sister, I think?" At the time it was a lot to get his head around and he couldn't possibly raise the subject of AIDS with Jordan when their flirtation was finally about to heat up.

Jordan turned back to Craig. "So you knew too." If he couldn't get Jordy out of hot water he could maybe push someone else in.

"I knew Alec and Jordy were hiding something, but I didn't know what. I asked Alec about it and I'll never forget his reaction. Can you believe for half a second I thought maybe *they* were fucking? Alec, the world's straightest man."

Jordan looked at Jordy and Jordy shook his head no, he and Alec were only friends. Roommates. Nothing else went on behind closed doors. "Craig, why tonight, why stir the pot after all this time?"

"You're not honestly defending him."

"What am I missing?"

Craig clasped his hands together. "Only the pact crumbling before our eyes!"

"You mean this is a get-out-of-jail-free card?" Jordan scoffed, pointedly employing the reference to prison. "And all you had to do was throw Jordy under the bus."

"Don't," Jordy said. He didn't want anyone coming to his aid. "I deserve to be thrown under it." Jordy looked down from Craig's windows just in time to see Naomi exit the building and take off down the block. "They're going to blame me for Alec's death."

"Don't be ridiculous."

"If Alec killed himself, there was a reason. And I knew it and none of the rest of you did, so it was up to me to stop him."

Jordan pushed back in protest. "That's not a reason. HIV's not a death sentence."

"In 1995?"

Jordy was right. The FDA had just approved the first protease inhibitors later that same year, ushering in an era of powerful cocktails. But the hope they brought with them hadn't yet taken root. They were all afraid of HIV, perhaps none of them more than Jordan, who, until he connected with Jordy, was the only one among them having gay sex.

"It was needles, by the way." Jordy sat down on the floor next to Jordan. "Not sex. Alec never had as much sex as you all thought."

"Not according to Alec," Craig said, trying to protect what was left of their friendship. He wanted to believe that some things Alec had told him were true.

"Yeah, well. He liked being thought of as a player," Jordy explained. What twenty-two-year-old wouldn't?

Jordan kept his focus trained on the loft's front door. "Do you think they'll be back?"

"They will," Craig assured. "But maybe not this weekend." He finished clearing the table like the visit was indeed over, which visibly annoyed Jordan. "Oh, don't give me that look, I didn't ask for any of this. This is funeral by ambush."

"Because we were worried about you! And not just about this weekend, by the way. We've been worried about you for a while."

Craig mindlessly flicked a light switch near the kitchen; he'd never figured out what it did. "Well, don't be. I've got it all under control."

"Sure you do," Jordan said.

You alone?" Marielle asked as Naomi caught up with her.

"Of course," she replied. She knew better than to bring any of the guys. In the dark, cool evening the city looked almost blue, the only warmth from bubbly groups huddled in conversation brushing past them on their way to late dinners. Marielle eventually spotted a jewelry boutique and pretended to look in the window.

"Are you mad?" Naomi asked as she stood on her tiptoes to rest her chin on Marielle's shoulder.

"At Jordy? You bet."

"*At Alec.*"

Marielle sighed. "I've devoted enough of my life to being angry with Alec." Her face flushed with embarrassment as she realized most of the jewelry had been removed from the store's window display for the night; she could have pretended to get lost in any boutique's store-front and she chose the one that was empty. "I'm tired of fighting to keep this group together."

"I know."

She focused on her reflection in the window. "I'm releasing every-one from the pact." She said it as if she had a magic wand that un-shackled them.

"You don't have to."

"It was bound to end sometime. You and I are the only ones who used it anyhow. The boys could be at death's door and we'd never hear a word."

"*Boys,*" Naomi agreed, as it was impossible to think of them as men. Men were in touch with their feelings. Men were responsible and cared for the feelings of others. Or at least in a more perfect world they would be.

"Truthfully," Marielle began, "I just want to give him a hug."

"Jordy?"

"Ew. No. Alec. He must have been so scared."

"It doesn't change anything. It doesn't mean his overdose was on purpose."

Marielle pulled away. "It makes it that much less likely it wasn't."

Naomi walked a few doorways down to sit on a stoop, and Mari-elle followed. A streetlamp lit them in that way that makes so much of New York feel like a movie set. "There's a third option," she offered.

Marielle turned to face her. "What's that?"

"That he was just, I don't know. Cavalier."

Marielle bowed her head. That was the most likely cause. That Alec figured his life would be short no matter what, and in a moment of weakness didn't care if he lived or died, deciding to leave it up to a metaphorical coin toss that came up tails. "I want to go back."

"To Craig's?"

Marielle looked at her like she'd lost her mind.

"To the hotel," Naomi corrected.

"To Oregon."

"You just got here!"

"My animals need me." Her animals never disappointed her in the way people continually did.

"*I* need you," Naomi said, taking Marielle's hand. "Come on. We're here in New York. We suddenly have the whole weekend free. What do you want to do?" She rattled off every possibility, from seeing a show to having a meal in a Michelin-starred restaurant to taking a carriage ride in Central Park.

"I heard they mistreat the horses," Marielle said.

"Okay, well, no carriage rides then. But come on, girls' weekend." To Marielle that did sound nice.

"Okay." She finally relented and Naomi helped her rise. "But just you and me. I mean it when I say the pact is done."

Naomi offered her hand to shake in agreement.

Hand in hand they stepped off the stoop and headed back in the direction of Craig's loft. A group of young women bustled past, brushing Marielle's shoulder. She looked at them wistfully, wishing to be them once again. Young. Happy. Carefree. Was life better then? Or did young people just have the energy to better deal with its crushing disappointments? Either way, she yearned for another time and place and was so lost in that longing that she almost didn't notice until it was too late.

"Mia?" she said.

And when one of the young women turned around, Marielle was standing face-to-face with her daughter.

When the women returned to Craig's loft to tell him the pact was dead, Craig surprised Marielle by triggering it. "I'm using my turn for real." And then he looked just past them to a shy-looking young woman with Marielle's same wild hair, which fell across her face in a way that temporarily disguised her. "Who's this?" he asked of their guest.

The young woman waved sheepishly. "Hi. I'm Mia."

Craig's jaw dropped in surprise. Marielle protectively put her arm around her daughter and, in the way mothers do, pushed the hair out of her face. "Mia, this is Craig, and over there Jordan and Jordy." She said Jordy's name with contempt. "*The Jordans.* And Naomi you already met. Everyone, this is my daughter, Mia." She winced as if this were already a mistake.

There was a flood of pleased-to-meet-yous, coupled with handshakes and hugs as the guys turned to Naomi for an explanation.

"Don't look at *me*," Naomi protested. She was just as surprised as any of them.

"Complete coincidence," Marielle professed. "We ran into Mia and her friends on the street."

Craig looked at the empty space behind them for these supposed friends.

"I told them to go ahead to the club," Mia said, and indeed she was dressed to go out. Her dress had long sleeves and was modest on top but was hemmed short to show off her long legs.

"Club?" Marielle protested. "It's bad enough you're in the city alone."

"Mom, I'm twenty-two. And I'm not alone, I'm with friends." She looked up at the others to explain. "We took the train down from Boston." She had that embarrassed look, one they knew from once having been young.

"What club?" Craig asked, making conversation.

"Concept, I think it's called?"

"Concept is great," he assured her. "Decent music. Good space. They do a lot of private events. Still figuring out what they want to be."

Mia smiled. "I guess that's why it's called Concept."

They laughed, but not Marielle, who was imagining men Craig's age in the same nightclub as her daughter. Craig in particular was drawn to Mia, not because she was attractive (although she was), but because she was not at all what he'd pictured. He imagined (or maybe hoped) he would recognize Alec in her if they met, despite Marielle's consistent denials. He didn't, but she was familiar nonetheless. Mia likewise was enamored, putting faces to people she'd only heard stories about.

"All right, well, that's enough staring," Marielle said, and Craig blushed.

"I didn't mean to interrupt," Mia interjected. "I just couldn't pass up the opportunity to say hello. I mean, you're the funeral people, right?"

"Celebrants," Jordan said awkwardly. *Funeral people* felt cold, and not how you'd like to be thought of.

"Maybe I should try it with my friends."

Marielle shook her head with an adamant no.

Jordan smirked. "This is all too Courteney Cox."

Craig whipped his head around. "Why Courteney Cox?"

Jordan looked to the others for backup. He usually got the Courtney Scale right. "I guess because Courteney Cox has a daughter?"

"Courtney Love has a daughter," Naomi interjected. "With Kurt Cobain."

Marielle held up a finger to cut Jordan off. "Do not say meeting my daughter is too Courtney Love."

"Okay, I barely know who any of those people are, but I'm sure you'll explain it to me later," Mia said, amused, and it was sweet to see how she humored her mom. "I should get back to my friends. You seem busy? I heard something about triggering a pact."

"It was already triggered," Naomi said.

"No, Marielle did so on my behalf, which is why it didn't work. But now this is me. I need my funeral. I need it right now." Craig stomped his foot in a little tantrum.

Mia looked at them like adults were terminally weird.

"There's nothing to trigger," Marielle insisted. "I dissolved the pact. You're all free."

"When?" Craig was surprised. Even the Jordans seemed startled.

"Just now. Outside. Right before we ran into Mia."

"You can't do something like that alone."

"I was there," Naomi volunteered.

Marielle turned to Mia and smoothed the shoulders of her daughter's dress. Her face soured when she noticed how short it was. "My evening is suddenly free. Maybe I'll join you at Notion?" She offered Mia a hopeful look.

"*Concept*, Mom," Mia corrected, "and over my dead body."

Craig leaned in. "Fun! We can do your funeral next."

Marielle was not amused.

"What else are you doing while you're in town?" Jordan asked, stepping in to make things less awkward. "Would you like to see a show? We could help you and your friends get tickets."

"That's true, they could," Marielle realized, although she was not quite ready to accept favors from Jordy.

"We're seeing *Book of Mormon* tomorrow," Mia informed them. "But actually my day is free."

"That's great," Naomi said. "Maybe you'd like to join us to tour the Cloisters."

Mia looked at her mother to see if that was okay; despite her misgivings, Marielle wasn't going to say no to a day with her daughter. "I guess that would be okay."

"We're going to the Cloisters?" Craig asked.

"Shhh," Naomi said. "Let me take it from here."

And it was just the shot of epinephrine their pact needed to bring it back to life.

After Mia left, Marielle held firm; they would have to conduct the rest of the weekend without her. She was met with immediate and unanimous pushback, especially from Jordy, whose words were couched in great shame. The part of her that still wanted to believe the best in people finally caved, and she postponed her departure at least long enough to spend some time with her daughter. Sensing his part in keeping them together and holding their fragile peace, Craig dropped his defenses, sharing with his friends the incredible stress he'd been carrying. He broke down at the mere mention of him serving time, stating over and over again that he wasn't prepared for this. He never set out to defraud anyone, he was just doing his job, allowing himself to buckle under the pressure of the demands placed on him. Was he guilty of bad judgment? Yes. Even he would admit that. But a *crime*? Every night he went to bed hoping to wake from this recurring nightmare in which he felt so helplessly trapped.

Craig was so emotional and honest and naked, and the attention had shifted so rightly to him, there was no room for Jordy to jump in to apologize. Even when Naomi had explained her inspiration for the Cloisters—taking Craig back to the basics, surround him with art to inspire him again—and it was clear that the weekend was not ending, at least so far as the pact was concerned, Jordy was not able to find the moment or the words to approach Marielle.

So now, more than twelve hours on, they boarded the A train and rode to Fort Tryon Park in Washington Heights to make their way to the Cloisters. Craig sat in the half-empty car with Naomi and Marielle and Mia, who had followed through on her promise to join them, while Jordan stood as a buffer between them and Jordy, as tensions were still running high. They exchanged pleasantries with Mia but mostly avoided each other, asking about life in Boston and her work in the mayor's office. (It was an exciting time, Mia explained, Boston electing more and more women to all sorts of positions.) "Politics," Jordan observed as their train pulled into the Dyckman Street station. "Just like your mother." Marielle smiled weakly; it had been a long time since she worked in government.

The Cloisters housed mostly European medieval art, but it was governed by the Met, so there were also rotating exhibits. On current display was a collection of Winslow Homer paintings, an artist who was in Craig's collection of favorites for both Homer's monumental seascapes in oils and the fact that he was largely, like Craig, self-taught. His color palette was something Craig greatly admired—it separated Homer from other Americans working at the time. Homer's subjects were sturdy, his seas rough, and wandering through the exhibit at this turbulent moment in his own life gave Craig newfound appreciation for his composition, and he understood more than ever how Homer's style strongly influenced the next generation of American artists. He died in his studio, which Craig found impressive—true commitment to a life's work; his painting *Shooting the Rapids* remains to this day unfinished.

"Did you know the city of Winslow, Arizona, is named after Winslow Homer?" Naomi was hammering out a text on her phone but still managed to sing "Take It Easy" by the Eagles until she got to the verse that referenced the town. Mia thought this was a particular delight.

"Aunt Naomi!" she giggled, trying that on for size.

Craig shushed Naomi. "Please show a little respect." He then leaned in toward Mia. "Homer died in his studio."

"Just now?" Mia asked in a hushed tone.

"No, like a hundred years ago."

"Then why are we whispering?"

Craig laughed.

"Seriously, though. That's impressive," she said.

"Right?" Craig was delighted that she took such an interest.

"The commitment," Mia mused. "I hope I remain as passionate."

Marielle eyed them suspiciously. "Sometimes you develop new interests as you get older. It's okay if your passions change." It was a defense of both her current life and her daughter's future choices.

Naomi glanced at the others. "It's too quiet in here. I don't like it." This wasn't church. There was no rule that they couldn't speak in the exhibit, and in fact the guards would tell you that on some days the museum could be quite noisy: babies screaming, sneakers pounding, adults lecturing in any number of languages, elderly people coughing or reading the gallery panels out loud to no one but themselves, phones ringing, laughter echoing, and so on. It just so happened that today's crowd was an observant one, and Naomi found it unnerving. She moved ahead at a pace she found more satisfying and Marielle trudged forward to join her. The others likewise wandered the exhibit in pairs.

Craig showed Mia the exhibit's centerpiece, *The Gulf Stream*, in whose presence he felt overwhelmed. The experience of seeing it in person was nearly religious.

"Painted in 1899," Craig whispered, and then added "Sorry" in a more normal tone. "The final year of the century."

"Wouldn't that be the *penultimate* year of the century?" Jordan said in passing, and Craig shot daggers his way.

"Look at his expression," Craig continued. A shirtless Black man lay on the deck, propped up on one elbow as sharks were circling, and indeed his manner was magnetic. "Heroically resigned to his fate. It's hypnotic." He had hoped in pleading guilty he'd find a similar peace, resigning himself to his own fate, but his brain instead kept railing against it.

Mia stood with her sweater draped over her arms. She looked more like her mother in casual clothes than she had the night before. "But there's another ship. Do you see it? There, in the background. Maybe he knows he will be rescued." She pointed to a second ship with tall sails near the horizon.

"Ah, you're an optimist, then," Craig stated. To him the second ship was so recessed in the background it offered little hope.

"I try to be. It's harder for my generation."

"I think every generation feels that way." And then he added, "I used to feel that way, at Berkeley at least. Like our parents had fucked everything up." Craig still felt just in that diagnosis; boomers hadn't done the world many favors.

"So it's only fair then we think that of you," Mia teased.

"Well, no," Craig laughed. "Gen X just wants to be left alone."

Mia pushed him playfully. "The world's on fire. Get off the sidelines." She looked back at the painting. "Tell me more."

"About my generation?"

"About the painting, Grandpa." Craig laughed. He would never graduate from "Nana."

Craig took a step forward toward the canvas and the gallery's guard took notice. "See the black cross on the foreground of the ship's bow? The open hatch, a tomb, the torn sail a shroud. It's all very funereal."

"How fitting for your weekend." Mia looked down at him; in her boots she was an inch taller.

"Right." Their pact suddenly seemed embarrassing now that Craig was seeing it through the eyes of an outsider.

"I still don't quite understand what you guys do. Maybe it's a middle-aged thing."

That knocked the wind out of Craig, who often dated women not too much older than Mia was now. *Grandpa, middle-aged*—he suddenly understood how they really saw him: old and a little bit sad. He wanted to remind Mia the pact was something they came up with when they were her age, but what good would it do? "Maybe," he said, given that only Marielle had called for her funeral before forty.

The painting, however, *was* appropriate for this weekend. Instructional, even. Struggle and conflict, two common themes in Homer's work. He *should* surrender, like the man in *The Gulf Stream*, and just ride stoically through his own trough between waves even though in the painting the man was surrounded by sharks. Maybe it was the only way to find peace despite the predators circling. Naomi wandered by, still texting. "Naomi, get off your phone."

Naomi didn't look up. "Mind your business." Craig took a swipe at her phone, but her reflexes were quick and she snatched it away just in time. "Try that again and you die."

Mia laughed. "You remind me of my friends." It made Craig both happy and sad to hear this.

After wandering the exhibit, they took some time to stroll the museum's tapestries and illuminated manuscripts; after the Homer painting, and now that his eyes were open to it, Craig saw many allusions to death. He was captured by an image in one of the manuscripts, the Psalter of Bonne de Luxembourg, which was from fourteenth-century France. *The Three Living and the Three Dead*, it was titled, three bodies in different states of decay painted against a stark blue sky, and it made him think of the six of them. Right now only Alec was gone. One day they would be three and three. Then another they would all be dust and the count would be zero and six. *How maudlin*, he thought, but the idea lingered.

When the others caught up, they sat in the Gothic Chapel, which had been built to house stained glass and some of the larger sculptures. Tombs, effigies, sarcophagi. The funeral imagery was now unavoidable, and Craig, overwhelmed, begged for some air.

"Come on, kid," Naomi said to Mia. "Let's check out the gift shop." The two of them sauntered off to browse.

Marielle joined Craig outside, and when she asked what was up he couldn't tell if he was more overcome with the finality of death or with the thought of confinement, imprisonment, as he would likely face that first, and his reaction was a latent claustrophobia taking hold. So they sat on a bench and admired the plants, which a plaque informed them were accurate to the time, overseen by a team of historian horticulturalists who specialized in both greenery and gardening techniques of the thirteenth and fourteenth centuries.

It was years since he'd been to the Cloisters, months since he'd been to a museum at all. Craig wondered when he stopped being enchanted by New York, when the endless jackhammering of the city overtook his sense of amazement. It made him sad, as he remembered promising himself years before that he would never allow that to happen. And yet it had. But perhaps that wasn't so different than the rest of life. You stopped being amazed after a time with the taste of coffee, the connection with a new friend, the beauty in a building's edifice. The stately grandeur of a tree. Perhaps that was what vacations were supposed to be for.

"What were you and Mia talking about?"

He smiled mischievously, knowing that it would drive her mad. "What were you and Naomi talking about?"

Marielle hated when people answered questions with questions, and for a moment declined to respond. Eventually, she relented. "She wanted to know if there was anything I could think of to tell you to make you reconsider."

"Pleading guilty?"

"She thinks, *we* think, you should fight it."

Craig was alone in so much of his life that he liked knowing someone cared. "I was telling Mia about the painting. She humored me while I told her why I loved it so much."

Marielle shook her head. She knew her daughter. "Mia doesn't humor anyone."

Craig sensed that things between them were strained. "You don't like that we get along?"

"I don't want you filling her head with ideas about Alec."

He smirked. "So what did you tell Naomi?"

Marielle looked at him confused.

"Did you think of anything that might change my mind?"

"I stole your toothbrush," she blurted.

Craig was confused. "Last night?"

"In Mexico."

Craig was taken completely by surprise. "Which lured me into a life of crime?" And then she held his gaze until he understood. "Oh." She was after his DNA. "I wasn't sure if you remembered that night in Big Sur. We never talked about it."

Marielle leaned forward a bit. "I didn't. Not really. Until my funeral and your thinking Mia might be Alec's."

"She isn't, is she."

"No," Marielle admitted.

Craig could see where this was going. He turned to her, waiting for her to share some lab result that would change his life. He closed his eyes to picture Homer's painting again. *Remember the calm between waves.* "And?"

"I never did anything with it. I threw the toothbrush away."

"Oh," he said, disappointed.

"It felt like a violation."

It was a violation. But in this moment he wouldn't have minded. "Would you like my consent?" he offered. "Perhaps a strand of my hair?"

Marielle kicked a pebble with her shoe and watched it tumble across the path. "I don't need it," she said. It was so clear to her now that she had witnessed them together; she couldn't understand how she hadn't seen it all along. *"She's you."*

Craig's eyes welled with tears. They were connected in such meaningful ways, all of them, and had been since the night they first met. He was so much more than the kid his parents couldn't be bothered with, pawned off on distant family to raise. So much more than a guy whose best friend killed himself long ago, sentencing him to a lifetime of difficulty fostering relationships. He was the beating heart of a family, *this* family, a family of friends, and they continued to give him so much. All this time he had thought of their association as it related to death, when in fact the bond he had with these friends had everything to do with life.

Thom Romero was waiting outside Craig's building upon their return and Naomi greeted him with a hug. "TUFFY!" she screamed, like he was a long-lost member of their circle. He had neck tattoos that crept eerily close to his face and was a full head shorter than any of them save for Naomi. "Right on time. This is the Craig I was telling you about." Naomi yanked at Craig's sleeve until he was standing in front of this diminutive, but nonetheless imposing, figure, while the Jordans and Marielle looked on confused.

"Tuffy, was it?" Craig asked. His head was both swimming and barely there.

"To my friends," he replied.

Craig squinched his eyes and drew his mouth to one side as if to ask, *Are we friends?*

"Isn't he exactly how I described?" Naomi marveled to Tuffy as she pushed Craig toward his front door. "Stop being such a nerd and let us in," she said before turning to the interloper and adding, "You have your work cut out for you with this one." Craig looked to Marielle for support; whatever this was, the two of them had more pressing things to discuss. Mia had departed the group at Union Square to meet up with her friends for their night at the theater, and he was hoping to get her mother alone.

Upstairs, Craig flipped on lights as Naomi ushered them inside and onto the couch and then faced them hand in hand with this stranger. "Do you need anything for your presentation, Tuffy? A whiteboard? Dry-erase markers? An overhead projector?"

"I have none of those things," Craig said flatly. While his patience was wearing thin, Naomi's enthusiasm remained undimmed.

"I'll just talk, if that's all right. And if they want to take notes, they can."

Naomi turned to the group and said, "You're going to want to take notes."

The rest of them growled. It had been a long time since they had been in school, and springing whatever this was on them when they were hungry and tired was not helping.

"Okay, just listen really carefully then, and you can jot down some of the key points later."

"*Naomi*," Jordan protested.

She pointed to him and Jordy and said, "The Jordans," and Tuffy nodded knowingly, as if he had been forewarned. "And over there is Marielle. That takes care of introductions."

Tuffy coughed politely in his hand.

"Oh, right!" Naomi turned to their mystery guest and slapped her forehead. "This is Thom Romero, also known as Tuffy. He's the drummer for garage punk sensation Guff, one of the bands on our label."

"I've never heard of Guff," Jordan said to Naomi, before turning to Tuffy. "Sorry."

"No need to be." He studied Jordan's polished demeanor before clapping back. "You're not exactly our key demo." Naomi screamed like it was the funniest thing ever said.

"Ignore him. He still listens to Erasure."

Jordan stood up to leave, but Jordy yanked him back down.

"It doesn't matter if you've heard his music, although you should so you don't seem older than Moses. Tuffy also has a side hustle. Are you ready for this?" Naomi clasped her hands together like she had the most exciting news. "He's a sought-after prison consultant."

"Oh, hell no." This time Craig stood to leave and it was Jordan who prevented him.

Jordy turned to Jordan. "Shouldn't music be his side hustle?"

"Why would music be his side hustle?" Naomi furrowed her brow.

"It seems more lucrative. Consultants make really good money."

"GUFF MAKES REALLY GOOD MONEY!" Naomi exclaimed. "They just finished a world tour."

"Did you go to Dubrovnik?" Jordan asked, elbowing Craig.

"I'll get you a concert T-shirt if you want the lineup so badly, but right now Tuffy is going to teach us all how to survive in prison. I thought it would be a fun activity for Craig's funeral!"

"Naomi," Marielle protested. She reached across the Jordans for

Craig's hand. "We *have* an activity, and that's letting Craig know how we feel."

"Well, I feel he needs to listen to Tuffy."

"Okay, this has gone on far enough," Craig said, putting an end to things before they could go any further. "Naomi, could I have a word in the kitchen?"

Naomi stood her ground. "No."

"NO?"

"No. Because this isn't for you, it's for everyone."

Jordy scratched his chin. "Why is this for everyone?"

Naomi pointed to Jordy, as this was an excellent question. "Because this is America and soon it's going to be illegal to be anything but straight and white and cisgender male. Do I need to paint you a picture?"

Tuffy turned to Naomi, impressed. "Maybe we should get *you* a whiteboard."

Naomi swatted him away playfully. "Craig was our one shining hope in that department and here he is the first one of us to be tossed in the crowbar hotel, so let's all take a breath and let Tuffy speak."

Marielle turned to Jordan, confused. "The what now?"

"The clink," Jordan said. "Prison."

"Actually, your friend is more likely to end up in federal prison *camp*."

"Oh, that sounds fun," Jordy said, suddenly interested, and he looked around for something to take notes. "Maybe you'll make lanyards."

"NAOMI!" Craig shouted firmly. "KITCHEN. NOW."

He grabbed Naomi by the arm and dragged her over to the area that designated his kitchen space. "What are you doing?"

"I got you a present."

"I didn't register for any presents."

"OOH. A funeral registry. What a great idea."

"*Naomi!*"

"You can't plead guilty without knowing what that actually means! Now will you please sit down and shut up and trust me? You might actually learn something useful."

"From someone who was named after a *cat*?!"

"He was named after his uncle who played in the NBA!"

"I don't care!"

Tuffy cleared his throat. "Actually, he played in the NFL."

"GODDAMMIT WHY DOESN'T THIS PLACE HAVE ANY WALLS!" Craig bemoaned as he banged his head against a cabinet in protest. When he turned back to Naomi, his forehead had a red mark.

"Just hear him out. And if you still want to plead guilty, your friends will at least know you made an informed decision and we will stand behind you all the way." She begged with her eyes, and for the first time he recognized genuine concern. He had been thinking of his decision as a way to end his current suffering, but he hadn't thought about how it might affect others, Mia now among them. He could at least do this for her.

"Fine. TUFFY? Let's do this." Craig marched himself back to the living area and plopped himself down on the couch. "Federal prison camps. What are those?"

Tuffy looked to Naomi, who gave him her blessing to continue, along with assurances that he wouldn't again be derailed.

"Federal prison camps are mostly white-people prisons. Martha Stewart country-club shit. That's where you're probably headed, if your sentence is not suspended. That or these minimum-security satellite camps they have nowadays on the grounds of higher-security jails."

Craig turned to the Jordans and swallowed hard. The latter seemed less ideal.

"No, this is a good thing. FPCs are where you'd rather be."

"No offense, Tuffy, but all things considered I'd rather be on a beach sipping rum."

"Then you'd better give real thought to what losing your freedom means."

Craig hung his head. That much was true. "All right, I've been sent to prison camp. What's the first thing I do? Sign up for activities? Join a gang? Earn a merit badge making moonshine out of toilet water?"

Tuffy crossed his arms and looked at his shoes, disappointed.

Naomi stepped in. "He jokes when he's nervous. You can't blame him for being overwhelmed."

"Get it out of your system," Tuffy warned, like he was babysitting a toddler he was waiting to tire. "Smart remarks will get you in trouble behind bars."

"Trouble, right here in River City," Jordan said, quoting *The Music Man*.

Naomi slapped Jordan upside the head. "Tuffy is only in town for one night and I was lucky to nab him for an hour while the rest of Guff is out getting shitfaced with fans. So trust me when I say he has better things to do with his time."

"Actually, most of Guff is sober," Tuffy explained.

"No one cares, kitten."

"Can you all just give me a minute?" Craig pleaded. "I don't know how I'm supposed to be taking this."

"Take it with a grain of salt," Tuffy offered. "I'm just here to share my experience."

"I take it with an *ocean* of salt, that's not the problem."

Tuffy shrugged. "Either way. I'm being paid the same."

Naomi could have sprung for anything, Craig thought: a limousine, spa treatments, high-priced call girls. *This is what she came up with?* Craig slunk back into his couch, wishing the oversized cushions would envelop him completely until there was none of him left. But deep down he knew there was something here to learn. "I'm sorry, continue."

"Right off the bat you've got a couple things going for you. One, you're not famous—"

"We can't all be the drummer of Guff," Craig muttered to Jordan.

"NANA."

Craig waved at Naomi apologetically. "I'm sorry! It's out of my system. I promise."

Tuffy eyed Craig suspiciously before continuing. "Your crime is not sexual in nature."

Christ. "*Alleged* crime." He hadn't pleaded guilty yet.

"Alleged crime," Tuffy corrected.

The fake Förgs happened to be nudes, but Craig thought it best not to cloud the issue. "What else?"

"You don't have any underlying health conditions. Or at least not any that I can see."

"Did you bring any latex gloves?" Jordan asked. "You might want to look under the hood." This time it was Craig who shushed Jordan; he was finally prepared to listen.

"The first few days are when you have to be the most diligent. All eyes are going to be on you, as the newcomer. Inmates will be skeptical of you; they will all want to know your deal, and if you're going to fit in or if you're going to make trouble. Everything you do is important. Keep your head down, but don't keep too much distance. Don't talk loudly on the phone. No one wants to hear your personal business. No cutting the chow line. Don't show anger, ever. In fact, don't even bring it in with you if you can help it. Anger is of no use. It doesn't change anything, and it makes terrible decisions on your behalf. Same goes for pity. Someone always has it worse than you."

Craig knew in his heart that was true—many had it far worse than him—but in the moment it seemed hard to swallow. Anger Craig knew he could manage, he was often frustrated, but not outright mad. Pity, however, was already taking root. He'd be, what, gaining a daughter and losing his freedom both in under a week?

"Hand in hand with that: do not attempt to bully. Anyone. I don't care if you think it makes you look tough. What are you, a buck-fifty?"

"One sixty," Craig corrected, and he squeezed his biceps to demonstrate there was at least a little meat on his bones. Tuffy, however, looked doubtful.

"Still. It's not a good look and it will almost always backfire. Don't be a pushover, either. And be careful who you befriend, they might later try to extort you for protection."

"I thought we were talking Martha Stewart country-club nonsense," Craig protested. With each passing moment prison camp felt indistinguishable from prison.

Jordy leaned forward. "Never underestimate Martha. I've seen the way she holds pinking shears."

"Which brings us to another thing. Don't think you'll get protection from the guards. In fact, don't get chummy with them at all. Don't piss them off, but no one likes a kiss-ass—least of all the other inmates. Do you believe in God?"

Craig was taken aback. Questions were being lobbed at him faster than he could take them in. "No."

"You don't?" Marielle asked.

"You *do*?" This was the kind of conversation most people had *before* having a kid. He looked at Marielle, not sure why it mattered. Their child had already been raised.

"I'd keep that to yourself. As well as any political opinions you may have. Eyes open, ears open, mouth shut. That's always what you want to strive for."

Tuffy continued to lay out his rules: don't change the TV channel without asking permission first; don't sit on anyone's bunk without permission; don't reach across someone else's food tray; don't rat out an inmate—for *any* reason. Ever. A lot of don'ts. Not many dos.

"Is it me, or does this sound an awful lot like dorm life?" Craig looked to the others, who seemed to agree. "Except with less freedom and a lot fewer drugs."

Tuffy mentioned there were no good days in the mess hall, just days that were less bad. That lined up with Craig's memories of Berkeley, and the day he emptied an enormous bowl that held six bunches of bananas, filled it with Fruity Pebbles, and brought it over to the milk dispenser to convey his disgust. Visitor days were never as good as you thought they might be; they agitated the population for all kinds of reasons. Just as parents' weekends would dredge up all kinds of feelings on campus—family dramas you were sucked back into, or jealousies of other, better families if your parents didn't see fit to attend.

"Oh, and wash your hands after using the bathroom."

"Excuse me?" Craig laughed. Did that have to be spelled out?

"I said wash your damn hands. Inmates have a real hang-up about that. Doesn't matter what type of prison we're talking."

Tuffy's best advice was his most sincere: find a way in which you could make a mark and offer something to the population at large. To Craig, this meant teaching an art class, either appreciation if he had access to slides, or painting itself if he could requisition the proper materials. He thought it funny, the idea of him teaching. What if, while in prison for his role in art forgery, he instructed a new generation of forgers? All while under the watchful eye of law enforcement and the guise of rehabilitation? At least it gave him a laugh.

In the end it was Marielle who took the most meticulous notes, always an eager student. But Craig knew that she was doing this for him, for his protection, or perhaps Mia's. If the two of them were going to have a future relationship, Craig would have to survive whatever came next. So the more Tuffy talked, the more engaged Craig became and he found himself asking sincere questions. Does time go by slowly? Does it help to have a routine? Is it possible to make actual friends? Tuffy did his best to answer, and what started as a confrontational and combative hour ended with awkward hugs, Craig careful not to lift his instructor off the ground when they embraced.

"See?" Naomi began after she had seen Tuffy out. "I think we all learned a lot."

Craig hugged her tight. He had no qualms about lifting her.

"Besides," Naomi said when he set her down. She opened her purse and pulled out a sandwich bag filled with withered caps and stems. "Look what Tuffy left us!"

Marielle swooped in for a closer look. "Mushrooms? God, I haven't done mushrooms in years."

Jordy took the bag from Naomi and held it up to the light. "I guess now we know what he went to prison for."

"He went to prison for falsifying financial information."

Well, sure. That's how they got Al Capone.

Naomi rolled her eyes. "You guys are so square."

Craig flopped back on the couch, exhausted. "I don't know that I have it in me tonight." He looked at Marielle, still hoping to get her alone. "Today has . . . Been a day."

"There's always tomorrow," Naomi said. And while she meant it literally, it was also a beautiful statement about hope.

The following morning Naomi booked them five premier tickets to the Circle Line Cruise, a two-hour half-island excursion that included highlights from Manhattan's skyline, the Statue of Liberty,

Ellis Island, DUMBO, South Street Seaport, and the Brooklyn, Manhattan, and Williamsburg Bridges.

"Oh, great," Craig joked. "Burial at sea."

Thirty minutes before the arrival of their Uber XL, the guys each consumed a portion of Tuffy's mushrooms with an equal handful of raw almonds divided from two two-hundred-calorie snack packs—almost the entire contents of Craig's pantry; the nuts helped mask the sour taste. Marielle, concerned about her weak constitution, steeped hers in boiling water and made a sort of tea, which she aggressively sipped once cooled. Naomi, honoring her sobriety, abstained to chaperone. By the time they had exited the Dodge Durango at the entrance to Pier 83 and lined themselves up in the queue, the psychedelic ingredient in mushrooms, psilocybin, had started to kick in. Craig, Marielle, and Jordy were all appropriately giddy; Jordan was paranoid; and Naomi was characteristically annoyed.

"Mushrooms are a class A narcotic," Jordan whispered; beads of sweat were forming on his brow. He eyed a lanky teenager in a red polo shirt with suspicion as he worked his way down the line.

"A-plus, if you do them right," Jordy replied, feeling relaxed for the first time that weekend, even though Marielle had still refused to engage.

"Class A drugs are punishable with up to seven years in prison."

"Good," Craig said. "I could use the company."

"Keep the line moving," Naomi scolded, encouraging Jordan to act natural. Jordan, however, was fixated on the security checkpoint ahead. "Just be normal." But telling someone under the spell of psilocybin to *be normal* was deeply unhelpful; in fact, Jordan looked at his arms and couldn't remember how they usually hung from his shoulders. They had brought a few extra caps and stems with them (Craig was out of almonds, but the ship had a snack bar) in case they weren't feeling the proper effects and needed to up their dose. But Jordan now desperately wished they hadn't.

"Security, security, security," Jordan whispered repeatedly until Jordy covered his mouth.

"Oh my god, you're sweaty." Jordy pulled his hand away from his husband's face and wiped it on his jacket.

"Securi—!"

"Stop saying 'security'!" Jordy gripped Jordan's shoulders. "They're looking for weapons, not fungus. Besides. This whole place is staffed with children. They wouldn't know what they were looking for if it bit them."

Jordan was wary. To him a New Jersey high school kid might be exactly who recognized their stash for what it was. He was about to grab Naomi's bag and bolt from the line when the teenager in the red shirt reached their group.

"Welcome to Circle Line Cruises." The kid introduced himself as an ambassador, although ambassador to what, no one was certain, and imagining what it might be (Belgium? The UN? A brand ambassador for Target?) sent them into fits of giggles. "May I see your tickets, please?" The ambassador's hair was limp, too long for his gaunt face, and while his skin was clear it was surprisingly oily, like it had just come out on the far side of a yearslong battle with acne.

"You're a what now?" Craig asked.

"I'm an ambassador. For the cruise line."

"Is that an official diplomatic status?" Jordy asked to everyone's delight but Jordan's.

"Don't challenge his authority." Jordan's eyes darted directly to Naomi's bag, where the drugs were tucked inside a Fendi sunglasses case.

Jordy continued undaunted. "Is that Ambassador Extraordinary or Ambassador Plenipotentiary?"

Marielle, having spent years in Washington, couldn't stop herself from intervening, despite the silent treatment she was still giving

Jordy. "Somebody please tell the oaf that ambassadors are extraordinary *and* plenipotentiary."

Jordan whipped around. "Oh my god, SHUT UP!"

Craig's curiosity was piqued. "What does that even mean?"

"'Extraordinary' means of the highest rank and 'plenipotentiary' means invested with full powers. Didn't anyone here take civics?" Jordan grabbed Marielle's face and squeezed her mouth open like a fish and studied her like she had just been speaking in tongues.

Naomi pried his hands off Marielle. "Is that being normal?"

Jordy turned back to the ambassador and asked, "May we see some ID?"

"There seems to be some sort of misunderstanding," the kid said, visibly confused. "I'm asking to see *your* ID. In the form of tickets. Please." When no one made any effort to show him their tickets, he relented and pointed to his name tag, which read *PETER B., AMBAS-SADOR.*

"Ah, yes. The diplomatic name tag." Jordy grabbed it for closer inspection. "Everything seems to be in order!"

"Jordy, stop it."

"*You* stop it."

Naomi stepped between the Jordans as the lone functioning adult. "BOTH OF YOU STOP IT."

Jordy protested. "It's not every day you meet an ambassador. It's exhilarating." His eyes sparkled with excitement.

Marielle pointed to the name *PETER B.* on the kid's name tag and turned to face the group. "Perturb. His name is Perturb."

"*OH MY GOD!*" Jordan pleaded, convinced they would be detained at any moment.

Craig doubled over in fits of laughter, so much so that Naomi had to usher them a few steps back. When she turned her attention back to the ambassador, she said, "I'm sorry. Please ignore them. We're here to honor a friend who died. He . . . Loved the Circle Line Cruise." She grabbed on to Craig's sleeve. "Before he was violently murdered. Here. The tickets are on my phone." She held up her screen and Ambassador Peter B. swiped through to make sure all five were in order.

When he was satisfied that they had all prepaid, although perhaps against his better judgment, he ushered them through security and reluctantly welcomed them aboard. They were shown seats on the upper deck so they could enjoy the views alfresco, and he gave them each a bottle of water; Jordan drank his in five gulps. ("I got it!" Craig exclaimed, once Peter B. was out of earshot. "He's the ambassador for thirst and the quenching thereof!")

Ten minutes into the cruise, Craig noticed the city kept changing colors. Not the buildings themselves, but the atmosphere near where Manhattan kissed the sky. "Does anyone else see that?" he asked, but he could have been asking about anything in the busy tableau before them.

"That's it. I'm going to the snack bar." Naomi clearly didn't like being left out of a party that she herself had arranged. Perhaps she could find pleasure in an old candy bar they were sure to have, like a Whatchamacallit or Charleston Chew.

Jordan focused on his arms, which he held zombielike in front of him. "Is anyone else feeling paralyzed?"

"Paralysis can be a side effect. Just be chill," Naomi instructed as she calmly left. Jordan's eyes grew wide.

"Temporary," Craig offered, hoping that would make Jordan feel better. "*Temporary* paralysis."

Jordy chewed on a mouthful and raced to spit it out before someone else could beat him to the joke. "Paralysis plenipo*temporary*."

"Extraordinary and plenipo*temporary*." Craig and Jordy then stiffened their bodies like they were frozen, thawing them just enough to high-five.

Marielle looked back wistfully at the shore. "What kind of mother would name their child Perturb?"

Jordan mumbled, "I'm going to beat every one of you to a pulp. As soon as I can move my arms." He swung his shoulders from side to side in a vain attempt to regain control of his limbs.

"Violence is never the answer," Marielle declared, and then she nuzzled against Craig's arm. She still eyed Jordy with suspicion, but the mushrooms were having an effect and she too was beginning to thaw. She remembered what Naomi told her at her own funeral—she had spent too much of her life being mad at the past. And the past no longer mattered. Not when she'd finally spoken to Craig and an enormous weight had been lifted. "You know, we have animals to thank for magic mushrooms."

"Do we?" Craig asked.

"We do." Marielle explained how she had gone hunting for mushrooms with a new friend when she had set down her own roots in Oregon. Where psychedelic mushrooms grew in the wild they were selectively eaten by critters and their spores were more widely spread; it didn't take an expert to find them, if you knew what you were looking for. If the psilocybin these mushrooms produced was originally intended as a defense, as a deterrent against being eaten, it roundly failed in the wild. Whether they had a psychedelic effect on woodland creatures was a matter up for debate, but Marielle liked to think they did. She imagined fawns and squirrels and foxes prancing about and communing while high as kites.

They walked to the railing on the port side to watch the sunlight refract off the waters where the Hudson met the East River as their cruise plowed toward Ellis Island.

"The water is alive," Jordy whispered. It was not hard to imagine glowing organisms science had yet to discover performing elaborate choreography just beneath the water's surface.

Naomi returned with a stale 3 Musketeers. "What are you losers doing?"

Craig spotted her candy bar. "The Three Musketeers!" he announced, excitedly pointing to all of them.

"There are *five* of us," Naomi said flatly, but the rest of them seemed to think this observation brilliant.

"Her face is moving," Craig remarked when their boat passed in front of the Statue of Liberty. "Why is it doing that?" Liberty was on duty, looking out into the harbor, but she couldn't help but steal glances at them, looking down with great sorrow and disappointment.

Marielle clasped her hands over her eyes. "Oh my god, she's looking at *you*. What did you do?!"

"I DON'T KNOW!" Jordy hid behind Craig, crouching there like a child.

Craig spun around. "What's gotten into you?"

They were almost right under her now as they took a close pass of Liberty Island. "There are spikes coming out of her head," Marielle stated. "That has to hurt." But it made sense to her, as women were more likely to suffer from migraines.

Jordy took another look at Lady Liberty and gasped. "Oh my god, *it's my mother.*"

"NOOOOOOOOOOOOOO." Confused, Jordan whipped around to look for his mother-in-law among the passengers. Jordy had to point up before he finally understood.

Marielle lowered her hands. "Why is she green?"

Against the cobalt-blue sky, the patinized copper, after years of oxidation and exposure to water, was the most striking color Jordy had ever seen. He suddenly understood why she was looking at him with such disappointment. "I told a lie," he said with deep shame.

"You kept a secret," Jordan said. That was different. He went to comfort his husband with a hug but still struggled to raise his arms. They hung limply by his sides, so he flailed them around like a Muppet. "WHAT IS WRONG WITH MY ARMS?"

The boat was now rocking a bit much for their liking as it drifted close to the island's retaining wall, where waves were actively breaking.

"Whoa," Craig said as he put his arms out to steady Marielle. Naomi eyed them suspiciously like she had the Jordans when they first became a thing.

"I don't like this," Jordan said. "I don't like this one bit." He lurched and grabbed the railing, then started pulling himself toward the stern.

"Guess his arms are working again," Craig observed.

"I'd better . . ." Jordy motioned to go after him.

"Stay," Marielle said. The silence had gone on long enough. It was time for the two of them to talk.

Craig and Naomi saw this as their cue to make themselves scarce and invented some urgent reason they were needed on the far side of the deck. When they were a safe distance away, Craig said, "I heard there's a new guy in your life."

"Heard it from who?" *Marielle.*

"Is it Tuffy?"

"Ugh. No, it's not Tuffy. Gary's much more like you."

"*Gary,*" he repeated, before asking how.

Naomi started to giggle. "Boring."

"I'm a felon! You can no longer think that I'm dull." Craig gave an embarrassed wave in passing to two older women who overheard.

"That's true," Naomi agreed. "Gary just sells insurance."

"Like, car insurance? Oh my god, is he the gecko from GEICO?"

"No, he doesn't sell car insurance." She launched into an explanation about how he sold completion guarantees for feature films, which helped protect investors from cost overruns.

Craig pretended to snore.

"STOP IT!" Naomi smacked him on the arm.

He acted groggy and confused, like he had just woken up. "Oh, sorry. I think I dozed off there for a minute. Tell me again about the world of bonds and guarantees. It sounds like such a magical place."

"Oh, fuck off."

"I hope you're being careful."

Naomi's face soured. "Like using protection?"

"Gary sounds like the name of a serial killer."

"It does not."

"Or a shop teacher." Craig's mind was scattered. "Gary teaches seventh graders in clear goggles how to use a drill press."

Naomi laughed. "Look." She pointed. In front of them, gulls were circling over the water. Craig reached out as if he could touch them, and they squawked louder and louder. "What do they want?" Naomi asked, finishing up the last of her 3 Musketeers.

"Maybe they found the body of one of Gary's victims."

Naomi growled. "No way. Gary punches holes in his victims with his drill press so they sink straight to the bottom." Just the idea of it made her like Gary even more.

Craig laughed. "Just when I thought there were no more good serial killers." He had consumed hours of true-crime documentaries since the gallery first put him on leave. They held a strange grip on him now that he was part of the criminal element; it was also comforting knowing there were far worse delinquents than him. "But Gary, he'll meet women at a bar, tell them about the world of film finance, and they'll literally lose the will to keep living."

"In all honesty, he's not who I imagined myself with. But he's good for me," Naomi admitted. "Really." And then she paused before adding, "My parents would have liked him. Even though he's Black and not Asian."

Craig smiled. "As long as your parents aren't the reason you're with him." He turned and leaned back on the railing. The boat was approaching the South Street Seaport on the other side.

"Not even a little bit. I'm with Gary for me." Naomi stepped gently on his foot. "So listen. I'm going to pay for a new attorney and I don't want to hear another word about it. I have more money than I can ever spend, and this is what I want to do with some of it. I can't promise it will keep you out of prison. But you're getting screwed here and we want to see you fight back."

Craig looked down at the foam that surrounded the boat. He couldn't tell if the waters were particularly rough, or if the drugs were messing with his equilibrium. Either way, he felt off-kilter. "Okay," he finally agreed. Naomi looked surprised. *That was easy.* She expected him to protest. "On one condition."

Naomi waited silently for his demand.

"I want to have my funeral right now."

Marielle and Jordy stood awkwardly as the boat sailed by South Street Seaport and under the Brooklyn Bridge. Jordy pointed at one of the piers. "The first pier was built by the Dutch West India Company. The seaport was a center of trade for several hundred years before falling into decline. Eventually ships started docking on the Hudson side of the island."

Marielle didn't say anything, but she did stare at the seaport as they glided past, although it was impossible to make out all of its charm, the open-air markets and the cobblestone streets, from the water.

"Just a little local insight." He was waiting all weekend for Marielle to explode and for them to hash it out, but this was now just awkward for awkward's sake.

"I'd prefer an apolo—"

"I'm sorry," he said before she could even finish.

Marielle felt sad, the weekend taking its toll. The other funerals, hers and Naomi's, had left her invigorated, but this one had just about drained her. "There's a morality to keeping secrets," she began. "Telling someone a secret invokes trust. Alec clearly trusted you. Maybe even more than me. I can accept that. And keeping a secret makes you feel worthy of that trust. You may have felt honorable, even. I can accept that too. Your reputation remains intact. You hang on so tightly, because breaking that trust means you risk losing a person."

Jordy closed his eyes and saw Alec, the two of them late at night tossing a ball back and forth from their dorm room beds. They were like brothers that way.

"But what you did, Jordy. That was dishonorable. Both to me, *and* to Alec . . ." Marielle trailed off, shaking her head. "You broke my trust, Jordy Tosic. And now you risk losing me."

They were gliding between the bridge's two Gothic suspension towers. It was a sight to see, overwhelming almost to sneak underneath a suspended structure with so many cars and bicycles and people flowing across like they were in some alternate, upside-down world. But Jordy kept his eyes focused on the water, partly in shame, partly because it was making endlessly fascinating foam around their boat and there was enough in his dose of mushrooms keeping hold of his thoughts. "I thought I was doing the right thing," he managed.

"You thought you were doing the *easy* thing."

"I *know* I was doing the easy thing," he said, and Marielle was happy he at least didn't deny it.

"You should have told me. Point-blank. You should have told me immediately. We could have kept it between us, but I could have been tested, and we could have got Alec some help."

Jordy nodded, and said he wished more than anything he could turn back time. Then Marielle nodded and they were quiet again. Because they couldn't. It was the reason for their pact. They could only prevent things moving forward.

"I don't miss this," she said as they emerged on the other side of the bridge.

"New York?" He didn't know she'd ever spent much time here.

"Just . . . *This*." She made a gesture that encompassed everything. Instead she missed her animals, and the quiet of her new life in Oregon. A certain color green that surrounded her place. The way the air smelled. Trees. She was missing quiet, and the honest people she'd met—not many, but enough to grow a little community. She missed wide-open spaces. She missed hearing birds (other than the seagulls overhead and the sound of pigeons taking flight). She missed how people could spread out, be alone, not have to deal with each other if they didn't want to, could hold a grudge, could take their time to forgive.

But she was also grateful that she was here. At least in this moment. And she knew she would long for her friends again as soon as she was home. Life was funny that way. "You should come see me. In Oregon."

Jordy looked surprised. "It's not exactly Jordan's scene."

Marielle persisted. "You don't always have to do everything together."

And in this moment, under the influence of psychedelics, the very idea of Jordy without Jordan seemed incredibly profound. The world dropped away, except for the desultory sounds, which amplified and grew louder until they were roaring in his ear like a jetliner taking off overhead. He stepped back from the rail until his back was pressed against the ship's cabin. "I want to feel safe," he said.

Marielle observed him do this, and the panicked look on his face subside, and so she too stepped back, pressing her own back against the cabin wall, which was warm from the sun. It did make her feel safe, like her father's hand on the small of her back when she was first learning to ride a bike.

And that was how Naomi found them, pressed up against the cabin for dear life, looking like a gargantuan tentacle had just swooped up on deck trying to grab them to pull under the sea.

"What," they said in unison when they felt Naomi's disapproving stare.

"We're having Craig's funeral in the bow."

"NOW?" Again, in perfect chorus.

Naomi shook her head yes. "Hurry. And someone find Jordan. Before we get back to the dock."

Marielle and Jordy looked at each other and then slowly inched their way along the wall in the direction Naomi had come, their backs never leaving the safety of the cabin wall.

Here, I brought something," Craig said once everyone had gathered. They found a spot to themselves on the Manhattan side as they headed up the East River. The boat was starting to slow and then turn, and Craig sensed they were running out of time. He produced a dented spice tin from Dean & DeLuca from his jacket pocket, the metal dulled with age, and handed it to Marielle.

"What's in this?" she asked. The white label, smudged from grease, read *paprika*.

"My cremains," Craig said with a totally straight face, and Marielle dropped the tin where she stood; it hit the deck with a thud.

Fortunately, the tin was old and had been in the back of his cupboard for years with a few other mostly unused spices and the top tended to stick, so the contents stayed neatly inside. Craig managed to grab it just before it rolled under the railing and over the side. "I thought we could scatter them."

"What's in the tin, really?" Craig now held Naomi's morbid attention.

"Oh. I severed a toe this morning before you got up and cremated it on the fire escape."

"You did WHAT?" Marielle looked to the others like they already knew this and she was just catching up.

"Not one of the big ones. One of the ones in the middle. I thought it might keep me out of prison."

Naomi glared. "It's not like getting out of the draft."

"This little piggy went to market, this little piggy stayed home. This little piggy had roast beef, this little piggy was tossed into a burning Folgers can on Craig's fire escape." Jordan smiled, pleased with himself.

Marielle reached for the tin and read the label closely. "Is that what paprika is? Smoked toes?"

"I didn't burn a toe, you guys. I burned something else."

"Evidence?" Jordy asked, wondering if they too might now be implicated in a crime.

Craig gave him a disapproving look. "Not *evidence*. Something else. Something symbolic." They all stared at him skeptically, and so he had to relent. "An old painting, if you must know. A small canvas. Something I painted a long time ago."

Everyone exchanged approving looks; this was finally starting to make some sort of sense. "It's a funeral, right? I wanted to say goodbye to my old talent so I could make room for the emerging new artist within." Craig imagined for a moment someone else inside him, stretching, reaching, yearning to break free. It was disquieting, itchy even, but exciting nonetheless.

Naomi was skeptical. "So like, performance art?" She had never much cared for that sort of thing and didn't want to be part of any.

"Art is about discovery," he offered, snatching his tin back from Marielle. "It's well past time I got back to painting. Now can someone hurry up and say a few words before this boat returns to port?"

They scrambled to assemble in some sort of formation that didn't appear too somber; Jordy found himself squeezed to the front of the group and all eyes landed on him. "Fine," he said. He had been the source of much friction this weekend and hoped he could rise to the occasion and contribute something that might wipe away lingering negative thoughts. "Here we gather to remember Craig Scheffler, the old—"

"The felon," Naomi interjected as she kicked Craig. He had better uphold their agreement about new legal representation.

"—who served his, hopefully very short, debt to society," Jordy added, pulling Naomi in tight to keep her from interrupting again. Craig held up his crossed fingers. "The Craig whom we loved with all our hearts, despite his being heterosexual and male—*no one's perfect*—often grumpy, and hardened to some of the things life has to offer, and to become acquainted with Craig Scheffler the new, the artist, the version connected again to his soul, the version who is free, in all the definitions of that word. It is in reconciling these two, our old friend and our new, that we celebrate today and scatter these ashes." Jordy then pulled his phone from his pocket and opened his Notes app to read from some thoughts he had saved. "Death is the starlit strip between the companionship of yesterday and the reunion of tomorrow."

Jordan and Marielle huddled together in awe, while Naomi unburied her face from Jordy's chest. The rest of them ooohed in unison;

whether it was the mushrooms filtering the words in a profound way or if they were genuinely touched, none of them were sure.

"No, don't *ooh!*" Naomi lectured, disappointed in them. "What does that even mean?"

"It's Mark Twain," Jordy clarified.

"It's bullshit, is what it is."

Jordan glanced over at Jordy's screen. "You just have that saved in your phone?"

Jordy scrolled through his Notes app. He had a number of quotes that he'd started collecting when Marielle had first invoked the pact and he realized it might be useful at a moment's notice to have something profound to say. "For the pact. I have a collection of inspirational quotes. This one seemed the most meaningful."

Craig grabbed Jordy's iPhone. "It's written first." Craig started scrolling.

"So?"

"So this is the *most* meaningful?"

"YES. That's why it's written first!"

Craig was still skeptical. "There's a quote in here from Mister Rogers."

"He was a minister!"

"And is this . . . JULIA CHILD?! 'A cookbook is only as good as its poorest recipe'?"

"Bon appétit!" Marielle declared.

Jordy snatched his phone back.

"I guess I should consider myself lucky I didn't get Bob Ross." Craig turned to Jordan. "Well, this is *your* problem now."

"Because I live with him?"

"No. Because Marielle, Naomi, and I have all had our funerals and he's not going to read these quotes for himself, so the rest of these gems are for you."

Marielle stepped forward to end their bickering. "I want to say something. From my heart."

Jordy jokingly offered his phone for inspiration, but she pushed his hand away. When she stood next to him she had a full view of the southern tip of Manhattan and was lost for a moment, watching the afternoon's light glint off the towering structures. She was reminded of the collection of glass figurines she'd curated in childhood and had a flashing image of the skyline not as buildings, but as the glass animals she kept as a girl. Giraffes and hippos and a gorilla that wore a pink tutu.

"Marielle?" Naomi prodded.

"Right." She snapped back to attention. "Craig. We were a balanced group in many ways when we formed. Two women, two straight men, two others who found each other. But when we lost Alec, we also lost that balance and in some ways you've been without your partner in this friendship, almost since it began. That's also at times put you at the center of everything. The apex, the balance, the midpoint between two ends. I'm loath to put a man at the center of any frame, but there you have it. I don't even know if you've been aware of it, but I admire you and always have." Marielle took Craig's hands in her own. "You see the world with an artist's eyes and sensitivity. I'm excited to see you take on new things."

Fatherhood, Craig thought, catching a lump in his throat.

"I know you will do them with your whole heart, and you will be loved for it."

Craig's eyes were wet. He moved to the center of the group. "I want to say something too."

The cruise almost over, no one objected.

"Maybe it's because I was given up by my parents, who seemingly just couldn't be bothered. That has an effect on you. You look for meaning. You look for connection. You look for family. And you see the beauty in all of those things. And maybe it's just the mushrooms talking, but you are my family. All of you. You have been since the day I met you, and you forever will be." An announcement over the boat's loudspeakers meant an imminent end to their afternoon. Craig wiped his eyes and held up the paprika tin. "Anyone want the honors?"

Jordan smiled. "I think it should be you."

"Me?"

"How often does one have the chance to scatter their own remains?"

Craig twisted the lid slowly, careful not to pry too hard when the lid became stuck, wary of ashes flying everywhere. When he had the lid free, he held the open tin between them, sheltering it, at least in part, from the wind. "Do I throw the whole thing in at once? Or keep the tin and scatter a little as we go?"

"You've never done this before?" Jordan asked.

"HAVE YOU?!" Craig was growing impatient.

Jordan took him by the arm and led him gently to the railing. "Nana." Craig cupped one hand in front of the tin like it was a birthday cake and he was trying to keep the candles from going out before a wish could be made. "Any last words?"

Jordan looked out at the water, and the others joined him, clasping the railing on either side. "There is an appointed time for everything, and a time for every affair under the heavens. A time to be born, a time to die. A time to plant, and a time to uproot the plant. A time to kill and a time to heal. A time to weep, a time to laugh, a time to mourn, a time to dance."

Jordy cocked his head, surprised.

Jordan faced Jordy and Marielle. "A time to stay silent, a time to speak." He then turned to Naomi. "A time to trip on mushrooms, a time to be sober." He at last focused on Craig and placed his hands on his friend's shoulders. "A time to embrace, a time to be far from embraces. A time to scatter stones, and a time to grow a new pair."

Craig slowly angled the tin until its contents started to spill from within, held aloft momentarily from the water's gentle breeze until they started to fall in an almost funnel-like shape, a tornado of his past and the man he used to be touching down on the waters below.

Jordy was stunned. It was plastered across his face. "Okay, well, that wasn't Mark Twain."

"Ecclesiastes 3:1–15, with a few alterations." And then when they still continued to look at him baffled, he added, "Oh, big surprise, the Latino kid was raised Catholic. News at eleven."

"I knew you were raised Catholic. I just didn't know you had all of that still inside you."

"There's not like a colonic for that," Naomi pointed out.

"Craig, is that all of it?"

Craig peeked inside the tin. Some of the ashes remained. He then raised it just as the wind shifted, and a cloud of ash blew back in their faces. Marielle coughed as the others swatted away soot with their hands.

Jordan groaned. "We look like the road company of *Mary Poppins*."

"The ambassador won't like this one bit," Jordy muttered.

"He's going to be perturbed for real." Marielle spit some ash from her mouth, hoping it wasn't toe.

They stayed in the bow until the boat docked back at the pier. Eventually they were ushered back onto dry land by another ambassador who was not Peter B., which made Marielle wistful. She would have genuinely been happy to see him again, but it was just as well. They had all left a bit of themselves on the river and were ready to start anew.

THE
JORDANS

There was no specific reason the fight erupted when it did, in fact both Jordans were having a perfectly pleasant day enjoying New York in the way residents sometimes forget to. Spending less and less time at the office—their employees had been granted discretion to handle things that didn't rise to the level of urgent—they were able to see a Wednesday matinee after lunch at their favorite Japanese spot. They hadn't told the staff exactly what Jordan's diagnosis was, but it was June and Tony season was now done and what was the point of owning their own PR firm if they couldn't take a step back in the summer? Leaving the theater, they agreed the play they'd just seen was overhyped, but it starred Judith Light, who was, if possible (since she had won just about every major theater award for the performance), undersold. In short, it was almost a perfect day.

Almost.

After the play they stopped for a drink at Joe Allen's, where they'd had dinner the night of their wedding.

"Are you sure?" Jordy asked when Jordan had suggested a cocktail. It had already been a long day and he worried about Jordan pushing himself too hard.

"Just one martini."

"A martini might be a bit much," Jordy suggested gently. Together they'd cut back their alcohol consumption of late.

"Just to sip," Jordan insisted. "I don't have to drink the whole thing."

Don't have to, Jordy thought. *But you will.*

They sat at the bar and for a while it was like old times. They talked about other shows that were mediocre and coasted to a successful run on a brilliant lead performance, and then they argued the opposite—great shows that were perhaps miscast or deserved more from their star. Jordan sipped his martini slowly at first to savor it, remembering he was quite literally now a lightweight. But then he drank with more abandon as he and Jordy grew more impassioned in their debate. They were bickering about *The Boy from Oz* and if it could be revived without Hugh Jackman as Peter Allen (no according to Jordy, but Jordan thought yes—in a few decades with Troye Sivan), when Jordan realized he was drunk. He swirled his three olives in the remnants of his vodka as the bartender came to refill it. Jordan pushed his drink forward, but Jordy reached out and placed his hand over Jordan's glass.

"One is probably enough, thank you."

The bartender looked surprised because they never used to stop at just one, but to make his point Jordy handed the bartender his credit card.

"Don't do that," Jordan said once the bartender had stepped away to close their bill.

"Why?"

"What if I wanted another?"

"You can't have another."

"Who are you, my mother?"

"I think Carmen Vargas would agree with me."

Jordan stopped and sulked on his barstool in awkward silence until the bartender returned with their check.

As Jordy added a tip and signed, Jordan announced, "I'm going to discontinue my treatment."

Jordy stopped midsignature. "Your cancer treatment?" he asked, as if Jordan could have been talking about a hot oil remedy for his hair or microdermabrasion.

Jordan nodded.

Jordy threw up his hands in disbelief. "May I ask why?"

"This is why." Jordan made a broad gesture encompassing first his martini glass and then everything. "I'm tired of being managed by people, treated like a child."

Then Jordy said the wrong thing. "You're tired, period. Let's just get you home."

The reaction was immediate. Jordan banged his fist on the bar, drawing the attention of the people around them. The bartender looked over and Jordy waved to him that they were okay.

"Can we talk about this at home?"

"We can talk about it here."

Jordy acquiesced. "Okay, hotshot. I'll make you a deal. Trigger the pact. Call for your funeral, and you can stop your treatment."

They locked eyes and neither looked away.

"What does that have to do with anything?"

"I don't think this is a decision you should make unilaterally."

"Then *you* trigger the pact," Jordan said. "If you think you need reinforcements."

"I'm fine. You're the one giving up! I think the least you could do is sit through your funeral and listen to how your death will make your friends feel."

"It doesn't matter how it makes anyone feel. It only matters how it makes me feel."

"And how do you feel?"

"Tired. But I'm *not* giving up."

"Like hell you're not. You promised you would fight! You promised you would fight to the end!"

Jordan placed his elbow on the bar and used his hand to prop his head up. "I did. I did fight. I fought valiantly, and what's more you know that I did because you were there. I fought to the end and this is the end."

"No." Jordy pinched the bridge of his nose, as he felt a headache bearing down; his body was physically rejecting Jordan's words.

"I want you to promise me certain things. I want you to keep swimming." Jordy tossed back the last of his drink. This wasn't happening. Jordan took his martini glass from him and set it next to his on the bar. "And not in vodka. You've been a different person since you've been back in the pool. I want you to stay in touch with my parents. Just once in a while. My brother only, if you want."

"It's not possible that this is the end."

"What difference does it make to you? You're 'fine.' And since you are, I want you to fuck around. A lot. You didn't get to do that when you were young." Jordan paused when he saw Jordy's eyes glaze over. "And then I want you to settle down."

Jordy spun on his stool to look at the other diners. A pre-theater crowd mostly, people grabbing an early dinner before the evening performance. Only a couple of blue-hairs who caught a matinee, like them. "You know what? Sure. No problem. Once you're gone I'll sleep my way through the good boroughs before settling down with a nice guy. Against all odds, his name will be Jordan too, but I'll make our friends call him Also. People will come up to us and say 'I'm so sorry to hear about Jordan,' and I will say 'Thank you,' and then turn to my new fella and say 'This is Also . . .' I won't even have to finish that sentence because it will be so crystal clear and then we'll all have a good laugh."

"You can't just change his name to Also."

"Why not? You changed mine." It was still a point of contention. *Jordy.* Did he look like a Jordy?

"There couldn't be *two* Jordans. It wasn't believable!"

"It was my name!" Jordy could feel himself getting genuinely angry. "You're tired of people fussing over you? I'm tired of people fussing over me! Telling me what to do! Do you know what it's been like? *How's Jordy doing? Jordy should talk to so-and-so. Jordy should do that. How's Jordy going to endure?* Maybe 'fine' was too strong a word. But is there a part of me that is excited to be Jordy and not half of the Jordans? To figure out who I am on my own? To maybe even be Jordan again?"

"I'm sorry this has been so rough *on you.*"

Jordy's head was pounding, like a hangover that came on all at once. "I don't want to make this about me. But we've been together our whole lives. And yes, people have a right to be concerned. But also, no one gives me enough credit. *You* don't give me enough credit. I'll swim if I want to. I'll fuck if I want to. This is sad and awful and I would give anything to change these circumstances. But in the end, I don't need the pact. I don't need people telling me what to do. I will survive."

Jordan added his second elbow to the bar, needing both hands to remain upright. Someone next to them was complaining that the trains in Kyiv ran better than the subway here, and Kyiv had been through a war.

"Sorry. Poor choice of words," Jordy finally said. *Survive.* Jordan didn't respond. The bartender took their empty glasses. "Jordan?"

"Yeah." Jordan snapped back to attention. "Don't worry about it. I was just singing the lyrics to 'Eye of the Tiger.'" One elbow slipped off the bar. "I think I'm drunk."

"Feels good," Jordy said, even though his head was still pounding. What he meant to say was that it felt like old times.

Jordan thought about his husband's words. It *was* like Jordy to survive, strength defining so much of his nature, at least on the outside—the athlete wanting to outpace any threats that were clipping his heels. But he knew Jordy better than anyone else, and to his trained eye his husband was protesting too much. For even with champions, someone or something eventually catches up. "Fine. You win. Give me my phone."

"I don't have your phone. Why would I have your phone?"

Jordan gave the front of his blazer a pat-down and found it in the breast pocket. As he produced the device from his jacket he noticed their bartender looked like Alec. And then he blinked, and the bartender *was* Alec.

"Hey," Jordan said, legitimately happy to see him.

"Hey yourself," Alec said in his happy-go-lucky Alec way.

Jordan closed his eyes and focused on clearing his head of its martini fog. When he opened them Alec was gone and the bartender was himself again, but they did bear a striking resemblance. He wondered why he and Jordy hadn't noted the likeness before. It had been so long, more than half their lives since they'd seen Alec last. Ages. And here Jordy had maybe half of his life still to live. If Jordan had to leave him now, he very much wanted to leave him okay. So he opened his Messenger app and started typing.

"Who are you texting?" Jordy asked, confused by Jordan's behavior.

Jordan didn't have to answer; Jordy watched as he added the names one by one.

Naomi.

Craig.

Marielle.

And then last, but not least, Jordy.

YOU'RE THE
NEAREST THING
TO HEAVEN
THAT I'VE SEEN

(JORDY, 2023)

When Jordan came down Sur la Vie's stairs, Marielle was the only one awake. She had found an old desk lamp that looked like the Pixar logo and was positioning it just so over the kittens' nest. The light it emitted was brighter than expected, which made Jordan wince, but Marielle somehow opened her eyes wider. He cocooned himself in a blanket from a wicker basket at the foot of the stairs, waiting for his eyes to adjust.

"You alone?" she asked.

"Aren't we all?" he replied. The honesty of his answer cut deep, and there was no rebuttal Marielle could offer, at least not in the cosmic sense.

"They like the heat," she explained as she lowered the bulb even closer. Jordan peered into the laundry basket and the kittens were snuggled together so tightly he couldn't tell where one ended and the other began; they looked so fragile, he was surprised they had made it through the night. "I made coffee."

"You're a godsend." Jordan went to the kitchen and flipped through the familiar cabinets until he found mugs, no two of which matched. The pot was brimming, waiting for others to wake, and he poured himself a cup. He took a sip and winced again.

"Too strong?"

"Too hot," he said, even though he was freezing. He was always freezing. He missed his old life, power walking uptown blocks gripping thirty ounces of iced latte as fuel. Now he would microwave mugs of hot water at home just to hold them in his hands or place his face over the steam.

"I don't know if there's cream, but there's kitten formula I just mixed."

Jordan stared at Marielle with intensity, drinking her in the way a lover might, searing her image into his memory. "Black is fine."

Marielle fussed over the setup, centering the kittens under the most direct heat, then stroked their fur with the back of one hand. "They should be fed, but I don't want to wake them. I mean look. Have you ever seen anything so perfect?"

Jordan peered again over the side. One of the kittens yawned, showing the sharpest, tiniest teeth. Their eyelids were mostly closed, but they weren't sewn shut in the way they might be if their eyes had been surgically removed; the result was a bit of glistening red tissue that was both visible and slightly alarming. He didn't see perfection, at least not as Marielle did, but understood in that moment why she chose her current life. The kittens weren't perfect, but caring for them somehow was. "You don't ever miss life in D.C.?"

"I miss Mia when she was young."

Jordan tried another sip of his coffee.

"Someone once said of motherhood, the days are slow, endless even, but the years go by quickly." She curled her finger, tucking it between one kitten's tiny paws so it rested against its white belly. "I found that to be true."

Jordan lifted his coffee mug under his nose and inhaled, feeling like the actor in that Folgers commercial where the adult son returns home early Christmas morning and awakens everyone with the aroma of coffee.

"It's back, isn't it," Marielle asked matter-of-factly; it was a statement as much as a question.

Jordan swallowed, stifling the urge to cry. "Yeah."

Marielle looked right at him. "And it's bad?"

Jordan indicated it was.

"How long?"

"How long has it been back?" Jordan then understood what she was asking. "How long do I have."

Marielle shuddered as she waited for an answer.

"Six months. Maybe nine. No one can say for sure." The calendar had already ticked off eighteen weeks since he was given his prognosis, so he had even less time than that—talk about a year that would pass all too quickly. Part of him was still in the doctor's office, receiving that bracing news, as if he were two different people—the man he was before, and the one he was now. (*Dead man walking*, he'd said to Jordy when they emerged from his oncologist's office.) Jordan had a sudden urge to trade places with the kittens, to curl up under a heating lamp, to be bottle-fed and kept safe. The kittens were blind, without eyes, but they were young and there was still so much time for them to see.

Marielle's eyes watered, but she remained stoic. "Come here," she said, and she hugged him until he collapsed his full weight in her arms. They stayed like that for a time, how long neither of them knew, and then Jordan pulled back and she said, "Here. Come feed them

with me." She then gently lifted one of the kittens from the box as it
mewed its displeasure and handed it to Jordan.

He set his coffee on the table and awkwardly accepted the tiny
thing, cupping his hands the whole time so it wouldn't fall. "How?"

Marielle pointed at two bottles sitting on the table that looked like
they might be for dolls. The kitten sank its sharp claws into his shirt
and clung to his chest and Jordan readjusted his hands to reach for
one of the bottles, and then held it under the lamp, as if it might
somehow make more sense when illuminated. "Were these in Naomi's
cabinets?"

"No, silly. I brought them." Of course she had brought them, there
were probably a dozen more in her car. "Let me show you." Marielle
grabbed a dish towel and swaddled the other kitten so that only its
front paws were free, and held the little thing tightly against her chest;
it squirmed, but only for a moment. She shook the bottle and then
dabbed it on her wrist before offering it to the bundle of fur. She
pressed the nipple lightly against the kitten's lips, until it relented and
accepted the formula. It took a few tries for the kitten to stop biting,
but with patience, Marielle got the thing to eat.

Jordan repeated these actions as best as he could, Marielle paus-
ing to offer guidance as he wrapped his charge.

"You're a natural," she said as she tilted her head toward the kitten
nestled against Jordan's chest. Sure enough, it was happily feeding, its
eye sockets open and empty in a way that turned his stomach the
night before when they were dancing to Karen Carpenter and arguing
about food but didn't seem so horrific now.

"Would you look at that," he said, proud of himself. The kitten was
not even wriggling the way Marielle's had, and he loosened the make-
shift swaddling.

Jordan was at peace, holding this fragile life, and yet oddly discon-
certed, as if he had stepped into some sort of Greek play. This blind

kitten, an oracle of sorts, calm in his arms because it could sense his strength leaving him. He was not to be feared, as his life was waning, his journey almost through.

"There's a job opening for you at the rescue if you ever want it." Marielle smiled, and her offer made Jordan think of all the parallel lives he could have led.

"Oh, I'm not a smart hire." He would barely finish orientation. Jordan closed his eyes and heard nothing but the sounds of an old house contracting and settling in the cold of a new day. Soon there would be footsteps. The flush of a toilet. Maybe water running for a shower. But right now it was just the house and the two of them, and two kittens gently taking to bottles, one resting on his chest; who was warming whom was anyone's guess. "I like the quiet of early mornings."

Jordan thought of his mother. In his family, the two of them were the early risers. She recently had a birthday and raved on the phone when he last called about how good she was feeling, how age was just a number, how she felt stranger about having a son that was fifty than herself being eighty-two, about how just that morning she and his father had completed a five-mile walk. He let her live in this excitement because soon he would have to tell her the news from which mothers did not recover.

Jordan glanced down at his kitten, who bared its teeth before closing its mouth around the nipple again. He held the bottle higher to make sure formula continued to flow.

"Ever done this before? Bottle-feeding, I mean."

He thought about that for a moment. A friend's baby? His niece? "I don't think so."

"Isn't that the thing about life? We can have new experiences even at our age." Marielle caught the expression on Jordan's face, a wistfulness coupled with fear, but she didn't remark on it.

Finally, the dreaded creak on the stairs. It was Jordy in sweatpants topped with, Jordan could see, all three of the sweaters he'd packed.

"Morning," he said, and then blew on his hands to warm them.

"There's coffee," Marielle offered, but when Jordy approached the table he crouched next to his husband.

"Are you bottle-feeding a kitten?"

"What does it look like?" Jordan answered, challenging him to reply. During his first course of chemo several years back, Jordan's doctors had told him to steer clear of animals, particularly unfamiliar ones, and two feral kittens certainly qualified as unfamiliar. He waited for Jordy to tell him that helping Marielle in this task was not a good idea, but to his credit he kept any opinion he might have had to himself.

"I think your little guy's done," Marielle observed. Jordan pulled the bottle away while the kitten kept opening and closing its mouth. He unwrapped it from the tea towel, careful to not tug at its claws, which had embedded in the cloth's weave, and laid it gently back under the lamp.

Marielle looked at her bottle; it too was empty. She placed her kitten back with its littermate and they nestled together as one. "They don't need to feed again for a few hours," she said to Jordy. "But if you're jealous you can help me fire up the nebulizer."

Jordy furrowed his brow. "The what now?"

Marielle laughed as Jordy stood to rummage for a coffee mug.

Within the hour the whole house was awake and sitting quietly on the deck in the blast zone of Jordan's news. Naomi wore sunglasses pressed tightly to her face despite the early cloud cover and stared out at the horizon. Craig was flat on his back on the deck's wooden slats, looking up at the sky; he kept reaching for his coffee but never actually lifted the mug to take a sip. Marielle moved the kittens from one spot to the next trying to find a fleeting patch of sun, keeping a watchful eye open for owls and hawks while sweeping away dry pine needles as they fell. Jordy avoided eye contact, not wanting anyone's pity. They were so much like themselves at twenty-two in this moment, stunned by the prospect of death. Yes, they had aged, that was unavoidable, but surely they were still invincible. *Weren't they?* With Jordan's news they were left to wonder if the pact had done them any good at all.

Jordan simply listened to the sounds of the woods on either side of them, the gentle dancing of the leaves, the creaking of stately trees that were here long before them and would stand tall long after, a small creature scurrying to store acorns underneath the wooden deck. Occasionally they would hear a car drive by, reminded once again that civilization had not ended, that they were surrounded by normal people doing normal things on a normal day. Some running errands, some on their way to the beach, some to admire the redwoods scattered around Big Sur. It was cool in the shade, and Jordan kept his blanket wrapped tightly around him, but it was the kind of cold that reminded him he was alive, like jumping in a lake formed from glacier runoff or the first night in November when you thought there might be snow.

"I'm thinking of selling this place," Naomi said, finally breaking the silence; she was almost certain it was the right decision. Too many memories, not enough of them good. "Gary loves it, but he'll just have to deal." She fidgeted mindlessly with her engagement ring; sometimes she liked it, sometimes it was a foreign presence on her finger like a wart.

Jordan poked his bare feet out from under his blanket. "If you sell this place I'll haunt you."

Marielle pushed the kittens next to Jordan and sat. "We're not coming back here without you."

"Oh, yes you are!"

"Oh no, we're not."

Jordan shook his head. It was all so childish. "Then just have me stuffed and prop me up in a chair." He had read once of important figures whose bodies were embalmed and still on display, like Lenin and Ho Chi Minh. He didn't see why such a custom should be reserved for world leaders.

Naomi raised an eyebrow, as if a corpse in the corner might be just the thing to renew her interest in Sur la Vie.

Jordan nudged his husband with his foot. "Big Sur must be full of amateur taxidermists."

"What?" Jordy asked, and then it registered with him and he said, "Yeah." They used to love a website called Bad Taxidermy, which was filled with hilarious photos of dead animals grotesquely posed with frozen expressions of permanent surprise. They would screenshot their favorites, the most mangled and outlandishly bizarre, and use them to text back and forth. Jordy imitated the stunned face of one of their favorites, a bug-eyed fox whose muzzle had been flattened so that it resembled the bill of a duck. Jordan laughed.

"We need a whole new Courtney for this," Naomi said, not understanding the faces they were making.

"Charles Courtney Curran," Craig said after a moment of thought. "Who?"

Craig seemed surprised he'd said that out loud. "He was a naturalist painter. His work was, I don't know—*too* real."

"We don't need any new Courtneys, and you're not selling the house." Jordan did his best to play cheerleader. "Come on. Thinking about you guys coming back here after I'm gone is one of the few things that makes me feel okay. Don't take away the one itty-bitty thing that brings me comfort."

"I just don't see it," Naomi said.

Marielle crept her toes into a new sunny spot. "The pact is almost over anyhow. Then I suppose there's not much reason to return."

"I thought you might say that." Jordan wanted his friends to stay together after he was gone and for the pact—or the spirit behind it at least—to live on. "So I came up with a plan." He reached out and lifted Jordy's chin so that they were looking eye to eye. "I'm giving my funeral to you."

Jordan thought it was the perfect scheme when he came up with it after their fight in the bar. He would give his funeral to Jordy and then die without triggering the pact for himself and thus the pact would remain binding forever. He'd given it much thought and realized he'd already gotten everything he'd needed. There were no rituals designed to make peace with the fleeting nature of life. We celebrated people after they were gone in a manner designed to bring closure to those left behind. But closure was not what was needed when it comes to death and dying; openness was. Acceptance that we share the same fate. Having these funerals, as silly as they might have seemed, allowed Jordan to come to terms with the fact that his time on Earth was finite. His allotment of it might be shorter, but had he lived any less? Had he not received more time than many others? Than Alec? Was he going with things left unsaid? No. Then why should the end be the most difficult part of his life, something worthy of their pact? It wasn't. Jordy was in the more precarious spot.

Of course, Jordy saw things differently. "You can't just give your funeral to someone else."

"I'm not giving it to you so much as *loaning* it to you; I'll have another soon enough."

They were quiet before Marielle piped in, "There *is* precedent." She leaned her head back to look at them upside down. "For triggering the pact on someone else's behalf."

"She's right," Craig agreed, having been the victim of this in the past. "The bylaws have changed."

"THERE ARE NO BYLAWS!" Jordy took a deep breath to calm himself. "Look, I know you're all concerned about me and I appreciate it, I really do. But I'm onto you, Vargas. I see what you're doing."

"What is he doing?" Craig asked confused.

Jordan tried his best to look innocent.

"Don't you see? He's trying to con us into staying together. If he dies without having used the pact for himself, it will never be finished, the circle will never be closed. Our little pact will outlive us all."

Marielle's face brightened. "A loophole." She looked at Jordan, impressed.

"I'm not conning you into anything; you're friends, for god's sake. If anything I'm conning you into acting like it."

"Oh god," Jordy groaned. "You've been planning this all along! That's why you were grinning at me on the plane. Why you got a van at the car rental. They weren't out of midsize sedans, you are up to something!"

Jordan laughed. "I can't believe you fell for that. There were like a hundred Hyundai Sonatas on that lot."

"You even have an itinerary planned, don't you."

Jordan rested his head on Jordy's shoulder, playfully elbowing him in the side.

"Lay it on me, I guess," Jordy sighed, resigned. He wasn't prepared to be at the center of their weekend but felt that protesting would dig his grave deeper. He looked up at the sky; the clouds were just beginning to part.

"We're going to San Francisco," Jordan announced. "Bright and early tomorrow."

"For what?"

"You'll see."

"What about the kittens?" Marielle asked, concerned.

"The kittens?" Jordan hadn't expected there to be kittens when he'd hatched his plan. "They'll just have to come with."

They loaded into the van at five thirty the next morning; the first sunlight just visible through the trees. Naomi insisted on driving even though she looked comically small behind the oversized vehicle's wheel. Jordy would normally have driven, but he was too nervous—he had a big day ahead. He leaned against the van's passenger window, looking wistfully at the house as they backed out of the drive. He was suddenly nineteen again, back on a bus at Berkeley headed to his first swim meet; he even felt the familiar rumbling of his stomach and his heart racing with excitement. He turned back to Jordan, who was bundled in blankets and splayed across the back seat. His eyes were closed. *Let him save his energy*, Jordy thought. Marielle and Craig shared a seat in the rear.

"You ever bottle-feed a kitten?" Marielle asked.

"Oh, for god's sake," Craig replied.

"Why are you so cranky?"

"Besides it being the ass crack of dawn?" Craig looked nervously out the front windshield as the van picked up speed down Route 1. "You guys are literally taking me back to jail."

Jordan had divulged his plan over pasta dinner the night before, so that Jordy could carbo-load. The race was called the Escape from Alcatraz swim, aka the Alcatraz Sharkfest, and this year was the thirtieth annual event. Jordan had balked at their including *shark* in the title when he was researching things for Jordy to do, but he supposed that sort of thing appealed to extreme athletes. The course mimicked the path brothers John and Clarence Anglin took, along with Frank Lee Morris, when the three inmates broke out of Alcatraz prison on the night of June 11, 1962. They had fashioned themselves a rubber raft made of raincoats and entered the bay late at night, never to be heard from again. Clarence Anglin's grandson had once claimed that only his grandfather survived and that the other two were eaten by sharks, but that was probably a tall tale. Or at least Jordan hoped that it was. Still, he had googled "sharks in San Francisco Bay" and while he was alarmed to read that the bay was in the notorious red triangle where forty percent of the country's great white attacks have taken place, he was comforted that the sizable shark population mostly stuck to the open waters outside the city's cove. Entrants wouldn't have the benefit of rubber rafts after all, even ones made of raincoats. They would have to swim.

But Jordan knew that his husband needed to do something big to shake things up; it was how he had dealt with difficult challenges all his life. In many respects he'd been training for something like this since he got back in the pool a year ago, even if he said at the time it was to strengthen his aging body.

The drive into the city was smooth at that hour and they arrived with plenty of time to find parking. They checked Jordy in on the first floor of the Maritime Museum at Aquatic Park. Jordan had secretly included what his husband would need when he'd packed their bags in New York: a swimsuit and goggles and the cap that came with registration. When Jordy, who was uncharacteristically quiet for most of the morning, saw a sandwich board that listed today's water temperatures at sixty-two degrees, he balked and asked, "Shouldn't I be wearing a wet suit?" Sixty-two degrees was a lot colder than the pool at Chelsea Piers.

"Then you would be placed in the wet suit category, and no one wants to win like that." Indeed, those who wore neoprene garments for warmth were judged separately, since they could be performance enhancing. And it just seemed uncouth, like a seal thinking it should take first place. "You're in the non–wet suit category. That's where all the glory is."

Jordy was in the age group marked 50–54. He started jumping in place like a kid with a pogo stick, both to stretch his cold legs and to manage the adrenaline. When he clocked the other entrants in his age group, his confidence ticked up. "I can do this," he said, throwing a few jabs like a boxer.

"Damn right you can," Jordan replied.

A ferry had been arranged to take entrants to the eastern edge of Alcatraz Island; family and friends were not allowed on board. Jordan had looked into booking a regular prison tour in order to hitch a ride to the island and watch the start of the race, but he was afraid with the tour boat schedule he wouldn't be back in time to see Jordy finish—and that was what he really wanted to do. Jordy hugged his friends tight, and Jordan noted his husband's hands wrapped around each of their backs; they were marked with his entrant number, 158, just above the wrist. Jordy embraced his husband last. "Thank you for this," he whispered in Jordan's ear.

"Don't thank me," Jordan replied. "This is all you."

Tears welled in his eyes as he stepped onto the ferry. He found a spot on the boat's upper deck and did his best to enjoy the ride as he watched the city recede. He tried not to read too much into Jordan getting smaller and smaller in the distance as the boat picked up steam in the bay, but over the last three weeks it had been impossible not to feel him slipping away. It was up to him now to fight his way back.

It was a perfect day for a race, and the sun even felt warm on his skin as they cruised out to Alcatraz, notable for a city that—even in August—never seemed all that hot; by the time he entered the water,

the cold might actually feel invigorating. He watched as the full skyline revealed itself the farther they pulled back from shore and the
Golden Gate Bridge likewise came into view. San Francisco was a
beautiful place and he wished he'd taken the time to know it better
when they were at Berkeley. But he was deeply closeted then, and he
ruefully remembered that any mention of the city in the early nineties
could invite speculation about one's sexuality.

When the wind picked up and they were out in the bay, Jordy
shifted his gaze to the other racers. Younger bucks deeply focused,
fidgeting with goggle straps to get them just right, making adjustments
to their swim caps to make sure they were on tight. He recognized the
enthusiasm of youth: Someone had to come in first place, and they all
felt why not them? Older men were laughing in groups; this was as
much a social event as a race, something to brag about Monday back
at the office or at a neighbor's future barbecue, like taking part in a
New Year's polar bear dip. The women, he admired. They radiated
courage and confidence, ready to take on the men. They most reminded him of his old swimming days, cycling through a familiar
series of warm-ups, getting themselves into a zone. Straight arm
swings to loosen the shoulders, say twenty-five on a side, then a
streamlined hamstring stretch to keep the legs from cramping. Jordy
unzipped his track jacket and followed suit, his old personal routine
coming back—a well-rehearsed combination of static and dynamic
stretching to limber him up for a race. He enlisted the ferry's cabin for
a wall press, and watched as Alcatraz prison grew near.

As the boat rounded Alcatraz Island and the city disappeared
from view, they were summoned for a last-minute briefing. Swimmers
were to jump from the ferry and immediately swim toward the start
line, which was marked by a line of kayakers. The faster they lined up,
the quicker more swimmers could enter the water, the sooner the race
could be under way. The finish line at Aquatic Park Cove sat due

south of Alcatraz Island, and they were to aim two hundred yards left
of the entrance. If they swam straight for the entrance itself, the ebb
tide would sweep them right past. Fifty lifeguards on kayaks would
monitor the race and a dozen more support boats were on standby for
any swimmer in distress; all they needed to do was stop and raise a
hand. The route had a notorious reputation, organizers admitted, but
there was no need to worry—they had over the years ushered fifteen
thousand entrants safely ashore and today would be no different. They
were given landmarks to aim for, determined by a test swim the day
before during identical tidal conditions. The race's start would be announced by the ferry's horn; the captain gave it a good blast so everyone could hear and the deck erupted in cheers. Jordy slipped out of
his sweatpants and put them along with his jacket in the bag he was
given marked with his entrant number. It would be waiting for him
back at shore.

This is it, he thought, standing in just his Speedo, his racer's spirit
coming back like an old friend. It was go time.

B ack on shore Jordan and the others walked to the tip of Municipal
Pier, Marielle hauling the kittens in the small carrying crate she'd
transported them in, and it did a good job of shielding them from the
most direct sun. She hugged the crate tight to her chest so that it
wouldn't jostle about as they made their way through the crowd.

Jordan hollered ahead to Craig. "Hey, Jean Valjean. Did you ever
think of anything like this?"

Craig turned back to Jordan, annoyed. Jean Valjean. *Really?* "Did
I ever think of busting out?"

"Yeah. Making a run for it." Or, *swim* for it in this case.

Craig thought back to his time in the pen. Now that it was over it
didn't seem half bad. The law firm that Naomi had hired worked a hell

of a plea. Indeed the feds wanted to make an example of him, as art forgery was on the rise, but he was hardly the image of a criminal or someone who deserved to spend much time behind bars. He'd made an honest mistake. If it hadn't been for the mess at the Knoedler gallery and its fake Jackson Pollocks the year prior, and that gallery's owner and director both escaping prosecution, he probably would have avoided criminal charges. But that wasn't the world they lived in. Craig surrendered himself thinking ten months was something he could make peace with; in the end he served only seven. "Every single day."

"Well, I'm happy you didn't," Marielle said, imagining the additional hot water he'd have been in. "And happier still it's behind you."

Naomi noticed Jordan out of breath when they were only halfway to the pier's end. "Here, let's stop for a minute," she said, and she held Jordan upright in case he felt faint.

"I hate this," he confided, clearly winded. Jordy was about to swim from Alcatraz to shore, and he couldn't even walk to the end of a pier without stopping. And it was only going to get worse from here. He looked back at the skyline, knowing it would be the last time he would be here. If there was other travel he wanted to do beyond Colombia, he had better start planning it now. His knees started to buckle and Craig reached for his other arm.

"Easy now."

Naomi tightened her grip. "Maybe you should have gone with Jordy. You could have been the shark bait."

Jordan laughed. There was almost something appealing about just getting it over with. "I'm easy pickings," he said, as if sharks were known to like a challenge. "Not enough meat on my bones."

Marielle set her carrier down, fished in the backpack Craig wore, and pulled out a bottle of sunscreen. She offered it to Jordan.

He pushed her away. "You think I'm worried about getting cancer?"

Marielle frowned. "Just let me put some on your face." Jordan relented because he didn't have the energy to fight.

The crowd cheered from the end of the pier that jutted farthest into the water, and they scanned ahead to see the commotion. Craig raised a pair of binoculars Mr. Ito had kept for bird-watching up to his eyes. "The swimmers must have entered the water," he assessed.

Jordan perked up with a second wind. "We won't make it to the end of the pier in time. Let's watch from the beach."

The water was a shock that reverberated through Jordy's body, a defibrillation of his heart. He remained fully submerged for only seconds but could hear the faint splashes of people plunging into the water around him, distant explosions in a dream. Then instinct took hold and he starting kicking as hard as he could, taking an enormous gulp of air once he surfaced. His eyes had been tightly closed, an old reflex he still held from his days diving off starting blocks, and when he opened them it was to a world tinted blue from his goggles. There were more splashes around him as other swimmers leaped from the boat, coupled with a few piercing screams as racers felt the shock of the cold. He remembered his instructions and breaststroked away from the boat, keeping his eyes above water and scanning for the kayaks that marked the starting line. When he saw them, he put his head in the water and picked up his pace to get a spot near the front of the pack.

"First time?"

Jordy turned to an older swimmer who wore a neoprene hood under his cap, looking like a knight in a joust. They were both treading water and it took him a moment to realize the swimmer was addressing him. "Yeah," he replied sheepishly, lifting his goggles onto his forehead and wiping salt water from his eyes. "Any advice?"

The man smiled. "You're already taking it."

Jordy tilted his head, confused.

"Do as many things as you can to remind yourself you're alive." There was a glint in the man's eye that was visible through his goggles.

Jordy nodded. And suddenly the salty water in his eyes was not from the San Francisco Bay. He spun around to see other swimmers lining up right behind them. The air was filled with the murmur of excited chatter and encouragement. He lowered his goggles to get ready to race and the man put his hand on Jordy's shoulder.

"Escape from Alcatraz," he said. "Is there anything more exciting than that?"

The racers settled into a line to wait for the starting horn and Jordy did his best to expend just enough energy to keep him from drifting in the current; now was not the moment to overexert, even if adrenaline and his competitive nature were telling him to fight his way to the best starting spot. Back in his swimming days at Berkeley everyone had their favorite lane, either from superstition or personal preference. Historically, world records and gold medals were won in the middle lanes, which were assigned by qualifying times. But there are exceptions to every rule and some swimmers he knew liked lane one or lane eight on the far outsides, so they could monitor the entire field with one breath. Jordy was partial to lane five. Lane four was always given to the fastest qualifier, lane eight the slowest; lane five allowed him to keep pace with the heat leader, and maybe pick up a little speed from their wake. In his current position, Jordy imagined himself in lane six, and that was good enough for his needs. He looked up at the sky and down at the water and everything was blue. He gave his goggles one final adjustment.

———

The blast of the horn could be heard from shore; Jordan, Naomi, Marielle, and Craig all cheered from their spot on the pier. Through the crowd they couldn't see much, at least not yet, but there was clearly commotion near the island's eastern shore. Jordan's heart raced as it always had when he would watch Jordy compete, and he closed his eyes and imagined them both back in school. *It all went by so fast.* It was hard not to feel wistful.

Marielle held the crate with the kittens with one hand and linked her free arm with his. "You know who would have done this with Jordy?"

Jordan smiled. "Alec."

"It's too Courtney Love for him to resist," Naomi agreed.

Jordan laughed. "I'll tell him all about it when I see him."

"Don't say that," Craig moaned. He found such talk defeatist.

But Marielle took it quite differently, and she leaned on Jordan's shoulder. "Do you really think you'll see him?"

Jordan offered a thin smile. He was still an avowed atheist, but sometimes letting his imagination drift brought him comfort. "Different roads. Same destination."

They pressed on toward the beach, absorbing the crowd's excitement.

It's long been said that a smart athlete knows when it's not their day, and Jordy wondered in the first moments after the starting horn if the reverse couldn't also be true. Does a smart athlete know that they are performing at the top of their abilities and when victory is theirs for the taking? Jordy was surrounded by younger athletes; he wasn't delusional enough to think he could seize the grand prize. But the top three swimmers in each age group medaled, and he felt good about where he stood in his pack. Stroke after stroke he could feel himself glide through the water as if he were floating slightly above it. It could have been the temperature (warmer water always slowed swimmers down), the buoyancy of salt water versus fresh, or simply the fact that he had always had the heart of a champion swimmer, even all those years he spent on dry land. Jordy found a rhythm to his freestyle that had eluded him in the pool at Chelsea Piers, breathing every third stroke so he could gauge his competition on both sides. His body was warm, the result of his blood vessels dilating to bring heat toward the skin's surface to release it. In short, he was feeling powerful.

The bay churned with swimmers, its usually placid veneer looking like snow; it wasn't until he was a third of the way into the race that there was enough distance between him and his competitors that he could see more than bubbles below. The water was murky, but it began to settle and the sunlight pierced the surface, illuminating just enough of the water below him that he started to see images in the way the light danced with its rays. He saw his old municipal pool, where he first fell in love with swimming, his parents waving from folding metal bleachers. He saw the Berkeley campus from above, like he was swimming over a giant map. That morphed into a Ouija board, then a parachute floating between puffed cotton clouds. He saw Alec and Jordan. Smiling Jordan, young, healthy, cupping his hands together over his mouth to yell his support from the stands and then enthusiastically waving him on. He knew it was the sun playing tricks on him, or aerobic respiration kicking in and mental and physical exhaustion—he didn't care. There were lessons to be drawn from each of these images, each of their funerals: to live in the present, to live for yourself, and that we were never as alone as we thought. His heart beat faster to bring oxygen to his muscles, to bring Jordan closer to him. Maybe if he swam fast enough, he could even turn back time.

One two three breathe. One two three breathe. One two three breathe.

When he put his face in the water to grind out three more strokes, a dark shadow wriggled beneath him, erasing these images, making the seawater murky again and his heart race even more. *What was that?* He was suddenly very aware that as much as he felt at one with the water he was the outsider here; there were plenty of creatures that made the ocean their home and might not take kindly to hundreds of humans disrupting it. He breathed to his left. No one seemed alarmed. One, two, three. He breathed to his right. Likewise he saw no signs of panic. Could it have just been the sun passing behind a cloud, causing the water to go dark? When he turned his head to his left again he could see a swimmer with his arm in the air. This is what they were told to do if they were in trouble. A cramp. Exhaustion. Numbness from the cold. If you veered from the course and found yourself in an unbeatable current. Do not panic. Raise an arm and help would be on its way. This was normal, he told himself. Things were happening just as they should. There was now one less entrant he had to beat. He returned his face to the water to see if he could spot the shadow again.

The water bubbled and churned as swimmers started to come into view, and the beach erupted with excitement. Spectators pointed and cheered; the first half of the race happened too far from view for fans to be truly invested. But as the wave of swimmers approached, friends and family and even strangers who came to witness the spectacle became energized with their own shots of adrenaline. People hollered and jumped in place, making both empty promises ("I'm going to sign up to swim next year, just you see!") and realistic plans ("Should we get ice cream sundaes in Ghirardelli Square after this?"). In the midst of the commotion, Jordan turned to his friends.

"Binoculars," he demanded, like a surgeon asking for a scalpel. Craig surrendered them to Jordan, who held them up to his face, focusing them to his vision. After surveying the water, his face drooped. "Something is wrong." He then took off down the beach to push his way to the center, Marielle, Craig, and Naomi chasing after him.

"I CAN'T RUN WITH THE KITTENS!" Marielle cried as she tried to keep them from jostling in their crate.

"Nothing is wrong!" Craig called after Jordan, trying to get him to slow down. The real danger was a weakened Jordan overexerting himself.

"I have to be there when he comes out of the water!" Jordan had imagined this moment like a sped-up version of evolution—Jordy would swim until he could touch bottom, then crawl from exhaustion, then pull himself out, stumbling erect on land, where Jordan would be there to wrap him in both a towel and the biggest hug anyone had ever received. But now he wasn't so sure.

Naomi and Craig caught up with Jordan first and slowed him to a walk. "Everything's okay, Jordan," Naomi said. "I promise." She then stepped ahead to make a path like a tiny plow clearing a field. "How did you even know about this race?" In her line of work she always knew about the hottest artists and trends before anyone else did and hated being the last to know about something that seemed popular with anyone else.

"The internet," he replied. How did anyone know about anything? "When I read about it, I just knew."

"Knew what, exactly?"

Jordan put one hand on Naomi's shoulder to rest, and she stopped and turned around. He heaved a few deep breaths. "That grief can be a prison. And at some point in the future I wanted him to look back on this day and remember that he has the strength to break free."

Naomi burst into tears.

"What?! What is it?" Marielle and the kittens finally caught up. "Is everything okay?"

Jordan gathered his friends around him. "Promise me you'll be there for him after I'm gone." He scanned their eyes to make sure he had their attention. "I want you to cheer him on, always, like you have today. Even if—even *when*—he meets someone else. Because he deserves nothing less."

They mumbled their agreement, but to Jordan that wasn't enough. Pacts for them must be clearly defined and spoken.

"Promise me."

"We promise," Marielle said.

"You be happy for him. And know that I will be too."

Craig unzipped his backpack and pulled out a beach towel they'd brought from Sur la Vie, and handed it to Jordan, who clutched it tightly to his chest as they pressed on.

As hard as it was to navigate the pier, it was even harder to walk on dry sand, and with his feet sinking with every step Jordan thought, *This is how it's going to be.* From here to the end, the journey was going to become more arduous. It would take more of his energy, more of his strength, until there was none left. But this was for him to worry about another day, as the first of the swimmers had already entered the cove.

Jordan scanned the splashing water looking for a yellow cap that read 158, but he couldn't make out any numbers, as most swimmers had dug deep for their last bursts of energy and kept their heads in the water as they barreled full speed for shore. Wild screams on the beach fell into a coordinated "GO! GO! GO!" Jordan squeezed Marielle's hand. "You hear that?"

Marielle smiled in recognition and in unison they shouted Alec's rallying cry, "S'GO! S'GO! S'GO!" until Naomi and Craig joined in, and Jordan imagined if Jordy could hear their screams through the crowd he would break into a smile big enough to power him across the finish line. Of course, there was no way he could with the thunderous splashing, but Jordan kept his eyes peeled for a swimmer picking up almost supernatural speed.

The first swimmer stood when the water was as deep as mid-thigh and charged his way across the finish line to thunderous applause and pats on the back. He was young, maybe twenty-eight, and his muscled chest heaved as his entire body shook with exhaustion. Down the beach a woman screamed and came barreling toward him as the second- and third-place finishers staggered ashore. Jordan's heart sank. It occurred to him that the beach was long and the cove was wide and family and friends were spread the entire length of it. He had so clearly envisioned Jordy stepping out of the water and into his arms, but the odds were just as good he'd step out of the water clear on the other side of the beach. Jordan scanned the shore to think where Jordy might land. *Lane five*, he remembered. That was where his husband would be.

"Do you see him?" Naomi asked.

"Lane five. Lane five. Where do you think that would be?"

Naomi cupped her hands over her eyes to block the sun. "Lane five?! The supermarket?" She had no idea what he was saying.

Jordan divided the beach into eighths and knew he had to move just right of center. "Number one fifty-eight!" Jordan instructed for the eighth or ninth time, and he ushered them down the beach.

"WE KNOW!"

A dozen racers had now stumbled ashore and the woman closest to them managed to stammer "Shark" to anyone who would listen as she labored to catch her breath.

Jordan grabbed Craig's arm to make sure he was hearing her right. "Did she say 'shark'? There was a *shark*?" He then pushed his way toward her.

The woman was spent and water dripped down her face. "Swimming underneath us . . . Huge." She then turned back to the cove and her face fell, either from exhaustion or genuine concern. "I hope . . . Everyone's okay."

Jordan turned to the cove and his heart pounded as if he were in the final strides of his own race. There were many swimmers past the breakwater now, but the last third of the pack was still in the bay. Any second he expected to see racers plucked from the surface and the water run red with blood like in a grisly documentary about dolphin slaughter he'd spend the rest of his life wishing he could unsee. "JORDY!" he screamed, and lurched forward into water up to his knees.

"Goddammit," Craig said as he dropped the backpack and ripped off his shoes and socks. He went into the water to stop Jordan from going in deeper. There were now swimmers exiting the water all around them saying things like *Did you see that?* and *It was huge!* while nearly knocking them over.

Marielle, not knowing how else to help, began plaintive cries of "One fifty-eight! One fifty-eight!" like she was one of the mewing kittens.

To which Naomi replied, "Shut up! Shut up!"

Jordy made good on the prerace instructions and had aligned himself perfectly with the entrance to Aquatic Park Cove. He picked up his pace as the swimmers on either side of him closed the distance to navigate the narrow opening. This was it, the home stretch. Jordy felt every one of his fifty years, but there was still enough of the college athlete in him to close this race strong, even if he collapsed on the finish line. That'd show Jordan. *You want to give me your funeral? Then let's make it a funeral you won't soon forget.* With each stroke he became angrier and angrier at his husband. For not taking his early symptoms seriously the first time around. For delaying his screening last year without consulting him so that they could go to France instead. For accepting his fate without wanting to burn the world down. For leaving him here. For not fighting longer. For being such a huge part of his life. His identity. For having his name. Once through the bottleneck, swimmers began to fan out. Not him; he refused to cede an inch as he plowed ahead straight for shore. Stroke, rage. Stroke, rage. Stroke, rage. He could feel himself picking up speed along with his fury, even if he had no desire for the race to be over; as long as he was in the water he felt untouchable, as soon as he was back on dry land the world would come crashing around him again. But he wouldn't allow himself to slow down. Come what may, he was going to barrel across the finish line, for that was Jordy Tosic's way.

One fifty-eight.

The cap was still partially submerged, but Jordan recognized his husband right away; he couldn't explain it, he just knew it was Jordy. He was overcome with relief, and then with pride. His love outswam a massive shark. He grabbed on to Craig, digging his fingers into his arm.

"Ow!" Craig flinched.

"There he is, there he is, there he is." Jordan then screamed back at the women, "THERE HE IS!"

They jumped up and down, going nuts, and it was the first real happiness Jordan had felt in weeks. He looked to the sky and felt the warmth on his face and told himself to remember this perfect moment. "JORDY!" he shouted with all his might.

As if Jordan were wearing a homing beacon, Jordy torpedoed straight for him. He ticked off the estimated distance. Jordy was a hundred yards. Then fifty. Then twenty-five. Ten. And just like that Jordy's enormous six-foot-four frame emerged from the water like a kaiju, his shoulders and arms swollen, looking twice their normal size against the sparkling waters of the cove. Without slowing his pace he charged across the finish line and ripped the goggles from his face. Jordan had just enough time to fall in love all over again before the whole world went black.

Jordy caught his husband in his arms and scooped him up in one fluid motion. His muscles were exhausted but he was still alarmed at how thin Jordan had become. He carried him onto the beach, laying him gently on the sand, where their friends crowded around. He gently slapped Jordan's face and called his name several times. Marielle thought of Alec and she tightly gripped Craig, and Naomi put her hands on Jordy's shoulders, just as she had done that fateful morning in their dormitory lounge. But today would be different and Jordan quickly came to, with worried faces peering over him like he was already in a casket. He wondered if this was all a dream.

"What happened?" he managed.

"You fainted," Jordy said.

Jordan turned to his friends to see if this was true. One of the lifeguards had sprung from his kayak and ran toward them with a bottle of water looking not unlike Henry Cavill. "Is he okay?"

"Oh my god, an angel from heaven," Jordan mumbled, fixated on the lifeguard's face. Jordy rolled his eyes.

"He's fine," Jordy scoffed. He had just completed the toughest race of his life and Jordan only had eyes for a lifeguard. "Maybe a little delirious."

Jordan tried to prop himself up to a seated position but came crashing back down.

"Whoa," Jordy said, and he cupped his hand under Jordan's head just in time. "Too much excitement and sun."

"Have him drink this," the lifeguard said. "Slowly. And then get him into the shade."

"Is it true there was a shark?" Craig asked.

Jordy and the lifeguard exchanged looks. "Where'd you hear that?"

"Some of the swimmers were saying." Craig pointed to a few, but none of them looked familiar.

The shadow. It swam right beneath him, the specter of death always near. So as not to put any further stress on Jordan, he said, "The only shark out there today was me." He smiled, and water was dripping from his hair onto Jordan's face, which irritated Jordan as much as it reminded him how irresistible Jordy was.

He felt pressure on his wrist and realized the lifeguard had been taking his pulse. "I'm fine," Jordan assured; he hated appearing weak in front of this super-man.

"Okay." The lifeguard relented. "But there's a lifeguard station just over there if you need us."

Once the guard stepped back, Marielle opened the water bottle and she and Jordy lifted him up so he could sip.

"This is for you. But if you can, save a few capfuls for the kittens." She felt silly asking, but really they could use a drink.

For his part, Jordan could not keep his eyes off Jordy.

"What?"

Jordan smiled. "You escaped from Alcatraz."

Jordy looked back out to Alcatraz Island. From their vantage point on the beach, it looked so far away. "I did," he said. He was so much stronger than anyone knew.

'm so embarrassed," Jordan mumbled when they were just outside the city. The ferry had returned Jordy's clothes and they made a beeline straight for the van. Naomi drove again; Jordan lay with his head in

Jordy's lap, and Craig and Marielle tended to the kittens on the way back.

"You fainted," Jordy said as he ran his fingers through Jordan's hair. "It's nothing to be embarrassed about."

"Did you really see the shark?" Craig asked.

"I saw something pass underneath me, that's all. A shadow. It actually reminded me of that painting we saw at the Cloisters. The Homer?"

"*The Gulf Stream*," Craig reminded him.

"That's the one." Jordy smiled in spite of himself. These funerals had gifted them so many things.

Craig let out a sharp exhale. "Well, I for one am never going in the water again."

"You spend a lot of time in the water now?" Marielle challenged.

Craig thought of Mia, grateful that she was grown. There were still plenty of things to worry about when it came to her, especially since he was new to the idea of being a father, but not nearly as many things as when she was young. He couldn't imagine a child at, say, the beach, with all the dangers it held. "Thank god Jordan didn't hear about it until you were almost ashore. He would have been beside himself with worry."

"Nah," Jordan managed. The van and the events of the day had lulled him almost to sleep.

"Nah?" Jordy was almost offended.

"I gave you my everything a long time ago. That includes the five or six lives I have left."

When they returned to Sur la Vie, the Jordans were ready to nap and Naomi was likewise exhausted from driving. Craig had softened his stance on the kittens during their ride and agreed to help Marielle feed them.

"They really are very small," he said when he saw how he could hold one in the palm of his hand.

Marielle was touched by how gentle he was with them and wished she'd had the opportunity to see him with Mia when she was young. If she could do things over, she might like a go at living a life with him.

"How long do you have to bottle-feed them?"

Marielle looked at the cat she was feeding. She wished it could see the love in her eyes, but she knew it felt cared for nonetheless. "Not long. They'll learn to eat on their own very soon." And then added, "They grow so fast." She could have been talking about Mia.

Craig felt the kitten's paws tighten around his finger. It was surprising how sharp its claws already were, but the kitten's grip wasn't firm enough to feel unpleasant. "So I was thinking. What if I came to Oregon for a spell?" He braced himself for a sour response, like he had overstepped some sort of bounds.

Instead Marielle asked, "What's a spell?"

Craig wasn't sure. "Now that I'm a free man, I'm looking for someplace quiet to start the next chapter of my life."

"You're asking what I think about you *moving* to Oregon."

Craig chewed on his lip like this was just occurring to him. "I didn't really think about it in those terms." Was that what he was asking? "I need a change from the city; everything there just seems tainted now, and no gallery will hire me. I'm getting back to my painting, and could use new inspiration."

He looked at her hopefully to see if she'd agree; her expression was hard to read, but she didn't seem off-put. Someplace like Oregon would be good for him. "There are lots of places to start over. Is there a reason Oregon specifically sprang to mind?"

Craig gently placed the kitten in its nest and took Marielle's hand in his own. "I wouldn't mind being closer to you, if that's what you're asking." He was under no illusion that they were a family, he and Mia and Marielle, and yet the idea that they *could* be intrigued him.

Marielle squeezed his hand twice. "It just so happens I have plenty of space. If you could stand to share a house with me and a few animals in need. And maybe pitch in with the occasional chore."

Craig didn't have a lot of options currently; he wasn't working and had been selling part of his art collection to live. But Oregon wasn't on the table by default, it was genuinely where his heart wanted to be.

"Mia's not there, you know. In case this is just about spending time with her."

"It's not," Craig said. For better or worse she had a father who raised her and that wasn't him. She had a busy life of her own, something Marielle was proud of, and something he was proud of too, even though he had no part in shaping it. He pushed her hair back from her face, revealing one of his deepest loves. "Marielle. This is about spending time with *you*."

They held Jordy's funeral that evening. It already felt different than the previous times they'd assembled. Somber. More sacred, as if there was pressure to get this one just right. The air was especially still. Jordan stepped onto the deck and slapped a mosquito on his neck. The others turned, startled, and he immediately wanted to slap them too.

"Why so glum?" Of course he knew why. He might have given his funeral to Jordy on paper, but he was aware they were very much there to honor him. It was the last one of these he would attend. "Oh, come on. You can't possibly miss me when I'm standing right here!" It was just enough to break the ice.

Jordy's condition for granting Jordan's wish was that they not go overboard. He didn't need flowers, or a special meal, for them to dress up, or for anyone to go out of their way. So they stood on the deck in a circle, like children playing a game. It began almost Quaker in nature; they stood silently, speaking not in turns, but instead only when they were inspired.

"Jordy was too damn tall," Naomi said, to everyone's delight except Jordy's. "I say 'was,' because I've gotten used to it. But at the beginning? I thought you took up too much space, and I was afraid you'd be one of those white boys who mistook their size for importance. But there you were, right from the starting gate, deferring to others, listening, asking us questions about each of our lives. You even polled us one by one to see if we were going to shower before dinner that first night so that you wouldn't be the odd man out."

They laughed at that memory.

"You were intense, and after today I can see that you still are. But intensity can be a form of passion. Come on, who else would get up at five a.m. for practice, or swim through shark-infested waters to prove a point? You eat more than your share of food. Honestly, Berkeley should have doubled your charge for room and board. Remember how you would eat before a race? You'd scarf down half of everything in the dining hall. I'm surprised you didn't eat a bench. The rest of us learned soon enough to get there ahead of you at dinnertime, but I don't think that one Scandinavian exchange student had a thing to eat the entire time he was there. Antoine?"

"Anton," Craig said, smiling. "You starved him all the way back to Finland."

"I'm not sure how this is a *nice* story about me."

Marielle reached up and pinched his lips closed. "The dead don't speak."

"I had a point," Naomi said as she grasped to remember it. "Oh, yes. I thought, 'That boy has an appetite!' And you have proven that's still true. Not just for food, but for *life*. It's something that always stuck with me. Have an appetite for life, coupled with a genuine interest in others. That's the secret to a successful life. There. That's the longest I'm capable of being sincere." Naomi scanned the group, looking for anyone else willing to speak.

Marielle raised her hand. "I was angry at you after I last saw you, and I held on to that anger for a long time. But you checked in on me, repeatedly, and I want you to know that that helped me. You took the easy way out once, and you could have done it again, but people change and they grow and you demonstrated that for me. For better or worse, I wouldn't have survived this life without you, all of you. Just as I don't want to endure what comes next all alone."

In the intermittent silence a pine cone hit the deck and rolled off the side.

"One time I was really drunk and I considered doing gay stuff with you." Craig looked up to blank stares. "Did I just say that out loud?"

Jordan shoved him playfully.

Craig cleared his throat, signaling he was about to be serious. "I was really moved by what you did today. You were a swimmer in college, and you are a swimmer still. I was an artist in college, but for so long I told myself it was something I had outgrown. Put too much distance between that version of me and the man I am today. But we are still capable of amazing things, and we are not so old that past versions of ourselves are long gone. There is fire in us still." He took Jordan's hand. "In all of us. And there will be right up until the end. Nothing is over until it is." He smiled at Marielle. "I don't have access to Jordy's library of inspirational quotes, so forgive me for mangling an old Buddhist concept I read while locked up. Thousands of candles can be lit from a single one, and the life of that candle will not be shortened. That's what you do for others. You light their candle with yours."

As if he hadn't heard the rest of Craig's speech, Jordy asked, "What kind of gay stuff, specifically?"

"No, stop it. I'm being serious."

"So am I! Like, just with hands?"

Craig waved him off. "All of you and your candles . . . They do that for me." Craig glanced at Naomi. "Except yours."

Naomi beamed with pride and her lips curled into a devilish grin. "My candle will burn your house down."

Everyone looked to Jordan as if it was his turn to speak, but he stood quietly with his eyes closed.

Jordy nudged him. "You don't have to say anything if you're not up for it."

After another moment, Jordan opened his eyes. "I was just remembering something Tuffy said when he was preparing Nana for jail."

"Tuffy," Naomi sighed.

"The best way to make it through is to find your purpose. He was talking about incarceration, but I think his point still stands. It's all about having a purpose." Jordan turned to his husband. "My purpose, in this life, has been to love and spend it with you."

Jordy put his hand over his heart.

"And I want to spend the time I have left with you too," Jordan continued. "I don't want us to be sad. Or bitter, or angry. I want to celebrate until it is over. And, when I'm gone, I want you to celebrate again because it happened."

Jordy hugged him tight and then the others stepped forward until their arms were enmeshed and they were all one like they were when they had agreed to the pact around the table at Sur la Vie almost thirty years before.

"Ow," Jordan exclaimed.

Marielle and the others leaped back, afraid they were crushing their infirm friend.

"It's a joke! I'm joking," Jordan said. "I'm not *that* fragile."

They fell back into their hug. Jordan imagined a day soon when he would no longer be there. The pact would live on, he'd made sure of that, but they would no longer need it. None of them would leave this Earth without knowing that they were loved. And even though he had given his turn to Jordy, that was very much true for him too.

To think about life is to contemplate death—it's what makes living so valuable. Our time here is limited, gone in the blink of an eye. Jordan thought of the water park he used to visit summers as a child after his family had moved to the States. The waterslides were a perfect ride. He would be sloshed side to side on a little blue mat that kept his young body from sticking to the smooth surface as he barreled down toward a pool. It was scary, but not too, exhilarating but not exhausting, draining—but also surprisingly invigorating. He would squeal with delight as he hit the shallow pool, then run back up the concrete path for another turn until his feet were raw and his mother had to drag him away in the last of the afternoon light. And now here he stood again, under the setting sun, and the urge crept in to run back up the hill for just one more ride from the start. But he let the need go as gently as he could, released it like a balloon in the sky.

You only live once.

That was the truth of it.

But if you do it right, and he felt that he had, once is more than enough.

JORDAN AARÓN VARGAS

Veteran public relations executive Jordan Aarón Vargas, who worked on campaigns for a number of Tony-winning theatrical productions including *Once*, *A Gentleman's Guide to Love and Murder*, and the revival of *Anything Goes*; countless independent feature films and books; as well as corporate clients and theater companies, died on Friday after a battle with cancer. He was fifty-one. His husband, also Jordan, Jordan Tosic, released the news through the PR firm they ran together.

Broadway producers, filmmakers, actors, clients, and reporters alike all loved working with Jordan and turned to him for both professional and personal guidance, and he was known for his sharp eye, creative campaigns, and skills in crisis management. He was a member of the Public Relations Society of America and the Broadway League and twice served on the board of directors of the Human Rights Campaign.

Jordan was born in Bogotá, Colombia, and immigrated to the United States at age eight. He studied at the University of New Hampshire before transferring to the University of California, Berkeley, where he graduated in 1995.

Jordan was known for his love of theater and his work with

numerous charities, as well as the unique pact he entered into with four of his college classmates. After the death of their friend Alec Swigert before graduation, they banded together with a promise to throw one another living funerals so that none of them would ever be left to wonder what impact they'd had on the others. Their mission: leave nothing left unsaid.

He is survived by his husband, Jordan Tosic; his parents, Carmen and Miguel Vargas of Portsmouth, New Hampshire; a brother, Luis, and niece, Camila, of Framingham, Massachusetts; and dear friends and the other members of his pact: Naomi Ito of Los Angeles, and Craig Scheffler and Marielle Holland-Scheffler of Boring, Oregon.

In lieu of flowers, Jordan Tosic asks that people honor his husband by telling a loved one the positive impact they've had on your life so that they are never left to guess. He promises you'll be glad you did.

ACKNOWLEDGMENTS

Writing the acknowledgments for a book can be a fraught endeavor; there are many people to thank and in the past I've worried about overlooking someone deserving. But in the context of a novel celebrating the meaningful people in your life and telling them exactly how you feel? This time I relish the task.

Sally Kim is a visionary editor with an open heart and I'm thrilled every single time we get to work together. We live in divisive and challenging times; progress is slow and painfully incremental and plagued with periods of backslide. But when things do get better—and they do—it's in part because diverse voices are allowed to tell their stories. Sally has trusted me with an enormous platform as a storyteller while simultaneously making me better at my craft. For that I owe her a great deal.

My agent, Rob Weisbach, has made dream after dream come true for me and is a genuine partner in everything I do. He's a valued creative voice, a trusted reader, and a bona fide friend. We may not be lifelong confidants like the characters in this book, but we sure have packed in a lifetime of successes, thrills, and fun.

The team at G. P. Putnam's Sons is the best in the business, and I continue to benefit from their expertise. Thank you Ivan Held, Alexis Welby, Katie McKee, Ashley McClay, Molly Pieper, Samantha Bryant, and Tarini Sipahimalani. I'm also indebted to both Tal Goretsky for his cover design and Sanny Chiu for her illustrations. I won the cover lottery.

To the extent that my previous novel *The Guncle* found its audience, it's in large part due to Bookstagram and I'm in awe of that community of readers. They invest so much of themselves championing books, writing reviews, and curating the most incredible images—all for the love of books. I hope you know how much your work and creativity mean to authors. Likewise, thank you to the many readers who have stuck with me through four books, and the innumerable booksellers who have placed one of my novels in a reader's hands. You are all so wonderful.

A book has many friends and it's so rewarding when those friends are also mine. Manuel Betancourt helped me find Jordan's voice. Nicholas Brown, Chris Neuhaus, and Roswell Encina introduced me to Puerto Vallarta and inspired a love of Mexico. Jordan Moblo and Jordan Cerf allowed me to lift their names and David Clark Smith and David Ruperti indulged my questions about being a same-named, same-sex couple. My own friends from Emerson College were with me in spirit every time I sat down to write. You know who you are; it's not an exaggeration to say this book would not exist without you.

Thank you Raindrop and Shirley for getting me out of my chair and eating just enough of my lunch when I've prepared too much. Likewise to Kevin Amell for reminding me that physical activity fuels creativity.

And finally to my husband, Byron Lane. I never thought I would be married, let alone to a dreamboat like you. Thank you for the laughs, thank you for the love, thank you for this incredible life.

DISCUSSION GUIDE

1. Author Steven Rowley describes the end of college with the anti-climactic feeling that sometimes accompanies it as adulthood dauntingly approaches and friends disperse toward new adventures. At which point in your life did you meet your closest friends? How do you keep memories of fond early days alive?

2. The celebrants in this story make a pact to throw each other living funerals "so that none of them could ever question exactly what they meant to the others." Do you think anyone truly knows how much they're loved? Discuss.

3. Throughout the story, Rowley ponders the interrelation between beginnings and endings. He writes, "[A]ll that begins, ends." Later, "[E]ndings are also beginnings." The book's epigraph is from *Chocolat* by Joanne Harris: "Life is what you celebrate. All of it. Even its end." What is Rowley saying about this connection, and how do the living funerals illustrate this point? Discuss if and how endings are crucial to living a fulfilled life. Can celebration and grief coexist?

4. Alec is described as the life of the party and as the heart of the group. In what individual ways did Alec bind each member to the larger group?

5. At one point, the celebrants decide to use a Ouija board to

communicate with Alec. What purpose does the board serve for them? If you could talk to a lost loved one, would you?

6. When it comes time for Naomi's living funeral, it doesn't quite go as planned. What do you think Naomi needed from her friends in this moment? In what ways was she extending herself outside of her usual pattern?

7. Through grief, change, and acceptance, *The Celebrants* also touches on our need for control. Which celebrant had the biggest challenge with this, and why?

8. Like Naomi's, Craig's living funeral is marked by surprises of its own. What did you make of the way Craig's funeral was triggered? Was it successful in fulfilling, for Craig, what the pact intended?

9. Alec and Mia, through different means, are two elusive figures in the story. They're mentioned frequently, but rarely seen on the page, if at all. Discuss how they play important roles in specific moments in the story.

10. Later in the story, Rowley reveals a shocking truth about Alec. How would you have handled the situation if you were in the know? Which character did you feel the most for in this scene? Discuss the impact of secrets on the relationships in the book.

11. In true Rowley fashion, the author touches on hefty topics with humor and heart, aptly titling this story *The Celebrants*. Discuss the meaning of the title, relating to the characters in the story and the idea of connection. What did each of these characters have to celebrate?

12. As the celebrants' motto goes, "Leave nothing left unsaid." In honor of Alec, Jordan, and celebrating love and life, turn to the person next to you and tell them about one positive impact they've had on your life.

Patrick O'Hara removed the cloche from his room service breakfast with a flourish it did not deserve; he grimaced at what lay beneath. *You have to hand it to the Italians*, he thought as he sat on his terrazza overlooking Lake Como. They hit lunch and dinner so hard there was never anything left for breakfast, unless you count the driest pastry you'd ever seen as a meal (and Patrick did not—this particular brick looked like it should be on display in Pompeii). He sighed. Neither the pastry nor the acrid coffee that came with it would alleviate the pounding in his head or the uneasiness of his stomach, as he ached for a good, greasy American breakfast to help him sop up the disaster that was the previous night.

"Why is your coffee so small?" Grant bellowed from inside his uncle's hotel room. The boy was eleven now, and had mostly outgrown his lisp, even if Patrick's trained ear still caught echoes of it—*tho thmall*—every now and again.

"Why is your voice *so loud*?" Grant and his sister, Maisie, had the magic ability to amplify his every hangover. Patrick took a sip of his caffè normale and winced. The boy's question was a decent one (as far as his inane questions went), but it had an easy answer: the espresso was so bitter he wouldn't survive a full cup. He was so hungover, even his hair seemed to hurt.

"What's wrong with you?" Grant asked.

"I prefer a French breakfast, if you know what I mean." They didn't, so Patrick scrapped the rest of the joke—*a roll in bed with some honey*—as it would most likely go over their heads and he didn't have the energy to explain double entendre.

Grant lifted the room phone from its cradle. "I'll see if they offer one." The kid had become far too adept at ordering room service over the course of their travels.

"See if they offer euthanasia."

Below, two passengers made their way down the hotel's docks and stepped onto the back of a wooden speedboat. Patrick squinted as diamonds of sunlight rippled off the lake; slowly his brother, Greg, came into focus, as well as Livia, his brother's soon-to-be wife. Or *maybe* soon-to-be wife. Too many things remained unresolved in the wake of a disastrous rehearsal dinner. He watched as they settled onto the boat's rear vinyl seat, Livia fanning her patterned Marimekko dress as she crossed her legs just so, Greg extending his arm around her, whispering in her ear until she giggled. They seemed genuinely happy. Patrick had to hand it to her. The night before he was certain Livia was a cooked goose, but she was an absolute bird of paradise in the fresh light of day. Patrick narrowed his eyes further until he could see his brother pouring two flutes of prosecco from a bottle that sat in an ice bucket between them—he extended his arm, as if reaching for a glass, his best hope a little hair of the dog that bit him. But as the boat's motor gurgled and churned, the only bubbles before him were in the water as the boat pushed back from the dock.

"Look at them," Maisie scoffed without glancing up from the phone she'd been given when she turned fourteen.

"Oh, you *are* talking to me." Maisie had been giving her uncle the silent treatment all morning, mortified still by the absolute spectacles they had made of themselves at dinner. Of course, the kids had an excuse: it was difficult watching their father remarry. Patrick, as the adult, did not.

"How can you eat at a time like this?" Maisie's question dripped with teenage judgment.

Patrick took a bite of the pastry and it disintegrated down the front of his hotel robe. "Not well, clearly." He let the dry crumbs roll off his tongue. Then he said in his most confident tone, "We can fix this."

"Why would we want to?" Maisie asked, and Patrick motioned toward Grant, who approached them with his game console; he wasn't sure if Maisie saw.

Grant sidled up next to his uncle. "They didn't have what you asked for, but I got us a pitcher of grape juice."

"Wonderful. I'm sure the conversation it inspires will be just as intoxicating." Patrick stood up to wipe himself clean over the edge of the terrace before taking a swig of Acqua Panna, turning what little of the pastry was left in his mouth into some sort of wallpaper glue.

"Don't you have any feelings?" Maisie had finally looked up from her phone.

Patrick laughed, recalling Goldie Hawn's answer to that question from *The First Wives Club*. "Yes, I have feelings. I'm an actor. I have all of them." His niece didn't think that was funny.

They were at the Grand Hotel Tremezzo, an iconic art nouveau masterpiece on the western shore of Lake Como, for four nights of a planned six. The wedding was to be that evening, followed by a day of rest, and then Patrick would take the kids home to the States while their father and Livia honeymooned in Greece. Or at least that had been the plan. Patrick had a hard time grasping that any of this was real. The wedding. The setting. His whole family in Italy. Now it was all one big mess.

Maisie tucked her phone into the shallow front pocket of her cut-off shorts; it did not fit all the way inside.

"Did you finally reach the end of TikTok?" Patrick mocked, but in all honesty he should thank the Chinese for keeping her calm.

Maisie leaned awkwardly in the doorway with one arm at her side, her left hand clasping the wrist on her right, looking not out at the floating pool in the lake, which was an incredible sight for its unnecessary opulence (a swimming pool *in* a lake?), but instead like she'd rather disappear from this place. "I just don't see it. Dad and *Livia*?"

Everyone needed a nemesis; Patrick had instructed Maisie well. And if Walt Disney himself had taught children anything it's that stepmothers are wicked, even if Patrick no longer found Livia to be all that bad. But it was long past time for his niece to ease up.

"The connection between two people is not always something others are meant to see." Patrick thought of himself and his ex-boyfriend Emory, and how many on the outside could think them mismatched. "Like fireworks in the daytime." Since ending their nearly five-year relationship, Patrick had never felt so alone. It used to be his default setting, but now solitude was an ill-fitting garment once-trusted cleaners had shrunk.

Grant's game console made a sound like something swirling a drain and he groaned. "Why can't Dad marry Palmina?"

Speaking of nemeses, a cold chill ran down Patrick's spine. "Palmina's a lesbian, you know that."

Grant didn't seem to view that as disqualifying. "Yeah, but gay marriage is legal now."

"Yes, for gay people to marry *other* gay peop—Why would you want your dad to marry Palmina?"

Grant shrugged, but they all knew the answer: Palmina was the very definition of *sprezzatura*. In every way, she exuded an effortless cool. "Maybe *you* should marry her."

"Gay men can't marry lesbians," Patrick said, appalled.

"Oh no. Here come the Guncle Rules." Maisie stuck out her tongue in protest. Guncle Rules were Patrick's little bon mots and instructions for living that he previously doled out like candy—*brunch is awesome, when a gay man hands you his phone look only at what he is showing you, bottomless mimosas are not the same as pantless mimosas*. Those sorts of things.

Grant pressed, undeterred. "Why not? She's gay, you're gay. You just said!"

"BECAUSE THAT'S NOT HOW IT WORKS!" Patrick swallowed the rest of his coffee like a bitter pill and motioned for Grant to sit. "That's not a Guncle Rule, that's just common sense." As their gay uncle, Patrick had once been the apple of their eye. Now he had been swept aside in favor of Livia's younger lesbian sister, Palmina, who just seventy-two hours earlier had crashed down on his world—an asteroid wiping him out like the dinosaur he was. Over was the era of the guncle; behold the dawn of the launt!

Grant circled three times like a dog and plopped down next to his uncle with such force it caused Patrick to rise an inch off the cushion. "I want you to understand something. Your mother would welcome this day. She wanted your dad to be happy. It's been five years and that's a respectable amount of time and we should celebrate your father and Livia."

Maisie disagreed. "Mom never could have imagined this day."

Patrick glanced up at the sun's yolk; colors seemed more saturated in Italy. "Well, no. Not *this* day, exactly." Even he could not have foreseen his lawyer brother representing the American business interests of an Italian noble family, then falling for his client's daughter, a marchesa of all things, and Patrick's imagination was quite robust. But Sara, his best friend from college, had planned for a lot of contingencies that others had not, including his summer with the kids in Palm Springs immediately after her death, when Patrick had been thrust into the role of caregiver, cementing their special bond; he was loathe not to afford her due credit. "But I know she would have been happy about it. Remember I knew her before any of you."

Maisie held firm. "I don't like the way I feel inside."

Patrick tried to make light. "Too much pasta and formaggio. That has nothing to do with your father."

Maisie's face soured. "It's not that."

Patrick had been warned by Maisie in stark terms not to inquire about her period again. But it was all still new and some things couldn't be helped. "Do you need another . . . "women's aspirin'?" He grimaced as he pulled the bottle from his robe pocket and tossed it for her to catch; it landed like a baby's rattle on the floor.

Maisie stomped her feet and Patrick jumped, knocking over his tiny coffee cup. "I swear to god, if you say women's aspirin one more—!"

"Okay! I'm sorry. I just want you to know I'm an ally. I've read almost everything by Judy Blume."

"Who's Judy Blume?" Grant asked.

Patrick's head pounded anew as he reclined back onto his chaise. *Are you there, god? It's me, Patrick.* But he was also clearly relieved. If it wasn't Maisie's period it was grief, something he was more adept at handling, as he'd helped the kids navigate so much of it when he had custody of them in Palm Springs. "That pit you feel in your gut, that's just love persevering." He looked solemnly at the kids to make sure each understood. "Remember our summer together? In many ways that was just the beginning."

"And this is, what? *The end?*" Maisie sneered. That was the thing about grief, none of us wanted to travel with it, exactly, but the suggestion that we would or should be over it was somehow an even more unwelcome passenger.

"Of course not. Maybe the beginning of a new phase."

"When *does* it end?" Grant asked, nestling against Patrick's side. Patrick tousled his hair and imagined that his nephew was still six. This is the kind of question that would have thrown him for a loop when the kids first walked into his life, but now he was able to answer honestly.

"It doesn't end. Not really." Patrick spoke from experience. His first love, Joe, died in a car crash fifteen years prior. In the wake of Patrick's recent breakup with Emory, Joe had been on his mind again. "But here's the good news. You get so much stronger." He tackled Grant and the boy burst out in fits of unguarded giggles. It made Patrick happy, as if it were proof that Grant survived the last five years with his childhood intact. "Now drop and give me ten."

Grant flexed his biceps, his arms two noodles like always. He then fell to the floor and completed seven push-ups, then three more from his knees. "TEN!"

"Come on. You can't be this unhappy. I mean, look where you are! George Clooney has a house just down the shore, and he could live *anywhere*." Patrick gestured at the crystalline waters and then across the lake toward Bellagio. "And yeah, I know—who's George Clooney." He'd walked himself into a trap. "He's like the reigning Spencer Tracy." Patrick stood to his full height, tightening the hotel's robe over his sleep pants, and then held a finger aloft before Grant could inquire about Spencer Tracy. "Look. You remember the Bellagio hotel when I took you to Vegas? The one with a lake built in front?"

"It had dancing fountains." Grant's eyes grew wide with the memory. "That was a *great* lake!"

"That's *this* lake! Or it's supposed to be."

"This lake has dancing fountains, too?" Grant ran to the edge of the terrace, as if he might have to fight for the perfect spot to catch the next water show.

"No. Just *that* lake has fountains."

"You said that lake was this lake."

"A re-creation of it."

Grant peered down over the edge, having lost total interest. "Oh. Then that lake was better."

"No, this lake is better because it's the real deal. The other one is for tourists who wear matching tracksuits and need to breathe oxygen from a tank." Patrick scuttered into the shade.

"We're tourists," Maisie pointed out.

"We're not *tourists*." Patrick said it with the disdain the word deserved.

"What are we, then?" she challenged.

Patrick leaned in the doorway of his suite. "Well, wedding guests, for one. Beyond that, itinerants, birds of passage . . ." Patrick disappeared inside to look for a cold compress and instead stumbled upon the room service menu Grant left on his bed. "The French would call us bon vivants!" He wondered aloud if a Bloody Mary, light on the tomato juice, might do the trick.

"Why do you need a drink at ten o'clock in the morning?" Maisie asked, following him inside.

Patrick gave her a loving jab at the nape of her neck. "Because I suffer from a rare condition where my body doesn't produce its own alcohol."

There was a knock at the door. Grant's pitcher of grape juice. "Un momento," he said as he fished for euros to tip. The door opened and his sister, Clara, waltzed in.

"Patrick. It's not even noon. What a surprise to find you upright." Clara's look had softened since her divorce (with Patrick's help she'd found a hair color and style that worked), and Italy had done even more to suit her. His sister's demeanor, however, was sharp as ever, as she was wearing a surprising amount of makeup.

"What's with the war paint?"

"Oh! Livia brought in a makeup artist for the wedding party." Clara touched her face gently like a silent-era star. She was clearly ready for her close-up.

"Does that mean . . . ?" Patrick asked. Maisie braced herself for an answer.

"I talked to Greg, but your guess is as good as mine." Clara gently tucked Maisie's hair behind one of her ears. "But it never hurts to be ready. Perhaps they have a bronzer they could use on you, Patrick. You look tired."

Patrick glared at Clara. "That's because you and Harvey Wall-banger kept me up half the night."

Even under Clara's makeup, Patrick could see his sister's face redden; it was unlike her to have one-night stands.

"You heard us?" she asked, horrified.

"We share a wall. Not that it matters. *Belgium* heard you."

Grant tugged on his aunt's sleeve. "Aunt Clara, can we go to the buffet?"

Patrick saw an opening and he nudged his family toward the door. "Yes. Take these ankle biters down to breakfast and secure us a table. The pastry they brought to my room leaves something to be desired."

"Only if we can find seats in the shade. I don't want my face to melt."

"Like in *Raiders of the Lost Ark!*" Grant pumped his fist. Face melting was right in his wheelhouse.

"All of you, out. I promise I'm right behind you." He closed the door on his family, revealing he was anything but.

Silence at last.

Alone, Patrick ran a washcloth under cold water and pressed it against his forehead, then stepped out onto the terrazza and inhaled deeply. He gripped the balustrade, his fingers curling tightly over the edge, and looked intently over the lake. He watched as a young couple ran across the narrow street toward the lounge chairs near the beachfront. Beach club employees were just starting to raise the umbrellas for shade from the intense July sun, their orange-and-cream-colored stripes and scalloped edges looking like delicious ice cream treats from above. "*Would* you be happy about this?" he whispered to Sara, less certain now that she would be than he was before. *Yes*, he thought, *of course she would*. What was good for her family was always best for her. But he wished he could know for sure that she agreed Greg and Livia were a match. It was the sad truth about losing someone—your certainty about who they were faded with memory.

Patrick stepped back into his room and frowned at the side of the bed where the kids had at with their shoes. Their European adventure was drawing to a close. Soon he would be returning to the States to start over, at the age of forty-nine, alone.

A knock on the door startled him. Grant's grape juice at last. Again he tightened his robe, and as he reached for the door he instinctively stepped aside to allow his server to enter. Except it wasn't a porter standing in front of him with a pitcher of juice, but rather someone else—someone who took his breath away.

"*It's you.*"

Photograph of the author © Byron Lane

STEVEN ROWLEY is the *New York Times* bestselling author of *Lily and the Octopus*, a *Washington Post* Notable Book; *The Editor*, an NPR Best Book of the Year; *The Guncle*, winner of the twenty-second Thurber Prize for American Humor and Goodreads Choice Awards finalist for Novel of the Year; and *The Celebrants*, a *Today Show* Read With Jenna book club pick. His fiction has been translated into twenty languages. He resides in Palm Springs, California.

VISIT STEVEN ROWLEY ONLINE

stevenrowley.com

MrStevenRowley

MrStevenRowley